BECAUSE YOU LOVED ME

BETH MORAN

Boldwood

First published in Great Britain in 2023 by Boldwood Books Ltd.

Copyright © Beth Moran, 2023

Cover Design by Debbie Clement Design

Cover Photography: Shutterstock

Every effort has been made to obtain the necessary permissions with reference to copyright material, both illustrative and quoted. We apologise for any omissions in this respect and will be pleased to make the appropriate acknowledgements in any future edition.

A CIP catalogue record for this book is available from the British Library.

Paperback ISBN 978-1-83751-330-7

Large Print ISBN 978-1-83751-326-0

Hardback ISBN 978-1-83751-325-3

Ebook ISBN 978-1-83751-323-9

Kindle ISBN 978-1-83751-324-6

Audio CD ISBN 978-1-83751-331-4

MP3 CD ISBN 978-1-83751-328-4

Digital audio download ISBN 978-1-83751-322-2

Boldwood Books Ltd
23 Bowerdean Street
London SW6 3TN
www.boldwoodbooks.com

In memory of my dad, David Robbins. It was an honour. And to George.
Thank you for the tea.

1

'Who are you?'

My first thought was to lie. To not be me. I hesitated.

The girl in front of me, so desperately trying to be an adult with her dark make-up and uneasy piercings, looked up for the first time. Her expression from behind the counter said it all. What type of person doesn't know who they are?

A dozen names zipped through my brain. The women I wished I could be. Amelia Earhart. Emmeline Pankhurst. Lady Gaga.

The girl began tapping her biro on the book in front of her, jabbing angry marks on the white page.

'Marion Miller.' This is my real name. I was here (and not standing behind my own counter at Ballydown Public Library) to discover what that name meant.

She checked her book. 'You aren't on the bookings list. Did you reserve a pitch or a caravan?'

'No. I haven't reserved anything—'

She slammed the book shut, shoving it to one side. Scowled through the inch-long spider legs glued to her eyelids. 'It's August. We're full.'

I was about to explain that I only wanted directions to the Sherwood Forest visitor centre. But before I could, the outside door opened and a woman *sashayed* in. Apart from her tiny frame, nothing about her appearance said 'girlish'. All of her, from the top of her platinum-blonde chignon to her sleek heels, declared her a lady. Her simple red dress wrapped her perfectly, emphasising curves where curves are meant to be. I couldn't guess her age. Thirty-five? Forty? Fifty, possibly? It felt crass even to consider how old she might be. For a woman like this, years and the passing of time are irrelevant. She was breathtaking.

She turned to me and smiled. 'Hello. Welcome to the Peace and Pigs. I am so sorry, but an emergency has occurred and I require my daughter's assistance immediately. Have you booked in yet?'

A voice of pure honey. Made with pollen from the sweetest of North American flowers. Deep and rich. A Southern Belle.

As I opened my mouth to reply, the girl who must be her daughter answered. 'She hasn't booked.'

'I'm not here on holiday. I...'

The woman grabbed my wrist with her French-manicured nails. 'You must be Becky Moffitt's niece – Jenna? You made it! I'm Scarlett. You are so very welcome! To be honest, I was beginnin' to think you decided not to show up, but better late than never, today of all days. Now please, I don't mean to throw you in at the deep end, but as I mentioned, we are in the grip of an emergency. Would you mind very much taking over from Grace and supervisin' check-in? All you need do is welcome arrivals, find their pitch number in the book, make sure they've paid and hand them the information leaflet.'

As she spoke, the woman steered me behind the desk. She patted my arm and turned back to her daughter. 'Little Johnny escaped again. Valerie has him cornered with a broom by the bottom wash block, but he is squealin' like a great big baby; we need an extra pair of hands.'

For a few beats of silence, Grace didn't move. I could feel tension swinging like a pendulum between them. Scarlett reached up her hand to smooth a non-existent stray hair back into place.

'Please, would you come and help?'

Grace rolled her eyes and plodded out to join her mum. The door slammed shut behind her, leaving me standing on the wrong side of the counter. A prickle of sweat popped out on my forehead, due to a lot more than the stifling August heat.

For the first few minutes, nothing happened; the only sound my breathless prayer, muttered over and over again, as if saying it more times made any difference. 'Please let no one turn up. Don't make me have to speak to anyone else.'

The bell on top of the door jangled, and my heart accelerated to triple time as a man and woman stepped in. Crumpled and sticky, like the old sweet wrappers inhabiting my car footwells, they barely glanced up as they handed over their reservation details. I checked the name on the piece of paper against the entry in the book.

'Pitch fourteen.' My voice had been replaced with that of an elderly toad.

'Excuse me?'

I coughed to clear my throat. 'Pitch number fourteen.' I pointed out the map on the back of the welcome leaflet I had been memorising for distraction purposes. 'Just here, by the play park.'

'That's great.' The woman swiped at the hair drooping in her eyes. 'The kids have been stuck in the back of the car for five hours. They can play while we put the tent up. You might have genuinely saved us from committing murder. You know what it's like.'

Nope.

They had already paid in full and I couldn't think of anything to say, but they stood there expectantly. I fought past the seven-year-old mute who grabs hold of my vocal cords whenever I am forced into making conversation with people I don't know. Remembered to do my mute busters: *breathe out, drop shoulders, pause. Breathe in, open mouth, speak.*

'Um. Have a nice holiday. And if you need anything, feel free to come and ask.'

The couple smiled and nodded as they opened the door to leave. I held my breath the whole time and then, as the door swung shut, my mouth opened all by itself and yelled, 'I'm not Becky Moffitt's niece!'

The man pushed the door back open and stuck his head around it. 'Sorry?'

Shaking my head quickly from side to side, I tried to smile. It might have been more of a grimace. He raised his eyebrows, glancing back at his car impatiently. 'You shouted something. I didn't quite catch it.'

I swallowed, and managed to mumble, 'I'm not Becky Moffitt's niece.'

The man stared at me for a second. 'Okaaaay. Well. Thanks for letting me know. I'll bear that in mind.'

I waited for him to climb back into his car before banging my head a few times on the reception desk.

* * *

An hour or so later, Scarlett poked her head around the door. Her eyes swept the room before coming to rest on me. I hadn't yet died of fright or done a runner. This is despite the fact that every time the bell jangled, my central nervous system pumped out an adrenaline rush big enough to send a shuttle into orbit. I could, by now, smell my own body odour and had agonised for a very long forty minutes about whether or not to take a cold drink from the fridge behind me. What on earth was I doing here?

'Y'all okay in here?'

I nodded yes.

'Anybody showed up?'

'Six.'

'Helped yourself to a drink and an ice-cream?'

'No!'

'Well, then, how can you be all right, sat in this sauna in *jeans* with nothin' to cool you down? Take somethin' quick before you pass out on me. I don't want suin' for maltreatment of my employees.'

Tentatively, I pulled a bottle of water out of the fridge and held it in front of me in both hands, trying to find the courage to own up before the real Jenna walked in the door. Embarrassment won out – I smiled instead.

'Well, just wanted to check you were still here, and managin'. We're chock-a-block busy this weekend, and I could do with Grace stayin' out here with me, so you just carry on here and I'll come by later. Reception closes at seven.'

She'd gone. There were three more hours until seven. I hadn't eaten since my emergency lunchtime banana. At six, I plucked up the courage to take a flapjack from the shelf of food items that made up the campsite shop, but I also had nowhere to sleep that night and only £17 left in my purse. If I confessed to being Jean O'Shay, Maureen Sheehan, Paula Callahan, Aoife Briggs, Danny O'Grady, and Liam O'Grady's niece but not Becky Moffitt's, would Scarlett pay me enough to rent one of her caravans? Or report me to the police for impersonation of a holiday park employee?

* * *

At five to seven, Scarlett swung in through the door. I don't know what she had been doing all day, but her appearance suggested she spent it being pampered in an air-conditioned beauty salon. Must be something they teach you in Southern Belle School. How not to wilt. In Ballydown, we call it a hot summer's day if it stops raining long enough to dry a load of washing, and if the wind is strong enough to give you chilblains but stops short of frostbite. So I was past my best after a long afternoon in the Peace and Pigs Holiday Park complimentary steam room.

But when she came to stand next to me, I saw that in fact her eyes were creased with tiredness. Opening the book, Scarlett scanned the page. 'How'd it go?'

I garbled my answer, wound up so tight my muscles were humming.

'I'm sorry,' Scarlett drawled. She looked right at me, emphasising each word. 'I only speak English.'

I repeated myself, replicating her slow enunciation. Trying to iron the Irish out of my vowels.

'All the reservations in the book have arrived. There were no problems.'

Scarlett narrowed her eyes. Not mean. Suspicious. 'Where you from, honey?'

'Northern Ireland.'

'Hmmm.' She examined me sideways on, starting with my dark, scruffy ponytail and moving right down to my supermarket trainers, via an ill-fitting pair of jeans that I had stolen from my cousin Orla when she put on two stone after having three babies in four years.

It is a rare day that doesn't have me believing I am a little girl trapped in a woman's body. Under Scarlett's gaze, I shrank down to even less than that. An adult who has taken neither the time nor the effort to learn how to become a woman. An insult to my gender. A disgrace to females throughout the globe. I felt sure she could see through my 'I'd rather be reading!' T-shirt to the body armour of my grey and sagging underwear.

She let out a long, smooth sigh. An iced tea of disappointment.

'I was led to believe the Troubles were over. You are something akin to a war zone, sugar.'

About 98 per cent of my red blood cell supply rushed up to my cheeks and neck.

Scarlett's face softened. For one fraction of a second, I glimpsed what it must feel like to be her daughter. To be Grace.

'Well. If you are plannin' on stayin', better start to slow down your words some. And Scarlett's lesson number one: dress that pretty face with a smile once in a while. Peace and Pigs people do not want to be greeted at the reception desk with your broken heart.'

'Are you...' I took a breath. Slowed down my words some. 'Are you offering me a job? Because there is something I have to tell—'

'Sugar, I know you ain't Jenna Moffitt. I don't need to know who you are if you don't want to tell me. Although it might make things easier in the long run. I do everything by the book here, but if you want to work for your board and keep, we can work out the rest.'

'No! I don't mind telling you my real name. I'm not running away.' I became flustered under Scarlett's raised eyebrow. 'Well, not from anyone who matters. I mean, everybody matters, of course, but not anybody – um – legal. I mean...'

Scarlett held up her hand. She waited for me to look up and meet her eye, then moved her hand forward to shake mine. A business gesture. To seal a deal. But with one infinitesimal squeeze, Scarlett said much more than that. She told me I was welcome. Even with my awful clothes and clumsy words. My undisclosed past and shattered spirits were invited to rest on the porch swing of her hospitality for as long as they needed. A tiny whisper, faint as a last breath, dared to wonder if I might find a home here, under the oak trees where the sunlight dappled and the air carried a scent of honeysuckle, and with it hope.

My new employer, gracious and charming to a fault, left the room. In her absence, my tears spilled over, carving clear, clean pathways through the grime of my facade.

I managed to calm down after about twenty minutes. Only after I had wiped my face on my T-shirt, blown my nose, and stepped outside did I realise Scarlett had been waiting for me the whole time. Sitting on the stylish oak bench outside the reception building, she could have been a classic sculpture. A masterpiece carved from a single block of marble by an impassioned master craftsman. I stood hovering for a few moments until she looked at me.

'Better?'

'Yes, thank you.'

'Come on then. I need to eat.'

I fetched my bag from the car, introduced myself properly, and we began walking across the site. The whole park had only ten vans for visitors and three for staff, but throughout August, it would accommodate one hundred tents. We strolled past the wash blocks, laundry room, and playground, locations I had memorised on the map. The pitches were dotted in between the oak trees, clustered in friendly groups around brightly coloured flowerbeds, tucked away in seclusion by the edge of the forest – nothing regimented into grim rows. On the west side, where the sun would be setting in a couple of hours, Scarlett pointed out Hatherstone Hall. Maybe a quarter of a mile from the park's boundary, beyond a field full of sheep, it rose magnificent on the skyline. Built of eighteenth-century grey stone, it appeared solid and unfussy, but beautiful nonetheless. Though trees shadowed the front of the house, I could make out three storeys, the second complete with balconies in front of the two largest windows. Ivy covered all the ground floor.

'Does anybody live there?'

'The Hall? Oh, yes. Lord and Lady Hatherstone spend most of the year here, with their son. Reuben runs an organic veg box business from produce grown on the estate. And there are two employees living in the annexe behind the main house with their three kids. Still – a big enough place for eight people to be rattlin' around in, if you ask me. More trouble than it's worth. That place positively eats money.'

Scarlett continued to fill me in on the details of the estate until we reached a smallish static caravan, set apart on its own at the borders of the woodland, surrounded by a white picket fence. Next to it grew a flourishing vegetable garden, probably three times the size of my ma's yard back home. I recognised lettuce and some raspberry canes. Besides that, I was clueless. Ireland might be green, but it rains far too much in Ballydown for anybody I know to consider gardening as a hobby. Not when you can get a tin of peas at Joe's Food and Fancy Goods for 29 pence.

'This is all we have, so I hope you ain't fussy. I kept it back for Jenna Moffitt, but I'm assumin' she won't be requirin' it. It's clean, and there are some basics in the fridge to see you through to next weekend. Payday's Friday. It only takes one eye to see you need some time, honey. But Grace and I are in the blue home. Stop by whenever you're ready for company.'

She handed me a key and turned to go. I had a million questions, but managed to find the courage to ask just one: 'How is Little Johnny?'

'That hunk of ham! I could cook and eat him as soon as spend half my life in swelterin' heat chasing him around the wash block. Don't worry yourself, Marion. That pig will outlive us all.'

2

I was too tired to manage any more than a cursory glance at my new home. It had one tiny bedroom, with barely enough space to put my bag on the floor, but the bed and the wardrobe contained a multitude of drawers and compartments, more than enough room for my belongings. In one of the bedside drawers, I placed an A5-size brown envelope containing a photograph that continually drew me in – my own personal centre of gravity.

Next to the bedroom, I discovered a bathroom with a shower. A galley kitchen opening onto a living area took up the rest of the van. Here two sofas flanked a small table. I saw a CD player with a radio, but no television. More cubbyholes and cleverly designed shelving filled the walls. I had nothing left to put in them.

I found bread, milk, cheese, and salad in the kitchen. A small packet of pasta and some bottled sauces rewarded my investigation of the cupboards, but even that seemed a challenge too far at this point in my day. The small fridge included a freezer compartment at the top, just big enough for some frozen peas and two ready-meals. I heated up a frozen curry in the microwave, and ate it propped up in one of the plastic sun loungers outside, a grey woollen blanket tucked around my legs. I sat on the far side of the caravan, looking out into the trees beyond the fence. The sound of children playing gradually died down as the twilight faded into night, replaced by the hum of crickets and an occasional burst of laughter from the groups of adults gathered around the dying embers of their barbeques.

The air felt deliciously cool following the mugginess of the day, carrying a thousand scents as fresh and new to me as this sitting on my own in the dark. Not once in my life had I faced a night alone. Every thirty seconds, I jumped at a movement in the shadows, or rustling in the forest beside me, clutching the blanket up around my face until I could convince myself that it wasn't Little Johnny, out on the loose again and looking for trouble.

By eleven o'clock, the sounds of holidaymakers had all gone, and the night hung dark and deep. I reached an uneasy state of watchfulness, proud to manage fifteen minutes without goose bumps or white knuckles. Calling this a positive end to a momentous day, I went to bed. Sleep has never come easily to me, but caravan creaks and the lumpiness of a cheap old mattress turned out to be the tonic my restless mind had been awaiting all these years. I slept deeply, and dreamed of my father.

I am six years old. Daddy is sick again. The sour smell of it tugs at the hem of my dress, like octopus arms wrapping themselves around my legs until I can hardly climb the stairs. Ma smiles, smoothing my hair away from my forehead. She tells me everything will be all right; we just have to do our best. But all the time she is talking, I cannot help staring at the worry behind her eyes. Ma is afraid.

Auntie Jean comes to take me out of the house because it is no place for a child, and for pity's sake, my mother needs a rest. I scream and kick as she tries to put on my baby-blue anorak while Ma shakes her head, holding a handkerchief to her mouth. I struggle free and run upstairs to the bathroom. I lock myself in, even though I'm not allowed to touch the key, and sit on the toilet lid until I hear the front door bang shut.

When I come out, Ma says nothing. She is ironing, her lips pressed together, thin as jelly laces. Auntie Jean's eldest, Roisin, is sent round with a video, so I know I am forgiven. When Ma is downstairs talking on the phone, I do the Naughtiest Thing, creeping into the big bedroom where my daddy is resting under a mountain of blankets in my parents' bed. He opens his eyes when I climb onto the empty side next to him, placing my cool hands carefully each side of his thin, hot face. I am not allowed to disturb my father, but this is something I do most days when Ma is busy with her housework. Daddy always says no medicine in the world can beat a kiss from a princess, and if I keep disturbing him, he will be up and about in no time. I show him the video, begging him to watch it with me if I help him down the stairs and promise not to disturb him tomorrow. He says he will watch it with me only if I promise to disturb him twice tomorrow, and he can still just about get down the stairs on his own, thank you very much.

The film is about a fox called Robin Hood, who fights the bad lion and gives all his gold to the poor people. The lady fox is called Marion, like me. Robin saves her from the bad lion, who is a king, and we cheer. Daddy whistles through his teeth, but I can't do that yet, so I clap instead. Ma comes in from bringing the soaking wet laundry out of the rain and finds us on the sofa, Daddy lying across the back in his pyjamas with me curled up in front. She doesn't shout. She brings in a cup of black tea with three sugars for Daddy, and a mug of orange squash for me. Even though I have done the Naughtiest Thing, she gives us one of the cakes Mrs Lilley brought round in a tin with snowmen on it. Then, instead of dusting the ornaments or cleaning the floor, she sits on the sofa with Daddy's feet in her lap, watching the video with us right up to the moment the screen fades to a black crackle.

This is the last time my daddy comes downstairs.

3

I woke early. The sun burned through the flimsy curtains, blurry shadows dancing across my bed. I showered in the tiny bathroom, and pulled out the coolest clothes I owned: cropped cotton trousers and another T-shirt, deep blue this time. I remembered the day I was given it – my twenty-fourth birthday – and being told it matched the colour of my eyes. A wave of nausea bashed against the lining of my stomach as I thought about the person who had bought it for me. I took it off, squished it to the back of a drawer, and put on a plain white top.

I ate outside again, soft brown rolls and butter. Hot tea in a tiny cup. The air already felt thick and warm, and I reluctantly dragged my sun lounger into the shade of the caravan. I watched the woodland, alive with insects and birds darting in and out of the trees; where meadow grass met the brown forest floor, a border of wild flowers grew. I didn't know what they were called but loved their colours – blue and yellow, rose pink and deep purple. I made a promise to myself that before I left here (tomorrow? Next week? A year?), I would learn the name of each one. As well as the names of the small speckled bird hopping about on the ground, and the large grey one swooping and diving from branch to branch. I would understand where the crawling insects were trying to get to and what kept the flies under the shade of the leaves.

I had an hour until I needed to be at reception, and spent as much of it as I could sitting there, soaking it in. Trying to figure out how the forest could be so still, and yet flourish with life and constant movement. On this static canvas, a million tiny dramas, a billion scenes, played out unceasingly in every corner, under each rock and crevice. I have always been small, and here my smallness became a good thing. I am just one life in a world teeming with others. My problems, my past, the questions about my future, seemed so inconsequential – insignificant – among all this *doing*. All this *being*.

I left it so late, I had to hurry to meet Scarlett at eight, breathless by the time I pushed open the door. Scarlett perched on the stool behind the counter, tapping into a calculator and jotting numbers into an accounts book. She wore narrow tortoiseshell glasses today, her hair swept up in a French pleat. She closed the book and set it aside, looking me quickly up and down before removing her glasses, carefully folding them into a leather case.

'Good morning. You look as if you slept well. That's what the forest air'll do for ya.' Scarlett moved out from behind the counter, gesturing for me to sit on the stool. 'Could you man the desk again for me today, sweetheart? We have fifteen new guests due in. Sunday is always our busiest day for check-in, and Grace has the mornin' off. While you wait, you can check the stock for me; make a list of anything that looks low. I'll send Valerie over to fetch it later. You'll like Valerie. She's a little different, needs extra help with some things, but is very special.'

She left me with a notepad and pen, and I set to work. What did she mean, 'anything that looks low'? Did three packets of rice count as low if there was no more room on the shelf? What about the boxes of matches? There were eight left, but a big space behind them. I spent a while fluttering in front of the shelves counting the same rows of goods over and over again. When the bell jangled to announce the day's first arrivals, it came as a relief.

Three check-ins later, the door swung open and a young woman bounced in. She came to land six inches from my face and grinned at me.

'Hi.'

'Hello.' I pulled back, a little disconcerted.

'I'm Valerie. You're Marion.' She giggled, jiggling up and down on her toes. 'You look scared.'

'I'm not scared.' *Lie. I'm always scared.* But I admitted: 'I am anxious.'

She stuffed one of her blonde bunches into her mouth and chewed on it.

'Why?'

'I'm supposed to be making a list for Scarlett, but I haven't started it yet.'

'Why not?' Valerie gazed right at me, letting the draggly hair drop out of her mouth. Something in her eyes, so clear I could almost see right into her soul, dissolved the tension in my throat.

'I don't know what to do. Look.' I crouched down beside the bottom shelf, and Valerie squatted next to me, a frown creasing her forehead. 'There are six tins of tuna, with space for maybe two more. Is that enough, or should I write it on the list? Have these poor six tins been sat here for years collecting dust, down on the bottom shelf where no one will notice them? Are they desperately hoping nobody buys any more new, flashy tins to stick right at the front? What if the new tins are dolphin-friendly, or tuna steak, not plain chunks? What if these faithful, trusty tins of chunks reach their best-before date, doomed to never be opened? A mummy tuna fish is swimming around in some sea somewhere, endlessly searching for her lost baby tuna fish. Broken hearted! And if I order too many tins to sit on this shelf, the lost baby tuna fish will have been sacrificed for nothing.'

Valerie looked sideways at me. 'The average female blue-fin tuna fish releases thirty million eggs at a time. Each baby tuna has a one-in-forty-million chance of reaching adulthood.' She snorted. 'You need help.'

I sighed and shook my head. Her disarming candour convinced me I had an ally in Valerie; I couldn't help trusting her. 'If only you knew.'

It took Valerie five minutes at most to point out what stock needed replenishing. Then she helped herself to an ice-cream from the freezer cabinet, handing a second one to me. She bombarded me with the obvious questions. Where did I come from? How old was I? Did I like her sparkly flip-flops? Where was my mum? As she neared territory I felt uncomfortable thinking about, let alone discussing out loud, I turned the conversation back to her.

Valerie was nineteen. She had lived with Scarlett at the park since her sixteenth birthday. Before then, home had been with her mother in the nearby village of Hatherstone. Her mum had kept hold of her as long as welfare benefit could be claimed. Even then, she told me (between long licks of vanilla ice-cream), most of her evenings and weekends had been spent here, helping Scarlett, for as long as she could remember.

'Mum hates me because she thinks I'm stupid.' She shrugged. 'But I'm not.'

If it were possible, my estimation of my new boss grew even higher.

'Do you have a dad?' Valerie dabbed absent-mindedly at a dribble of ice-cream with her thumb.

'I did, but he died.'

Her eyes grew round. She stared at me, blinking back tears.

'It's all right.' I rubbed her arm, awkwardly. People rarely knew how to react to this information, but nobody had started crying on me before. Valerie screwed up her face, now turning blotchy. 'It was a long time ago. I hardly miss him at all any more.' *Lie.*

She leaned in and put her arms around me. I could smell baby lotion. Her body shuddered as she began to sob. 'That's terrible, Marion. I never had a daddy, and Grace's daddy was a no-good dirty rotten crook, and Scarlett's Pop did Bad Things to her and made her run all the way to England to hide from him. And your daddy died. Where are all the nice daddies, Marion?'

We stood like this for a couple of minutes. I could feel the sticky mess from Valerie's mouth pressing against my cheek. Thinking so hard, processing this new information, I forgot to answer her question. Only when she mumbled it again, 'Does anybody have a nice daddy?' did I disentangle myself, pulling her over to the window.

'Look.' I pointed to a grassy space where a young man played rugby with two boys. They squealed with delight as he wrestled the ball off them and they collapsed in a pile of laughter.

On the path to one side, a small girl swung from her father's hand as they ambled across to the toilet block. Another pushed his child on a tricycle, draping his spare arm around the pretty woman walking beside him. As I watched, the ache in my chest swelled, pressing hard against my ribs. Valerie stared through the glass, transfixed. She reached out, absent-mindedly, and wrapped her fingers around mine.

A motor-home big enough to intimidate a space shuttle rumbled up the drive, pulling to a stop in the car park. My new friend beamed again. She raced outside to greet the newest visitors (two nice daddies, and a granddad), and I got back to work.

After lunch, Scarlett ushered me outside. She declared that I would be gardening that afternoon, primarily because my pale, pasty, damp-pickled complexion was screamin' for some sunshine like a baby for its mother. The garden fork dangled awkwardly in my hesitant grip as Scarlett directed me to a large flowerbed dug in the shape of a heart.

'Here we go. Scarlett's lesson on weeding. One: remember a weed is just a plant growin' where you don't want it to be. Grass here' – she waved at the lawn, her nails deep purple to match her tailored shorts – 'wonderful. We love it thick, lush and fertile. Now here' – she pointed back at the bed – 'it is oversteppin' its welcome. Yank it out!

'Pretty much any living thing is accepted at the Peace and Pigs, with the exception of certain human specimens. But we respect each other's personal space. And some plants are just too greedy!

'They reproduce like my old Pop – without a care or a thought for what their offspring are gonna eat or who is gonna suffer because of their greedy, philanderin' ways. Like these dandelions here.'

I gave myself a mental pat on the back for recognising the dandelions.

'Exercise some common sense, and dig 'em up. Two: if it's got shallow roots, it's a weed. Rip it out! Most healthy, respectful, worthwhile plants need to put down decent roots. They shrivel otherwise.

'Three: just make it look nice and pretty. Everything benefits from a bit of thought, care and attention to tidy it up. A critical, independent eye.'

I wasn't sure if we were still just talking about plants.

'If it looks dead, pull it up. Brown means dead. Peace and Pigs is a place of life and livin'! No room for dead weight or dead wood or what's past its time. Haul it up. Four...'

The whole time she was talking, Scarlett had been gazing at the flowers. Now she turned and fixed her strong eyes on me.

'I don't care an owl's hoot if you mess it up. Just get stuck in and use those womanly muscles hidin' somewhere underneath that pale, pale skin. They'll thank you for it later. And remember lesson number one. Now enjoy yourself.'

Training over, I tried to get stuck in. My womanly muscles were soon swearing at me in protest, but I did begin to enjoy myself, so I pretended to be my new boss and told them to quit whinin' and knuckle down. The first half hour was easy. I pulled up every dandelion. Then I pulled up the stray grass. Then Valerie walked past and pointed out the weeds called buttercups and shepherd's purse.

'Be careful, Marion. Each shepherd's purse has an average of 4,500 seeds. And their seeds can last for thirty-five years in the soil. That's a long time!'

I picked up one of the tiny seedpods and balanced it on the end of my finger. It was the shape of a heart. Thirty-five years. He would have been here then. In the forest. I tucked the pod in my pocket. Even though I knew that heart could only grow weeds.

An hour in and my endorphins were buzzing. I wondered why I had never gardened before, Northern Irish rain notwithstanding. Another hour passed and I realised why. Too much time to think. I had pondered about Scarlett, Grace, and Valerie, replayed and analysed the last two days and wondered what I might have for dinner and if there was anywhere in the village I could buy some cooler clothes. I had even designed the logo for Marion's Landscapers and Outdoor Design, the friendly, stylish garden team with a Celtic twist. But inevitably my thoughts then began scuttling back over the Irish Sea. I only knew one good way to drag them back. Clapping my hands together, adjusting my balance on the knee protector mat, I smiled cheerfully at the flowers in front of me, politely (yet firmly) requesting their attention. I then recited word for word my personally chosen Ballydown Public Library's story of the week as I cleared their home of greedy, selfish invaders. I think the roses particularly enjoyed Chapter Three, 'Escape in the Knickers of Time'.

Stories saved my life. Trapped in my prison of silence, doctors and speech therapists and child psychologists could not reach me. The love of my mother was too feeble to pull me free. I lived alone in a swirling, writhing smog of fear that clamped across my mouth with its cold, dank fingers. Stories provided enough light to show me the way out.

Happy ending successfully concluded, I clambered to my feet and stretched the ache out of my back. As I tossed the last few weeds into a wheelbarrow, a man ambled down the path toward me from the reception building. He wore a red polo shirt with the campsite logo on one pocket. Stopping next to me, he smiled, dark eyes crinkling in the late afternoon sunlight.

'Marion?'

'Yes.' I wiped my face with my arm, self-consciously trying to erase any smears of dirt. The man looked younger than me, early twenties, with sun-bleached hair and a knowing tilt to his mouth. I suddenly became very aware of my filthy clothes and having spent the afternoon working up a sweat.

'I'm Jake.' He paused, waiting for me to say something. I didn't, so he carried on. 'Scarlett says if you take the tools back to the shed then you can finish for the day.'

'Oh! Okay.' I leaned down and picked up the fork and trowel, bending my stiff legs as little as possible.

Jake watched, his smile broadening. He grabbed the handles of the wheelbarrow, now full of weeds. 'Coming to Fire Night?'

'What?'

'It's Sunday. Scarlett always puts on a barbeque for the staff over at her van. Everyone brings something to share. We chat, eat chicken, maybe have a bit of entertainment.' He nudged me with his elbow. 'Come on – it's fun.'

Help!

'I haven't been invited. I don't have anything to bring. I'm pretty tired.'

'I'm inviting you. And you won't be expected to bring anything. There's always far too much anyway. Come on.' He gestured with his head over toward the staff caravans. 'Just stay for a beer and a burger.'

I hesitated, not sure how to say that sitting around feeling obliged to make small talk with a bunch of people I don't know, who all happen to know each other, while pretending to enjoy it, is in my top ten list of things to avoid at all costs.

'I'll come and knock for you at eight.' He strode off, pushing the barrow with practiced ease.

4

It was that moment every Ballydown girl has been dreaming about her whole life. My dress too tight, my heels too high, my hair forced against its will to three times its usual volume, I was swaying awkwardly in the middle of the dance floor when the cheesy ballad screeched to a stop. A hush fell over the crowd. Out of the corner of my eye, I spotted Auntie Jean clutching hold of my mother's arm, tissue at the ready. My mother did not require a tissue.

The man in front of me dropped smoothly to one knee. For a brief second, I wondered if he had been practising in front of the mirror. He gripped my hand, which was damp with nerves, and squeezed it reassuringly. I was not reassured. He lifted up his other hand. The ring held between his thumb and index finger sparkled, dazzling. I couldn't imagine where he had found the money to pay for it. He cleared his throat. I tried to ignore the lace on the dress I did not choose myself, scratching beneath my arm. The catch of the town, my gorgeous, newly qualified doctor boyfriend, in front of all our family and all his friends – just about everyone I had ever known – asked me the question. Well, sort of.

'Marion. You've been so patient waiting for me all these years.

Putting up with long shifts and all those nights alone when I had to study. But we finally got here, and on this special night, when we celebrate the result of all that hard work and sacrifice, I want to make it official and let everybody know that you are still the one for me. I can't wait to spend the rest of my life with you by my side.'

If that speech made me sound as if I had spent seven years while he attended medical school sitting about on my growing backside picking out wallpaper patterns, then it was pretty much spot on. Except I couldn't be bothered to pick out wallpaper. I did pick my nails.

He wriggled the ring onto my finger, and the place erupted with the sound of cheers, whistles and Bruno Mars crooning 'I think I wanna marry you' in a rare Ballydown foray into the twenty-first century. My future in-laws rushed over to smother us in hugs, vodka-soaked kisses, and manly slaps on the back, and the rest of the party soon followed them. I was left spinning in a whirl of congratulations. Someone shoved a glass of bubbles in my hand, and my Uncle Danny tried to pick me up and spin me around before realising that he was far too old and drunk to get me off the ground. I smiled, and said thank you a hundred times, until my cheeks ached with lies told and words swallowed back with cheap wine.

Nobody noticed that I hadn't said yes.

* * *

At 8.15 p.m., I handed over my hastily assembled pasta salad to Scarlett, who received it with unwarranted grace. Particularly considering I had put it together using ingredients found in the caravan kitchen, which she had paid for. Having been introduced to two other people and promptly forgotten their names, I perched awkwardly on a plastic chair, trying to fade into the background. It's my party trick.

Jake took command of the barbeque, a vast brick construction along one side of the meadow Scarlett had fenced off to form her garden. Trees surrounded us, and just out of sight I could hear a stream cascading into the lake. Scarlett busied herself fetching glasses, plates of salad, and buttery potatoes. Chicken breasts and fat ribs sizzled over coals. She batted away my offer of help. I am sure she knew I would prefer to hide in the kitchen, but decided I should mingle instead.

'Katarina, Sunny – did you know Marion is from Northern Ireland? Didn't you go to Ireland one time?'

'Ooooh, yes!' Katarina was a huge, Viking, forty-ish woman with pale-red hair rippling down her back. She stood six feet tall (at least) and her circumference couldn't have been far off that. Barely covered by a strapless mini dress, she displayed the type of pillowy breasts grown men sob into.

'Come sit! Come sit!' She yanked over my chair – with me on it – and leaned forwards, thrusting eight inches of freckly cleavage under my nose.

'Sunny! Fetch Marion a drink!'

Sunny resembled a beanpole version of his wife, only younger. He brought me a glass of water (with ice and lemon for the poor, hot girl) and I braced myself to negotiate the minefield of small talk. Fortunately, Katarina seemed happy to chat about herself, one of those conversationalists who only part way through one story remember another, and then realise it makes sense only if they digress into a different story for explanation. Like panning for gold, here and there a flash of useful information gleamed among the mountain of words. I did manage to piece together that Katarina worked as the groundswoman at Hatherstone Hall, while Sunny balanced working part-time as housekeeper with taking care of their three children.

At one point, Katarina called out in a different language – it sounded like something Scandinavian – and three tiny people with hair the actual colour of carrots appeared from a clump of bushes at the far end of the meadow by the water, all of them plastered in mud. Literally, they were walking mud pies in mud shorts and T-shirts. Bright teeth glinting in unapologetic smiles, they scampered up to their parents. It was hard not to flinch away from the dripping, splattering mass of skinny arms and legs. It was harder still to decide whether to laugh, or join with Katarina in her frown of disbelief.

'What is this?' She held up both hands in surrender. 'What is the explanation for my darling children being exchanged for the scariest, most dangerous-looking mud monsters? What are you doing here? And what have you done with my beautiful, clean children?'

They wriggled with laughter. The smallest child tried to climb on her mother's knee, leaving two smeary handprints of dirt on her leg.

'No, no! I will not have this! My knee is not for nasty, squelchy blobs of dirt. Then my nice, spotless little girl and boys will no longer want to sit there. Go away and don't come back. And tell my precious, immaculate, good children that if they want any pudding they must return in ten minutes.'

The children exchanged glances.

'Ten minutes. Not a second more. Or no pudding. Be sure to tell them this message now, won't you?'

They nodded that they would tell them, and dashed back in the direction they had appeared from.

Katarina huffed. 'See, this is what happens when a man is left in charge. My children are roaming free like wild animals. Looking for every possible means of making mischief with no thought of the consequences. What shall become of them, Marion?'

At this point, Sunny returned with another piece of chicken for his wife. I couldn't understand any of the rapid words that flew between them. But when they had finished, Sunny grinned and sat back down on the grass, shrugging his shoulders. Katarina tutted and tossed her hair, but no translator was necessary to interpret the twitch at the corner of her mouth as she grabbed her husband's head and wiped her knee on his cheek.

Ten minutes later, three children came charging out of the bushes. Not a speck of dirt remained on their skin. They had solved the problem of their filthy clothes by leaving them behind, including the girl's nappy. Sunny made origami pants out of paper napkins and tied tea-towel cloaks around their necks while each of his offspring ate giant bowls of ice-cream, without letting a single drip end up anywhere but in their mouths. He then retrieved the clothes and kissed Katarina soundly on the lips. I sat there, watching all this, amazed and bewildered that no cross words, no slaps on bare behinds, no threats or tears or whining had occurred.

I decided I liked Sunny. And Katarina. Their attitude rocked. I was actually – maybe – possibly enjoying myself.

A short while later, we heard a car pull up on the other side of Scarlett's caravan, then the sound of a door slamming followed by the screech of wheels accelerating off way over the five miles per hour campsite speed limit. Valerie appeared, a wispy husk of the girl I had met that morning. It looked as if the real Valerie had shed her skin, and this was the old, dead exo-skeleton drifting into the garden.

'Oh, honey!' Scarlett put down a bowl of bread and was next to her foster daughter in three strides. She wrapped herself around the Valerie-shell and buried her face in her hair. For a long, long time they stood there. Scarlett poured out love into that girl like sunshine onto the water. I have never seen two people stand so together and so still for so long. Jake flipped chops and swigged from his beer bottle behind them.

Katarina leaned over to me and whispered, loudly enough for the family on the other side of the lake to hear: 'First Sunday of the month. Valerie visits her mother. It is not good! She sucks all hope and happiness right out of her own child. Drains all the good feelings and the knowing that she is smart and beautiful and loved – drains them right out! Gone! To feed her own despair and pathetic failure. But Scarlett knows that strong arms can rebuild a shattered heart. Valerie remembers who she is again – watch!'

She was right. Valerie grew three inches inside that hug. By the time Scarlett let her go, she was bouncing again. Scarlett sent her off to check there were enough napkins, and only then did she allow the cost of loving Valerie back to life pass across her face. Scarlett closed her eyes, briefly, and let her shoulders sag, just half an inch, for a couple of seconds. Then she tipped up her chin and shook off the pain with a flick of blonde curls.

I didn't know why I had worried so much about coming to the party. Whether Scarlett had briefed everyone beforehand, or they were just used to strangers coming and going, I didn't figure out. But no one asked me anything about home, or my previous life, or how on earth I ended up working at the Peace and Pigs when all I wanted was directions to the visitor centre – the one I still hadn't visited.

Grace stomped in about nine o'clock, tightening the muscles along her mother's jaw. She grabbed a beer and plonked herself down on a chair next to Jake. Over on the other side of the meadow, Katarina raised her eyebrows at Scarlett.

'I know, Katarina, I know. But it's just one beer and she'll be eighteen in five months. To be honest with you, I'm more concerned about where she's been since ten this mornin'. A super-

vised drink I can deal with. Drugs in the woods with grown men –
that's what bothers me.'

'No! Is she at this again? I still say she is not too old for a good
walloping across her alternatively dressed backside! Are you
working her hard enough, Scarlett?'

'Oh, she works hard enough. And I honestly don't know what
she's getting up to any more. She promised me what happened
before was a one-time thing. I don't think I can really follow her,
can I? When I was her age, I lived on my own in the city, workin'
three jobs to save up for my plane ticket outta there. I just wish she
could still talk to me.'

'She is very angry with you, Scarlett.'

Scarlett sighed, and shook her head. 'I know. She's angry with
the whole world. But that don't make her daddy into a man worth
knowin'. And as long as I live and breathe, I will spare her that
heartache.'

At that point, another man joined us, tall and broad, wearing
workman's boots with worn jeans and a faded checked shirt. His
hair and beard shone pure white, and his face gleamed as brown as
polished walnut. Moving with the confident ease of a man who
knows and likes himself, he bent and kissed each of the women in
turn – except me. He reached out and took my hand instead, intro-
ducing himself as Samuel T. Waters.

'So, are you here for the summer?' He settled down on a tree
stump, stretching out long, straight legs in front of him. 'Or maybe
longer?'

'Yes. I think so.' I hesitated. 'I'm not really sure...'

'Oh ho! A lady of mystery!'

'She's only been here two days, Samuel,' Scarlett scolded.

'Ah yes, but does she know that you and your campsite of peace
and pigs are irresistible, dear Scarlett?' He winked at me. 'I would
move in here myself if the big boss-woman would employ me, but

she refuses to give me a job. Says I'm a shoddy worker. I tried getting her to marry me instead, but she won't have it. Says I'm too tall to live in a caravan. Ah, Marion, just look at her. Wouldn't it be worth a crick in the neck, waking up to that glorious vision of womanhood every morning?'

'Will you behave yourself?' Scarlett stood up and swept over to the food table. 'Now, for mercy's sake, plug that ridiculous mouth of yours with some chicken before I have to turn the hose on you.'

When the shadows had settled into every corner and the piles of food had been reduced to scrapings and bones, as the air hummed with crickets and the breeze called for our cardigans, Fire Night began in earnest. Jake and Samuel built up the fire in its pit. Grace, I noticed, hovered in Jake's shadow. Valerie brought out skewers and bags of marshmallows, with mugs of thick, steaming chocolate or rich coffee. Sunny told me there were usually more musicians at Fire Night but, being August, they'd gone on holiday elsewhere. Still, Jake had brought his guitar and sang songs we all knew well enough to join in with. Katarina thumped time with a stick on a wooden crate, and Valerie danced with Samuel. If we had replaced the forest with the dark walls of a pub, and the fragrance of coffee and wood smoke with Guinness and cigarettes, I could have been back home.

I remembered with an ache in my throat that it would be my youngest cousin Maggie's first communion in two weeks. There I would sit in the back room of Doherty's and listen to all the old stories, the fresh gossip. My aunts would ask my mother (not me) what flowers had been chosen for the wedding, whether Wee Kitty would still be a bridesmaid after what she'd got up to with Finny Brown. They would shake their heads, marvelling that such a good man would turn his head toward our Marion. I would feel safe, being with people I had known forever in a place where I had always lived. But at the same time, I would feel small, useless, and trapped. I decided then and there that I would not be at Maggie's party. They could talk about me instead.

It had been a long week, and by midnight, I felt more than ready to scrunch back along the gravel path to my caravan. It was a clear night, but under the trees the darkness gathered into a thick black blanket. Without a torch, I gratefully accepted Jake's offer to escort me home. We had spoken only briefly during the course of the evening and there had been little opportunity for one-on-one conversation. I had enjoyed just sitting in the group, listening and joining in the songs. Now we were alone together in the dark, the presence of this man next to me felt slightly overwhelming. I could hear his breathing, faintly, and when I stumbled over a stone and he grabbed my arms to stop me falling, I could feel the warmth of his hands through my sweatshirt.

I started to panic. Help! Why had I let him walk me back? What did it mean? Had I inadvertently promised him something at the end of this walk? Was I supposed to ask him in for coffee or – please, no – more than coffee? I tried to focus on the path in front of me. *It's just a walk, for goodness' sake. We're colleagues. Scarlett must have rules about her members of staff sharing late-night coffees.*

Jake stopped at the little white gate and I began praying he couldn't hear my heart hammering as if I had just run ten laps of the park. His perfect teeth glinted in the moonlight as he smiled and I tried very hard to open my mouth and say something appropriate.

'Well. Thank you very much. I had a really nice evening...' Stop shaking, voice! He'll think you are trembling with pent-up passion! He'll do something out of pity for the frumpy, shy girl and you don't have enough courage to fend him off.

Jake took a step closer. He slipped his hands out of his pockets, and tipped his head to the side. I really, really did not want this man to kiss me. For ten thousand reasons. Mostly good ones, like hardly knowing him, an attempt at self-respect, and not actually being sure if I was engaged to somebody else at that moment. Some not so critical, like the tiny kernel of corn on the cob wedged between my teeth.

Just as, in super-slow motion like on the films, he reached the point of no return, the 'Yes, I am moving in to kiss you now, make no mistake about it' moment, and I stood like a small animal mesmerised by a predator, a sudden shrieking noise interrupted the slick smoothness of his move. Jake froze, his head bent down about eight inches from my face. The shriek came again, louder this time. We turned toward the direction the shriek had come from. My caravan.

Instantly, my need to get away from Jake seemed a lot less urgent. I clutched hold of his arm and shuffled along behind as he approached the caravan. He gestured for me to stay at the bottom of the veranda steps, and stealthily moved up to the door. I didn't stay. It was my caravan, the first place I had lived in by myself, and my initial moment of fright gave way to indignation. I'd locked up before leaving for Fire Night but, as Jake cautiously tried the door, it opened now. He slowly turned the handle, waiting for another wailing cry before he threw the door wide open, disappearing inside. I followed a millisecond behind him. And then sort of wished I hadn't.

It was one of those times when your eyes see something so awful your brain can't get the message down the nerve endings to 'Stop looking! Turn away! Turn away!' That image has about thirty seconds to burn itself onto the back of your retina only to forever pop back up at the most inappropriate moments...

Okay. So maybe I overreacted, but I had never seen two old, wrinkled, hairy, *dangly* people naked before. Naked and *entangled*. Except that the man still had on a pair of socks held up with those old-fashioned garters. Pink socks.

Jake twizzled around, facing me. Thankfully, that broke the hypnotic spell and I was able to take my eyes off the sight in front of me. He grinned.

'Good evening, my lord. My lady. Can I pass you your clothes?' he called over his shoulder.

Lord and Lady? Hatherstone?

'Good evening, Jacob.' The man spoke. He sounded like an English aristocrat from a cheesy sitcom. 'Good Fire Night? We were on our way, but got slightly diverted. I am afraid our clothes are in the forest. No problem! We'll get them. Looks as if we weren't the only pair wanting to make use of the spare caravan. Nothing like a change of scenery to add a bit of rumpy to your pumpy!'

I was still temporarily speechless. I had never seen two people naked and rumpy-pumpying before. Ever.

'This isn't the spare caravan, Lord Hatherstone. Marion is living here now. I was just walking her home.'

'Oh! Right. Well, pleased to meet you, Marion.' The lord and lady helped each other up and reached around Jake to shake my hand. Lady Hatherstone leaned forward and kissed me on each cheek, prompting her husband to follow suit.

Do not look down! Do not look down!

Of course I looked down.

5

It was the day of my father's funeral. For the past three days, the body that had belonged to Daddy had been laid out in the dining room. He wasn't in it any more. People hadn't stopped coming and going the whole time. They kissed the face that used to be his, and stroked his hand. My aunties cried and my uncles said: 'One of the best,' and, 'Don't worry, son, we'll see the wee girls right,' and blew their noses. My mother sat in the corner chair twisting one of Daddy's hankies round and round in her fingers. She seemed tinier every time I looked at her. There was only a little bit of her left. Her sisters tried to press cups of tea into her hands, but she wouldn't take them; she just kept twisting the hanky. She had not looked at me. This was because she knew it was my fault. Nobody else did, but I knew and Ma knew, and so she could not look at me any more.

Right now, there was nobody here. Auntie Jean had gone back to get the boys smartened up for church. I had put on my blue dress with the matching cardigan. It was too short and the collar pinched my neck, but it was the one Daddy liked best. I sat on my bed and listened to the sound of my mother moving about in her room. After a long, long time, she opened the door of my bedroom and stood there, watching me. At first, I thought this was better, but then she spoke. The voice that came out was not my mother's voice. It was twisted and raspy and thin.

'You did this. With your constant noise and banging about. Running up and down the stairs like a herd of elephants! And you never left him alone. How many times did I tell you to leave him be, let him sleep? Chattering on about this and that. Stupid nothing-talk that wore him out and drove him to his grave. As if a man in his condition wanted to hear about spelling tests and silly little girls' parties. You sucked the life out of him. He was too good to tell you to stop bothering him. Too kind. And you just wouldn't let him rest. Didn't I tell you this would happen? I will never forgive you for this, you selfish cow. You talked your own father to death. Every time I hear that whiny little voice of yours, I remember what you did like a blade through my heart. I will never forgive you.'

She left the room. I did not cry. She had told me a hundred times to leave my father alone, to stop bothering him. That it was the Naughtiest Thing. But Daddy loved me, and when he asked me to come, I had to. I knew my stories made him tired, but I told them anyway. Now he was gone. I had killed him and I would never see him again.

I did not speak again that day. Or that week. Ma didn't notice, lost in her anger and grief. My other relatives tried to coax words out of me. They all thought they knew best how to get me to talk. One hugged me for hours and hours, smashing my face tight against her enormous chest. Some tried sweets, or put their babies in my arms. One talked sternly at me, told me to pull myself together, and that's not what my daddy would have wanted, now, was it? Life goes on. They pleaded with me for my mother's sake. They did not know. My words had killed my father. I would not kill her too.

* * *

Thursday was my first day off. I didn't want it to be. I had spent Monday learning how to look after Little Johnny, his wife Madame Plopsicle, and two daughters, Louisiana and Mississippi. Valerie showed me the ropes. Did I know that pigs are the fourth most intelligent animal in the world? And that pigs have no sweat glands – that's why they roll around in mud, to keep cool?

Tuesday I was back in reception, and had a lesson from Scarlett on cleaning bathrooms that have been messed up by someone other than myself.

'Think glorious sunsets over the ocean. Walkin' through crisp, fresh snow. Dancin' in the moonlight in a strong man's arms. Do not, whatever you do, think about what you are scrubbin', scrapin' and scoopin'. Focus on the hot and happenin' dress that you are goin' to buy with the money you are earnin' right now. Do not let yourself wonder how that hair got where it did, or what that glob of somethin' might be. For the next half hour, your body is a machine, operatin' on automatic. Your mind, sugar, had better take itself somewhere else.'

Wednesday I was on chicken duty. Did I know the chicken is the closest living animal to the tyrannosaurus rex? No, but I have learned that they are nearly as scary, and chicken pecks leave a bruise. I weeded, sold ice-creams, and picked up litter. My muscles got so sore, but the ache that dragged deep within my bones melted away in the sunshine. And the evenings! Three nights sitting counting stars, a good book, and a soft blanket over my knees.

I must have opened my bedside drawer a hundred times and peeked inside the envelope. I was not ready to do anything about it yet. Soon. Getting sooner.

When Scarlett announced I could have Thursday off – I *must* have Thursday off – I had to try to cover up my disappointment. I spent an hour cleaning my caravan, did a load of washing and finished my book sitting in the sunshine, but I was starting to wake up, and it felt so good that I daren't stop or slow down for even a day. I would have gone shopping. My fridge was just about empty, and had it not been for the bag of leftovers firmly placed into my hands after Fire Night, I would have been living off stolen ice-creams by now. But I didn't have enough money to do a decent shop, and with payday coming up, it made more sense to wait.

I could have gone to the Sherwood Forest visitor centre. But I tried that idea on and found it too big a fit for me that particular day. Soon. Getting sooner.

I fidgeted and faffed about for another half an hour until I spotted Jake making his way down the gravel path toward my caravan. I had managed to successfully avoid him for most of the previous three days. The times we had crossed paths, I had scuttled past and mumbled something about an urgent message for Scarlett, or hidden behind a tree. He smiled at me as if I were an amusing puppy, and left me to my fumbling blushes. But here he came now, and he had caught sight of me through the window before I had time to duck into the bathroom.

He knocked, and walked straight in. He wasn't wearing the campsite T-shirt today, just a plain white shirt and a pair of khaki shorts.

'Hi.' He glanced around, his eyes settling on the middle of the floor. 'Bit quieter than last time I was here. Seems more spacious too.'

'Yes. Thanks again for, you know...'

'No problem. Not the best timing, though.'

Oh, dear.

He looked up and levelled his gaze on mine. His eyes were hazel, with long, thick lashes. I got the feeling he had used this look once or twice before. 'What are we doing today, then?'

I stood up and pretended to hunt for my shoes. They were in the bedroom, but honestly, to go into my bedroom in that tiny caravan with a man who had just looked at me without blinking for at least thirty seconds standing right there – I daren't do it.

'Well, actually I have the day off,' I mumbled, poking my head under the table in my feigned search. The room was empty. Only a fool would be scrambling around under there, but if he decided I must be an idiot, maybe he would leave me alone.

'I know. I thought we could go into Nottingham, maybe. See what's on at the cinema. Grab some lunch. Visit the castle.' My heart stopped for a second. The castle! A ripple of yearning spread through my insides, sending goose bumps down my bare arms. I *hungered* to visit the castle. But not today. Not with Jake. I pulled myself upright.

'That sounds great. But I have some things I need to do. Some shopping to get. Boring stuff. *Women's issues.*' I have seventeen male cousins. I knew that the mention of *women's issues* would squash his manly urges quicker than a Polaroid of Lord and Lady Hatherstone rumpy-pumpying on the brown lino. I slipped on my sandals, one glance confirming it was now safe to open the bedroom door, and grabbed my bag from the sofa.

'Sorry about that. Maybe another time?' *No! Not another time! Shut up, Marion!*

'Yeah – sure. I'll see you later?' He was out of the door and backing down the steps. 'Maybe not today, I mean if you're – like – busy. Um, Fire Night?'

'Okay. Bye, Jake.'

He was gone.

To keep up the pretence of going out, even though I no longer had anybody to pretend to, I walked up to my car, still parked at reception, and clambered in. The steering wheel was so hot, I thought I might have blistered the palms of my hands, and I detected a faint stink of warm rubbish. So when I turned the engine on and found I had nearly run out of petrol, I felt glad of the excuse to scramble out again. I couldn't take the car out when I had no money to refill the tank. Scarlett poked her head out of the reception door. Her hair was up in a bun today. She looked like the principal dancer in a royal ballet from somewhere stylish and European.

'Car trouble, honey?'

'No. I just decided I might prefer some fresh air.'

'Where you off to?'

'I don't know, really.'

'Well, why don't ya check out the village? It's two and a half miles – a fair way to trek on a scorcher like this one, but you can take Pettigrew.' Scarlett emerged from the doorway in a pair of soft grey linen trousers and a silk top. Leading me around to the side of reception, she introduced me to Pettigrew the bike. The sort of bike that deserves a name: rainbow striped, with a gold basket on the front and shiny plastic flowers clipped to the wheel spokes. The tyres were turquoise, and the seat and handlebars orange. Streamers adorned the basket, and on the handlebars an enormous clown horn replaced the usual bell. I stepped back, held my breath. Scarlett met my eye, her face set firm.

Well. I wanted to stop being invisible. This would do it.

'There is a slight problem.'

Scarlett narrowed her eyes at me, preparing to swat away any excuse.

'I sold my bike after I failed my cycling proficiency test at school when I was ten. I used the money to buy a copy of *Little Women*.'

'Hmm. What did you fail on? Somethin' dangerous?'

'I don't know specifics. The examiner just wrote an exclamation mark on the test sheet.'

She smiled, and wheeled Pettigrew over to where I hunched in the shade of the reception wall.

'Scarlett's lesson on ridin' a bike. One: don't witter, waver or worry about wobblin'. Get up, get on and get goin'. Just keep pushin' one foot in front of the other. Don't stop, don't slow down and – whatever you do – don't look back. Do not turn to the side, do not focus on any obstacles in your way, look to the wide-open spaces and roll right on through 'em. It's all about keeping *balanced*. Two: feel the wind whistlin' in your hair. Shoulders back, chin up! Breathe in and breathe out, open your eyes and take it steady over the bumps. Three: and most important of all...' She lifted her hand and tucked a stray lock of hair behind my ear. Her voice grew soft. 'Be free.'

I wheeled Pettigrew over to a break in the treeline where a signpost told me the small wooden posts with blue arrows would lead me to Hatherstone village. A bag containing my purse and caravan keys sat in the basket. Buried underneath them I had tucked the brown envelope containing the photograph. Moving it from the drawer to my bag felt like a big step. I whispered a prayer into the woods that I was not kidding myself; that I would not slink back to Ireland one day with the photograph untouched and unseen.

Scarlett tactfully returned to her post at reception and, peering into the darkness ahead, wishing my phone had not been tossed into a bin at Dublin Docks, I braved the saddle for the first time in fifteen years.

'Okay,' I huffed to myself twenty metres down the path. 'It's true, I haven't forgotten how to ride a bike. I'm still dangerously incompetent.'

Initially I creaked and teetered through the trees so slowly I felt tempted to get off and push the whole way there, to save time. I jerked to a stop at every sharp turn or fallen branch, failing to notice anything beyond the dirt path in front of my nose or the blue arrows every few hundred metres. But eventually, as I eased off my white-knuckle grip on the handlebars, I began to get the hang of steering while keeping my balance; my shoulders relaxed. The thrill of being entirely surrounded by the forest – *this* forest – wrapped itself around me.

I could have been the only person alive. It was fabulous. The trees rustled and rasped with the wisdom of a thousand years, and it seemed as if every other creature kept silence in honour of their age and beauty. I soared through dozens of miniature spotlights, where the sun's rays flickered through chinks in the verdant roof above my head, illuminating the insects in their dance shows, warming my skin with an ancient blessing. Nothing mattered for those two miles. My messy life unravelled like a snagged jumper behind me as I pedalled on, swallowed up by the mystery and grandeur of a road well-travelled. Nothing like a few hundred-foot oaks to help you find perspective.

The path led right up to the village. Hatherstone consisted mostly of a main street lined with imposing red-brick houses and a handful of shops. A shabby looking pub, an old church and a village hall interrupted the row, and on the forecourt of the hall I saw a cluster of market stalls. I rode proudly along the street, managing to smile at a bunch of holidaymakers ambling along, licking ice-creams.

I dismounted at a market stall laden down with tourist items. One corner displayed expensive woollen sweaters, trinkets, and ornaments that nobody would buy unless they were on holiday. The rest of the stall was crammed with Robin Hood souvenirs. Plates, spoons, felt hats, wooden swords, and teddies dressed up as Robin or Marion jostled for space alongside wimples and old-style maps of Sherwood Forest. I hovered there long enough for the stall-holder to ask me three times if he could help me. Worried he would think I was waiting for an opportunity to pilfer a plastic Little John tankard, I quickly searched for something worth spending my dwindling pennies on.

'Do you have any postcards?' My voice was a creak, and I had to repeat myself before he could understand my accent. Oh, yes, he had postcards. Racks of them. Merry men and evil sheriffs, a dozen different pictures of the forest itself, Hatherstone village, even the campsite. And a selection of legendary graves. Nice.

I bought one with a red English telephone box on the front.

Wheeling back down the path, I paused by Robin Hoode's Tea Shoppe to try to picture myself relaxing at one of the plastic tables outside, sipping an iced coffee while I wrote the postcard. Sitting by myself in a café seemed as impossible right then as riding Pettigrew to the moon, ET-style. And I was about as ready to write that postcard as I was to enter into the Irish Olympic cycling team.

I did go inside to buy a bottle of water. A reluctant purchase, but I knew I wouldn't survive the return journey without it. As I stepped back out into the glare of the sun, it took me a couple of moments to realise that my bag had gone from the basket. I had taken my purse with me into the café, and as I frantically searched the street either side, I could see where the thief had pulled out the remaining items from the bag, dropping them onto the pavement every few metres.

The market trader who had sold me the postcard barrelled over, while his friend chased down the road in the direction of the strewn items. As I stood there, frozen, he called the other stallholders to help gather up my keys and emergency box of tampons, along with some dirty tissues, a melted mush of old toffees and other assorted pieces of embarrassing rubbish. One trader, a middle-aged woman with a frazzled brush of deep pink hair, picked up the envelope, which had been ripped open, and the photograph, lying next to it. I clutched one of the plastic tables as the relief threatened to knock me over. It felt like an omen. The photograph should have stayed in the drawer.

My rescuers clucked and fussed, sitting me down and bringing me a cup of sweet tea with a custard doughnut. As much as I protested that I was fine, my hands were shaking as I picked up the mug. The burly man who had chased after the thief limped back, my now empty bag in his hand, but with no sign of the perpetrator.

'D'you wanna call the police?' the waitress, a younger woman called Jo, asked me.

'No. Thanks, though.'

'You're not from round here, are you?'

I shook my head.

'You that new girl working for Scarlett?'

'Yes.'

She picked up my empty mug and turned to go back inside. 'See you around, then?'

I nodded, but she had gone.

The pink-haired woman handed me back the photograph, tucked inside the ripped remains of the envelope. She looked me up and down but said nothing, scraping back to her stall on heels as high as her pencilled-on eyebrows.

* * *

I had spoken nine words since the day of my daddy s funeral, nearly a year before. Four of those were by myself, where no one could hear, so they didn't count. Each word was a tick of a bomb, counting down to the Bad Thing that would happen. I didn't know how many ticks the bomb would have, but it would be my fault if it reached the end of the fuse. Because I did not talk, nobody wanted to sit next to me at school any more. My old friends had stopped knocking to see if I was coming out to play. At first, the grown-ups were kind. 'Give her time,' they told my ma at the kitchen table and in the queue at the Post Office. My mother was happy to give me time – and space – enough to form my own universe. She did not hug me or look at me. She had not said sorry. She had not forgiven me. For a long time, she pretended everything was fine, but the curse she had spoken grew between us like a thick fence of poisonous thorns. So I kept quiet, and when the doctor tried to cajole sounds out of me with sweets and books and promises of a trip to the beach, I shook my head, and shrugged my shoulders, and smiled to tell him that things were better this way.

But now Ma wouldn't get out of bed. For three days, she had not left the bedroom except to go to the toilet. She hadn't eaten the sandwich I made for her, or the crisps, or the biscuits. She hadn't drunk anything. The bedroom smelled. Different to when my daddy was in it. She lay on the bed and stared at the ceiling. I had been eating cereal and bread with ham and salad cream, but Ma hadn't been shopping properly for weeks and now there was nearly nothing left. The phone rang four times but I daren't answer it. I wanted to tell somebody, so badly, that my mother wouldn't get up and we had no food left and we needed a new card for the electricity box. But she was lying in bed and wouldn't move and there couldn't be many ticks left. I thought she was nearly dead. I stuffed my pillow into my mouth to keep the sobs from getting out, but hot tears squeezed from my eyes, and my throat ached and ached with the pressure.

I didn't know what to do. It was four weeks until school started again. Maybe I would be dead by then too.

I wanted my daddy.

* * *

I was still trembling when I ducked back under the cover of the forest. It was late afternoon, still warm, only the heat felt oppressive now, its caress no longer comforting, but claustrophobic. The quietness was foreboding, the shadows ominous. I battled the urge to keep looking behind me, convinced I would see some creeping enemy in pursuit. Every rustle sent a jolt through my tight nerves, causing the bike to veer off to the side until I controlled myself enough to pull it back onto the track. I muttered as I rode, berating myself for picking up the breadcrumbs of my neuroses as easily as I had scattered them aside that morning.

It didn't help that I felt tired, and my backside was sorer than I could have believed. It wasn't as if I didn't have ample padding. How do professional cyclists manage days in the saddle? Do cycling shorts have special sewn-in cushions? I picked up speed, grimly aware that by the end of this journey I might indeed be suffering from *women's issues*, when a streak of brown shot out of the trees to my right and rocketed in front of me. I panicked, weaving from side to side while the brown something flashed in and out of my peripheral vision. Then a fallen log blocked the path ahead; I careened off the track and into the brush, crashing through ferns and bouncing over the uneven surface. The wood sloped sharply downwards, and I began to speed up. My feet left the pedals, and I totally lost control. Even worse, the brown blur was still running alongside me, dashing toward Pettigrew's wheels before veering away again.

I yanked on the brakes. Nothing happened. I really was in trouble now. Up ahead I could see a brook, racing toward me at a frightening rate. I was going to end up very wet if I couldn't pull this together. What would a rider on a runaway horse do in this situation?

I screwed my eyes shut, and screamed. Just at that moment, Pettigrew hit a tree stump. I flew over the handlebars and soared through the air, crashing into the stream, sending shockwaves juddering up my outstretched arms. Well, my head and torso were in the stream. My legs landed in a pool of stagnant swamp mud.

I lay there, my body submerged, head tilted up so I could breathe. Every movement caused my legs to squelch a bit further into the sludge, and it was too much of an effort to even think about pulling myself up. Perhaps I could sleep here. It was cooler than the caravan, and nice and quiet. I closed my eyes and tried to pretend I was somewhere else for a minute.

But while I was still nowhere near finished my imaginary walk up Mount Fuji, a pair of rough hands yanked me out of the mud and plonked me on my feet.

A man, a few years older than me, stood there, shaking his head in disbelief. He was carrying a small brown dog, a Labrador puppy. Was it really that tiny? It had seemed a lot bigger when it was leaping up at me at a hundred miles per hour. The dog lay still in the man's arms, one leg sticking out at an awkward angle. It was whimpering softly.

Oh, no. I had broken his dog.

'What was that? Are you completely insane, or just a total idiot?'

He was dressed in running clothes, hair almost black with perspiration, and his broad shoulders were heaving. From exertion or because he was really, really angry, I wasn't sure.

'Sorry.' I wiped my wet hands on my trousers. They came off sticky with mud.

'Sorry? Oh, that's all right then. I am so sick of *tourists*.' He said this with an impressive sneer. 'Trampling about the forest, damaging the wildlife, dropping litter, starting fires, leaving gates open, winding up our livestock, provoking the local kids... they are so infernally *irritating*.'

I stood, wide-eyed, not sure whether to point out that I wasn't actually a tourist.

'You've probably broken her leg!' His voice cracked, and I

realised he was more upset than I was. 'Sorry? Of course you are. Isn't there a law about stupid city girls who don't know what they're doing, riding bikes if they can't control them?'

Woah! I don't react well to being called stupid.

'Isn't there a law about letting a dangerous animal unsupervised on a public footpath where it can attack members of the general public? I was perfectly in control of my bike until you lost control of your dog! Who do you think you are, telling me what to do in a public place?'

He pulled his head back, surprised.

'And – I'm not a tourist, not from a city and I got the top score out of my *whole school* in the cycling proficiency test!'

There was a tiny flicker at the side of his mouth. 'Wow. The top mark in the whole school. You must be very proud. And this isn't a public place. This is my land. So, as the landowner, I'm asking you to leave before I have you arrested for trespassing, damage to *private* property, and seriously harming my dog.'

I had run out of bluster. I felt terrible about the puppy. Hauling up Pettigrew, who had thankfully landed in soft earth and appeared undamaged, I scanned the forest, trying to get my bearings. The mud was beginning to set on my legs and backside. It was freezing cold and so was my wet top. I was exhausted. My bag had been stolen. I had cuts and bruises to complement my aching muscles and sore buttocks, and I didn't even know which direction to take to get back to the path.

A tear popped out of the corner of my eye and slipped down my cheek. The man sighed and shook his head again. He took my bag out of the basket and handed it to me. Then, gently placing the dog in Pettigrew's basket, he started wheeling the bike through the trees. I had to scurry to keep up with him, stumbling over roots and scratching myself on poking out branches. He ignored me until we reached the edge of the woods and I could see the campsite only a few hundred metres away.

Passing me Pettigrew, he scooped up the dog, who responded by licking his hand furiously. 'Next time, keep to the path.' He strode off, calling over his shoulder, 'And tell Scarlett I'll fix her brakes on Fire Night.'

I leaned on Pettigrew, inching my way forwards one slow, squishy step at a time, only glancing back when I heard the bark of laughter coming from the woods. The man stood, one arm braced on a trunk for support, helpless with mirth, his dog dancing around his ankles.

6

I woke in the pitch black, jolted out of deep sleep by a noise. A crash. My blood hammered so loudly in my ears that I had to strain to hear if the noise, whatever it was, sounded again. I lay in bed, every muscle rigid. Waiting.

My eyes fixed on the shadow of the doorknob as the shapes of furniture and belongings emerged from the darkness. I tried to keep my breathing slow and even, ready to feign sleep if the door began to open.

Silence. The initial panic gradually subsided and I inched up the bed, rustle by rustle, until I was in a sitting position. I carefully leaned over to peep through the chink at the edge of the curtain. A pale face loomed at me from the glass, sending me careening out of the bed into the tiny space by the door. I realised, too late, that the face was my own reflection. Furiously swiping at the tears on my cheeks, I scanned the darkness for a possible weapon.

2:53 a.m. Ten minutes crept by on the digital alarm clock. For most of those I stood, braced against the door, SuperValue hairdryer in hand, wondering if I should stay there until the sun rose. But it is incredible how quickly fear can turn into boredom.

Propelled by an urgent need to empty my bladder, and pretending what had woken me must have been a bird on the roof, I whipped open the bedroom door. I charged into the kitchenette, hollering like Grace O'Malley, the Pirate Queen of Ireland. Bouncing off the sink, I stumbled forwards into the living area. Here I crouched, jerking the hairdryer from side to side in front of me as if I was going to blow-dry the intruder back to where they had come from.

There was nobody there. I collapsed onto the brown sofa, my legs shaking so hard they tap-danced the rhythm of my panicked heart on the lino. Placing my hands flat either side of me, I concentrated on sucking air back into my lungs. Only as my body stopped trembling did I notice the tiny stones under my palms. Not stones. Chips of glass.

Jumping up, I half fell over to the light switch. Squinting in the glare, I found what had caused the crashing noise. Somebody had thrown a rock the size of a tennis ball through my window. It had bounced off the sofa and landed underneath the table. Wrapped around the rock and held on with elastic bands was a piece of A4 paper. On the paper was written, in harsh capitals, the words,

BACK OFF

After the hastiest possible visit to the bathroom, I swept up the glass, wrapped the rock and the note in a carrier bag found in the bottom of my wardrobe, and went to bed, where I stared at the ceiling until morning.

At 6.30 a.m., I dragged myself into the shower, managing to swallow down half a cup of black coffee before leaving the van. I stuffed every precious possession into my bag as a precaution against further intrusion, but had no real plan. I just needed to get away from the ugly, jagged scar in my window; somewhere I could quieten the angry swarm of bees that had built their nest in my skull during the night.

I hurried up the path to reception, nodding hello at the occasional camper making an early-morning trip to the wash block. A baby cried in one of the tents, and the scent of frying bacon wafted through the trees. Business as usual at the Peace and Pigs. Chickens scratched, pigs oinked, and birds tugged at worms in the dewy earth. The air was mercifully fresh and light, in stark comparison to the dread squatting in my stomach, as cumbersome as the bulging bag slung across my back.

I planned on waiting at the bench until Scarlett showed up, but as I rounded the top of the slope to the main block, I saw a police car parked on the gravel. Confused, wondering how word could have reached the authorities so soon even in this close-knit community, I went straight into reception.

I found Scarlett inside, pacing up and down in the small space. She had scooped her hair into a rough ponytail. I hadn't seen her without make-up before. Her eyes, heavy with purple shadows, stood out in her pale, drawn face. A policewoman sat at the counter, nursing a mug of steaming tea.

I stopped in the doorway. Scarlett sighed, closing her eyes briefly.

'Hi. Brenda, this is Marion, who stepped in for Jenna Moffitt. Can I fill her in?'

Brenda stood up and placed one hand on Scarlett's arm. 'I'll explain. You go and check on Valerie, and phone that list.'

Scarlett hesitated, but Brenda ushered her past me out of the door. Returning to her seat, she gestured for me to sit at the stool behind the counter before picking up her mug again.

'How well do you know Grace?'

'Grace? Not very. I've only been here since Saturday.'

'But you have spoken to her?'

'Nothing much beyond work stuff. I might have asked her where something was kept a couple of times, or to pass on a message. That's it.'

'Did you ever see her with anyone else?'

'Only the other workers here. Jake or Valerie. Why, what's happened? Is Grace okay?'

'That's what we are trying to determine.'

Brenda refused to tell me any more, but her eyes sharpened when I described what had happened to me the previous night. She asked if I knew any reason why Grace might send me that message. I thought of the way she had lingered in Jake's shadow, remembering just how all-consuming teenage crushes can become. I didn't want to believe that Grace would have thrown a rock through my window. But the truth is, I couldn't believe that anyone else would have done it either. I told the policewoman about Jake, rambling on about how there was nothing going on between us, until she snapped shut her book and stood up.

'Let's take a look.'

By the time Brenda had finished examining the window, and the note, Scarlett had found us. Brenda left and I made us both another coffee. Scarlett told me Grace had taken a rucksack and vanished. Her bed hadn't been slept in and there was food and money missing. Scarlett had phoned Grace's two friends, only to discover Grace had barely seen them all summer. Brenda would follow up at the nearest train and bus station, out of kindness to Scarlett, but could offer little hope of police intervention for a seventeen-year-old leaving of her own accord.

I showed Scarlett my broken window, and the note. The creases deepened on her forehead. She shook her head. 'What is going on in your head, my sweet child? What are you thinkin'?'

'Could she have left because she did this, and felt bad?'

'I don't know.' Her voice, soft and gentle, cracked with pain. 'I just don't know any more.'

I reached out and took Scarlett's hand. She gripped on, tight. The coffee went cold.

It was Valerie who noticed Pettigrew was missing. My heart stopped when I realised Grace had taken a bike with broken brakes, but two hours later, Brenda found it at Mansfield Station. Maybe Grace had cycled the eight miles to the station without stopping or slowing down. Scarlett crumpled at the thought of Grace reaching Mansfield safely, only to leave for some other city, knowing first-hand the kind of men who wait for lonely, vulnerable girls to ensnare in their evil webs.

Katarina, who had been a tower of strength throughout the day, banged one fist on Scarlett's tabletop.

'Underneath all those studs and streaks, she is a sensible girl, Scarlett. She is angry but not weak. She will know what it is that she is doing.' She bent down and put her arms around Scarlett's shoulders. 'She is not running from a wicked father. She is not you. She knows she has a good mother who loves her here. If she is in any danger she will call.'

Saturday... Sunday... Monday... she didn't call.

Scarlett tucked her hurt behind a mask of glossy lipstick and large sunglasses, and got on with running her campsite. She knew very few people in the UK a train journey away, only one or two regular holiday visitors, and it took no time at all to make sure Grace wasn't with them. She had taken her phone and her laptop with her but, thankfully, not her passport.

Jake, grim-faced, replaced my window. He offered to sleep on my sofa, but as everyone assumed that Grace had thrown the stone, he let it go when I declined, sloping back, embarrassed, to his flat in the village. Samuel came by each evening and sat with Scarlett and Valerie. He brought them soup and simmering casseroles, tenderly coaxing Scarlett to finish at least a few spoonfuls before the sun set and he returned home.

For the holidaymakers, unaware of the drama, the campsite remained a place of laughter and sunshine.

As for me? Well, I heeded the note. I worked as hard as I could, head down, mouth closed. I filled up my car and restocked my fridge. I spent the evenings with my windows shut and door locked. I tried to sleep, wondering what on earth I was doing there and if it could really be coincidence that less than a week after my arrival, the Peace and Pigs campsite, once so aptly named, had become a lie.

Tuesday it rained. The campsite resembled a ghost town. Tents zipped up, families either huddled inside or went out to the cinema, shops or museum. The downpour turned the whole world grey. We scurried from one shelter to the next, accompanied by the unrelenting staccato of warm, fat drops drumming tirelessly upon the roofs of the caravans and beating time on the oak leaves. Water streamed off the ends of our noses and became one with the rivers running along the campsite paths.

The rain was familiar to me, yet different. Rain is rain, and we get all types in Ballydown, but I was unused to the mud coating my boots – and therefore any floor I stepped on – with dark, gritty sludge. The air reeked of it: a rich combination of sodden sky and earth. The forest seemed wild and harsh without the warmth of sunlight to lift it. When Grace stepped out from between the trees, it was as if she had summoned the wind and water to herald her return. A perfect manifestation of the storm that lived within her soul.

She disappeared inside her mobile home with Scarlett, emerging hours later to feed the pigs as if she had never been away. Her face was set in an expressionless mask, but the black streaks of make-up on her cheeks betrayed something of what had gone on behind the blue door.

Valerie found me scrubbing a caravan vacated that morning. Thankful for an excuse to put down the muddy cloth, I helped myself to the teabags left behind in one of the cupboards and put the kettle on.

'Grace is back, Marion. I can't believe it!'

'I know. Scarlett must be so relieved.'

'Relieved? She's hopping mad. Instead of shouting, she's whispering in this calm, creepy voice like a crazy bad guy. Grace is pretending not to be scared, but she is totally freaked out. She expected to be grounded or something, but this is way worse. She won't crack, though. Won't say where she's been, or why she went. Or who she was with, or anything. Just sits there. Scarlett tried being nice and Grace still won't say. Then she cried, and Grace got angry and screamed that she was sorry but if people just told her the truth, she wouldn't have to go looking for it. Scarlett went dead white then. I thought she was going to faint, but she asked me to give them some time, so I came to find you.

'What does Grace mean, about having to look for the truth? Scarlett doesn't lie, not ever. It's one of her lessons. When Grace lied about meeting Gregory Fisher in the woods, Scarlett taught her that lesson. And when the exchange student lied about the money in the till, Scarlett said he had to go back to France.' Valerie shook her head, cradling her tea in both hands. 'I don't understand why anyone would want to leave the Peace and Pigs. That's why all those visitors keep coming back every year, because it's so good here. They pay money to come and stay, and can only come for a week or two. Grace gets to live here for free, all the time. Why would she want to run away?'

'I don't know, Valerie. I think, maybe, when people expect you to stay somewhere – especially if it's the place you've always been – it can make you want to run away. Even just to see what somewhere else is like.'

'Did you do that? Did you run away?'

'I didn't run away, because I told my ma I was going. And I'm a lot older than Grace, so nobody will worry about me.'

'Will you go back, then? Back to Ireland?' Valerie looked at me, eyebrows lowered. Daring me to say yes.

'I don't know. But if I do, it won't be for a while yet.' I handed her a pair of rubber gloves. 'Come on. While you're keeping out of the way, you can give me a hand.'

* * *

It had been two days since the party. I had dragged that diamond ring about as if it weighed a thousand carats. My new fiancé had been in Belfast, packing up his student life and preparing to move back to Ballydown. Here he would lodge with his parents to save money, commuting to his new position at the local community hospital. He had texted me twice. The first text said:

CAN U RING HOTEL AND SEE IF THEY FOUND MY JACKET.

The second text was even more romantic than the first:

MA SAID COME 4 TEA ON SAT. DID YOU GET JACKET?

I rang the hotel and used up my lunch break retrieving the coat. I took a good long look at my new sparkly, shiny, caraty ring and decided to skip tea that Saturday. In fact, I decided to skip not just my future mother-in-law's house, but the whole of Ballydown. I packed a bag on Friday morning before I could change my mind, and phoned the library manager, Harriet. Despite being my boss,

Harriet was also my best friend. I even loved her enough to put up with her humming. All day, from the moment she opened the doors until she locked up in the evening, Harriet produced a continual tuneless drone without even realising it.

Harriet cheered when I told her I was handing in my notice. She hummed out a mini symphony of joy. She was the only person I had told about the photograph. After showing it to her last Christmas, Harriet kept depositing different books on my desk: *Sherwood Forest: A Visitor's Guide*; *Walks in the Forest*; *The Legend of Robin Hood*; *Robin Hood and the Battle of Nottingham*; *Where to stay in Nottinghamshire*. None of these books arrived at Ballydown Public Library by chance. When I returned them to Harriet, I pretended I hadn't read them. She pretended to believe me.

Harriet loves me enough to keep kicking me up the behind. She did not offer her congratulations at the party, but she did give me a present: a one-way, one-passenger ferry ticket from Dublin to Liverpool.

The ticket bought a place on the overnight ferry setting sail that evening. At one o'clock, I just got up and walked out the door. As I loaded my bag into the car boot, Ma walked up behind me.

'Going somewhere?'

I slammed the boot shut. I deserved this.

'Yes.'

'Coming back?'

'I don't know. If I do, it won't be to here.' I nodded my head at the house.

'Well. That's a load of stew I've got cooking in the oven wasted.'

'Bye, Ma.' I pulled open the car door, then turned to say something else – anything – but she already had her back to me, walking away. I drove off, more angry than sad; wondering how I could pretend to myself I had done something courageous for the first time in my life, when I knew that tucked inside the zip pocket of my wash bag was an engagement ring, and saved in the outbox of my phone a message not yet sent to the rightful owner of that ring.

However thoughtless and self-centred a man may be, he doesn't deserve to be told his fiancée has done a runner by her mother.

I drove the three and a half hours to Dublin without stopping. Despite the clear signs, I managed to get lost twice trying to find the port, adding another forty-five minutes to my journey. I grabbed a flabby sandwich from the café and ate it staring at my phone sitting on the passenger seat beside me. Four times I went through the buttons until I was one click away from sending the message. In the end, so fed up with myself I could have screamed, I pressed 'send'. Heart racing, I turned the phone off, darted over to the nearest bin and chucked it in.

A text message. I am not pretending this was in any way the right or decent thing to do. I was hot with shame as I huddled in my car, waiting for the port official to wave me up the ramp onto the boat. Harriet would tell me that it was exactly what he deserved. What would cause her to bristle with annoyance is not that I used such a cowardly means of communication, but that the message itself was a total cop out. After twenty-three drafts, my spineless message said:

NEED A BREAK.

(A break from what? Our relationship? My job? Ballydown?)

WILL CALL WHEN SORTED.

Which could be, let's face it, never.

I cried as I drove up onto the ferry. I was still crying when I ate my jacket potato at my table for one in the restaurant. I sobbed through brushing my teeth and putting on my pyjamas. I snivelled and blubbered as I crawled under the covers of the bunk bed. Not because my mother didn't say goodbye. Nor because I had walked out on the man who had been my boyfriend since I was seventeen. Or because I might never see my hometown again. I cried because I was finally here. And the shame and fear, the guilt, the pain and the great big giant piles of broken mess had come too. Because they were me. This was when I started to pray. *Oh, God, do not let me be this person any more.*

7

Friday afternoon I was sitting in reception when a lavender Volkswagen camper van pulled into the car park, completed a three-point turn at breakneck speed, and reversed under a large chestnut tree at the back of the park. It was Ada and May. They came every Friday to sweeten, style and spruce up the women (and men) of the Peace and Pigs. Valerie told me they had both celebrated their seventy-ninth birthday earlier that year. (Did I know that the Kray twins were born the very same year?) In expecting blue rinses and tightly curled perms, I couldn't have been more wrong.

A queue formed while Ada set up the simple chalkboard sign next to the van:

Hair £10
Hands £8

Women of all ages brought folding camp chairs and settled down to wait. Ada slid open the front of the van so that she could work in the sunshine. May set up her manicure and nail bar under the shade of the chestnut. I took a bottle of water and positioned myself on the bench outside reception. Technically, I was still manning the desk, but this way I could see the action. A fifty-something woman came first. She lowered herself into the lavender leather chair, took off her sunhat, and shook out her long, thick, deep-bronze tresses. She spread them carefully around her shoulders, gently patting her scalp. 'Just a trim please, Ada, to tidy up the loose ends.'

'Yes, dear.' Ada, whose own soft, white hair was cut in a snazzy layered bob, moved behind her customer. I could see no mirrors on show in the van at all. 'What's your name?'

'Catherine.'

'Catherine. Did you know it means pure? I knew a Catherine once. She was anything but! We skated together on the canals in Amsterdam...' As Ada began to spin a spellbinding tale of New Year's Eve in Europe, filled with fireworks and appelflappen, all-night dances and dodging randy dukes, she took a lustrous handful of Catherine's hair, her crowning glory, and chopped it off. About three inches were left still attached to Catherine's head. Ada expertly flicked the severed lock behind her, out of sight, and carried on, snipping and chattering while her customer, totally unaware of the growing mound of cuttings, closed her eyes blissfully and sank deeper into the chair.

Less than fifteen minutes later, Ada finished the story and put down her scissors. The women in the queue held their breath as she picked up a gilt-edged mirror and handed it to her customer. Catherine gasped, turning her head this way and that. She said a word that was not at all pure. A tear ran down the side of her nose, which now appeared a good inch smaller thanks to the way her stylish new cut framed her face. The woman who handed over a £10 note in stunned silence had been transformed into someone who looked ten years younger and twice as gorgeous. Were they magic scissors?

The next person in the queue leapt up into the chair.

'Good morning, Beatrice.' Ada started snipping immediately. 'Where's that lovely man of yours today? Not having a cut?'

'Oh, he's fine. But the test match is on; he's glued to the radio.'

'Well, he does love his cricket. Did I ever tell you about the time I toured Australia with the women's England cricket team? Oh, they were marvellous days...'

And off she went. Twelve customers took their place in Ada's chair that afternoon with windswept, tatty, tired hairstyles. Each of them left looking and feeling like a different woman. They strutted back down the path swinging their hips and glancing from side to side, just dying to be ogled. Ada accompanied each cut with a story more fantastical than the one before. We rescued tigers in India, intercepted enemy signals in the Cold War, kissed a rock star in the Vatican and delivered a baby in an igloo. I had no idea if any of the stories were true, but how I hoped they were. And how I longed for a tiny speck of Ada's spirit, and the magic touch of those scissors.

When the last customer, a teenage girl who sat down in the chair a wallflower and got up a calla lily, had left, Ada pointed her finger at me. She called out: 'You haven't had your hair cut in – hmm – two years at least?'

I had my hair, as always, scraped back in a ponytail. I said nothing, but nodded my head. Two years. Try doubling that and adding on a bit more.

'And even then, you cut it yourself, didn't you?'

'Yes.' She couldn't hear my feeble squeak, but didn't need to.

'Well, come on then!' She beckoned me over. I really wanted to sit in the lavender chair and have my hair cut. I longed to be able to stride across the campsite swishing my fabulous new hairdo, seeing the look of approval in Scarlett's eyes. But I shook my head as I got up off the bench and opened the reception door.

'Sorry, but I have to get back to work. Maybe another time?'

Ada squinted at me across the car park. 'All right, then. Scarlett will have you ready for me soon enough.'

I slunk behind the reception counter, trying not to watch as Ada and May tidied their things back inside the van. May had seen just as many customers as her sister, and each had left the Lavender Mobile Beauty Parlour glowing, but she had said nothing for the entire afternoon. Worse than that, her pursed sour-lemon lips and furrowed brow spoke disapproval and discontent just as loudly as Ada's stories shouted life and love. Now, packed away, she walked across to reception.

Looking me up and down, May almost stepped back, as if my frumpiness was contagious. She was rail thin, with severe short hair that I imagined suited her personality as well as it did her bony, jutting cheekbones. She was probably once identical to her sister, but while Ada's laughter lines were the story-map of a life lived with joy and wonder, May's scrunched-up, wrinkly face testified to years of bitter resentment. Like Ada, she wore a 1950s-style purple, spotty dress, but on her it seemed stiff and old-fashioned. I tucked my ragged, soil-encrusted nails under the countertop.

'Usually we are provided with iced water.' May could have dipped that cold tongue into a boiling hot kettle and the water would have frozen solid.

'Oh. I didn't know.' I rushed over to the fridge, banging my shin on the door as I wrenched it open.

'My sister and I are nearly eighty years old. *Eighty!* We have been toiling in this heat for over two hours. You didn't have to *know* anything! Have you no common sense? Or are you just cruel? Or selfish and thoughtless?'

'Sorry.' I blinked back the tears that sprang up, hot behind my eyes. I took two large bottles from the shelf and held them out to May. 'Do you need anything else? I mean, um, is that enough? Would you like an ice-cream, or a cake?'

May sneered at me. She didn't take the drinks. 'I shall be reporting you to your employer at the first opportunity. And if either my sister or I should suffer from any effects of dehydration, I shall be contacting my lawyer.' She pulled open the door. 'I partly blame myself for expecting anything from such a *shambles* of a girl. Your bra is a joke. And surely Scarlett pays you enough to be able to afford a better moisturiser? If by some miracle you haven't been fired by next week, I expect both situations to have been rectified.'

Slamming the door shut, May marched back to where Ada waited by the side of the van, swigging from a can of ginger beer, a frozen ice-lolly in her other hand.

Valerie had made me promise to come along to Fire Night that Sunday, the last one having been cancelled due to the sudden disappearance of Grace, who still denied any connection with my broken window. Rather than trying to make up my mind whether to believe her or not, I chose to cram it to the back of my brain behind all the other unresolved junk. Nothing else happened, and the coil of dread began to uncurl in my stomach as the days went by. However, I was nervous enough thinking about the evening ahead to drop the chocolate cake I had bought as I tried to tip it out onto a plate so I could pretend it was homemade.

Having wasted ten minutes trying to squash the broken pieces back together, even though it had been on the floor, I dumped the cake in the bin. Dashing outside, I filled a large bowl with raspberries from the vegetable patch next to my caravan, making sure I carefully closed the vegetable patch gate behind me. But I forgot to close my own front door. Leaving the bowl on the side, I jumped straight in the shower. Only when I turned the water off did I hear the clicking, scraping sounds coming from outside the bathroom. Wrapped firmly in the towel, I held my breath, listening for a few seconds. Something had definitely come into my kitchen.

The something clucked.

The chickens and I had not been best buddies in my time at the Peace and Pigs. The very sight of me irritated them. Feeding or cleaning them out involved me dodging about, whimpering in fear while chickens ran at me aggressively, jabbing their beaks at my ankles. During the day, the hens roamed loose in the campsite, led as a pack by Denver, the freakishly huge cockerel, lord of all he surveyed. He swaggered from tent to tent, stealing bread out of babies' hands, ripping up unattended cereal boxes, eating a few pecks of the contents until he got bored and wandered off, leaving his wives to form a frantic cloud of flapping feathers as they fought and jostled each other for the remaining cornflakes.

I had imagined hens to be gentle, docile birds, but these were like a gang of feral teenagers out on a Friday night looking for trouble. I had assumed the role of victim, and the chickens became my bullies. If I saw the mob making their way anywhere close, I would turn and hurry in the opposite direction. I found myself ducking behind trees and even scrambling up the slide in the play park in my attempts to avoid them. This doubly complicated my efforts to steer clear of Jake where possible. The previous Thursday, finding the pack of chickens approaching menacingly from one side and Jake from the other, I had actually hidden in somebody's tent, knowing the family had gone out on the lake in their dinghy.

I slowly opened the bathroom door. Just a tiny chink. A red eye, level with my own, leered at me from two inches away. I slammed the door shut and stood leaning on it while I caught my breath. I cracked open the door again. Denver, who stood at least three feet tall with both his scratchy, gnarly feet planted on the ground, craned his neck to look me right in the eye from his perch on the top of my fridge. How he got there, I don't know, but I suspect this particular cockerel is actually an escapee from a secret government experiment, possessing powers beyond those of an ordinary bird. He opened his beak to three times the width of his head, and released a war cry that would have made William Wallace proud. I stepped back, out of the range of his foul-smelling breath, but kept the door open, impressing myself but not Denver. He wiggled his comb at me and spread his wings. Seven of his ladies had crammed into the narrow galley kitchen, all huddled around the upturned bowl, gobbling raspberries. When their master crowed, they snapped to attention, waddling around to find me, their least favourite human, standing in the doorway, brandishing a bottle of shampoo.

Mercy, one of the most inappropriately named creatures there has ever been, ran at me, squawking. I leapt on top of the toilet seat. At Denver's command, the whole gaggle rushed into the bathroom, flapping and pooping and cackling like a bunch of crazy witches. I was trapped in a sea of evil, pecky sharks. I tried yelling and waving my foot around as if preparing to give them a good boot out of the door, but those crafty girls weren't fooled. They knew easy prey when they saw it. I didn't really think that they wanted to hurt me, or to eat me. But like any bullies, they were bent on humiliating me until I shrivelled up and cried.

I carried on hollering, clapping, and stamping up and down on the toilet lid until Belinda, a deceptively cute-looking black hen with gold eyes, snatched hold of my towel and began yanking it off. Admittedly, it had become partially unwrapped due to the scrambling and the kicking, but still. That was deliberate emotional abuse. Two of the other birds began to hop up and down on it, clawing it further away. We were engaged in a feathery, squawky towel wrestle when suddenly a voice shouted, 'Hey!' causing Belinda to let go of the towel, me to stumble backwards and fall off the side of the toilet, and every other chicken to cower on the floor in terror. It was as if the teacher had finally showed up at the start of class. For one moment, I really thought the voice was Denver's. That's how absolutely absurd the situation had become. When I saw who stood in the doorway of my bathroom, I almost wished it had been the cockerel.

It was the man with the dog. He coughed, his eyes wide with amusement. He did at least have the decency to duck his eyes as he passed me my towel.

'Out, girls! Now!' He pointed one straight arm in the direction of the outside door, and the hens meekly shuffled out in an orderly line.

'And you.' He swept up Denver and held him up to look sternly into his beady, blood-red eyes. 'You should know better.'

He tossed Denver out of the door and stood watching as he scampered off after his hens. I had hastily covered up my body with the wrecked towel, but no towel in the universe could have concealed my mortification. No man had ever seen me naked in broad daylight before (except for my da). I mean not even my boyfriend-slash-fiancé of eight years. And to be honest, if I had imagined the first time a man saw me naked, the scenario in my head would not have involved me wedged into the space between a shower and a toilet, the strip light glinting off the bird poo on my feet and dirty brown feathers stuck to my skin. (I would, however, have lost two stone and had a boob job.) I cowered behind the doorway, my eyes looking anywhere but at him.

'Are you all right? Did you hurt yourself?' He kept his head firmly angled toward the outside.

No! And yes! But I'm not about to tell you that I have a severely bruised bottom. Please go away and never come back.

'I'm fine. Thanks.' I began to edge the bathroom door shut, with me behind it.

'Do you want some help clearing up?'

'No. Thank you,' I whispered. *Go!*

'Okay. Well, I'll see you around.' He turned and looked me right in the eyes, catching me there for a second before I could drop my gaze. His eyes were deep blue, with flecks of silver. The colour of twilight in the forest.

Suddenly he grinned. 'I'm looking forward to it.'

He jogged down the steps, past my caravan, and into the trees beyond. I dashed out and whipped my front door shut, scrabbling through my bag for the keys to lock it. As I cleaned up myself and the rest of the mess, I felt, unaccountably, as flappy and flustered as the chickens.

If any man did ever get to see me naked in broad daylight for a second time, I maybe wouldn't mind so much if he looked at me with eyes the colour of twilight in the forest.

I had nothing left to take to Fire Night. It had grown late by the time I was ready to leave, and I felt tempted to simply draw my curtains and curl up under the covers to have my own little pity party for one instead. But, with a knock on my window, Valerie's voice called out: 'Where are you, Marion? I was worried about you. We're ready to start eating and you aren't there yet. Are you all right?'

I grabbed my bag, unlocking the door.

'Yes, I'm coming. I had a bit of an accident, but I'm fine. It just took a while to tidy up.'

'Six thousand people are hurt every year either tripping up over their trousers, or falling down the stairs while pulling them up.'

'Oh. Well, good job we don't have any stairs then.'

'Yes. Did you know you have a feather stuck to the back of your head?' Valerie reached up and plucked it off, blowing it away before taking hold of my hand. She jiggled and tugged me along to her garden, chattering the whole time about nothing much. That girl lifted my spirits more than she could possibly know. I felt entirely comfortable again by the time I reached the barbeque; maybe even a tiny bit confident. Until I saw how many people – and, more specifically, who – had come to the party.

His name was Reuben. He hadn't been joking about owning the land where Pettigrew and I came to grief.

He introduced me properly to Lord and Lady Hatherstone – his parents. I managed a stammered hello, although they seemed perfectly at ease with the whole situation.

'Oh, none of that lord and lady twaddle! They only call us that to wind us up.' Lady Hatherstone whacked me on the back. 'I think we are a little beyond formalities, all things considered. Don't you?'

She winked. I wondered if your cheeks could get so hot they burst into flames. Her husband tipped back his round bald head and roared. 'Ha! That's one way of putting it. No, we are Archie and Ginger to our friends, and anyone who has seen us deshabille had better be a friend, not an enemy!'

Reuben glanced at me, raising one eyebrow. A panic attack began swimming at the edge of my vision. He turned back to his mum and dad, shaking his head. 'Please don't tell me Marion has had to see you two at it. When are you going to learn to get a room? One with a lock on the door?'

'Oh, grow up, darling! Marion didn't mind. It's happened to all of us at one time or another!'

Ginger and Archie wafted off to another corner of the meadow, leaving me standing with Reuben, desperately trying to think of an excuse to walk away, if only my brain would stop buzzing enough to let me think.

He cleared his throat and ran his hand through his dark hair a couple of times.

'Well. Looks like we're even.'

I froze, horrified.

Reuben grimaced. 'Sorry. I take that back. No comparison...'

At that moment, Jake sauntered over, just to crank up the tension further. He slung one arm round my shoulder, beer bottle dangling from the end of it.

'Reuben,' Jake nodded, in a macho, chin-jutting sort of way.

'Jake,' Reuben smiled, sticking his hands in his pockets. He got the message. If Jake were a cat, he would have sprayed his urine on me about now.

'So – where's Erica?'

Reuben rolled his shoulders. As if Jake's hot, heavy arm was annoying him as much as it was me. 'Working. She'll be here for the festival.' He glanced at his own bottle. 'I'm getting a top-up. See you later, Jake. Marion.' Reuben walked off toward the picnic table laden with drinks, pausing to take Katarina's empty glass from her as he went.

Jake bent his head closer to mine. I could smell the alcohol on his breath. 'Erica is Reuben's girlfriend.' Of course she is. 'Her parents own the campsite land and live in one of the new houses on the edge of Hatherstone. She rents a flat in Nottingham, 'cos she's got some fancy job with a chain of designer shops, and the head office is in the Lace Market. Reuben is supposed to be finally popping the question at the festival next week. Don't know what he's waiting for. Erica's a fox.'

I had nothing to say to that. I was too weak and too stupid to remove Jake's tentacle arm for no better reason than not wanting the arm of a rude, drunk, presumptuous man pressing down on my shoulders, no matter how strong and muscular that arm might be or how good looking the man on the end of it. I did not want the whole of the Peace and Pigs, plus numerous guests, to imagine something going on between us. I especially did not want Jake to think that. Let alone Grace.

I pretended I needed the toilet.

* * *

Scarlett found me, much later on, hovering in her kitchen, moving dirty pots from one side of the room to another.

'Okay?'

'Yes, I'm fine. Just thought I'd better help out a bit since I didn't bring anything to share.'

'Well, that's very kind of you.' She crinkled her eyes at me. 'And there was me thinkin' you were hidin' from Jake. Don't judge him too harshly tonight. He had a very uncomfortable conversation with Grace today, followed by the news that his mother has been denied parole again. He don't know whether to celebrate or drown his sorrows, but either way, he'll only hate himself more in the mornin'.'

'I didn't know his mum was in prison.'

'Well, it ain't a secret round here, but it ain't exactly the kind of thing you share with the girl you're tryin' to impress, either.'

'So – do all your employees come from tough family situations?'

Scarlett wiped her hands on her apron. 'I don't know, sugar. Do they?'

I turned and began scraping leftovers into a goody bag for the chickens. 'I'm not very good at parties.'

'Most people aren't. That's why I have 'em every week, so we can get used to 'em. This is about the busiest it gets, though. With the festival comin' up, we always have extra.'

'The Robin Hood Festival?'

'Absolutely! It's the highlight of the Peace and Pigs year. We'll be full to the brim those three days; but on the last day – the Sunday –

reception is closed and all employees must attend the festivities. It's in everyone's contract.'

My breath got stuck somewhere behind my diaphragm. I thought about the photograph, and my head swam. All I could do was nod.

Scarlett gently took the plate out of my hand, and put it with the rest of the pile on the draining board. 'This isn't your job tonight. You are going to listen and put into practice Scarlett's lesson in survivin' party minglin'. One: never forget Scarlett's lesson number one.'

I smiled. It wasn't hard in the warmth of Scarlett's kitchen.

'Two: find someone who looks as lost and lonely as you feel, walk right up to them and ask them how they're doin'. Listen to their answer and respond accordingly. Ask intelligent, thoughtful questions, and keep goin'. If you can't see anyone lookin' lost and lonely, look harder. If you can't think of an intelligent question, ask 'em what they like to do and go from there. Never, *never* ask somebody, "What do you do?" It's dumb and rude to think that anyone can answer that question adequately by recitin' a job title, and most of us are far more interestin' than that. These days, goodness knows, enough people are spendin' every moment searchin' high and low for any kind of work, worryin' about how they're gonna pay the bills or buy their kids that mobile phone they want so they don't get laughed at in the playground. They cry, wring their hands in despair, and work their butts off tryin' to scrimp and save on every penny, meanwhile prayin' it will be enough to prevent the big fat bank manager from bootin' them out of the house they spent years makin' into a precious home for their family. Before he jets off to spend his big fat bankin' bonus on yet another luxury holiday to erase all that stress he gets makin' so much money off poor hard-workin' everyday folks.

'So don't ask 'em what job they do. Lift your head, look 'em in the eye, remember you are as worthwhile a human bein' as anybody else, with a unique story to share. Three: don't ramble, moan, bitch, gossip, drink too much, or agree with somebody just to seem nice when you think they are talkin' outta their patoot. Got it?'

'Um.'

'Good. Now go make some friends.'

8

I was on my first holiday at Auntie Paula's house. Except even then I knew holidays should be far away, not just past the Post Office. And you don't have to go to school. And they are actually fun. Auntie Paula told me I was on holiday because she didn't want to say, out loud, the truth that Ma was locked up in the hospital for crazy people having electricity zapped into her brain until her eyes span round. I knew this because my cousin Declan told me.

In a town of typically large Catholic families, Declan was the only boy in his class with his own bedroom. This status symbol somehow made up for him being mean and spoiled, and smelling of old chip fat from his parents' fish van. Now that I had come to stay while the doctors drilled holes in Ma's head, Declan had to share with his five-year-old brother, Benny. Benny woke Declan every morning at 5.30 by jumping on his bed, yelling. He broke Declan's model of a zillion-pound Lamborghini, and scribbled on his Italia '90 Republic of Ireland football cards. Declan hated Benny, but he blamed me.

The second day of my holiday, he picked his nose and wiped the snot on my battered cod. Two days later, he smeared dirt in my underwear so Auntie Paula thought I had messed myself. He didn't even try to be sneaky about it. He knew I couldn't tell anyone.

Frustrated at my continued silence, my aunt took me to see Father Francis. She figured that when all else fails, you had better try God. I hadn't been to mass since my daddy had gone, but I remembered Father Francis. He had a moustache. I liked watching it waffle up and down when he talked. His voice was soft and slow, and he always shook my hand and called me Miss Marion. He was my daddy's friend. Four times after the funeral, he came round and knocked on our door, but the first two times Ma ignored it. The third time she opened the door, threw the dirty dish water over him, and screamed at my daddy's friend: 'Get lost, you lying hypocrite. Go on back to your land of make believe.' The fourth time she phoned the police.

Mrs Dunn, the housekeeper, showed us into a room with fat, flowery sofas and an entire wall of shelving units crammed with books. Above a worn desk was a noticeboard covered in photographs. Radiant brides with their arms flung around grinning grooms. Babies in christening gowns, older children in smart suits and first communion dresses. Anniversaries, birthday parties, graduation pictures. And squeezed in between all these smiles and hats were dozens of cards of thanks and good wishes to Father Francis, who had cheered on every morsel of good news, and wept with every loss that touched his beloved parish.

Auntie Paula sat up straight and tucked her solid brown bag behind crossed ankles. I was wearing my best dress. Like all my clothes, it had got too small and I kept trying to stretch the skirt to cover a bit more of my skinny legs. When Father Francis came in, carrying a tray with a teapot and mugs and a sticky brown cake, Auntie Paula stood up. She nodded and smiled at the priest, and then suddenly remembered she had to ask Mrs Dunn about the next month's cleaning rota.

Father Francis waited for her to leave, then cut an enormous slice of cake and handed it to me. I took a bite, but the chewed-up crumbs stuck in my throat, blocked by the traffic jam of words. He sipped his tea and smiled at me. His moustache smiled too.

'How are you, Miss Marion? I haven't seen you in a while. We've missed you at mass, and Sunday club.'

I drank some tea to force the cake down.

'That's okay if you don't feel like talking. Do you mind if I tell you a story?'

I shook my head. I didn't mind. Stories were my favourite thing.

'Many years ago, when I was still a young man and not long a priest, I used to go fishing at the lake behind the Mullans' farm. Only on this particular occasion, I didn't know that two very naughty boys, who shall remain unnamed, had protested against my telling their mammies when I found wee Carla Bragg locked in the church cellar.'

My mouth twitched. Carla Bragg was now the captain of the women's rugby team. There were rumours that when the men's team were short, she donned a thin disguise and played for them. They always won those particular matches.

'Their protest took the form of a hole in my boat – tiny enough to make sure I reached the very middle of the lake before I noticed water seeping in to fill the bottom. I tried to scoop it out with one hand and row closer to shore with the other, but as a clever girl like you knows, you cannot row with one hand. You just go round and round in circles. Now, the lake wasn't all that deep, and I could swim well enough, but what I haven't told you is that on this particular afternoon, I had to conduct the funeral of James Herbert Hamilton Moore. The late husband of Miriam Hamilton Moore.'

I sat up in my chair. Miriam Hamilton Moore was the snootiest, bossiest, pickiest woman in Ballydown. I hadn't known she had ever been married. I felt a moment of pity for James Herbert.

'I had been a little bit foolish, Marion. I only had an hour or so until I had to be getting myself ready, and by the time I had rowed myself round and round in circles for a while, I had maybe time to change, but certainly not to shower stinky brown lake water out of my hair. Besides, there was a six-foot, iron-jawed old pike living in the lake in those days. I didn't fancy him nipping at my trousers as I swam past.

'So I was stuck in the middle of the lake in a sinking ship, with no way out that didn't involve me turning up to conduct a respectable man's funeral smothered in mud and whatever else you might find floating about in that water. I prayed a heartfelt prayer, I can tell you, asking God to forgive my reckless decision to fish on a funeral day, and to help me to forgive those two monkeys who right then I felt like sticking on the end of my fishing rod to use as pike-bait. I asked him to send me an angel to get me out of there dry, and just at that moment, a young man whom I had never set eyes on before appeared at the far side of the water. Seeing my difficulty, he called across to ask what my problem was. And so I told him. Do you know what that young man did, Miss Marion?'

I shook my head. What did he do?

'He pulled off his trousers and his jumper, and his shoes. He plunged into that freezing cold, murky lake in just his underwear and he swam through the pouring rain out to my boat, now eight inches deep in water. He climbed in with me, and while I bailed, he rowed us to shore. His arms were so strong, his pull on the oars so swift, that I didn't have to change more than my socks. And Miriam Hamilton Moore was none the wiser. Do you know who that angel was, Marion?'

I thought I did.

'Your da was a good man in every sense of the word. A great man. He was my best friend, and I miss him every day. I feel angry some days, and bewildered on others. Sometimes I just feel so very

sad. But I am always glad to have had the honour of knowing him.'
Father Francis told more stories about my father, and for that hour I
forgot about cancer, and mothers who smash plates against the
kitchen wall. I stopped thinking about fat cousins with glittery eyes
who spat in my lunchbox and laughed as they walked away. For the
first time in over a year, I forgot to feel scared or alone.

* * *

I remembered Father Francis as I stood, clutching the brown
envelope, while crowds of visitors jostled past me toward the
entrance of the Robin Hood Festival. My father was a great man,
loved by good people. There could be nothing to fear from discovering the truth about someone who dived into a freezing lake to
rescue a stranger from getting wet trousers. So he once had a
different name, a past no one was allowed to probe. A secret family
he never saw, or even mentioned. I knew how he felt.

It felt surreal, wandering down the forest path toward the visitor
centre. I had dreamed of coming here for months. I'd imagined the
people, hordes of children wearing green hats or garlands of plastic
flowers, waving swords and aiming arrows. I had pictured the
medieval encampment, the stalls of crafts, and the jesters and
bards. But I could never have predicted walking right up to the first
person I saw who looked vaguely something to do with the festival
and showing them the picture of my da under the Major Oak in a
Robin Hood costume.

The man looked at me and wrinkled his brow. 'What's this
then?'

I wrestled briefly but fiercely with the mute child who hides in
my windpipe.

'I was wondering if you might recognise this picture, or be able
to tell me anything about it.'

'Oh, right. It looks quite old.' He squinted through his glasses (did they have glasses in Robin Hood's day?). 'When was it taken?'

'I think between 1979 and 1984. That's all I know, except for what it says on the back.'

He turned the photo over. Written on the back in blue pen were the words 'Daniel, Robin Hood Festival'. The boy in the picture looked about sixteen, or perhaps older. It was slightly blurred, so I couldn't be totally sure it was my da. But if not, it was a very close relative. The image of my father was fading inside my head, to be replaced with only the smells, and the memory of the texture of his stubble, or his dressing gown, on my cheek. But I had spent hours comparing it with the last photograph taken of him before he got ill, and I had to believe this boy Daniel was the man I called Father. What I wanted to know was why everybody in Ballydown had called him Henry.

The obvious person to ask was my mother. Unless you had met her, of course. Then you would know that even mentioning his name would be a stupid waste of time, likely to end up with you covered in spaghetti Bolognese, or whatever else was near to hand. I threw away four ruined tops before I gave up asking.

'Sorry, duck. I wasn't around back then. Try the minstrel.'

Hidden in the trees, I found the minstrel. Under an ornate velvet canopy, surrounded by children squatting on blankets, he looked quite possibly old enough to remember the original Robin Hood. I waited on the fringes of his audience until he had finished his tale, accompanying himself with what I think was a hurdy-gurdy, and then shooed the children away.

He watched me, beetling his bushy eyebrows as I moved toward the blankets. I coughed at the blockage in my throat.

'Can I just—'

He held up his hand, palm facing me, like a policeman stopping traffic, then turned and lit a cigarette. He took a couple of long slow drags, eyes closed, and puffed the smoke out into the trees. I opened my mouth to speak again, but he grimaced and held up his hand, not bothering to open his eyes. Taking another drag, he pulled a flask out of his medieval tunic and tipped it to his mouth, wiping his sleeve across his face once he had finished drinking.

The minstrel opened his eyes and sighed. 'What?'

'Well, I was just wondering, if you don't mind...'

'I'm on a break. Get to the point.'

'Do you recognise this man?' I rushed out the words, thrusting the photograph forward so that it didn't matter if he could understand my accent or not.

He flicked his eyes down for the tiniest of seconds, long enough for his pupils to contract. 'No.'

'Are you sure? If you could just have another look, maybe you will recognise something else about the photo.'

'I said no.' The minstrel stared up at the sky without blinking. Now that I was finally here, something in me refused to be intimidated.

'I'm trying to find out when this photo was taken. Do you know anything about the festival in the eighties? Who played Robin Hood those years? Or anyone who might know something that could help me?'

He scratched at his stubble with yellowed fingertips. 'I can't help you.'

'Please. I think this man might be my father. I just want to find out who he was.'

'I said I can't help. Drop it. Go home.'

Not can't; won't, I thought as I walked away.

I spent the rest of the morning asking around, but the majority of the volunteers and entertainers were either too young or not around back then. The sting of the minstrel's rebuttal lodged in my mind, puncturing my initial enthusiasm. I decided to take a break for lunch, convinced that the one person who could actually help me, for some reason, wouldn't.

I bought myself a sandwich and wandered through the woods to find somewhere quiet to sit, eventually winding up back at the main event area. Here a dozen old-style craft stalls, and demonstrations of the different aspects of medieval life, ranged around a currently empty main stage. I recognised some of the market traders from Hatherstone, including the man who had sold me a postcard. He smiled and introduced himself as Jimbo. Next to him, glaring like a two-fingered salute to all the attempts at authentic history, was the woman with pink hair.

I took a few minutes to pass around the photo. It sparked a complicated discussion about everybody they had ever known called Daniel, but they concluded that all those Daniels were the wrong age, the wrong size or too ugly to be the young man in the picture.

A couple of older traders did admit he seemed vaguely familiar, so I gave them the phone number of the Peace and Pigs, and asked them to call if they remembered anything else. They seemed interested enough in helping me, but once home, I wouldn't be sitting around waiting for the phone to ring.

I found a spare bench and ate my sandwich opposite an enormous, ancient tree: the Major Oak, where Robin Hood supposedly hid from the evil Sheriff of Nottingham. It formed the backdrop to my father's photograph. Except that now, the tree's giant branches were held up by posts and metal supports – a protective fence preventing tourists getting close enough to touch it. In the photograph, the boy called Daniel leaned with one hand propped against the gnarled trunk. I watched the tree, wishing I could do the same.

A loud trumpet blast made me jump. The crowd turned their heads toward the sound of shouting from the forest to one side of us, and out of the trees galloped two horses, with several men running alongside them. The rider of the first horse called out.

'All hail the Sheriff of Nottingham!'

There were murmurings and a few laughs. One of the men on foot, who were all dressed as soldiers, pointed his massive sword at a man at the front of the crowd.

'Bow before your lord or face the consequences, peasant!'

The man, grinning to the people either side of him, bent over and tipped his baseball cap.

'All of you!' the first man on the horse hollered. 'Hail your Sheriff.'

Most of the visitors made some sort of gesture, either a quick nod of the head or, for the bigger show-offs, a more flamboyant bow. I huddled on my picnic bench and kept still.

The second man on horseback, dressed in black and silver, nudged his horse over to where I sat. He wore a large velvet hat tipped over half his face. He swung one leg over the side of the horse and jumped down to the ground, right in front of me. I gripped the empty sandwich wrapper in my fist. A shadow fell over the bench as the Sheriff stepped closer. The crowd watched all this, silent except for the occasional catcall or whistle. They thought it was part of the entertainment. I was in the preliminary stages of an anxiety attack.

'Pray tell' – the Sheriff spoke in a pretend medieval lord's accent – 'what beautiful maiden is this, who doth scorn me, the Sheriff of Nottingham, by refusing to bow? Name yourself!'

Oh, no. The voice belonged to Jake. I wriggled on my seat, and tried to find his eyes underneath the shadow of the stupid hat so that he would see my terror and leave me alone.

He drew a frighteningly realistic looking sword with a dramatic swish and poked the tip about two inches from the pulse that pounded in my throat.

'Your name.'

'Jake, please...' I whispered, while the crowd listened in, transfixed.

'Your name,' he shouted. 'Or shall we throw her in the stocks?'

This got a mixture of cheers and boos. The stocks were all the way over on the other side of the field. Right then, I would rather he kill me with that sword than drag me across the clearing and place me in the stocks. But a drawbridge had slammed across my voice box. As the crowd grew noisier, I panicked my way through my mute busters. Jake tipped back his hat with his free arm and peered at me.

'Come on,' he murmured out of the side of his mouth. 'I can't back down now. Just tell me your name, give me a bow, and I'll move on to the next bit.'

I forced a tiny whistle of air up through my throat. 'Marion,' I mouthed, waiting for the earth to open up and swallow me whole. It was much easier to bow my head forwards toward his feet. The hard part would be pulling myself up again.

Jake heaved a sigh of relief and put one hand on my shoulder. 'Sorry. Didn't mean to embarrass you,' he mumbled, smiling ruefully.

Calling out to his men, he took the reins of the horse now nibbling on the grass behind him. 'She yields! Onwards, men! We have a foul outlaw to lay hold of this night.'

But one of his men must have had supersonic hearing. Either that or he could read lips. Or was just mean.

'With all due respect, my lord, have you lost your mind?'

Jake snapped around. His eyes flashed.

'Did you not hear that this is none other than the Maid Marion? This is the lady who has stolen the heart of that dastardly fiend, Hood. Surely this would be a perfect opportunity to ensnare the evil criminal and rid ourselves of him once and for all?'

A murmur rippled through the spectators. A voice called out: 'Tie her to a tree and use her as bait.'

I saw who had shouted and wanted to rip out her hair one pink strand at a time.

Jake hesitated. The crowd liked this idea. Again, they thought it was all part of the show. A chant rose up. 'Tie her to a tree! Tie her to a tree!'

I braced myself, shifting back as far as I could on the bench. Weren't the people supposed to be on Robin Hood's side? Jake twisted around to find his men gathering closer. They began urging him to give the visitors what they wanted.

Jake bent down and took hold of one of my wrists. His touch was light but I flinched anyway, yanking my arm away.

'Look. It's only for fun. Robin's due here any second – he's probably waiting in the woods watching us already. I'll just walk you over to the tree and wrap some rope around, okay?'

No, it was not okay. However, I was way beyond speech. I looked at Jake and my eyes must have screamed at him not to do this. But I was one girl who had dented his pride. Behind him, a dozen men with swords and a mob high on candyfloss and Friar Tuck's home brew stood watching. He took hold of my hands, gently enough that they still had room to quake inside his grip, and led me over to the Major Oak. I would get to touch it after all.

* * *

When I was nine years old, on holiday for the third time, my delightful cousin Declan had tied me up and trapped me in the coal bunker. I was there for six hours before Uncle Keith found me.

When I was eleven, he enlisted the help of Benny to tie me up again. This time, they left me in the woods overnight.

I was thirteen, and wearing my first teen-sized bra, when he tied me to a tree and decided to unleash all of his hate and his evil, angry poison on a girl who would not tell of his crimes. My bra was ruined, but I decided it suited me better that way. I patched it up and carried on wearing it, wishing that my life could be held together with just a needle and a reel of cotton.

The next time Declan tied me up, someone found us. That someone beat Declan until he needed to spend three weeks in hospital. He made sure that Declan never came near me again. That is why, ten years later, when that someone pushed a diamond ring onto my finger, it was harder than it should have been to take it off.

As Jake coiled the thick, twisty snake of rope around my body, some sort of long-buried survival mechanism kicked in. I began to fight. Jake's handsome face was gone. All I could see were the shiny, gleeful eyes of my cousin. I kicked and bucked and hollered. I think I may have spat.

Gasping, frantic, with the desperate instinct of a wounded animal, I wrestled my way out of the hands that seized me, and fled back toward the shadows of the forest.

Twenty strides in, a pair of hands reached out from behind a tree and grabbed my shoulders. I screamed. The hands flipped me around, pressing my face against a leather-clad chest, stifling the sound. I found myself pulled behind the huge trunk, lost in panic and frantic fear. A muffled voice spoke just above my ear. 'Calm down. You're safe. I've got you.'

I couldn't calm down. A volcano of buried emotions had erupted. I pushed and wriggled, and tried to twist my head from side to side. I scratched at his wrists, stamped the heel of my trainer down on his foot. For a long time, he let me fight, repeating his words over and over again.

'You're safe. Calm down. Just breathe.'

Finally, spent, I stopped struggling. He loosened his grip.

'Are you going to scream?'

I shook my head.

He let go of my arms. I stepped away, keeping my head angled to watch him as my body bent double, gulping in air.

It was Robin Hood. I could tell by the outfit, which was an exact copy of the one that Daniel had worn. The bottom half of his face was covered in a dark scarf. His hood was pulled forwards, leaving the rest of his features hidden in shadow.

'Better?'

I nodded, too drained to feel embarrassed.

'You just had a panic attack.'

'I know.' I shrugged, standing upright, wiping my trembling hands across my face. 'A thing happened to me once. I guess I'm not over it yet.'

'Well' – Robin Hood's voice was grim from behind his scarf – 'not many people would have enjoyed being caught on the wrong end of Jake's overinflated ego.' He shook his head. 'He's a fool. He should be banned from volunteering.'

'Maybe.' I remembered the look of confusion and hurt on Jake's face when I raked my nails down his cheek. 'Do you think jumping out from behind trees and grabbing women is any better?'

'For the evil Sheriff of Nottingham? Absolutely not. For Robin Hood? Most women in this forest dream about having me wrap my arms around them.'

He tipped his hood back so that I could see his eyes for the first time, and winked at me, disappearing into the trees. *Darn.* Those eyes. Twilight in the forest.

I tramped back through the greenery, avoiding the paths, hoping I was moving in the direction of the exit. I still had the photograph in the back pocket of my jeans, but I had left my bag by the picnic bench. I didn't go back for it, trusting that Jake or one of the market traders would have kept it safe for me.

Jake. Now we had a reason to make working together even more awkward. I would have to tell Scarlett. Except she was bound to know what had happened already. I pondered what advice she might give about dealing with the situation. Apologise, forgive, get over it, move on. I could do that. Jake wasn't to know the scars I still bore from Declan's attentions.

I reached the visitors' centre and tidied myself up in the toilets. Finding my car, I managed to hold it together until I saw my bag on the passenger seat. Somebody must have made pretty good time to get there before me. My purse and keys were still inside. Opening up my purse to check if all the money was still there, I found a tightly folded piece of paper squashed in with my loose change. A note:

FORGET HIM!

I climbed out of my car, closed the door, ripped the paper into a hundred thousand tiny pieces and chucked them into the air like rotten confetti. I was back in my car and out of the car park before the last swirling, spinning fragment hit the ground.

But then came the finishing touch to round off my day, just in case it hadn't been rubbish enough. I don't believe in luck or fate. The reason bad things come in threes is because after the first two you are so stressed out, fed up, exhausted and distracted, thinking about ropes, crowds, crusty minstrels, pink hair and notes, to look where you are going. Your head hangs so low, you stop paying attention to the road in front of you, or, in this case, the person who steps out in front of you.

I ran over Maid Marion.

I was crawling along the road leading out of the car park, alongside a steady stream of visitors ambling in the opposite direction. The ridiculously tall, attractive woman bounced off my bumper and landed in the arms of the man who was behind her. One of quite a few men. The look on his face reminded me of when a ball flies into the crowd at a football match and someone catches it.

I climbed out of the car. Not quite as quickly as I should have done but, to be fair, much faster than I wanted to. The woman's hat had fallen off, revealing thick blonde hair.

'I am so sorry. Are you okay? Shall I call an ambulance?'

A small girl in an outlaw costume pointed her bow and arrow at me. 'You ran over Maid Marion. Robin's gonna get you for this.'

The woman delicately prised herself out of the man's arms. 'No, I'm fine, honestly. I wasn't looking where I was going. Really; all my fault. I should be the one apologising. I only hope I didn't dent your car.'

We looked at the car. It was impossible to tell which of the dents, if any, had been caused by today's accident.

'I bet she's working for the Sheriff. Traitor!' The same girl spoke again.

I was beyond arguing. My victim had to step in to defend me.

'No, no. It was an accident, I'm sure. Wasn't it?'

'She's probably jealous. Look at her. She doesn't even have a flower in her hair. And she's fat.'

How bad would it look if I just jumped into my car and drove away? I breathed for a moment.

'Can I take you to a medic? Is there a first aid tent somewhere?'

'I don't think so!' the man who had caught her said. 'We'll take her. Make sure she gets there safely.'

Marion's groupies began shuffling away, forming a protective circle around her. She limped gracefully, if that was possible. Like a bruised flower or a butterfly with a damaged wing. Smiling the whole time.

'Oh, thank you; you are so kind. No, I don't need you to carry me. I'm sure I can manage. Really, it was only a scrape.'

I hurried after them, handing the other, superior Marion a scrap of paper with my name and phone number on it. 'Here, just in case you need to contact me. And I am really, really sorry.'

She scanned the paper. 'Oh. You're Marion.'

This caused a murmur about concussion, and delirium setting in. The groupies shrank the circle closer. Maid Marion bent close to me, still smiling, and whispered, 'I'm Erica, Reuben's girlfriend. He's told me *all* about you.'

I thought about Reuben stroking that perfect glossy hair while gazing into those perfect blue eyes on top of perfect long, skinny legs and telling her all about me, and broken bicycle brakes, and ninja chickens.

I went home and, after eating an entire coconut cake, climbed under my duvet, planning on staying there for a very long time.

9

The day after the festival, a huge bunch of pink and white roses was delivered to my caravan door, with a note saying:

Sorry. I'm an idiot. Please forgive me. Jake.

I found him hammering nails into a fence supposed to prevent Little Johnny escaping: a token gesture for insurance purposes. In reality, Little Johnny did exactly as he pleased, wherever he felt like doing it. Jake banged at the nails with as much enthusiasm as he might use to build his own coffin. I tapped him on the shoulder, making him slip and hit himself with the hammer.

'Sorry!'

He jerked around, biting back his curse when he saw who it was.

'Don't be.' He held out the hammer. 'Here – take a swing. I deserve it.'

I ignored the gesture, instead waving my hand toward his face where three angry red lines scored down his cheek. 'I think I did enough damage yesterday.'

Jake grasped hold of my hand. 'I am really, really sorry, Marion. I never meant to upset you.' He grimaced. 'I was actually trying to impress you. But now you know the truth: I am a complete loser.'

'Woah. Don't start feeling sorry for yourself. That will get you nowhere.' I pulled my hand back and folded my arms. 'Anyway. Thank you for the flowers. And I accept your apology. I have issues with ropes that you weren't to know about. Let's just forget it ever happened.'

'Whatever you say.' Jake grinned at me, crinkling up his eyes. 'And for the record, I'm going along with whatever you say from now on. You were fierce, Marion. You should be a cage fighter. Or one of those ultimate wrestlers. Remind me never to startle you in a dark alleyway.'

'Do you have a computer?'

'What?' He frowned at my interruption.

'I need to use a computer, with internet access. Can I borrow yours?'

'Yeah, sure. Anytime. No problem.'

'Thanks. Are you off this Thursday?'

'Yes.'

'Okay if I come over around two?'

Jake thought for a moment. 'No. I'm busy then. It will have to be later. Come at six, and stay for dinner.'

I took a deep breath. 'Jake, I need to borrow a computer, from a friend. I don't want a date.'

He stuck his hands in his jeans pockets and rocked back on his heels a couple of times. 'I know; whatever you say, remember. You're the boss.' His mouth was a straight line but his eyes still crinkled. Hm. I needed to use a computer. I would just have to run the gauntlet of Jake's intentions to do it.

On Thursday, just after six, I propped Pettigrew, brakes fully repaired thanks to Reuben, against the wall outside Jake's flat before buzzing the intercom. Taking the bike had been a calculated decision. It would be dark by nine o'clock, which gave me a good excuse to leave before then if I wanted to take the shorter route along the forest footpath. I cycled a lot these days. It was cheaper and more pleasant than using my car, and muscle definition was beginning to show along my thighs and upper arms for the first time. It felt amazing being able to ride further and faster as the days went by without getting out of breath. As a child, I had careened between being a grey-skinned bag of bones and an overinflated punching bag, depending upon whether I had been living with my mother's neglect or Auntie Paula's fish suppers. But I had always been fat, or skinny, or somewhere on my way to one of those. Not strong. And never healthy.

I hitched up my trousers. If I carried on losing weight, I would have to do something about the state of my wardrobe. The deliberate layer of protective bagginess was progressing toward bag lady chic. And while I didn't want Jake to open the door, take one look at my outfit and start cooking up plans to wriggle me out of it, I had sprouted a tiny seedling of pride in my appearance. I didn't *loathe* the idea of somebody else noticing the muscles emerging from under my flab.

Jake buzzed me in, meeting me at the top of the steps leading up to his flat. It was pretty much as I had expected: a living area leading to a small, functional kitchen with a two-man table in one corner and a giant-sized television looming over the rest of the room. The decor was straight-down-the-line IKEA. He had no photos, nothing more revealing than a copy of *FHM* and his guitar propped up against the sofa.

'I like your herbs.' A tray containing five plants filled the kitchen windowsill.

Jake smiled. 'Come and look at these, then.'

He pointed outside another window, to a flat roof. On here he had at least a dozen large pots containing plants of varying sizes. Some had fruit to identify them: tomatoes and peppers, and what might have been cucumbers or baby courgettes.

'Oh! I love them! I didn't know you could grow all this without a garden.'

Jake pushed up the sash window and I leaned out, inhaling the Mediterranean smell.

'Here.' He leaned past, squeezing me into the corner of the frame, and plucked a cherry tomato from the nearest bush. 'Try it.'

'It's nothing like a normal tomato!' It wasn't. It was tomato to the power of ten.

'Wrong.' Jake grinned, pulling the window shut as we moved away. 'That's what a normal tomato tastes like. It's those plasticised, chemicalised supermarket freaks that aren't normal.'

'Point taken.'

We made a bit more small talk, then Jake opened up his laptop on the sofa and clicked onto a search engine. He passed the computer over to me, where I balanced it on my knees. I would have suggested using the table in the kitchen area, but had to keep pretending I hadn't noticed the two large candles and vase of flowers on it.

He excused himself to go and sort out dinner. Heart, stomach, and kidneys in my mouth, I began my search.

Forty minutes later, and I was still searching. I had found out some information about this year's Robin Hood Festival, and the previous couple of years, but here the path came to a dead end. Combining the name 'Daniel' with words like 'Robin Hood' or 'Hatherstone' or 'Sherwood' proved equally unsuccessful. There were way too many Daniel and Henry Millers online to search through them all, but none were local, and all of them seemed to be still alive. Then, just as Jake announced that the meal was ready, I found a tiny online article from a local newspaper talking about the history of the local Robin Hood enthusiasts' club. It mentioned a man, Morris Middleton, who had been the club secretary since 1972. How many M. Middletons could there be living in the area? The answer, according to Jake's phone book, was nine.

I copied out the numbers, scribbling as fast as possible, and joined Jake at the table. We helped ourselves to pasta and salad. The salad was incredible. I allowed Jake to pour me a small glass of wine.

'Did you find what you needed?'

'Maybe.'

Jake waited. He put down his fork. I squirmed on my IKEA chair. He had let me borrow his computer, even if there had been an ulterior motive. I had to give him something.

'I'm looking for information about my dad. He died when I was seven and I don't know much about his past. I think he came from round here.'

'You must have searched the internet back home? Or don't they have modern technology in the Irish backcountry?'

I laughed. 'They do in the library where I work. But... I don't know; I wasn't ready before. And then I had some holiday come up, so I thought why not come and see for myself? Then I would be here to follow up any clues I found online.'

'So you think there might be a mystery to investigate?'

'Aren't all families a mystery?'

Jake looked down. He took a large gulp of wine, muttering under his breath, 'No mystery required to be a total disaster.'

I changed the subject.

Dinner was nice, and I could chat easily enough to Jake as long as I didn't meet his eye and could busy myself with eating. But once the meal was finished, awkwardness crept back along with the dusk. I declined a coffee, and got up to leave.

'Thanks so much for letting me use your laptop. And for dinner. You're a really good cook.' I picked up my bag. 'Well. Work tomorrow. And I've got to bike back. I'd better go.'

Jake stood up. He moved out from around the table so there was nothing between us.

'If you want, I could drop you home. I can bring the bike back tomorrow. Then you don't have to rush.'

I glanced across at the empty bottle of wine on the table. Jake had drunk all of it except for one small glass.

'No. Thank you. I've got to go.'

He lifted one hand and gently brushed it against my arm, lowering his voice to almost a whisper. 'Stay for a bit.'

I stared at the floor. My face must have been redder than his oh-so-juicy-and-delicious tomato collection.

'Jake...'

'What? We're having a good time, that's all. It's not a date. I'm behaving myself. Honestly, Marion, I just love being with you. The fact that you are totally gorgeous has nothing to do with it.' He smiled and held his hands up, innocent.

The problem with living for eight years with a boyfriend who treats you like a pigeon he rescued from the side of the road, who never makes you feel special, or beautiful, or interesting, is that you are prone to fall for the first man who comes along and tells you something different. Jake was an expert flatterer. I felt terrified and bamboozled and most definitely flattered. So I did what I do when I don't know what to do. I ran away.

* * *

I was fifteen when I took my first steps along the painful, potholed path out of mutism. Declan lay in a hospital bed with, among other things, a smashed-up face and three broken ribs. Neither I, nor my rescuer, had said anything to anybody. I later heard that Declan had claimed a gang of men from some terrorist organisation tried to recruit him, and when he refused, they made him pay. *Everybody* saw through this hilarious hogwash. The local police officers, having had the displeasure of dealing with Declan on numerous occasions in the past, would rather have bought a pint for whoever beat him up than arrest them. Many stones were left unturned during the investigation.

But somebody now knew what had been happening to me. And he wasn't prepared to ignore the fact that my silence protected an evil, perverted sicko.

It was easy to find out where I lived.

'Marion!' my mother screeched up the stairs. I came down to find him at the front door. Eamonn Brown. He was a year above me at school. One of the popular kids, son of the local doctor who sent my mother to hospital on several occasions. He had, of course, never spoken to me before.

'Hi.'

I froze. What was he doing here?

'Would you come for a walk?'

My mother smirked as she hovered in the doorway. 'Good luck with that.' She curled her lip. 'And with her.'

I stepped out of the door, slamming it shut behind me, marching off down the path and down the road until I knew my mother couldn't see me from where she would be peering through a slit in the net curtains.

Eamonn caught up, matching me stride for stride on the outside of the pavement, as nice boys did.

'You have to tell someone.'

I shook my head, quickly. Tell someone what? That my cousin had pinned me down and shoved dirt inside me?

'I don't care if he says it was me that hurt him. He deserved it, and any jury would agree.'

Maybe so. But a trial for GBH would surely put a dampener on Eamonn Brown's plans to follow his father into medicine. I kept walking.

'Okay. Forget that for now. I came to tell you Ma has a job for you.'

What? I turned to look at him for the first time.

'She works at the library.'

I knew she worked at the library. I spent more time in the library than I did at my own house. With the exception of Father Francis's office, it was the only place I felt any peace.

'She says you can start whenever you like, but you'll need to be able to talk to the visitors. She can keep the job open until school breaks up, but then she'll have to offer it elsewhere.'

We walked a little further. Eamonn talked about his schoolwork and his plans to go to Belfast University. He told me where he was going on holiday and that his dad had got him some hours as a porter to earn enough money to buy a computer. How his football team had reached the cup finals. I barely listened. I was thinking and thinking about that job. About enough money to stop being hungry all the time. About somewhere to go that might become a stepping-stone out of here. About Mrs Brown's warm smile and how she always smelled of biscuits. I had seven weeks until the end of school. Seven weeks to heal the girl hiding in my throat.

We circled back and reached my front gate. Eamonn smiled, and nodded goodbye. 'See you around then, Marion? I'll tell Ma you'll let her know about the job. Bye.'

I stood and watched him saunter off toward the centre of town. The first boy who had called for me. The first *anyone* who had called for me. My mouth opened and closed again, blowing out a tiny, whispery husk of air. 'Bye.'

The following week, at exactly the same time, he called again. I was out of the door before he could hear my mother cackling about how he was a sucker for punishment, and we automatically turned to walk the same way, toward the river.

'I brought you something.' Eamonn held out a carrier bag. 'Don't look at it now. It's from Da's office, so I'll need it back. Thought it might help you with the job.'

I took hold of the bag, feeling the weight of the book inside it. Could it undo the curse my mother had flung at me? Bring my daddy back? Release the suffocating grip of memories that clamped on to my vocal cords? Unless it was a spell-casting, time-travelling, magic book, I doubted it.

Selective Mutism. The book lay on my bed. Why did I mind so much? Bitter bubbles of anger and humiliation fizzed through my veins, frothing up into my brain. It was one thing to suffer from a condition making you a weird misfit, with no friends and no life. It was another thing to have somebody name it. To see it in black and white. A tiny part of me knew Eamonn meant to be kind. The rest thought I was a fool. That he was laughing at me along with everybody else. If he felt anything at all for me, it was pity. I threw the book against my bedroom wall and the spine broke. I managed one word that day. It wasn't a nice one.

* * *

I like text messaging. And using email. However, the ability to communicate so quickly and easily without using my voice is one I try not to rely on too frequently. In my efforts to stay functional, and grow in confidence and courage, I occasionally bully myself into using the phone, or speaking to someone in person, even when a text message would do. In the past, when my throat has been tighter than usual for a few days, perhaps following a conversation with my mother when she has been particularly energetic in her insults, I have banned myself from using non-verbal communication. The threat of slipping back into my maze of silence still hovers in the deeper crannies of my brain, so I hack back the hedges with self-discipline and torture.

I promised myself I would phone one M. Middleton on the list each day, using the cheap pay-as-you-go I bought the week before. But I couldn't do it after a Friday spent on reception dealing with customers. Or Saturday, exhausted after making conversation with Valerie for the four hours it took us to clean the caravans. Sunday was Fire Night, and who wants to be interrupted by a strange person phoning you up with a load of questions on a Sunday evening anyway?

Jake laughed at my excuses until they were a quivering, pathetic blob of lies.

'Do you want me to call them for you? Find out if any of them are Morris?'

Yes. No. Yes. But that would be just another cop out... so...

'No. I'll do it... I just need to psych myself up first, get in the right mindset.'

He laughed again, not unkindly.

Scarlett floated past, carrying a platter of salmon decorated with lemon wedges and what I now knew to be dill.

'Okay, so here's the lesson in makin' yourself do somethin' you don't want to do, instead of lettin' it hover over your head like a giant spider wavin' its hairy legs and snappin' its poisonous fangs as it dangles on the end of its web.' She handed the plate to Valerie, waving her over to where Samuel tended the barbeque, and put her hands either side of my shoulders.

'Oh, for your own sake, just do it, Marion! Don't stop, think, debate, imagine. Do *not* bargain with yourself! Never negotiate! Right now, this minute, today. No questions, excuses or waitin' 'til a more convenient time. Don't worry or witter about what may or may not happen. *Do not* allow the possibility of uncomfortable consequences to be a reason not to do what needs to be done! Tell yourself you are strong, capable and confident. Because underneath all that wibblin' and waverin', *you are.* And I will tell you this. Life is too short and too sweet to waste any of it puttin' things off. Why would you think so little of yourself that you would let another day – another *hour* – pass by with the big ugly shadow of a spider hangin' over your head? I can promise you that whatever it is, it is better done so you can get dealin' with the consequences than frettin' about what they might be. Pull up your socks, take a deep breath, and just do it.'

Monday evening, I closed my curtains, pulled up my socks, whizzed through my mute busters and just did it.

Nine phone calls later, I was nauseous, exhausted, and ready for a very big piece of cake. It had got harder, not easier, with each conversation. Six of the numbers were a straightforward 'no'; they weren't Morris Middleton and they weren't related to Morris Middleton. No, they hadn't heard of Morris Middleton. No, they hadn't ever been involved with organising the Robin Hood Festival. No, they didn't know Daniel Miller... and who was this again? One number rang and rang until I hung up. Two were answerphone messages. I left my name and number and asked them to call me back.

So that was that. I would retry the three numbers that hadn't answered another day. Probably.

Friday came. Ada and May returned, and I was on duty at reception. Nine women, including Valerie, received the attentions of those magic scissors. Ada told her incredible stories, and every time May glowered at me, killer rays shot out of her beady eyes and zapped at my self-esteem. Valerie swished her new choppy blonde cut and waved at me. 'Come on, Marion! I'll sit on the desk. Come and have a cut. Your hairstyle is rubbish.'

It was. My hair was a nest of rubbish. I smiled and shook my head. 'No, thanks. Maybe next time.'

10

The Peace and Pigs' high season officially finished in mid-September. All but the die-hard campers packed up and left, though the caravans would remain full with pre-school children and older couples right through until November. Grace was back in sixth form and Valerie had a part-time course at a local college for adults with learning disabilities. That left me tackling monster chickens, cleaning duties, and the three phone numbers in my back pocket.

The last Sunday in September, Fire Night moved up to the Hall for the Hatherstone Harvest Supper. Following tradition, the villagers arrived at dusk carrying pots of steaming stews and soups along with potatoes baked to the perfect combination of crisp shells and fluffy centres. Every child came bearing an armful of wood for the fire – sticks from the garden or broken pieces of unwanted furniture.

Valerie and I spent the afternoon stringing red and orange bunting between the rafters of the big barn. We entwined white fairy lights around the beams and pillars, placing vases of late summer flowers along the rows of trestle tables lining the edges of the room. At one end, Jake joined another guitarist, a drummer, and a fiddler as they set up amplifiers and trailed wires about. Scarlett and Ginger had laboured as Sunny's kitchen assistants for the past two days, and by the time the guests arrived, the tables creaked under the weight of apple tarts glistening with caramelised sugar, towers of crisp meringues stuffed with cream and berries, and dozens more pies, strudels, and cakes in keeping with the season. As usual, Grace had disappeared.

By 8.30 p.m., all the 200 or so guests had found a drink and gathered with mock solemnity around the enormous pile of wood. Archie guided Katarina's eldest boy, Lucas, as he carefully placed his bunch of sticks at the bottom of the bonfire, before turning to salute the crowd.

'People of Hatherstone!' he called out, standing nobly in a green and brown tweedy suit. 'Thank you one and all for your contributions to the 169th Hatherstone Hall Harvest Supper and Fire Night! Now, if you would be so kind, may I ask for your participation and cooperation in one more very important thing? That is—' and here he paused for dramatic effect, twisting his head from side to side as he scanned the crowd, until Ginger shouted, 'Oh, get on with it, do!'

'That is – for each and every one of you to have a rollicking good time!'

A cheer went up, glasses chinked and small children skipped about. Archie lit the fire with a flourish, and Fire Night began.

Each and every one of us did indeed have a rollicking good time.

Squashed in next to some of the locals I recognised from the village, I ate my supper. I saw Jo from the café, and the usual gaggle of market traders. It helped that everybody already knew me. The trick was remembering who I had actually met before, and who just knew of me through the local grapevine.

When I had done enough chatting, I listened and drank, by

which time the floor had filled with dancers, so I had a go at that as well. It might seem strange that a socially inept, ridiculously shy person, with what might be classed as self-esteem issues, would dance in front of a whole load of people, most of them strangers. But, aha! I have learned that dancing is an excellent way to avoid conversation. And if I pretend that I am enjoying myself hard enough, sometimes I actually do.

When the band took a break, I grabbed a glass of punch and found a spare bale of hay to flop down onto. Jake joined me. For once, he was drinking Coke instead of beer.

'Having a good time?'

I thought about it, realising with much less surprise than I would have felt a month ago that I was.

'Yes. I love your band.'

'You're a pretty good dancer.'

'No, I'm not. But it's nice to be able to keep dancing for more than one song without getting out of breath.'

'So you didn't used to dance much back home? I'd have thought you'd be well into those Irish jigs.'

'No.' I picked at a loose piece of straw poking into my leg, trying not to think about the last party I had been to. I couldn't help noticing, peeking out from behind the big splatter of guilt, how different this evening had been compared to then. How different *I* was now, compared to the floppy, feeble mouse at my engagement party.

'How's the mystery solving going? Made any more progress?' Jake lowered his eyebrows at me. 'Tell me you have called all the Middletons on the list.'

'Yes! And called back the ones who didn't answer the first time. I've spoken to all of them except for one, who never answers. So I'm at a bit of a dead end. I've tried the library and asked everybody I can think of locally if they recognise the photo.' I frowned, pulling on another stem of straw. 'I sometimes get the impression somebody knows something, but they aren't telling me. Maybe because I'm new here.'

'Have you asked Ada?' Jake nodded his head across to where she perched on a stool, dressed in pink silk, a cluster of listeners leaning forward to catch the full spectacle of her storytelling. 'She's lived here at least twenty years. Or May? She might remember.'

I had to wait a while before Ada took leave of her audience to visit the 'room of refreshment and relief'. The ladies got to use the bathrooms in the main house, while the men made do with the outbuilding and the hedge, so I hovered in the hallway until she came out.

'Why, hello, Marion.' Ada cast a swift, appraising glance over my hair, which I had at least washed and brushed for the party. It had started out in a neat plait, but become slightly dishevelled during the dancing. I felt some knots untangle under the sheer power of her gaze. Tension buzzed as Ada restrained her hands from grabbing hold of my head and giving it a good sorting out. 'Are you enjoying the party?'

'Yes, thanks. You look magnificent, Ada.'

'Why, thank you! You know, I'm a great believer that what's on the inside counts.' She paused, smoothing a non-existent wrinkle in her dress. 'And I think maybe you feel the same way. But once you have spent some time working on the gift which is the inner you, there is nothing wrong with giving a little attention to the wrapping.' Ada smiled, and her eyes twinkled. 'I can see you are learning to respect yourself, girl. You'll be ready for me soon enough.'

We began to walk back through the hall toward the party.

'Ada, can I ask you something?'

'Fire away, girl. What's on your mind?'

I paused in the grandiose entrance hall, and Ada, realising that this wasn't merely a simple question relating to haircare, suggested we take a seat on a dark-blue sofa beneath the staircase.

'I'm trying to find out about my dad, who I think might once have lived around here. All I have to go on is this.' I pulled out the photograph from its zipped sanctuary in the inner compartment of my bag, Ada rising above commenting on the excruciating blooper of bringing my everyday bag to a party.

She scrutinised the photograph, crunching up her bright eyes to tiny wrinkles. 'He looks familiar. But if I do know him, I haven't seen this boy for a very long time. When was the picture taken?'

'Sometime in the early eighties, I think. But my dad moved to Ireland before I was born, so you wouldn't have seen him for at least twenty-seven years.'

'The Robin Hood Festival. It must have just been starting then.' Ada snapped her head up. 'You need to speak to Morris.'

'Morris Middleton?'

'Yes.' She narrowed one eye. 'Or have you already spoken to him?'

'No. But I did call every M. Middleton in the phone book.'

'Oh, no, girl. Morris won't answer his phone. He doesn't hold with modern technology. He only has a phone line because his daughter insisted on putting it in, but he won't answer.'

'So how can I get hold of him?'

'I'll take you to him.' Ada folded her hands neatly in her pink silk lap and fluttered her eyelashes at me. 'In return for an hour with your hair sometime.'

I looked at Ada. She pursed her lips and lifted one perfect eyebrow. She was right. It was time.

'Done!'

By one o'clock in the morning, the band were packing up and most of the partygoers had weaved and wobbled their way back down the drive to the village. I stood at the sink washing up while Grace dried, which was fine. I felt ready for some silence, and its stony quality left me unfazed.

Scarlett tapped in, the only person in the whole grounds still wearing six-inch heels.

'Marion, honey, will you take some of this pie?'

'Yes, thanks.'

'Rhubarb, apple, apple and rhubarb, blackberry, apple and... oh, no, actually, that one's all done. Peach, pumpkin...'

'Any is great. They are all a million times better than the supermarket pies I grew up on.'

'Your mama don't make her own pie?' Scarlett must have had too much wine. She never asked personal questions.

'No. Her cookery style mostly involved taking frozen food out of packets and putting it in the oven. Though she did make Irish stew. And cheese on toast.'

'Well, honey! That ain't cookin'. How did you learn? Did you teach yourself, or have a grandma do it?'

I concentrated on scrubbing the large pan floating in the sink. 'No, not really.'

'So how did you learn?'

I shrugged.

'You can't cook, can you?'

I shook my head.

'You can't cook *anything*, can you?' Scarlett clapped her hands together. She was definitely on the squiffy side. 'That's it! That's the answer! I've been rackin' my brains thinkin' about how we are gonna finally get your petals to open up so that the world can see what pretty colours you are hidin' inside yourself. Everybody needs an outlet of creative expression to creatively express themselves, and I knew we would find yours eventually. *Sunny!*'

Sunny appeared, hefting a saucepan that had probably, when full, weighed more than he did. 'Yes?'

'Marion needs cookin' lessons, Sunny. As soon as possible!'

Sunny glanced down at the small, red-headed boy clinging on

to his leg. He swung to the side, revealing his two-year-old daughter clinging, half-asleep, to his back like a bush baby.

'This is how I cook, currently. Except usually there is Lucas also, tripping me up as he steals my ingredients to make stink bombs. And once they are in bed, which can be anytime between half past six and eleven, depending on what time Katarina finishes work, there is washing, ironing, dusting, polishing. I am frequently taping my eyes open. If you can wait three years until they are all at school...'

Scarlett frowned. 'Forgive me, Sunny. I forgot you spent your days drowning in a sea of boiling hot chaos. Remind me to tell you about my lesson on how to bring up your kids, instead of letting them bring you down. Now, there must be someone else that we can ask.'

She grabbed my arm. 'Leave that! Leave that! Come with me.' She pulled me outside, where we found Reuben watching the last of the bonfire with the remains of the stragglers.

'Reuben!' Scarlett peered into the shadows. 'Is Erica still here?'

Reuben called her over and she floated up on a puff of air, wrapping her arms around his waist. She wore a yellow sundress with Reuben's jacket on over the top. Her hair tumbled down around her shoulders, white gold in the moonlight, framing her perfect features like a Greek goddess.

Scarlett patted my hand. 'Don't you mind too much,' she murmured behind my ear. 'I bet she'd swap that hair for your boobs.' She smiled. 'Hey, Erica. Marion needs cookin' lessons. I remember that dinner you cooked last New Year's at your parents' place. Pure heaven! Could you maybe spare some time to show her the ropes?'

Erica lifted her head off Reuben's chest and scrunched up her nose.

'I suppose I could. I'm no expert or anything, but it sounds like it might be fun. Although my flat is tiny; we couldn't do it there. And I don't suppose her caravan is much better...'

'Hmmm. What she really needs is a fully equipped kitchen to practise in.'

Erica unwrapped herself from Reuben, clutching one of his arms while taking hold of Scarlett's. 'Reuben! We could use the Hall!'

'What?' He glanced over at me. 'I don't think...'

'It would be perfect. Ginger won't mind. It gives me another excuse to come over and see you, and we could raid the leftovers from your veg boxes. You could even help us.' Erica rubbed her hand up and down Reuben's arm. 'Reuben is an *amazing* chef, aren't you?'

Reuben didn't look convinced.

'Well!' Erica clapped her hands together. 'That's settled, then. You're free Tuesday, Reubs, aren't you? Yes. I'm sure you are. Why doesn't Marion come over around six? Then we can eat what we've made for supper!'

'Wonderful,' Scarlett drawled. She swayed back toward the house, tugging Erica with her.

Reuben stood and watched them for a few seconds before turning back to poke the fire. 'Do you always let people treat you as if you are invisible?'

'What?' I jumped. 'No, um. Scarlett's just had a bit too much cider... she never normally would...' My voice trailed off to a mumble. 'I don't mind, really.'

Reuben looked up in my direction. Even though his eyes were hidden in shadow, I could feel his gaze burning through all the rubbishy excuses. He saw me. And it scared the life out of me.

On Tuesday evening, at quarter past six, I knocked on the kitchen door of Hatherstone Hall. Erica whipped it open, her eyes gleaming.

'Marion! Come in! How amazing to see you. We're all ready to go. Reuben, will you take Marion's coat? And please see to the dog.'

Ah, I see. Erica's playing at being Lady Hatherstone.

On one end of the enormous kitchen table sat three carrier bags and several plates, spoons, and other kitchen equipment laid out next to them with military precision. Still dressed in his muddy farming gear, a five o'clock shadow sharpened the angles of Reuben's face. He hung my coat on a hook behind the kitchen door and leaned back against the worktop, folding his arms. His dog, who must have doubled in size since last I saw her, padded across the kitchen tiles to lie on his feet.

'Hi.' I pulled a face, apologising for taking over his kitchen.

'Hi, Marion.' He smiled, resignedly, and I remembered he knew this wasn't exactly my idea.

Erica looked at the dog. 'Reuben! She can't stay here. Aren't you going to put her outside?'

'She's fine.'

'It's unhygienic, having an animal in a food preparation area.' Erica whisked over to the door and opened it, calling for the dog, Lucy, to come. Lucy didn't move.

Erica wouldn't give up. She kept slapping her hands against her thighs and calling Lucy's name. This felt like a bigger issue than food hygiene. In the end, Reuben clicked his fingers, and Lucy ambled to the far corner of the room, where I saw a massive cushion tucked into an alcove. She curled up onto her bed, resting her head on her paws.

Erica paused for a tiny moment before straightening up and fixing a breezy smile on her face. 'Right. Shall we get started?'

She ushered me up to the table and pulled out a stool to perch on, leaving me standing. I had dressed in my increasingly baggy jeans and a grey sweatshirt, fully anticipating the spills and splatters of my comprehensive ineptitude. Erica wore a Cath Kidston apron over a knee-length, cream, woollen dress.

'First things first! You've washed your hands?'

I nodded, hating myself for blushing. Hating myself more for stooping to answer the question.

'Right. Well, today I thought we would start with a simple tomato pasta dish, followed by crème brûlée. Okay?'

'Sounds good.' I hoped that dress wasn't as expensive as it looked. Then I sort of hoped it was and that Erica slopped a load of sauce on it. Then I mentally slapped myself on the wrist for being a bitch.

'Have you ever cooked pasta before, Marlon?'

'Um. Yes. But mostly I use a ready-made sauce, from a jar. By the time I get home from work...'

'Don't worry, it's pretty easy, really. I brought my pasta machine so we can make the dough from scratch. You're going to be amazed at what you can achieve when you try!'

For the first time in my life, I wanted to punch someone. By seven o'clock, I was ready to grab her bouncy, glossy, naturally blonde hair and stuff it into the rollers of the pasta machine. Then a miracle happened. I stood slicing onions while Reuben chopped celery opposite me. Erica, who had been *supervising*, had a phone call. She disappeared into the pantry, returning five minutes later, pale-faced.

'That was work. The ad campaign has just come back and it's a *disaster*. The title font is cerise, when I specifically ordered raspberry. It's riddled with mistakes. I'm going to have to go and fix this.'

She slipped off her apron. 'I'm so sorry, Marion. I feel awful about having to leave you in the lurch. You were doing so well. Reuben, do you mind helping Marion finish her lesson? It would be such a shame for her to have to quit now and go back to tinned meat and fish-fingers.'

Reuben put down his knife. He looked up at Erica. 'Don't worry about us. Will your work be okay about this? You'll be able to sort it out?'

Erica smiled, showing most of her perfect white teeth. 'It'll be fine.' Then, for the first time, I saw her smile waver. 'Well, I hope it will.'

'Thanks anyway, for going to all this trouble,' I said, continuing to chop the onions. 'Shall we save you something for later?'

'No.' Erica kissed Reuben goodbye. 'It'll take forever. But hopefully I'll be done by Fire Night. See you then.'

Erica left, and facing Reuben across the table, I almost wished she'd been able to finish the lesson. The first thing he did was turn the radio on. Nottingham Forest playing football. He stood and listened until the commentator announced the score. Forest were one-nil up. As if someone had thrown a switch, his tension vanished.

'Okay. Let's get on with it. Grab a pan and heat up some oil. No – not that much oil! Just enough to coat the onions...'

It was hard to tell if Reuben was any good as a teacher, because I was such a disaster as a student. He intimidated me. I still hadn't forgotten the chicken incident, and he just seemed so *big*. Not so much physically, but he seemed to take up so much space with, I don't know, his personality or something. Not the most graceful person at the best of times, I became clumsy, awkward, and scatter-brained to the point where I felt ready to bash myself over the head with the antique copper frying pan.

Reuben grew increasingly impatient and frustrated, though to his credit, he did try not to show it. At 8.30 p.m., I finally tipped a plate of stuck-together spaghetti clothed in watery-yet-burned tomato sauce onto two plates.

We stared at the food for a few moments.

'Sorry. I've wasted your evening. And made a total mess of your kitchen. Maybe we should just throw this in the bin. I can make an edible cheese sandwich...'

'Sit down.' Reuben pulled out a chair for me to sit on. 'It's taken us two hours to make this dinner. I've been lugging vegetable boxes since half past six this morning, and I'm so hungry that this doesn't actually look too bad. Stick some cheese on the top and it'll be fine.'

We grated some cheese on the top. A lot of cheese. It was not fine. I managed to force down a few forkfuls.

Reuben had no such qualms, finishing his plate, and the rest of mine, before pushing himself back from the table and stretching his legs out. 'There. You can tell Erica your first lesson was a success. We made a pretty good team, even without her *supervision*.' He winked at me. I grabbed my water glass and hid behind it. Reuben smiled. 'Erica means well; she just gets a bit carried away sometimes.'

'I can see she really loves being here – at the Hall.'

His smile disappeared. 'Yes. Yes, she does. In small doses.'

We ate our sloppy crème brûlée without talking. It wasn't an uncomfortable silence, just the quiet of people too exhausted to bother making conversation. I cleared away the remains of the meal and washed up while Reuben, who dried, suggested what I could do to improve things next time. Did I want there to be a next time? I wasn't sure yet.

* * *

My visit to the home of Morris Middleton, who to my surprised dismay also turned out to be the minstrel, aka the unpleasant man who had been rude to me at the festival, counted as just about the creepiest afternoon of my life. I had known the kind of terror that turns your spine to water at the hands of my imaginative cousin, and grown accustomed to the drip drip of slow, steady, stomach-curdling dread that came as an inevitable side-effect of living with my mother. But this was just plain weird. Bad weird. Thank goodness for Ada.

I picked Ada up from the thatched cottage she shared with her sister and we drove through increasingly narrow, potholed lanes through the forest until we reached a tiny, semi-derelict ruin hidden under the eerie shade of towering pine trees. If Ada and May lived in a fairy-tale house, this had to be the home of the evil villain. I pulled up on the patch of dirt standing in for a driveway and switched off the engine. In the murky light under the trees, the gloom heightened the impact of cracked, peeling walls and rotten frames surrounding windows so grimy no one could have seen inside, not even once they had crept right up to the front entrance.

As Ada lifted her hand to knock on the door, a sharp cacophony of barking burst through the flimsy wood, then a heavy thud on the other side as a large animal threw itself against the inside of the door. When the next crash threatened to break the door down, Ada had to grip hold of me to stop me sprinting back to the car. She peered in through one of the filthy windows and shouted through the glass.

'Morris! It's Ada. Stop fooling about and open the door! And mind you get the wolves under control first. You don't want a repeat of what happened with Mrs Grant!'

What happened with Mrs Grant? I might have said that out loud, but I think my voice had reached supersonic frequencies that only the wolves – *wolves?* – could hear.

After a few more knocks and yells from Ada, a lot more barking, growling, snarling and scratching from inside the house and some muffled swearing, Morris Middleton opened the door.

He slipped through a gap just wide enough for his beer belly, slamming the door on the beasts trying to shove their way out after him, and gestured with his large, grimy head toward the back of the building. Without his medieval hat, I could see he had one of those heads with hair just about everywhere except on the top where hair ought to be. I didn't blame him that the hair was stained yellow in places, and lank and scrawny. It was probably a hard job to look after hair that long growing in all those places. His head must represent Ada's worst nightmare.

At the other side of the house, in between piles of wood, junk metal, and about a thousand empty beer cans, Morris Middleton led us inside a lean-to containing a bloodstained table on which lay three dead squirrels. One of the squirrels had its guts half pulled out. A bowl holding what looked like lots more guts stood on the floor beside it. A sink that may have once been white hung against the wall adjoining the main house. A high shelf ran along one wall, and a black, three-legged stool stood next to the table. Oh, yes, and a thick, buzzing crowd of fat, shiny flies swarmed on everything. I cannot even begin to describe the stink. Except it smelled of dead squirrels, blood, guts, filth, unwashed crazy forest man, and a zillion flies.

I stepped as far back into the (thankfully wide) doorway as I could without being actually outside again. My skin crawled, imagining flies already burrowing beneath my clothes. I tried to keep my features neutral, fighting the stench. Ada had no such qualms. She stuck a lace-edged handkerchief in front of her nose and scowled at Morris Middleton.

'This is repulsive, Morris! We can't talk in here.'

Morris squatted on the stool, tugging at the squirrel innards. I turned away, sucked in a lungful of relatively clean air and tried not to gag.

'I don't want to talk. I didn't ask you to come. If you don't like it, you can—'

'Mor-ris,' Ada sang, pulling a bottle of whisky out of her shoulder bag while still managing to keep the handkerchief pressed against her face. 'Let's not be too hasty, now. We know you are a busy man and your time is precious.'

He glanced at the whisky, then sighed. 'Wait five minutes.'

We waited on the scrubby grass behind the house, carefully avoiding the piles of dung. Hoping they were animal in origin.

The minstrel emerged, as promised, five minutes later, wiping his hands on a grey rag.

'What?'

'Good afternoon, Morris. How are you? Are you keeping well? The wolves? All healthy, hale, and hearty?'

Morris tucked the rag into the top of his woollen trousers. He folded his arms.

Ada smiled. 'Oh, Morris. Drop the hard man act, please do. You know I've been interrogated by far worse.'

He sniffed. I waited, trusting Ada knew what she was doing.

'Marion here is looking for information about the Robin Hood

Festival. From maybe the first or second year. She wants to know about this man.' With that, Ada offered Morris the photograph he had snubbed a month earlier. It was only a copy I'd made, but I still had to fight the urge to snatch it back out of his filthy, rank fingers.

'It's in the cellar.' Morris curled up the corners of his mouth. 'You'll 'ave to look yerselves.'

Ada looked at me. Her eyes shone. 'Well? What are we waiting for?'

I closed my eyes, which actually made no difference in the pitch-black cellar, thought about my warm, wonderful daddy, and edged forward down the slippery steps until I met the bare earth floor at the bottom. Ada, proving beyond any doubt to be indeed the fearless adventurer her stories suggested, followed behind me with a torch, the handkerchief now secured above each ear with a hairclip.

'Well, how interesting!' She whizzed the beam of the torch around the tiny room, revealing flashes of wooden crates stacked up against every wall. 'A veritable treasure trove of secrets could be hidden inside these boxes!'

It felt like forever before we found the right box. Each container had been labelled with the year of its contents, but the writing – messy to begin with, and done in charcoal – had rubbed and blurred, becoming almost illegible. The boxes were stacked in no particular order, and we had to turn some of them around before we could find the date. The cold, dank cellar air, laden with mildew, was suffocating. I felt profoundly grateful for Ada's cheerful chatter. Every time she paused for breath, the sound of rustling, scuttling feet was enough to make me light-headed.

When we eventually found the box for 1981, the first year of the festival according to another internet search on Jake's computer, it was too heavy and awkward for us to manoeuvre up the steps. We had to stay in the cellar while we rummaged through the mouldy contents, finding newspaper clippings, minutes of planning meetings and eventually what we had been looking for: an original programme from the Robin Hood Festival. A quick flick through in the torchlight revealed a photograph of my dad, again in Robin Hood costume, laughing with another young man dressed up as Little John. The musty cellar disappeared around me, momentarily lost in the dappled sunshine of the forest.

'Let's get out of here, girl! Mission accomplished!' Ada waved the booklet in the torchlight, triumphantly.

I stole a glance up the stairs. 'He said we aren't allowed to take anything.'

'Hah! Poppycock! He knows there's no chance of that.' She crammed the sheets down the back of her pedal pushers and kicked the box back toward the wall with her silver stiletto.

Stumbling back out into the hallway, we found Morris Middleton waiting at the front door, gripping the collar of a huge wolf-dog-thing in each hand.

'Found summat?'

'Yes, thank you, Morris. We found exactly what we were looking for, a very good stroke of luck.'

'Didn't decide to take owt?'

'Of course not. Now, if you will excuse us, we wouldn't dream of taking up any more of your time.'

Morris narrowed his eyes. He eased his grip on the animals, so they strained forwards eagerly, huge globs of saliva dripping onto the floor.

'Won't mind lettin' the girls check you over then.'

Ada rolled her eyes. I held my breath as the huge, soggy nose of the wolf-dog-thing probed about my person, leaving a trail of dog-meat-scented slime. I couldn't see what was going on with Ada through my scrunched-up eyelids, but she somehow passed inspection and we hastily made our exit.

We drove in silence without stopping until I pulled up outside Ada's cottage. She lifted up her backside and retrieved the stolen papers from her trousers. She then wriggled about for another minute, before removing a handful of garlic cloves. Where on earth had she hidden those?

Ada grinned, neatly placing the garlic inside a plastic sandwich bag. 'Never ignore the possibility of sniffer dogs, girl. I found that out smuggling illegal Bibles into China. That's a mistake you don't make twice!' She opened my car door and clambered out. 'See you Friday then. That barnet won't know what's hit it!'

I set off in the direction of the Peace and Pigs, creeped out, covered in canine slobber, the clinging stench of Morris Middleton's rancid house still pungent in my nostrils. But I felt my spirit flutter a good six inches off the floor – not quite soaring but a pretty good start, all things considered. I had been in one of Ada's scary, strange stories. I felt a teensy bit proud of myself. Turning off the main road into the campsite, it hit me: for the first time in my life, I no longer wanted to tell other people's stories. I wanted to live my own. I thought about my old boss Harriet, living every day to the sound of her own tune, and spent the rest of the day humming 'Who Let the Dogs Out?'

After Mrs Brown's job offer, I went to visit Father Francis. We settled in our usual chairs, mugs of tea in hand.

'It's been a while, Marion. Have you been doing all right, now?' This would be the point in the conversation where I would nod, or shake my head, or more often shrug my shoulders. I took a deep breath.

'Aye.' A tiny, breathy whisper. Father Francis pretended not to notice, but a light glowed behind his eyes.

'That's grand. Your mother has been out of the hospital for what, three weeks now?'

I nodded. He waited, hopefully. I sucked in another breath and fought past the screaming, angry, frightened girl squeezing the life out of my throat.

'Four.'

'Is she still looking after you? Are your aunties visiting often?'

I shrugged. Father Francis waited. I stared at the floor. I was done.

'I heard Colleen Brown offered you a job. Sounds like a grand idea to me. Will you take it?'

I looked up to meet his eyes, my own now brimming with tears. A moment of understanding passed between us. He knew how much I needed that job. For the rest of our visit, Father Francis chatted about the town, who was getting married, which babies had been born. Never gossip, only good news. We sat in silence for a while, and I ate enough cake to make up for having no supper to eat back home.

He let me out at six, when Mrs Dunn served his supper every night on the dot. 'Can you come back again tomorrow, Marion? After school? I have something to show you.'

I nodded my head, trying to hide my frustration and disappointment. Two words. Two more than last time. About two thousand fewer than I needed to manage if I was going to get that job and take my first step out of there.

I wandered round to the priest's house after school the following day. Part of me wondered if Father Francis had something to show me to do with my da. Mostly I was too depressed to care.

The something turned out to be a someone: a boy, maybe two or three years old, dressed in faded clothes far too big for him, with a pale, scabby complexion I recognised as due to poverty and neglect. He could have been my brother.

'This is Stephen. He's had a hard time of it lately, and really needs a friend. Someone who will understand how he's feeling. Not ask too much of him. What do you think?'

I looked at the priest. Seriously, what did he expect me to do? Pass on some tips about how to be a freak? Demonstrate how not to pick yourself back up when life knocks you down?

'Grand. I've just got one or two phone calls to make. I'll be back in a wee while.'

Stephen and I sat facing each other on our respective flowery armchairs. After a long stretch of nothing, I offered him a piece of flapjack from Mrs Dunn's tea tray. He ignored me, so I ate it myself. As the mahogany clock on the mantelpiece ticked round fifteen minutes, Stephen never moved or made a sound. My heart cracked – what was left of it. Two-year-old boys should be wriggling, giggling, racing, hollering, mini-elephant-warrior bouncy balls. What had happened to create this shell of a boy?

I moved over to Stephen's chair and put my hand on his arm. He tensed, but remained completely still. I saw a carrier bag tucked behind him. Gently pulling it out, I looked inside and discovered a grubby stuffed penguin, a dummy, a tiny racing car, and a book, *Pumpernickel Party*, about a baby penguin's birthday party. As I opened the book, Stephen's eyes swivelled around to land on the first page. I carefully took one finger and turned the page. His tiny hand shot out and flipped it back. Stephen briefly flicked his eyes over to my shoulder and down again, his hand still resting on the first page of the book.

He wanted me to read the story. This poor, wee, wretched boy wanted me to read the book. Aloud. A gathering rush of heat pressed at the back of my eyes. I forced my arms hard against my thighs to try to stop the tremor that jigged them up and down. Kept glancing back at the door. Where was Father Francis?

Stephen kept his hand on the book, his gaze downcast. One eye of the baby penguin peeked out from between his fingers. He suddenly sucked in a hiss of air and I realised he had been holding his breath.

Okay, that's it. I don't care any more. Forget my mother. I'm not listening to the girl inside me who thinks my words do nothing but harm. I am going to read this book.

'It was a very...' I stopped. Cleared my throat. Swallowed back the roaring rush of panic. Stephen flicked his eyes across in my direction again. His fingers trembled on the page.

'It was a very special day. For... for Pumpernickel Penguin...'

Page by page, one creaky, wheezy, halting croak at a time, I read the book. All six pages of it. Forty-six words. By the time I had finished, sweat dripped down my forehead and the blood pounded in my ears. Stephen turned the book back to the first page and patted it. I guess he didn't notice I was about to have a heart attack. By some strange coincidence, right then, Father Francis stepped back into the room. He grinned at me: a wide, open, honest beam of happiness. I ducked my head and nearly knocked him flying as I hurtled out of the door.

Late that night, hiding under my blankets, by the light of my daddy's electric torch, I opened up the spine-shattered *Selective Mutism* and started to read. I was still reading at seven o'clock the next morning when my alarm clock went off.

I didn't speak again that week. I was spent, empty, exhausted. But after school the following Tuesday, I found Stephen sitting in the flowery armchair, clutching his carrier bag on his knees. My journey out of the maze had begun.

12

Autumn exploded in the forest. Every tree – every leaf – reflected a different hue as it spun and crackled in the October winds. Rich clarets danced with copper and bronze, purples so intense they were nearly black, rose, gold and every shade of brown from soft fawn all the way to burned coffee. Squirrels skittered through the heaps of crispy vegetation, obsessively gathering the never-ending carpet of nuts. I had upped my regular walks through the woods to a jog, crunching past holly bushes sprinkled with crimson berries, entangling myself in vast networks of silken spider webs, sucking in the earthy, smoky scent of decaying nature with heaving lungs. I was in paradise, pounding longer and longer routes as I learned the secret footpaths of the forest, the tiny trails rabbits and badgers used. There were no other sounds but the scuff of my trainers through fallen leaves and the rasping of my breath, puffing out clouds of steam in the sharp morning air.

Early one Saturday, as I leaned on the trunk of an ancient oak tree stretching my calf muscles, I discovered Grace's secret. Never in a million years would I have guessed what she was up to as I watched her flit through the shadows. I followed behind her as far back as I dared, until I saw her disappear into a huge sprawl of rhododendron bushes. Creeping through the narrow spaces between the twisted limbs of the plants, I came right up against the tiny shed before I saw it. The door was closed. Moving around to the side of the rickety building, scraping my arm on a rough branch as I squeezed past, I found a window. I used the sleeve of my sweatshirt to scrape away the worst of the dust and the webs. Then I slowly moved my head across to peer inside.

A light came on. It reflected off the glass, casting the interior of the hut into distorted shadow. I could see Grace moving around. Was there anyone else there? Was this where she met her boyfriend? Or her drug dealer? I crouched back down underneath the window. What should I do? Pretend I hadn't seen anything? Go and fetch Scarlett? Wait until Grace came out again, then look inside?

I waited a few minutes, listening for the sound of voices, but heard nothing over the thump of my heart clanging in my ears. I began to make my way carefully back around to the tunnel through the bushes. This was not my business. Grace was not my friend. She clearly had issues, and I didn't want to become one of them (or more than I was already). If I discovered something awful in that shed, then I would have to decide whether or not to tell Scarlett. Right now, my best plan was to get away and then decide what to do next.

Except this plan didn't include me tripping on a tree root, crashing into the wall of the shed and punching a hole in a rotten panel with my fist. Grace screamed. I screamed louder. Half the birds in the forest whooshed up into the watery blue sky above us. I instinctively yanked my arm back, bringing a dozen jagged splinters with it in exchange for half the skin off the back of my hand. Grace flung open the hut door and stood there, staring at me, her tongue stud glinting in her open mouth. She recovered first.

'You followed me!'

I cradled my hand in the other arm and bit the side of my mouth to stop myself wailing as the damaged nerves sent shock waves up my arm.

'What. Are. You. Doing?' Grace was yelling now. Her face was a bitter white, a high spot of colour on each cheekbone. 'You're spying on me, aren't you? Did my mum send you? She did, didn't she? And you couldn't wait to follow orders, could you – for the *perfect, fabulous* Scarlett? *Yes, Scarlett; no, Scarlett; oh, please teach me your lessons on exactly how to think, Scarlett.*'

She smashed her own fist against the wooden wall, and let out a stream of curses. 'I should have guessed! This was the one thing I had for myself. I spend my life living in that blue shoebox with my mother and her latest reject. *Why won't she trust me?*' Grace's face scrunched up. She leaned her body forwards, hacking up sobs from somewhere deep in her guts. Her voice was like a piece of cloth being ripped in two. 'Why can't she trust me?'

I sat on the dry earth at the side of the shed and took a moment to pull off my sweatshirt and wrap it around my bleeding hand, wiping the dirt and sweat from my face with a dangling sleeve.

'Nobody sent me, Grace. I was out running when I saw you and was curious. Not curious. I was snooping and I'm sorry. But I was leaving when I fell.'

'So you wouldn't have gone running straight to Mum to tell her what you'd found?'

'I don't know. I would have thought about it first. Maybe asked you what you were using the shed for.'

Grace tossed her head. She knew I wouldn't have asked her about it. I adjusted my position on the dirt.

'So what now? Are you going to show me what's inside? I can't walk away and pretend I haven't been here.'

She slammed the door of the shed behind her. 'I'll have to move anyway, now you've broken the wall.' She scowled. 'I'll show you if you promise not to tell. Anyone. Not Valerie, or Jake.'

'I promise. As long as it's legal.'

She held out one hand to pull me up, then hesitantly began pushing the door open, before quickly turning back to face me. 'And you can't laugh.'

I smiled. 'You're not making an internet movie, are you?'

Grace didn't bother answering. She propped open the shed door with one boot, and reached over to turn the camping light the right way up. I stood at the doorway, speechless for a moment, before moving inside the room to take a closer look.

'Grace! These are *beautiful*.'

They were.

Shoes. Eight pairs of stunning, elegant, simply beautiful shoes.

They were stacked up along a short bench. Next to this stood an ancient deckchair, and a cardboard box containing plain, ordinary, pre-customised footwear. There was a large toolbox filled not with tools, but all the decorations and accessories for the shoes. Miniature silk flowers, hundreds of different coloured buttons, little paint pots, embroidery threads neatly arranged by shade. There were ribbons, squares of lace, butterflies, pieces of coloured glass in different shapes, beads, ruffles and even feathers. On an upturned bucket sat a glue gun and an old ice-cream box full of sewing equipment and cobbler's implements. In one corner sat a carrier bag with a multipack of crisps poking out of the top, and a pile of Coke cans. Every available inch of wall was covered in A4 pieces of paper filled with shoe designs. Some pretty, some spectacular, they ranged from flip-flops and sandals through to trainers and Wellington boots. I was absolutely astounded.

'Grace, this is amazing!'

Grace ducked her head. A hint of a smile creased the edges of her mouth.

'Can I touch them?'

She nodded. I squatted down in front of the bench. The first six pairs were simple ballet pump styles, all white or cream. Grace had decorated the first pair with thin, dark-green ribbon in a twisty vine design, then added burgundy metal beads, to create miniature bunches of grapes. She had continued the ribbon to make ankle straps, with more bunches of grapes dangling off these.

Another pair was entirely covered in brightly coloured birds, the embroidery threads intertwining with one another. She had given them shiny crystals for eyes, and added the smallest feathers, only a centimetre long, to every bird's tail, and around the edge of the shoe. A third pair was smaller, child size, and Grace had stuck on buttons in the shape of different sweets – jelly babies, dolly mixtures, mint humbugs and Liquorice Allsorts.

'Can I...?'

'What size are you?' Grace squinted at my feet. 'Here, try these.' She handed me a pair of six-inch stilettos in navy-blue satin. Tiny silver stars decorated the surface, including the heel, and the buckle was a crescent moon. I slipped them on, and we laughed at how ridiculous they looked with my jogging bottoms.

'These are so wonderful, Grace. How did you ever learn how to do this? Why did you start? Why are you keeping it a secret? Why do you always wear those boots when you have shoes like these?'

Grace lingered by the door while I laced my trainers back up. 'I don't want Mum making a fuss.'

'Where did you get all the tools and stuff from?'

She shrugged.

'Okay. But you can't keep working in here through the winter, even if we can patch up that hole. You'll go blind trying to sew with only a camping light.' I looked at her nervously picking at her nails, and realised what a gift she had entrusted me with, letting me in here. I took a deep breath.

'I've got loads of space in my van. Most of the living room cupboards are empty. Why don't you move all your stuff in and work there? We can hide everything away, and your mum will be really pleased that you're spending time in my caravan instead of roaming the woods with dangerous drug-dealers old enough to be your father.'

'I don't care what Mum thinks.'

'Don't tell her then.'

She narrowed her eyes at me, but I could see her wavering.

'So... what's in it for you?'

'A kick-ass pair of shoes.'

We waited until Sunday afternoon, when Scarlett and Valerie went out shopping and Jake was busy sorting out wood for the evening's Fire Night, then transported Grace's workshop to my caravan. We had to carry everything through the shrubbery by hand, before balancing as much as we could in a wheelbarrow lined with bin bags to haul back through the woods. We left behind the chair and the bench, returning the lamp to the shop in reception from where Grace had borrowed it.

Once everything was safely stowed away, Grace's drawings neatly filed in plastic sleeves in a folder, I put the kettle on.

'Can you stay for a drink, or will Scarlett want you to help get ready for tonight?'

'If I turn up on time, she'll only get suspicious.'

I made us both tea, and we sat on opposite sides of the living area.

'It wasn't me.'

'What?' I steadied myself, but not before I had spilled hot tea onto my lap. Grace found a dishcloth and threw it over at me.

'I didn't break your window.'

'Oh. No... I didn't think...'

'Yes, you did. You'd be stupid not to. But it wasn't me. My leaving had nothing to do with you.'

'Right. Well, thanks for letting me know. I suppose.'

'You suppose?'

'Well, if it wasn't you, who was it? And what the heck did that note mean?'

'I dunno. No offence, but you don't seem interesting enough to make that many enemies.'

I thought about it. 'May seems to think I'm pretty hideous. She told me I should be sacked because of my offensively ill-fitting bra.'

Grace laughed, splurting out some of her drink. I passed her the dishcloth.

'May hates everyone.'

'I got another note.'

'What? When?'

I told Grace about the festival, by which time she reckoned she had left it late enough to suitably annoy Scarlett. I gave her my spare key, a voice at the back of my head hollering, 'What are you doing?' and went to shower off the bits of rhododendron bush caught in my hair.

* * *

Scarlett was not impressed with the frozen cheesecake I had brought along as my contribution to Fire Night.

'What is this?' She inspected the plate at arm's length, as if it was rancid. 'Honey, it's nearly a month since your cookin' lessons started. I was hopin' to sample some of what ya learned back there.'

I took the cheesecake off her and slid it to the back of the food table. 'Erica's been really busy with a problem at work, so I haven't seen her since the first lesson.'

Reuben leaned past with a tray of kebabs, grinning. 'And believe me, Scarlett, you would not have wanted to try anything from that first attempt.'

'Reuben!' Scarlett smacked him on the arm. 'Keep your negative nose out of it. How would you know anyway?'

'No. He's right. And Erica's work thing kicked off in the middle of cooking, so actually Reuben took over as my instructor. I think it's fair to say his input was largely responsible for the failure of the lesson.'

Reuben winced in mock offence. 'Without my input, you'd have burned down the kitchen.' He opened his mouth to go on, but glancing at Scarlett, thought better of it.

'Reuben, darlin'. No one is expectin' Marion to be able to cook. That is the whole point of the lessons. Sounds like you need to practise teachin' as much as she needs to learn. I think you just volunteered yourself to continue the course. Next Fire Night is Bonfire Night, last one of the season. I expect you two to come up with somethin' finger-lickin' fabulous. And you know who I'll be blamin' if it isn't.'

She began to glide away, then thinking of something else, she called back over her shoulder: 'Oh! If you teach her well, you can get Marion to cook you a wonderful dinner as a thank you!'

Reuben raised his eyebrow at me. 'A wonderful dinner?'

I shrugged. 'Dinner, maybe. Wonderful sounds a bit ambitious.'

'I'm not going to do this if you've been bullied into it. As painful as it is to me, some people are content to spend their lives living on tinned carrots and frozen roast potatoes.'

I remembered Jake's salad pots. 'No. I want to. If you don't mind? It might be a lot of work.'

'As long as you don't hassle me about listening to the scores, or about my dog.'

I shook my head.

'Fine. I'll teach you how to cook.'

13

It was the first Friday in November. I had arranged a lesson with Reuben for the following afternoon, in time for Bonfire Night; but meanwhile, I had a deal to keep. With the high season over, the mobile beauty parlour only visited the campsite if somebody had made an appointment. That afternoon the somebody was me, and at one o'clock, I dragged my frumpy heels across to the lavender van. It had turned cold enough that May and Ada now both remained inside with the doors kept shut, each with a workstation at either end. Soft jazz music played in the background as I climbed the steps. Ada clacked her scissors together, brandishing them around her head.

'Get in here, girl! I've been dreaming about having a hack at that scrap heap since August. Unflattering, unstylish, unkempt. What a splendid challenge! What do you reckon, May?'

May didn't bother looking up from sorting out her nail polishes. 'I've seen more attractive hair on a corpse.'

Professional haircuts are torture for selective mutes, however far we may be along our road to recovery. The expectation to make small talk with a stranger, intensified by the stereotypical atmosphere of cosy gossip, creates pressure akin to diving into one of those black crevices deep under the ocean. Not being blind or an idiot, I knew how bad my hair looked when I cut it myself, but I would have chosen baldness over crossing the threshold of a hair salon.

Yet here I was. Knowing Ada helped, but I still closed my eyes from start to finish, gripping the arms of the chair to still my quaking body. I took slow, deep breaths and listened to Ada's story about when she had actually cut the hair of a deceased prince. She ended the story abruptly.

'Any luck with the stolen documents?'

'Not really. There's just that picture of my dad in the programme, laughing with the other guy, but the caption only calls them Robin Hood and Little John. I've hit a dead end.'

'Well, what else do you want to know?'

'I don't know. Where he lived. Why he kept his past such a secret. He must have had a reason for changing his name. I might have relatives in England. Grandparents, or cousins. And I'm sure some people know more than they're letting on. They remember Daniel Miller, but won't talk about him. Why not?'

The van was silent for a while, save for the rhythmic snipping of the magic scissors.

'You do realise that when it comes down to the bare bones of it, knowing the truth about your father won't help you find yourself?'

Oh, I do know that. I have no illusions about finding myself. It's losing myself I've been working on.

Half an hour later, I scuttled into reception, about two pounds and six million split ends lighter. Scarlett was shaking hands with Erica's dad, Mr Fisher. He picked up a briefcase and marched past me out of the door. She crumpled onto the counter, head in her hands, elbows resting on a pile of papers.

'What's happened?'

My boss inhaled sharply and flipped up her head. Her hands fluttered at her chignon before shuffling the papers, then darting back up to pat her hair again. I waited, and she composed herself, deliberately stilling her hands on the counter.

'Due to economical and recessional factors *beyond his control*, Fisher has increased our rent. Oh, yes – and being an evil, greedy, graspin', felonious leech who would suck the whole world to a lifeless husk if it meant he made some extra money out of it may have somethin' to do with it too!'

'Is it bad?'

'Bad enough that I ain't gonna sleep this week.' She shook her head. 'We'll think of somethin'. We always do.'

'Can you put up the price of the pitches?'

'Not enough to cover costs and remain competitive. We got peace here, and pigs, but we need a whole lot of bells and whistles if we want to charge much more than we do now.'

I tried to think of something helpful to say. Grace's secret shoes popped into my head.

But then Scarlett looked up from her muddle of papers, and her startled eyes focused properly on me. She gasped, and nearly vaulted over the counter in her effort to reach me.

'Honey, your hair!' She oohed and aahed, stroking and turning me this way and that. Her voice softened. 'Marion, you are so darn beautiful! I hope you can begin to hold that heart-stoppin', blood-whizzin', hormone-enticin' head a little higher now.' A steely glare entered her eyes. 'Hang bankruptin' rent rises. We're goin' shoppin'. There is no way you are insultin' such a hairstyle with that bargain-bucket wardrobe of yours. Let's go!'

Scarlett took me to Southwell, a small market town twenty minutes south of Sherwood Forest, full of quirky tourist shops and cafés serving tea made from real leaves in mix-and-match china. She marched me past a few clothes shops, their windows displaying yummy mummy tunics and drapey cardigans, only stopping when we arrived at the market itself.

'The Hatherstone lot are here on Fridays. They'll be somewhere near the back.'

She jostled expertly through the crowds of shoppers until we reached the last row, where I recognised Jimbo, his usual Robin Hood tourist tat nowhere in sight. Instead, he was manning an olive bar. He waved hello, offering us a sample olive on a cocktail stick.

'Crackin' 'air, Marion.'

'Thanks, Jimbo.'

I saw a clothes stall standing in the middle, but wondered why Scarlett had brought me to a market for my grand makeover. In my experience of market stalls (limited to Ballydown and watching TV soaps like *EastEnders*), the clothes they sold were for trampy tarts or old ladies. Or in the case of the pink-haired woman who ran the Hatherstone market clothes stall, a trampy, tarty old lady.

Okay, so she wasn't that old. Maybe in her fifties. But her orange tan plastered over a smoker's complexion, and pink zebra-striped jacket over a boob tube and wet-look leggings, made her look it. The top said 'Bite Me'. I tried to keep my face impassive. My mind screamed silently at Scarlett, '*What on earth have you brought me here for?*' My gaze flicked over a rail of plastic mini-skirts; bleached skinny jeans with rips where my knickers would show; garish, frilly crop-tops and that most unflattering outfit known to woman, a catsuit with horizontal stripes and a V-neck so low it would be impossible to wear with a bra.

Scarlett remained cool. She caught the attention of the pink-haired trader and introduced us. Icy cool.

'Marion, this is Amanda. Valerie's mother.'

Amanda smacked her chewing gum. 'We've met. All right?'

'Hi.'

She smirked at me. Her face was long and pointed. Like a snake's face. 'Come for a new image?'

I battled to keep my arms from crossing over my body. I had on my raincoat, excellent for keeping wild Irish weather at bay, but at the expense of some style, admittedly. Amanda looked me up and down with her snaky face and snickered.

'What size are you? Ooh – I reckon about a sixteen? Tell you what, let's go with an eighteen, save any embarrassment. You're obviously a girl who likes her cake. Nothing wrong with that, mind. Personally, I find most fellas like a woman with a bit of sommat to grab hold of.' She rolled her bony, saggy hips and leered at me.

Discovering that this odious woman was Valerie's mother did not surprise me.

'Amanda.' Scarlett's voice made a sharp, pointy icicle jabbing at Amanda's smug bubble. 'I'm sure you have lots of work to do. We'll browse in peace, if you don't mind.'

Amanda popped her gum again. 'Whatever.'

Scarlett took my arm, gently, and bent to mutter in my ear. 'As much as I loathe contributing to the profit margins of this business, she is great value for money, and her partner is a good woman who somehow ended up financially shackled together with a nightmare. If we look carefully, we'll find the stock she has bought in. There are gems hidin' in this trash heap. Now, a split-second lesson on transformin' your image from jumble sale don't-give-a-rat's-ass to I-love-myself fabulous. One: you ain't fat, so stop dressin' like you are. Two: pick those clothes the secret person that you dream of becomin' would wear, not what you think you deserve. Three: never try something on just because it's in fashion, what everybody else is wearing, or in the sale. Do you like it? Will it suit you? Is it well made? Real women are not slaves to fashion but free to be themselves. Four: life is too darn short to save your best dress for a special occasion. Far as I'm concerned, you need no better reason to look your best than simply celebratin' bein' alive on God's great earth for one more day.'

I spent five minutes uselessly dithering up and down the racks before Scarlett ran out of patience. She deftly worked along each of the four rows, pausing two or three times on each rail to whip out an item and toss it to me.

'Right.' She called to Amanda, who lounged at the back of the stall with a cigarette dangling from the side of her mouth. 'Still using Betsy's?'

Amanda shrugged. 'She gets a 20 per cent discount for it.'

Behind the market was a retirement complex. Scarlett led me to one of the entrances and rang the buzzer for a ground-floor flat.

'Hey, Betsy! How are you doin', sugar?'

We were buzzed in, and I soon found myself in Betsy's chintzy bedroom trying on clothes while Scarlett and her friend caught up. I picked out a cardigan, soft dark brown with a thick cable pattern down the front and a knitted belt. Judging it to be a safe, stretchy bet, I put it on over what I was already wearing.

I forced myself to take a look in Betsy's full-length mirror. I could see the cardigan was shaped well, and it felt comfortable. Did I like it? Did it suit me? It was a size twelve and it actually fitted. That seemed like a good enough reason to buy it.

'How ya doin' in there?' Scarlett poked her head around the door. She sighed. 'Honey. You can't possibly tell if that beautiful cardigan is gonna work if you are still wearin' it with those hideous jeans. Here...' She handed me a teal top and a pair of jeans apparently designed for a child.

'I don't think I'll be able to—'

'Put them on. They'll stretch.'

They did stretch. They were soft and fitted closely, but not tight enough to squish out my flab. What can I say? I looked like a woman. W.O.M.A.N.

I bought that outfit, and the rest of them. Scarlett had been right: they were great value. But I was still left with a very light purse, wondering if I could survive on the products of my cooking lessons for the next couple of weeks. I tried to care about having spent all my money on clothes. I didn't try very hard.

Saturday afternoon, I slunk into my cooking lesson. Not a sexy, slithery, sleek slink. A 'trying to be invisible so that a handsome, intimidating man won't notice my new image and embarrass me' slink. Reuben sprawled at the huge table, reading the paper with a mug of coffee, Lucy in her favourite spot on top of his feet. He looked up at me casually, then became very still for a few moments. My heart ricocheted about in my ribcage. He raised one eyebrow, and pulled out a stool.

'Ready?'

I nodded. Time to stop all this scintillating small talk and get cooking.

I made pumpkin soup (using the empty pumpkin shell as a soup tureen), steak and Guinness pie, and apple cake. Reuben had written out the instructions this time. Consequently, with the minimum necessary conversation (and no patronising, shouty orders from his girlfriend), I relaxed as I got involved in the tasks, and didn't make too many mistakes or cause any serious mishaps. Well, okay, I did set the frying pan on fire, so there was no bacon for the soup, but it still tasted good enough for me to take to the bonfire party. The pie and cake both had room for improvement, but were definitely edible.

Reuben had two pieces of cake. I turned away to hide my glow in the washing up, without success. I think my pride and delight lit up the fields all the way from the Hall to the campsite. I half expected a report in the *Hatherstone Gazette* about luminous aliens invading the estate.

I had swishy hair. I had clothes that actually fit me. I could make a cake worth a second helping.

And my alien sheen had nothing to do with spending two and a half hours in the company of twilight-in-the-forest eyes. Nothing at all.

* * *

It was the first Saturday of the long, nine-week summer holiday we have in Northern Ireland. Ironic, considering we barely scrape nine days of actual summer. Despite this, I left our house at 8.30 in the morning dressed in what was basically my school uniform. Faded black boot-cut trousers, a white blouse with an ink stain on the pocket, and a baggy black cardigan. No tie, no blazer – I wasn't a complete loser. A raincoat, of course.

I rang the bell at the side of the library door, as it was still locked. Mrs Brown came into view behind the glass and unfastened the bolts at the top and bottom. A thrill ran through me. I couldn't believe that I had made it.

'Welcome, Marion. How are you then?' Mrs Brown ignored my dishevelled appearance. 'It's great to have you here. Are you looking forward to it?'

I nodded my head, realised that I was on trial, and took a deep breath. 'Yes, thanks, Mrs Brown.'

'Please, call me Colleen, now we're workmates.' She walked me over to the tiny office behind the help desk. 'And somewhere in here is my assistant manager.'

Towering stacks of books packed the tiny office. From behind these floated out the sound of humming: the theme tune from *Neighbours*, I think.

'Harriet!'

A blueberry-coloured head popped up above one of the book

towers. Harriet crawled out on her hands and knees. I had never seen pink jeans before. I had certainly never met anyone who wore pink trousers over the age of eight, or teamed them with a red cardigan. Harriet, who I later found out was twenty-nine, hauled herself up by a spinny office chair. Her cardigan flapped open, revealing two rows of hand-sewn badges on her shiny top.

'Harriet.'

'Hi, Coll.'

'Are those swimming badges?'

Harriet brushed her hands over her chest and stuck out her not-inconsiderable breasts.

'Aye. What of it? I'm proud of my aquatic achievements. Thought I might inspire the weans with my hard-earned success.'

'Five hundred metres?'

'Aye. I can swim to shore. That's enough.'

'Harriet, why are you wearing your old swimming costume to work?'

Harriet hummed a few bars of Aretha Franklin's 'Respect' as she very deliberately buttoned up her cardigan.

'My washing machine's broken. I had no more clean knickers and I've done the inside out thing already. I'll buy some more after work. Sorry, Coll.'

The strange thing to me about this was not that I had met somebody who wore a swimming costume to work when she ran out of clean knickers, nor that she hadn't thought to buy either a new washing machine or more knickers before she used up all the dirty ones. It was that she was possibly the first person I'd met who hadn't got a ma, a granny, half a dozen aunties, numerous family friends she called aunties anyway, old school friends – *anyone* – who would put through a load of washing for her. My neighbours and relatives would have burned with shame had they known the many times my mother was too ill to wear clothes, let alone wash them. Nothing had me shipped off to Auntie Paula's house quicker than a creased blouse or a stain on my cardigan. I had grown very good at doing laundry.

My clothes may have been shabby, sparse hand-me-downs, but there was no disgrace in being poor. Being dirty, slovenly or downright disorganised, now that was another matter entirely. When they arrested Mary Milligan for running a brothel on the top floor of her bed and breakfast (which more than one of my male relatives had been known to frequent), my Auntie Jean commented: 'To be sure, it wasn't right what she did; but I'll say this much: those sheets on her washing line were always beautiful. The whitest on the street. A woman who gets her washing that white can't be all bad.'

'I hear you, Jean.' Auntie Paula shook her head in wonderment at whites so white. 'All those filthy bodies, rubbing themselves up and down, all hours of the day and night. I'd love to know her secret, that I would.'

I hungered for independence, craved escape from a town full of prying, well-meaning relatives. I dreamed of a world where I would be no longer labelled or judged. Where I could have a broken washing machine and nobody would know. Or perhaps, more significantly, wouldn't care even if they did. In the humming, pink-jeaned Harriet, I had found my hero.

How was my first day as a library assistant? Stressful, emotionally exhausting, awkward, uncomfortable, brilliant. I spoke 478 words. This both terrified and exhilarated me at the same time. I stomped on the little girl who kept screaming that I would kill my mother with my worthless chatter as I read a story to a baby. Squashed the breath out of her when Colleen invited me for supper that evening and I didn't even phone Ma to check if she was okay first. Punched her temporarily unconscious when Eamonn walked me home and I was the first one to say goodnight.

I walked in the door and found Ma not wondering where I had

been, or concerned about how my first day had gone. She was, on the contrary, seething with crazy, jealous rage that I had been working all day, and had not, as she'd predicted, been sacked for being 'a pathetic, wallowing, useless dud who creeps people out with attention-seeking behaviour and melodramatic moping'.

I had managed to push every one of her buttons by working for the doctor's wife, a 'manipulative, snotty camel with man's hands'. If ever I had doubted words were brutal weapons, one conversation with my ma during her plunge back down to serious illness could have convinced me. I prayed she would keep taking her tablets, hold on to the fraying thread connecting her to sanity until I was old enough to avoid another holiday. That she could find a way to love me. Or maybe that my words would spill forth until I killed her after all.

14

Over the next few weeks, life at the Peace and Pigs settled into a steady rhythm. We worked on campsite repairs and improvements when weather permitted, looked after the animals, dealt with caravan guests, and took bookings for the following year. Jake convinced Scarlett to let him design us a website, though since the campsite was often filled to capacity throughout the high season, this could bring only limited benefit to the holiday park income. Grace spent more and more of her time after school at my caravan, occasionally bringing her homework, usually working on her shoes. It turned out we had some things in common. Loneliness, mainly.

Initially, I worried Valerie might get jealous. She too often came knocking at my door on her free evenings (did I know the four largest doors in the world are in the Kennedy Space Centre and are 456 feet high?), but I'd underestimated the extent of her pure unselfishness. Valerie often annoyed Grace, who treated her as a pesky little sister with caustic putdowns and mass eye-rolling, but Valerie either didn't notice or didn't care.

I spent Saturday afternoons chopping and stirring, blissfully lost in the high of combining different ingredients to produce food that actually began to taste pretty delicious. Reuben, a hands-off teacher, let me rummage through recipe books and experiment by myself while he read the paper to a steady background drone of football commentary. I fell in love with the rhythm of cooking, the focus and patience the process required, finding it an unexpected balm on my turbulent soul. In a few short weeks, cooking became a secret garden where I could forget the world outside and lose myself in the pleasure of my senses. Engagement rings were hidden in the steam of a freshly baked loaf, the memory of photographs overpowered by the smell of herbs lingering in my hair, and the sour taste of threatening messages was drenched with a symphony of new flavours.

Threatening messages. Number three appeared the week after Bonfire Night. No words this time, just four slashed tyres. To claim on my insurance, I had to involve the police in the form of Brenda, thorough in her enquiries and quietly concerned that somebody might be trying to scare me out of the forest. I suggested they slashed my tyres because they couldn't bear the thought of me leaving; got my head down, kept breathing, tried not to get on anyone's nerves. I wasn't going anywhere just yet.

The 1 December fell on a Saturday. Valerie and I had spent the previous week stringing blue and white Christmas lights from campsite trees. We had created, following Scarlett's strict instructions, a Christmas trail through the woods, hiding a star, a robin, elves, and a present, along with other festive objects, leading a trail to where Jake was building a Christmas grotto. Archie turned up in his antique Father Christmas costume, ho-ho-hoing and proudly stroking his three-inch beard grown especially for the role. On Thursday and Friday, we displayed notices and placed leaflets around Hatherstone and a couple of other nearby villages. Elf

Valerie visited the local schools, winning them over with her sparkly, Christmassy exuberance.

In a jovial, buoyant atmosphere, we got everything ready, wrapping presents for the grotto, decorating inside and out. Even the pigs embraced the festivities, allowing us to stick antlers on the back of their heads. But as Scarlett tacked up the sign detailing our price list, her face looked drawn and tight.

This was business, not pleasure – at least, for all of us except Archie. We were throwing crumbs at a starving bank account. But it was a start; it was something. As the person responsible for keeping the bank fed put it: 'Sugar, if that moist-skinned bullfrog with a lump of concrete where his heart's supposed to be is goin' to take my Peace and Pigs offa me, I'm goin' to make darn certain that every day before he does, we fill this place with love, laughter, and gingerbread snowmen.'

Having worked late Friday night wrapping hundreds of tiny gifts, I was given the next day off. So, while carloads of children full of Christmas beans hunted for miniature reindeer and wooden angels, I hunched in my caravan, contemplating a postcard with a red phone box on the front and a swimming costume.

Harriet had given me her swimsuit on my sixteenth birthday. I unwrapped it in the library office, still shy of Harriet's gusto, and unable to quite believe she considered me a friend.

'Um, thanks.'

'Come on, Marion. Aren't you going to ask me why I've given you an old cossie for your birthday? On the face of it, it's not a great present.'

'Why did you, then?'

'Courage.' Harriet pointed one jewel-encrusted nail at my chest. 'Think about it, now!'

I thought about it. 'This is an adult-sized swimsuit. With all your swimming badges on it.'

'So?'

'So, either you transferred the badges from your school costume... which you would never have done because you couldn't be bothered... or you only learned to swim as an adult.' I glanced at Harriet for confirmation. 'Which needed courage. You were scared of water.'

Harriet lifted a heap of books off one of the plastic chairs and sat down. 'When I was six years old, I watched my brother get swept away at Bundoran beach. For the next fifteen years, I could brave nothing bigger than a bathtub. But I knew however much I buried fear under bravado, so long as I was scared, it had control of a piece of me. So I signed up for swimming lessons. For the first five weeks, I sat there like an eejit, shivering on the side. Then I paid the lifeguard ten quid to push me in.

'Life is too short to let fear make your decisions for you, Marion. Too much gets thrown at you as it is. So, I'm giving you my cossie of courage. I figure you could use it.'

'Thanks.'

'Well? Aren't you going to put it on?'

I did, allowing my fear of Harriet to make the decision for me, fantasising about how awesome it would be if some of Harriet's courage seeped out of the fabric into my pores.

Every birthday after that, Harriet ordered me to don the cossie of courage. She would wave her hands and preach about how it was time for me to stop existing and start living, to throw off the cloak of mousiness and run naked and brazen through the streets.

'Don't let yourself dither about one more year in this town, killing time and watching the clock tick by!'

'But I'm waiting for Eamonn.'

'Yes, Marion. I understand why you feel the need to wait for that handsome, presentable, nice young man to finish his studies. I accept that you want to hang about waiting for that lovely, boring, patronising, spoiled man. But why are you waiting for him *here*? You have sixty years to spend picking up his socks and cleaning his toilet, being a grand wee wifey. This could be your only chance. I'm booking two tickets this time. And yours will be one way only.'

I could have pointed out to Harriet that she too lived out her days in this small town, working at the same small library, dealing with the same small-minded customers. The difference was, every winter Harriet booked eight weeks off work and went on holiday. And these vacations did not include lounging by the pool – unless maybe a natural pool in the middle of some mountain where a near-extinct flower bloomed for the first time in a hundred years. The only occasion she went to the beach was to protect baby turtles from birds of prey as they flippered themselves to the sea. She had been to forty-nine different countries, never to the same place twice and always with an itinerary ensuring she spent each and every day 'justifying the use of every molecule of oxygen I breathe by doing something I can honestly call worthwhile'.

Harriet said she could only bear to look after other people's stories for a living if she spent the rest of her time creating her own. She remained my hero.

The postcard was not for Harriet. Once I had replaced my tossed-away phone, I texted her that I was doing fine. Her reply:

Of course you are. Now stop wasting time texting me and get yourself a life that is a lot better than fine.

I also sent her a photo of me wearing one of my new outfits, flicking my hair about (the reply: a photo of her with a load of children from the library story time all flicking their shoulder-length black wigs and sticking their thumbs up).

The postcard was not for Eamonn, either. I shrivelled up inside when I thought about what I had done to him. However much he had taken me for granted in the last few years, or thought only of how I fitted into his life – if he considered me at all – I had behaved appallingly. I had no excuse. Not cowardice, or selective mutism, or a rubbish childhood, or a mother who bequeathed me a thousand issues and taught me nothing about how to relate to people in an appropriate manner. And I knew that though my continued silence was not the answer, a postcard didn't cover it either.

Hi. How are you? Don't wish you were here. Don't know when, if ever, I'll be back. Weather is fine. From Marion. P.S. Are we still engaged?

I pulled the swimsuit on, slipping my new jeans and soft grey jumper over the top of it. I picked up a pen. This was not the first time in recent months I had attempted to write this message. However, this time would be different. It was my birthday, and I had on my cossie of courage. Go, me! I wrote:

Ma. I hope you're well at the moment. I think about you a lot. I'm doing grand here. I have a job, and a nice wee place to live, although it's very different from home. Sorry I haven't been in touch sooner. I can't come home yet. I hope you can try to understand. Please send my love to everyone, and wish them a happy Christmas from me. Marion.

I put it in an envelope, knowing my mother would be livid if she thought every postie between here and her letterbox had feasted their eyes on her personal business. I felt fairly certain she would rip it into tiny pieces and chuck it into the fire, cackling as it burned to ashes. Whether she read it first or not was impossible to predict. But I had written it. I would send it, and I would feel no guilt whatsoever regarding my relationship with my mother. She had plenty of people to support her and take care of her, to help her through the more serious bouts of illness. At twenty-six years old, I could finally accept that however much I longed for it, however hard I tried, until my mother chose to forgive me, I could not be in her life.

I was late for my cooking lesson by the time I had composed myself. Writing that postcard had felt like taking a meat fork and jabbing the prongs into my liver with every word. I threw on my old raincoat to ward off the sleet tumbling down from steel skies, and trudged in my new fur-lined boots through the fields to the Hall.

Hallelujah! Yet again, Erica had been unable to come over. Her excuse, passed through Reuben, was that she was flat out throughout the Christmas season at work. I understood this, but noted how conveniently that enabled her to avoid facing an employee from the holiday park plunged into crisis following her father's decision. I also felt relieved because Erica, underneath her sugar coating, was patronising, dictatorial and frustratingly intimidating. Reuben, left with the task of teaching me the arts of haute cuisine, dumped a side of beef, a box of muddy vegetables, and some suet on the table, and let me get on with it.

* * *

It was all going well. My casserole was bubbling nicely in the oven. I made us each a mug of coffee, after which I planned to start on a Christmas cake, which, according to Ginger's antique copy of *Mrs Beeton's Book of Household Management*, must be baked by 1 December at the absolute latest so you can then spend the next three weeks feeding it brandy.

But my foot caught on an uneven flagstone. I lost my balance and the scalding hot coffee flew out of the mugs and drenched my new jumper. Wrenching it off, I ran over to the Belfast sink and started running the tap. Reuben startled me with a hand on my shoulder.

'Marion, you need to take this top off too. You're getting scalded.'

'What?' Only then did I notice the searing pain of freshly boiled water soaking through my top. The adrenaline kicked in, and I dropped the sweater, panicking.

'Here. Keep your arms still.'

I couldn't keep my arms still. I was burning. Reuben tried to pull my top up, but it wouldn't budge.

'Your top's stuck.'

I started to cry. Big, jerky sobs. Lucy stood up on her cushion and began to join in with anxious whines. I put my hands to my top and when my fingers hit the fabric, I remembered.

'Oh, no.' I could see my alarm mirrored in Reuben's eyes in front of me. His may have been for slightly different reasons.

'I have to take my jeans off.' No longer sobbing. Too mortified.

'Your jeans are fine. You need to get your top off – now!'

I undid my belt, wrestling my skinny jeans down – a manoeuvre I hadn't yet managed to perfect without falling over. I tugged them over my big feet like a child yanking her wellies off, wanting to cry again when Reuben grabbed one trouser leg to speed up the operation. By now, he had realised that the rainbow-striped garment covered in badges ranging from 5 metres to 500 metres in distance was, in fact, a swimming costume. All this, although long enough for me to have died a thousand deaths, had only actually taken less than a minute. The coffee must have been cooling by this point, but my chest was on fire.

'I have to take this off.' I was gabbling. 'Sorry.'

During emergencies such as this, when trying to avoid causing yourself serious bodily harm, while simultaneously plummeting into new depths of humiliation, a small part of the brain always remains detached, as if observing the catastrophe from outside the rest of the head. This part of my brain took a moment to be very, *very* thankful I had kept my bra and knickers on underneath the cossie of courage.

This separate, objective bunch of brain cells similarly, two seconds later, reflected on the irony of having removed my pluck-producing one-piece, because in the next few moments, I would need a lot more courage than dealing with a mug of hot coffee required.

I don't think it was unreasonable of me to have been making some noises while Reuben dabbed at my chest with a freezing cold tea towel. Yes, they were quite groany, and it wouldn't be inaccurate to have described them as breathy. If somebody had decided to stand and eavesdrop from around the side of the pantry, yes, they could, with a suspicious imagination and lewd mind, possibly interpret the sounds that I was making as being caused by something altogether different from a scalding accident. Maybe, if that person then decided that they had done enough earwigging and wanted to see for themselves what was going on, and they discovered their boyfriend rubbing the ribcage of a woman wearing only her brand-new push-up bra and matching knickers, they might not instantly comprehend what was happening, and form an entirely erroneous assessment of the situation.

Well, Erica did, anyway. Reuben turned to face her, one hand still pressing the tea towel against my raw skin.

'Erica!'

'Reuben!'

Erica had blanched the colour of her perfect teeth. She tried to spin around, her heels skittering on the stone floor. Frantic, she grabbed a metal jug containing meat juices from the table. Before Reuben could move to stop her, she flung it at me. I stood and let the cold blobs of gelatinous stock plop off my shoulders and hair onto the flagstones. Erica wasn't finished.

'Bitch!' She grabbed the large jar of self-raising flour and threw that, continuing to scream insults. Reuben tried to grab her hands, but she fought him with all the fire of a woman scorned. Those next few minutes, as Reuben yelled explanations over Erica's shrieks and Lucy's whining crescendo, and my throat clamped up tighter than an oyster's shell, were akin to a hideous nightmare. To be called a 'flabby, fat slut' and an 'abnormal, ugly, boring troll', confirming most of the worst fears I held about other people's opinions of me, felt unpleasant. To have it spat at me from a stunning, successful woman while I stood there in my underwear, my skin blistering – that brought things down to a new low.

Eventually, Reuben managed to drag Erica away to calm down. Disregarding the greasy meat stock dripping from my hair down my burned chest, I pulled on the swimsuit with trembling hands, dragging my jeans on over the top. Hurriedly finding my coat, I put on my boots, and left. This time, however, I left a very sincere note apologising for making a mess in my host's kitchen and an even greater mess in his personal life.

15

The Christmas trail proved a runaway success. Scarlett began selling mulled wine and mince pies in the evenings, with chocolate cake for 'all those regular people who know the reason we eat mince pies only once a year is 'cause they are revoltin'.' She arranged for Jake's band to play jazzed-up carols and Christmas songs, and soon we had parents dragging their teenagers along just to have an excuse to enjoy the festivities (the teenagers then came back, bringing more of their teenage friends). Some adults started bringing nieces and nephews, neighbours' kids, even the children of their work colleagues. We added jacket potatoes and hotdogs to the menu, and before long, the adults were coming on their own too.

Archie dusted off an old wagon languishing in one of his barns and gave rides through the forest. We decorated it with lanterns, strung battery-powered fairy lights around the wheel spokes, and twisted ivy and red ribbons along each side. I persuaded Scarlett to trust Grace with decorating the ten-foot Christmas tree, and she spent hours creating baubles out of spray-painted tennis balls, weaving ornaments from twigs she also sprayed silver.

Had we known then what New Year would bring, would we have been determined to laugh more? Would we have paused more often to wonder, gaze at the stars, make each moment of her last December sacred? Or would every greeting and farewell, each frosty breath, have been coloured bittersweet, tainted with aching yearning for what could not be? Is it better to know? To have the opportunity to live your final winter certain it will be your last? Or is there blessing in a swift goodbye?

The 21 December, a Friday, was the grotto's last day. Scarlett, Grace, and Valerie were due to fly out to Florida for a fortnight on the 22nd, courtesy of Scarlett's brother, an obstetrician with five children of his own. Grace knocked on my caravan door early Saturday morning.

'Hi, Grace. Come in.'

She grinned.

'Grace!' I clutched one hand to my chest. 'You actually have teeth. I was beginning to wonder.'

'Mock all you want. I'm spending Christmas in an actual house, built with real bricks. With a bath and the internet and *privacy*. With palm trees and Disney World and family members who are my age and therefore normal and *interesting*.'

'Careful. It sounds like you might be teetering dangerously close to the brink of a good mood there, Grace.'

'So that's what this weird feeling is.' She flopped onto my sofa, flinging her arms out from her sides. 'I thought it must be all the coke I snorted with Archie in the grotto earlier.'

'Are you all packed, then?'

'Yes. I just wanted to give you your present.' She reached into her duffel bag and handed me a shoebox wrapped in Christmas paper. I held it up to my ear and gave it a good shake.

'Um… is it a gift voucher? Or a pair of earrings?'

'Don't shake them too hard!'

I sat on the other sofa and cradled the box as if it were a baby. 'Thank you. I can't wait to open it. But I will. It'll probably be my only present, so I'll resist until Christmas morning.'

'Are you really staying here by yourself?'

I nodded. Scarlett had made discreet enquiries about my plans already, reminding me that with Jake visiting his dad, I would be the only person on the site for more than a week.

'Yep. All on my ownsome; and I fully expect it to be my best Christmas for a very long time.'

'What are you going to do all week?'

'I'm going to cook and read and walk off all the mince pies I've been eating. And someone has to dismantle the grotto and pack up the decorations. I'll give Samuel a hand with the pigs and chickens. Well, with the pigs.' The chickens were quite capable of looking after themselves, in my opinion. Samuel wasn't so much looking after them as preventing them from taking over the campsite and turning it into an independent poultry state.

I stood up and went to put my present under the two-foot-high tree I had dug up from the forest behind the caravan and planted in a green and gold stripy pot.

'What do you normally do at Christmas, then? Don't you have any family to go and see?'

'There is no normal in my family.'

'So what did you do last year?'

'I think you'd better get on, Grace. You don't want to miss your flight.' I reached out and hugged her. 'Scarlett has packed your present from me. Now go, and have a really wonderful time!'

* * *

Last Christmas, I woke late to find my mother huddled in front of our coal fire, a bottle of Guinness in her hand. I made myself toast, and sat across from her on what she still called 'Henry's chair'.

'Are you going to open your present, Ma?'

'Are you still planning on abandoning your own mother on Christmas Day? If so, I'll save it for later. It'll give me something to do when I'm on my own. Perhaps it'll stop me feeling so lonely.'

'Ma.' I closed my eyes, ground my teeth a few times. As had happened every single year my mother had been out of hospital for Christmas, Auntie Jean would pick her up straight after mass and take her to their brother Liam's house. They'd have dozens of relatives coming and going all day, a four-course dinner, games, music, and enough booze to keep even my mother happy. For the first time, I had been courageous enough to speak up and tell the rest of the family I would not be joining them. This ruffled a few feathers, and provided Ma with buckets of sympathy to wring out from anyone unfortunate enough to blunder into her sphere of bitterness.

The postman must have been sick of hearing about her selfish, stuck-up daughter who would rather leave her widowed mother all alone on Christmas Day and traipse off to that doctor's house. Might as well grovel on her knees and beg that boy to marry her, she's that brazen. Always considered herself too high and mighty for her own family. Too grand for the likes of us. And who'll she come snivelling back to when he decides he doesn't want a weak, freaky sheep for a wife? Who'll be expected to pick up the pieces then?

I spent the morning sitting with Ma while she pointedly looked at the wall behind my head and worked her way through two more bottles. She informed me, several times, that seeing as I was ditching her for such a grand family, they could buy me a present while they were at it. This had limited impact since I hadn't received a gift from my mother in eighteen years. There was always something under Liam's tree with a tag stating,

To Marion, with all my love, Ma

but even at eight years old, I'd known the writing, and the love, was not my mother's.

Once Auntie Jean had been, I walked across town to Eamonn's house, where I spent the afternoon playing Monopoly and eating chocolate. We ate a late dinner, opening our presents in the early evening. Eamonn walked me home, and we kissed goodnight. As I climbed into my freezing bed, hoping to be asleep before my mother returned, Harriet phoned.

'So, how was Christmas without the screaming cousins and your mother's jolly wit?'

'It was fine, thanks. Peaceful.'

'Boring, you mean.'

'No. I missed the weans, but I had a nice time.'

'And? What did you get? Anything sparkly in a wee velvet box? Is your hand a little heavier this evening than it was when you woke up?'

'No.'

'Disappointed? Or relieved?'

'Neither! I wasn't expecting a ring, Harriet. We're fine as we are.'

'No, Marion. You are not fine. You're hanging all your hopes on this man rescuing you, yet again, from the clutches of the dragon witch.'

'Harriet!'

'Sorry. From *her* clutches. You're drifting about like an empty crisp packet, doing the bare minimum to classify yourself as animal, not vegetable. You have a job and a nice boyfriend. Big deal. Your life is not going to change once you marry Eamonn Brown. You'll still be round at your mother's every day, cooking her dinner and absorbing her evil spillage. You'll go nowhere you really want to go, do nothing you actually want to do and carry on pouring your life away like dirty dishwater. There is nothing wrong with living in the same town your whole life, sticking with a good job and marrying your childhood sweetheart. But Marion, you have no peace, no satisfaction, and you certainly aren't happy. You walk around this town with your head bowed and your eyes on the ground like that's all you're worth, all you're aiming for. You had a lousy childhood. A really lousy one. So have millions of other people. When are you going to stop letting that be an excuse to waste the rest of your life? Get over it. Move on. It's claws that hold you here, not love. Eamonn is not the answer. He's part of the problem because he gives you an excuse to keep wallowing in your swamp of a life.'

'He loves me! Eamonn loves me, even though I'm a complete mess. How can that be a problem?' My voice echoed down the phone. I felt shocked. Harriet had encouraged and cajoled me pretty much non-stop over the years, but she had never spoken to me like this before.

'He might love you for who you are. He doesn't love you for who you can become. Only you can save yourself, Marion. Only you can find a way to look at yourself in the mirror and feel proud of the person gazing back at you. I don't know exactly what's happened to you, or how Eamonn's helped you out, but I do know this: you are never going to be free until you get out of here.'

I didn't want to be free. I wanted to be safe.

Harriet called me back ten minutes later.

'I'm sorry. I've spent the day listening to my parents wondering why I'm not married yet. Ma told me over Christmas pudding that if I was a lesbian, that would be grand, as long as I was the girl one.'

'Happy Christmas, Harriet.'

'Happy Christmas, Marion.'

* * *

Sunday morning I got up, made myself a flask of coffee, wrapped up a cinnamon bagel, and trudged over to the grotto site. The ground was crunchy with frost. Droplets of freezing dew clung to the decorations and glimmered off every wooden surface. The sun shone but the wind slapped at my skin. I ate breakfast inside the grotto hut, perched on the large rocking chair Archie hadn't got round to collecting yet.

'So then, Marion, have you been a good girl?'

I poured myself a cup of coffee, offering a sip to imaginary Santa. 'Oh, yes, Santa, ever so good. Well, except for running away from home without telling anyone where I was going, leaving my fiancé in the lurch, and stealing a programme from a mad man's cellar. And having pleasant thoughts about someone else's boyfriend, and unpleasant thoughts about, oh, loads of different people, and—'

'Steady on, Marion, this isn't confession.'

'Sorry, Santa. I suppose you want to hear my Christmas list.'

'Yes, please. I am pretty busy at the moment.'

'Well, let me think. I'd like a new coat to show off my haircut, and some more books. I want to be able to run all the way around the estate without getting a stitch. But – honestly? What I really want is to find out who my da was. To feel… oh, like I know him again. What he cared about. If he was like me. And it would be great if you could give me enough courage to face the mess I've left back home. And to stop thinking about men who don't belong to me. Oh, yes, and a cookbook. Does that sound a bit much, Santa? I could do without the coat.'

I was about to reply to myself, when I heard a bark from the other side of the shed wall. Jumping up, I managed to avoid spilling my coffee, and looked up to see Lucy poking her head around the shed door, Reuben right behind her.

His eyes glinted. 'Is it just you in here, Marion? I thought I heard the sound of voices.'

I straightened my spine and pointed my chin up toward the roof. 'Yes. That would have been me. I was reciting poetry. It's good for one's soul.'

'Of course.' He nodded his head gravely. 'Good idea. What's your poem of choice for, um, soul improving?'

I stared at him for a moment. 'That would depend. But today it was, of course, a Christmas poem. By Christina Rossetti, actually: "Love Came Down at Christmas".' *Thank you, Ballydown library Christmas recital evening.*

'Love all lovely, love divine?' He furrowed his brow. 'Funny. I don't remember any lines about Santa.'

'Did you want something or are you just here to eavesdrop?'

Reuben grinned. A full-on beam of crisp December sunshine. 'Archie thought you might need some help. It was that or make stuffing with Sunny while his elves swung from my belt loops and bounced pigs in blankets off my head.'

'Are you ready then, for Christmas? Got all your presents?'

'Nearly. Erica usually writes me a list, but she refused to this year, and it's a nightmare trying to guess what she'd like. She thinks I should know her well enough to figure it out. I'm a bloke. I'll never figure it out. If ever I get it right, it will be a lucky fluke.'

'You really don't know?'

He leaned forwards slightly. 'Why? Do you? Has she said something?'

I sighed. 'Everybody in the whole entire forest knows what Erica wants you to get her for Christmas! It's the same thing she wanted last year. And for her birthday. And for Valentine's Day. And your anniversary. I can't believe you haven't cracked under the pressure. There was a sweepstake on whether you were going to do it at the festival.'

Reuben tightened his jaw. 'I don't know what you're talking

about.' Turning briskly, he stalked out of the doorway.

I took a few moments to make sure my bag was definitely fastened properly, checked it again for good measure, and having judged that to be long enough for him to have calmed down, I followed Reuben outside.

'What were you going to do first?' Reuben tugged at a star dangling from an oak branch. The rotten string snapped and it came off in his hand.

'I was going to undress the tree.' Even as I said it, a hideous flashback of my last cookery lesson slapped me across the face. I squinted at Reuben from the corner of my eyes, praying he hadn't noticed.

'Well...' – his voice was breezy – 'as long as it's only the tree getting undressed.'

Dumping a crate near the Christmas tree, I began tucking Grace's woven decorations into the nest of shredded paper. 'Archie said you'd managed to explain what happened. That you're forgiven.'

'Erica trusts me.' He stretched up to unhook some of the ornaments that I couldn't reach. 'And she trusts herself.'

'What does that mean?'

'She knows she's a great girlfriend and I have no reason to cheat on her.'

I thought about that for a few minutes, and wondered why, if Erica was such a great girlfriend, Reuben hadn't given in to expectations and asked her to marry him. Or move in, at least.

'Are you really staying here by yourself all week?'

'Yes. It'll be a blissful change. I might manage to get through Christmas Day without a relative-induced migraine.'

'So you wouldn't want to spend Boxing Day with us up at the Hall? There will be relatives, both immediate and extended.'

'Ah, but they won't be my relatives.'

16

I drove to Nottingham on Christmas Eve and spent a couple of hours wandering around the Winter Wonderland in the old market square, until the scrum of desperate last-minute shoppers drove me into a café. There was a pay phone in the corner. I sipped my hot chocolate and stared at it. The warmth of my drink couldn't melt the lump of ice in the bottom of my stomach. I made a decision. This would be my Christmas present to myself: doing the right thing. In the midst of all my mistakes, I could tick this one thing off my list. I picked up the phone and dialled.

'Aye?'

'Eamonn, it's me.'

There was a hard silence.

'What do you want?'

'I'm sorry. Really, truly sorry. It wasn't about you—'

'Is that it?'

'No, Eamonn, I...'

'Bye, Marion. Have a nice Christmas.'

I drove home, nauseous and wretched.

* * *

Sitting in the caravan on my bed, I opened the little box with the ring Eamonn had given me. I knew now that he did not love me – only the idea of loving me. I knew he thought of me only in terms of how I fitted into his life. He considered me too fragile, too small, to have hopes or dreams of my own. But he had genuinely believed it would make me happy to be the doctor's wife, to spend my life looking after him and being protected by him. He had believed I needed a safe harbour, a calm sea, after all the storms I'd endured before. He had never realised that the peace I needed would come, not from my surroundings, but through making peace with myself.

By 11.30 p.m., I still felt restless with remorse. Old habits die hard in guilty Catholic girls. I grabbed my bag, picked my way through the deserted campsite with a torch, and went to church.

I parked on the street outside Hatherstone village chapel. If the full car park hadn't confirmed my guess about there being a midnight mass, the warm glow of lights shining through the lead-paned windows would still have enticed me in.

From the outside, the chapel looked a typical English country church. Within, it had been surprisingly modernised. Rows of padded chairs greeted me instead of the pews I expected. The floor had warm carpet instead of old stone, and I could see no ancient relics or statues at all. Bright banners hung on the walls, and dozens of paper lanterns filled with coloured lights dangled from the rafters. None of the familiar landmarks I associated with church were visible – no altar or stations of the cross, no pictures of Jesus or the Virgin Mary. If it hadn't been for the box of white candles stacked behind the last row of chairs, and the wooden nativity scene on a table beside the door, I wouldn't have known where I was.

Most of the hundred or so chairs were occupied. The glass door from the porch creaked as I slipped inside, and about ninety of the hundred people there twisted round in their seats to see who had come in late. I recognised some of the faces, including Jo from the café. She pointed to the empty chair next to her and, grateful to squeeze in near the back, I scurried over. A teenage girl at the front was about to begin a reading, struggling with the clip on her microphone. I used the empty moment to send up a silent prayer:

Forgive me, God. It's been a long time. But then I guess you know that already. And what I did to Eamonn. I'm not sorry for leaving, but I am ashamed of how I did it. I won't make excuses for hurting him; I just wanted to say I'm sorry. If you can, help him to forgive me so he can move on without anger. Bless Ma, and the rest of them. Oh, and I hope you don't mind me being in this random church. I don't even know what one it is. It was the best I could do at short notice. Amen.

I settled back and listened as the girl began. It had been years since I'd heard the Bible read. Father Francis had moved to a new parish when I was twenty and I had rarely attended mass since, only making an exception for cousins' weddings, their children's baptisms, and maybe a first communion if it was someone I especially liked. The words washing over me felt familiar, stirring memories and feelings long forgotten, but at the same time, it was as if I'd never really listened to them before, never connected the syllables together to understand what they actually said.

'Don't be afraid! I bring you good news of great joy which is for all people.
Glory to God in the highest! And on earth peace, good will to all men.'

I thought about that: no longer being afraid. Having great joy. Finding peace. It all sounded so simple. I didn't know much about anything, but life was never simple – this I did know.

The girl sat down, and a bunch of musicians took her place. A woman sang a carol I hadn't heard before, and then an older man read some more Bible verses.

Somebody turned the lanterns off. The room went black. A hundred people held their breath. There was no sound except for the brief rustling of clothes, a child coughing. The room smelt of pine trees and polished wood. The man spoke again. His voice, though cracked with age, sounded resonant and vibrant in the darkness.

'The light shines in the darkness, and the darkness
has never put it out.'

There came the faint rasp and hiss of a match igniting, and a tiny flickering candle flame lit up the man's face in front of us. A child, maybe nine or ten years old, went to stand in front of the man, and he dipped his candle to one held in the boy's hands. Two flames now glimmering, the boy turned to light the candle of the young woman behind him, and so it went on, until every single person in the church held a glowing flame, the brightness shining all around us. The darkness fled.

At gone one o'clock, I still lay awake in bed, thinking about churches where people smile instead of tutting when you walk in late, and the person in charge (a priestess? A vicaress? I had no frame of reference for women who ran churches) has skinny jeans, high-heeled pointy boots, and a laugh that bounces off the rafters.

Then my thoughts skittered to a dead halt as I heard a crunch. Then another one. The soft tread of footsteps in the frost outside my window. Slow steps, hesitant, *secretive*.

I held my breath through the familiar wobble of the caravan as somebody climbed the steps outside. I waited for a knock. Or a crash. Neither came. I heard the door rattle, then a bump. The van wobbled again as whoever it was scrunched away.

Great.

I lay in bed a while longer, letting the adrenaline subside, wondering where my phone was.

'Was that you, Santa?' If it was, he wouldn't have been fooled by my bluster. And besides, my mother had made it very clear that Santa was a big, fat, jolly sack of reindeer droppings. *What are you crying for, you pathetic brat? Santa wouldn't visit a girl like you anyway.*

I flipped the covers off, forcing myself to get up. This worked; caravans in December being deathly cold. I dug out a thick cardigan, and carefully laced up my trainers, just in case I had to make a run for it, of course – nothing to do with putting off opening my front door. Peeking through a chink in the corner of my living room curtain revealed nothing; too dark to see. I carefully turned the key in the door, trying to be as quiet as possible even though I had heard the footsteps walk away, and gingerly opened the door a tiny crack.

Well, there was another one in the eye for my mother. Santa had been after all. The sack was a proper brown, Santa-y one, with a red ribbon tied around the top. Somebody had tried to hang it on my door handle, but the weight had caused it to slip off and thud onto the top step. Still cautious, I slowly took hold of the ribbon with two fingers and dragged it inside, slamming the door shut after it. I faffed about for a few minutes, poking the bag, nudging it with my foot, even sniffing it (to see if it smelled like a bomb?). I finally decided that, quite possibly, I had received a nice message for once.

I cut the ribbon to save having to unpick it with freezing fingers, and tipped the contents of the sack out onto my sofa. A large rectangular present tumbled out. Did I leave it under my two-foot tree like a good girl, ready to open in the morning? Of course not.

It was a cookery book, published in 1979: *How to Survive in the*

Kitchen by someone called Katherine Whitehorn. Hm. I remembered the conversation I'd had with my imaginary Santa before we took the grotto down. It wasn't hard to guess who was masquerading behind this Santa's beard. I could have killed him for scaring the pyjamas off me in the middle of the night. Except that as he took one final look at the murderous rage on my face, I wouldn't have been able to hide how embarrassed I felt that he had overheard me having a pretend conversation with Father Christmas.

I hugged the book to my chest for a few minutes. Who was I kidding? He had snuck across sub-zero fields in the middle of the night to leave a cookery book *in a sack* on my doorstep. I loved it.

17

I took an almond and clementine cake to the Hall on Boxing Day. Homemade. I was so eager to arrive with the cake in one piece, I drove the quarter of a mile up to the house instead of walking.

Parking my car in between an Audi and Erica's Alfa Romeo induced a brief reality check. I wondered, between mute busters, how many other guests found themselves glued to the seat of their swanky cars by an overwhelming cascade of inadequacy. I restarted the engine. My drug, the promise of solitary silence, pulled at me with its invisible cord. But I knew that leaving now represented a fall off the wagon no less injurious than a shot of vodka to an alcoholic. I closed my eyes. Fought. Breathed. Nearly had a heart attack when the car door flew open.

Reuben. He reached over and switched the engine off before standing back, holding the door like a chauffeur. I scrabbled to undo my seat belt and clambered out, lifting the cake from its protective nest of blankets in the passenger footwell. As I took a step toward the house, Reuben moved in front of me, barring my way.

'You need a minute.'

'What?' I was still dizzy with the scent of isolation.

'Take a minute.' He held out one hand, in a gesture of greeting. 'Hi, I'm Reuben. Nice to meet you.'

I shook his hand, which was dry and rough with calluses. 'Hello?'

Reuben smiled. 'There you go. That's all you have to do.' He led the way as we moved across to the front entrance. 'Oh, and you might want to do up the button on your trousers.'

The Hall looked like a set from a film. Pots displaying Christmas rose bushes stood on every step leading up to the front door. Half the garden shrubbery appeared to have been brought inside. Each room overflowed with winter greenery – lining mantelpieces and banisters, framing the vast mirrors, nestling on every surface. Tiny ornaments tucked among the foliage gleamed in splashes of silver and blue, and in the centre of the grand hallway, the tree took pride of place. I nearly laughed when I saw it. A fat, lopsided, scrubby fir tree, barely higher than my head, scrappy, dog-eared decorations too tacky even for Jimbo's souvenir stall covered it entirely.

'I love your tree!' I moved past Ginger, who had welcomed us in, and took a closer look.

Ginger stroked one of the decorations: a clay star with a point chipped, painted with messy gold brushstrokes. 'Our boys made these.' She smiled at me. 'They might be less than perfect, and showing the odd signs of wear and tear, but aren't we all, Marion?'

About twenty others gathered in the main reception room, drinking mulled wine, sherry, or fruit punch, chatting in small clusters as Sunny and Katarina weaved in and out bearing plates of nibbles and fancy-looking canapes. I took a deep breath. I tried to recall Scarlett's lesson on party mingling (something about fat bankers?) and wafted the throat-girl away with a sturdy exhalation. She still hung around, but I was winning the battle. No invisibility tricks today.

'Marion!' Archie welcomed me into his huddle, which also contained Erica's father, Mr Fisher, with his wife Olivia, and a younger woman I hadn't seen before. 'Is it too late to say Merry Christmas? *Was* it a merry Christmas? Out there in the forest all alone? Marvellous!'

'Yes, it was lovely, thanks, Archie. Very relaxing.'

This was true. I had opened my other presents: a scarf and gloves covered in pom-poms from Valerie, an elegant journal from Scarlett with a quote inscribed on the inside cover:

Fill your paper with the breathings of your own heart – William Wordsworth

an indoor grow-your-own-herbs kit from Jake, and my new shoes.

They were Sherwood Forest shoes: deep brown walking boots with a chunky heel and thick tread. Grace had embroidered them with leaves in three different shades of green: oak, chestnut, and birch. Around the thick rim of the sole, she had painted a tiny row of mushrooms. Among the leaves I found a ladybird, a spider's web, and a silver arrow. The laces had deer running up and down them, and inside, woolly white fleece lined my beautiful boots. I was to walk for miles through the forest in my Sherwood Forest shoes. They returned mud encrusted, but I knew that was how they were meant to be.

Erica sought me out through the groups of guests. Cucumber-cool in an ice-blue shift dress, she fondled the sapphire pendant dangling between her collarbones.

'Marion! I'm so glad you came. Not that I would have blamed you for staying away after what happened.' She widened her eyes at me. 'I don't know what came over me. I was so tired and stressed that for a moment, I actually thought that something was going on between you and Reuben. You! And Reuben!'

I sipped my drink.

'Anyway, all's well that ends well. I heard you spent Christmas in your caravan. You're so brave, Marion. I really admire how you don't care what anyone thinks and aren't afraid to show it. Although...' Erica eyed me up and down. 'You do look really nice today. And you've had your hair styled. It suits you.' She smiled. 'Perhaps I'll have to keep my eye on you and my boyfriend after all.'

Katarina rescued me with a tray of mini salmon tarts.

'Lovely, Katarina!' Erica helped herself to the decorative sprig of salad. 'Are we still all right for punch?'

Katarina swung around, leaving Erica face-first in the mound of her impressive back. 'Huh! Some guests need to remember that they are still holding the status of guest and not anything more than this yet.'

As always, Katarina's disgruntled mutter reached every ear in the room. 'And some young men should be realising they have plenty enough attractiveness to locate a woman who will not try to control their lives with their bossy and patronising manner.'

Erica's neck flushed purple. She blinked several times, her eyes darting around the room.

'Um...' I said, dumping my drink on a mahogany side-table. 'I'm going to the loo.'

We were in a part of the house quite new to me and, having retraced my steps back to the main hallway, I opened up the two nearest doors, leading into a study and a dining room respectively, before moving down a corridor deeper into the building. A white door with an iron latch opened onto a bathroom, and I nipped inside. These did not look like guest facilities. Towels had been left strewn across the floor. A pair of lacy pink knickers hung over a wicker chair next to an overflowing laundry basket. A tube of Anusol perched on the edge of the sink.

I was quickly washing my hands when a second door, one carefully designed and wallpapered to blend in with the stately decor, so that unsuspecting bathroom users wouldn't notice it, crashed open. The door swung toward me, momentarily blocking me from view. I instinctively ducked further behind it, as if that could make any difference. Panic overrode my rationalisation that nobody would really mind me being here.

Hiding didn't make any difference, because even if I had stuck the pink knickers on my head and performed a tap-dance on the terracotta floor, the writhing, steamy, conjoined couplet of Archie and Ginger wouldn't have noticed me.

They groped their way along the wall toward the other side of the room, murmuring frantic endearments into each other's mouths. Archie stumbled on a discarded towel and they tumbled to the floor in a burst of giggles. I took the opportunity to make myself scarce.

That second door led to a magnificent master bedroom. Yet everything about that room faded into a monochrome haze compared to the high-definition, technicolour photograph sitting on a chest of drawers, as splendidly alone as it was distinctive.

Little John. The Little John captured in the first annual Robin Hood Festival programme. The Little John with one arm around my father, the other one reaching over to grab his pointy green hat. He grinned at me from somewhere in the early nineteen-eighties and I saw, with the advantage of foreknowledge, Ginger's warm smile in the curve of his cheek and the arch of his lips.

With the sound of the lord and lady's tryst jarring in my ears, I wrenched my phone out of my bag and took a picture of the photograph. I had to unlock the bedroom door to get out, only hoping the couple wouldn't notice, or if they did, would blame it on absent-mindedness or other preoccupations.

I re-joined the partygoers now clustered around the grand piano. Fisher banged out some seasonal tunes, while those comfortable enough sang along. I sidled along the group until I reached Reuben and tapped him on the arm.

He broke off mid-line when he saw my face.

'What's happened?'

'Nothing. Can I talk to you for a second?'

He nodded, and we moved down to the other end of the room. My hands betrayed my agitation as I fumbled with the buttons on my phone.

'Do you know him?' Please, please, know him.

Reuben blanched. 'Where did you get this?'

I didn't say anything.

'Have you been snooping around?' The muscle in his cheek twitched.

'No. I was looking for the toilet, and then your parents came in – you know, *occupied* – and I snuck out through a different door. I wasn't looking. It hadn't crossed my mind to look here. But then, I couldn't believe it when—'

Reuben took hold of my wrist and pulled me out into the corridor.

'Slow down.' He shook his head. 'I don't want to know how you ended up in my parents' bedroom. I would like to know why you're asking about my brother, and why you have his picture on your phone.'

'Your brother? Little John is your brother?'

'His name was Henry.' Reuben's eyes were steel. My throat set like brittle toffee.

'I need to explain.'

He nodded. *Yes, you do.*

'Can I have some water?'

Reuben marched me through the maze of corridors to the kitchen. I poured myself a cup of warm water, and drank it slowly, facing the kettle, before taking my usual seat at the table.

'I'm trying to find out about my da.'

'I heard. Henry isn't him.'

'No, I know. But he knew him. I found a different photograph, of Da at the Robin Hood Festival, the first one, with another boy. Your brother.' I took another drink. 'There was no name. The caption called them Robin Hood and Little John, but they had their arms around each other. They were friends.'

'So, they knew each other. What does that tell you? Henry's dead. You can't ask him anything.'

'There's more to it than that. When Da left England, he changed his name from Daniel Miller. To Henry. That has to mean something.' Reuben said nothing for a long time. He ran his hands through his hair, took a gulp of my water.

'Henry died in 1981, in a horrific accident. He was eighteen. Mum and Dad still don't talk about it. Or him. I know they were broken, completely devastated, until I was born.' His eyes found mine. The pain there was startling. 'I'm asking you, Marion. Please don't mention this to them. There's nothing you can learn from their faded memory of one of Henry's friends that is worth opening that wound.'

I didn't want to say that I wouldn't ask. I knew there was something here. Reuben knew this too.

He sighed. 'All right. But will you wait? See what we can find without bringing them into it? Then decide?'

This I could do. We stood up to leave, just as Erica entered the kitchen, carrying a tray of dirty glasses.

'Oh!' She drew up short. I stood there for a brief eternity, knowing that the guiltier I felt about looking guilty, the worse it became; wondering why, even though I had no reason to feel guilty – and this was, quite possibly, the worst time ever to look it – I was growing hotter and hotter, despite the blast of Erica's icy glare.

'What are you two doing hanging around in here?' Her smile got so tight that her face looked close to snapping in half.

'Marion needed a glass of water.' Reuben kissed his girlfriend on the mouth, taking hold of the tray at the same time. 'Leave these; come back to the party with me.'

Erica took Reuben's offered hand, melting under his genuine affection. I followed them back to the drawing room, pretending to ignore the look Erica levelled at me over his shoulder as she stopped in the hallway and kissed him again. Message received, loud and clear.

I was proud of myself for going to the party. See, I told myself, look what happens when you take a risk and do something you're scared of, instead of wriggling back into the depths of your duvet. You stomp on your self-pity, giving yourself a chance to become a nicer person to be around, liking yourself a bit more and further reducing your self-pity levels, completing the cycle to go around again until you actually enjoy being a fun, fabulous, pity-free you. And not only that, but you might even have discovered some vital information unlocking the mystery of Da's past, securing hope and a fellow detective in one fell swoop.

Slightly carried away on the crest of my post-party high, I made a New Year's resolution for once aimed at neither losing weight nor resisting strangling my mother. I wrote it in the front page of my new journal:

I will take more risks and do things I'm scared of, instead of wriggling back into the depths of my duvet.

I read it back, and deciding that it wasn't specific enough I added an extra clause:

Never avoid a party just because I am scared.

Then one last line:

Never avoid <u>anything</u> just because I am scared. Fear will not control my life.

So when Jake asked me to go to the Hatherstone New Year's Eve party, I said yes. Later on, changing into my new jeans and silky top, I racked my brains for other reasons to say no, as fear didn't cut it any more. I could safely assume I was now single. I found Jake attractive. The heating wasn't working properly in my caravan. I had run out of books and had nothing else to do.

How about not wanting to give the wrong impression? I was not ready, or willing, for any sort of relationship. But then everything I knew about Jake strongly suggested that he had no interest in commitment either. I had come to the conclusion that I offered a reasonably interesting distraction for Jake. We got on okay, and my refusal to succumb to his charms intrigued him. Over the past couple of months, he had played it cool, restricting himself to the occasional flirty comment, but for the most part accepting that his advances only pushed me further away.

Jake and I had become friends now. It never crossed my mind he would take my saying yes to the party as agreeing to more than that.

A reason not to go? Eight pints of beer, countless shots, and a simmering rage of seasonal rejection.

Sometimes we do well to listen to our fear.

18

The party took place in the village hall. Most of the usual faces were there. Jake bought us each a drink, and we found seats. His Christmas had been tough, without his mum. The fragmented remains of his family had spent the holiday eating, drinking, and ripping one another to shreds.

The conversation widened during the evening as a few others came to join us, including Jake's band mates and their girlfriends. Reuben came over to say hello.

'Where's Erica, then?' Jake craned his neck at the crowd.

'She's gone into Nottingham with her flatmates.'

'What? You've let her out on her own on New Year's Eve? Man! You're brave. Or stupid.'

Reuben's jaw clenched. 'I'd be a lot stupider to spend the evening following Erica and her friends about on their tour of over-crowded, overloud, vomit-soaked nightclubs from hell just because you thought I shouldn't trust her. I'd actually rather be here. Even if it means having to talk to you.' This last sentence he said under his breath. Jake didn't quite catch it, but his expression soured as he watched Reuben walk away.

As Jake continued drinking, he touched me more and more often, his arm draping around my shoulders, or his hand stroking up and down my leg. He shuffled his chair until he was almost facing me, side-on to the table, and started whispering into my neck, drunken ramblings that sent bugs squirming down my ear holes and sweat prickling the back of my knees.

Jo invited me to dance with her and a few others. I gratefully accepted, feeling the weight of Jake's stare with every step.

After a couple of songs, he crept up behind me and snaked his arms around my waist. Spinning me around, he pulled me up against his chest. I tried to ease back, but his embrace clamped tight.

'Come on, dance with me, Marion. Loosen up, have some fun. It's New Year's Eve.'

'You're the one who needs to loosen up. You're crushing me.' I laughed, but it was shrill and hollow.

'Sorry.' He switched to a ballroom hold, swaying us across the dance floor, knocking into people and never quite in time with the music. I clamped my teeth together and waited for the song to end.

'I'll be back in a minute,' I muttered, making a quick exit.

Locking myself into a cubicle in the ladies', I collapsed onto the seat and tried to work out how I could get Jake to back off. I scrunched my eyelids together, refusing to cry. It was fine. Jake was my friend. He would be more embarrassed than anything.

Someone banged on the door, yelling at me to hurry up. I left, and spotting an open fire exit, I stepped outside to phone for a taxi. Before the call connected, a hand grabbed me. I dropped the phone.

'Jake!' My phone had split open on the concrete surface of the car park. I bent down to pick up the pieces. Jake shoved his hands under my arms and jerked me back up.

'Who are you phoning?' His face was right in mine, eyes burning, skin clammy with sweat.

'A taxi. I'm not feeling great. I think I need to go home.'

'What? It's not midnight yet. You can't go now.' He smiled, waving an unsteady hand at the sky.

'I know, but I'm really not feeling well. I'm not going to be much fun.'

'Oh, come on.' He leaned forwards, propping himself up on the wall beside me. I backed away, but hit another wall. I was boxed in.

Jake started stroking my hair. I could smell his hot breath: beer and whisky and something sour that I didn't recognise. 'You're lovely, Marion. I think about you all the time – about what it would be like to kiss you.'

'Jake! I said I'm not well. Don't do this now.' I wasn't lying. My skull was being hammered from the inside. I thought I might throw up.

He lifted his other hand to the wall, trapping me between his arms. Bending forward to kiss me, his lips pressed hard against mine, his tongue forcing its way inside my mouth.

Please, don't.

Lost in blinding panic, I was fifteen years old again and tied up in Ballydown woods. It was no longer brick scraping my back but the gnarled bark of an oak tree. I could smell the wet peat and Declan's rank sweat. My body had shut down. The only scream was the soundless cries from the girl inside my throat. Hands gripped my ribcage, working to push up my top. When the freezing cold air hit the skin on my stomach, I came to.

It's Jake. It isn't him. Move! You are not tied up. *You are not tied up.*

I brought my knee up, hard, between Jake's legs. He twisted to the side and relaxed his grip enough for me to get both my hands on his chest and push. He stumbled, losing his balance. I pushed again, harder, furious.

He lurched to the side, his head smacking off the wall next to us. 'What are you playing at?'

I was already moving away from the wall, gearing up to run. He stretched out his hand to grab hold of me, and I whirled away from his grasp.

There was a shout, a screech, a loud thud. Everything went black.

I woke up enveloped in the softest quilt, patterns of light filtering through shutters scattered across the wall beside the bed. The room was large, although warm from a lit fire that crackled and popped in the stillness. I could see a white iron bedstead, a white vanity unit, and chest of drawers, along with a bedside table and armchair. The walls were papered in soft pink, and I had the surreal feeling of having been transported back in time while I slept.

A clock on the table said ten to two. Judging by the light, this was afternoon, not early morning. Sluggish and disorientated, it took me a while to bring to mind where I was, and what had happened. The Hall. Of course. I vaguely remembered Ginger helping me into soft pyjamas, washing the scrapes on my back and leaving me with hot tea and ibuprofen. My head still ached, but only noticeably so when I touched it. I could feel bruises on my shoulders and back, and discovered more on my legs and hips, starkly purple against the ivory skin.

I lay in bed for a long time. When my tears had dried up, I swung my feet onto the polished floor. Cautiously lifting my body out of the bed, I slipped on the pair of fleecy slippers someone had left out for me, and the towelling robe I found hanging on the back of the door. I wanted to stay in this cocoon forever, but I needed to empty my bladder and, more urgently in my mind right then, I had to find out what had happened to Jake.

After gratefully locating the bathroom, I limped down the back staircase to the kitchen, where I found Sunny making soup. He said nothing, but brought me a mug of hot tea and some toast, resting one hand gently on my shoulder for a moment before going back to his chopping. I sipped the tea to soothe my throat, leaving the toast. Once I had finished, Sunny wiped his hands on his apron and sat down opposite me.

'Are you ready for the running of the gauntlet?'

I nodded. I wanted it over with so I could go back home. I would have simply walked back in Ginger's pyjamas, except that I knew they would come after me, and the thought of this invading my caravan was unbearable.

'Are you sure, now, Marion? You should be eating first.'

I took a bite of toast, which made it about three inches down my oesophagus before I threw up.

An hour later, just after sunset, I tried again. Having managed a few bites of a cheese sandwich, washed down with more sweet tea and ibuprofen, I sat with Katarina and waited for the lord and lady of the house. Reuben arrived a few minutes later.

I don't know if it was upper-class English reserve, or unusual wisdom and sensitivity, but – God bless them – Ginger and Archie got through the next two hours without tears, touching, flapping, or fuss.

Did I want to contact the police about Jake?

No, I did not.

Did I want them to speak to Scarlett?

I couldn't see any way around that. But, as ridiculous as it sounds, I didn't want Jake to lose his job.

'What happened to him?'

Ginger looked steadily at me across the table. 'Archie took Jake home.'

'How many people know?'

'Everybody knows you were hit by a van in the car park. Only us, Sunny, Katarina, and Reuben know it was something more serious than too much to drink that sent you spinning into the path of the van.'

My head seemed too heavy for my neck. I propped it up on my hands, letting my hair fall in front of my face. 'It wasn't anything more serious. That's all it was.'

'*That's all it was?*' Reuben's rough hand tipped up my chin, so my hair slipped to the side. He stalked away, returning a minute later with a mirror that he had taken from the cloakroom wall. He shoved the mirror in front of my face so that I had no option but to see.

I closed my eyes, too late. Angry to be crying again.

He slammed his hand on the tabletop. 'I saw you with him, Marion. You need to tell Brenda what that scum did.'

'Sit down, Reuben.' Ginger spoke softly, but she meant it.

'There's nothing to tell.'

Was that true?

'So what happens next time he gets drunk and does nothing again – to some other poor girl?'

I pressed my hands against the ache in my chest, sure the growing pressure would crack my ribs.

'Jake isn't a monster. Believe me. I would know.'

'So what, you do nothing? Let him get away with it?'

I shook my head, too battered to argue.

Archie moved his chair next to mine. 'You are absolutely sure you don't want us to contact the police?'

I nodded. Rightly or wrongly, I was sure.

'Okay. Well, whatever happened, I spoke to Jake this morning. He is going to stop drinking and attend counselling for his other issues.'

Reuben shook his head in disbelief. 'Do you really think, even if he could stop drinking, it would make a difference? You're either the kind of animal who is capable of this, or you aren't.'

Archie levelled his gaze at his son. 'You're wrong. Alcoholism and depression are fearful compatriots. Separately and alone, they can cause noble men to do terrible things. Together, unchecked, they can destroy any trace of the decent man that once was. If Jake will accept help now, after this first fall, he has a good chance of recovery. This can become the wake-up call to snatch him back from the brink of a very slippery slope to hell.'

'How can you be so sure? How do you know you aren't kidding yourself?'

Archie sat, back straight, shoulders squared. Ginger extended her arm and took hold of his hand.

'Because I have been that man.'

Reuben became very still.

'When your brother... when we lost Henry, I entered a very dark time in my life. I don't need to describe it, or who I became. But by the grace of God, and the astounding love of your mother, herself suffering beyond what any woman should have to bear, I was able to find restoration before any permanent damage was done. Your mother chose to forgive, and to believe. If Marion can offer that same hope to Jake, I am prepared to stand with them.'

'You're assuming Jake is going to go along with this.'

'Yes.'

'And if not?'

Archie frowned. 'Then God help him.'

I pushed my chair back and levered myself up. 'Please! Nothing happened. Jake tried to kiss me, I pulled away, and didn't see the van. Can't we let it go? Forget about it?'

Reuben left the room, slamming the door behind him. I then registered the bandage on his right hand.

'His hand?'

Katarina sat back and lifted her palms in the air. 'Oh, yes, Marion, did you not see? Jake will have black eyes and a broken nose to go along with his sore head today.'

I insisted on going home. Archie drove me as I was, still dressed in the pyjamas under a borrowed coat, the bag containing my washed clothes on the back seat. I shoved them, still in the bag, to the back of one of the cupboards.

In the caravan, Archie made me yet another cup of tea, which I left untouched on the table beside an uneaten piece of cake. He left soon after. With the door locked and every curtain closed, I stepped into the shower. I stayed there, my tears intermingling with the spray, until I couldn't stand up any longer. Pulling on my own jogging bottoms and sweatshirt, I fell into bed, knowing from experience that even though my bones sagged with exhaustion, I would not sleep that night.

I allowed myself three days of blurry, tear-streaked wallowing. I ate nothing but chocolate and the soup Katarina brought in a flask, poured out into a bowl, and threatened to spoon-feed me if I didn't take it myself. I lay in bed, on the sofa, curled up on the bottom of the shower. I said nothing, thought about everything, watched with fascination as my bruises turned black, then green. I forgave Jake. I forgave myself for trusting him. I read my ridiculous New Year's resolution and decided to keep it. On 5 January, I looked in the mirror at my brutal complexion and laughed.

'Get over yourself, Marion. You were groped. It happens to women every day, all over the world. So it brought back some foul memories? Just be grateful it wasn't anything close to what you had to deal with before. You know he's gone for good. Jake is not the monster. Just a rubbish date.'

* * *

I was seventeen when Declan was arrested for attempting to rape his twelve-year-old next-door neighbour. He hadn't realised her daddy, a lorry driver rumoured to have spent several years transporting unmentionable items for a paramilitary organisation in Belfast, was working nights that week. Declan broke into the kitchen where Anna Malone was eating a slice of pizza for her lunch. He grabbed her and held a knife to her neck while he communicated his intentions. As he pushed her to the ground, Anna grabbed the edge of the red and white checked tablecloth upon which rested her plate, a glass of orange squash, and a heavy metal oven tray she had cooked the pizza on. She managed to bring the whole lot crashing to the ground.

Anna's father, a man who slept the fragile sleep of a part-time terrorist, woke up. Declan had a broken arm, three broken ribs and a punctured lung on his admittance to custody. Two nights later, while I agonised about whether I should speak to the police or not, an unknown intruder sneaked into his hospital room – somehow, mysteriously, avoiding the watchful eye of the police guard – and stabbed a fillet knife into his heart.

It was yet another tragedy to befall my mess of a family. The collective view of the town was that Declan had 'always been a strange one'. Auntie Paula and Uncle Keith moved across town, then to County Claire, and finally Queensland in Australia, trying to escape Declan's ghost. His younger brother, Benny, dealt with the situation by joining the police.

The evening after Declan's death, Eamonn found me in the woods. He sat down on the log next to me. Without saying anything, he kissed me then, for the first time.

Later, I wouldn't hold his hand as we walked back through the town.

'It's weird, isn't it? Do you feel weird?'

I nodded. I felt like running into the sea until it reached above my head, and then keeping walking until I couldn't walk any more. 'Don't blame yourself, Marion.'

I ignored that stupid comment.

'Well, if you're to blame, then I am too. I'm more to blame than you are. I could've actually said something.'

We had reached the end of my road, where Eamonn usually said goodbye so we could both avoid my mother's barbs. I leaned against the wall there.

'It wasn't just once.'

Eamonn shrugged. 'I figured that much.'

'I knew what he was. What if there were others, Eamonn? It's been two years. Who's it been for the last two years?'

He kicked at a stone on the pavement. 'If you had told somebody, it would have been your word against his.'

I knew this. And back then, I had no words with which to stand against him.

'And your ma, Marion. She wouldn't have backed you up.'

'She'd have blamed me. Probably called me a slut with a guilty conscience.'

Eamonn rested his hands gently either side of my face. 'You had enough going on. You did what you could.'

My laugh was bitter. 'And what was that?'

'You survived. Which, considering the circumstances, was pretty impressive.'

I pushed off from the wall and made to go. Eamonn grabbed my hand, and began to move with me.

'What are you doing? Let go. She'll see.'

He stared straight ahead, carried on walking. 'I'm seeing my girlfriend to her door.'

Eamonn was no fool. He knew by picking that day, of all days, the last thing I thought about before I went to bed was not murder, or attempted rape, or wrists bleeding from burning ropes, or a ruined bra. It was the soft lips and gentle smile of Eamonn Brown. My boyfriend.

19

Scarlett came to see me a couple of days after she returned to England. I'd spent the day spreading mulch over the flowerbeds, and now stood at the kitchen sink, scrubbing away the dirt lodged under my nails.

'Hey, Marion! I brought dinner.' She placed a dish of lasagne on my tiny table, scooping out two portions while I poured juice into glasses and chopped cucumber and peppers to make salad.

We ate in silence for a while. I knew what was coming.

'I hear you are expectin' me not to fire Jake's ass, or to fire my shotgun at it, either.'

I put down my fork. 'You have a gun?'

'Keep eatin', Marion. This might take a while and Scarlett's Sunshine Lasagne is too good to let it go cold.'

'How is he?'

'Oh, I knew you'd be worryin' about him! He's crawlin' with self-loathin', not sleepin'. But I hear he's not had a drink since New Year's Eve. That's what, two weeks? It's a start. Archie's been lookin' out for him, arranged some support group in Mansfield for him to go see.' She fixed her all-seeing eye on mine. 'Can you tell me straight what happened? The Peace and Pigs is a place of second, third, and thousandth chances, but I will boot his backside right outta here if this was anything more than a lost, angry young boy with a perception pickled in alcohol. And I mean it about shootin' him.'

'I don't know. I'm terrified of making this into something it wasn't. But I'm just as scared of being one of those women who allows this stuff to go on by not speaking out.'

We spoke for a long time. Eventually Scarlett called Brenda for an off-the-record conversation. We talked some more, and finally reached a first step forwards. Scarlett would contact Samuel in the morning, to ask if he would agree to hire Jake for now. If nothing else, it would give us time to think. Before she left, Scarlett asked if I would mind hearing her lesson on surviving 'sweaty, fumbly fingers that squiggle their fungussy way into places they are not welcome and have no right to be'. I didn't mind. It was not Jake's fingers I was thinking about.

'You're doin' it, honey. Just keep on at it.'

That was it?

'You know it is never your fault, not something you did, or said, or wore. And you know not all men think they can push women around. Actually, most don't. I know you know there is nothing shameful here, or spoiled. It happened. It sucked. Sometimes you might need to talk it over, or cry, or kick a chicken. It'll make you a little wary of every man, but that ain't always a bad thing, as long as you can figure out how to move past it. Keep your chin up, and keep on keepin' on. Find a bunch of great women – and men – open a flashy box of chocolates and laugh with them so hard your diaphragm don't know what hit it.'

Scarlett pulled up one side of her mouth. Her eyes were deep pools of sadness. 'What else can you do?'

Once my bruises had faded through green and yellow to a faint smudge, I took Pettigrew and cycled to Hatherstone. Jake was shocked when I rang his buzzer, but what was he going to do? Leave me standing on the doorstep?

He looked as bad as Scarlett had said. Even worse than I expected. His eyes couldn't keep still, and his knee jerked up and down as he sat on the sofa facing me.

He cringed. 'I don't know how to say anything that won't sound like worthless excuses.'

'Say it anyway.'

He rubbed his hands over his hair, hanging greasy and unkempt below his collar.

'I'm sorry.' His voice cracked. He wiped his nose on the back of his hand.

'I forgive you.'

'Don't.' Jake released a shuddering breath. 'Every time my mum hit my dad, or threw a vase at him, or smashed his head into the wall, she would wait until she sobered up, then beg for his forgiveness. Every time, I prayed he would refuse. That this would be the time he threw her out, hit her back, pressed charges. He never did. And she always did it again.'

'Will you do it again?'

He stared at the floor. 'I went to the police.'

'To the station?'

'I asked them to arrest me.'

'What happened?'

'Brenda signed me up to see a shrink – said there was nothing she could do if you denied anything happened.' He shook his head. 'I'd rather face a judge.'

There was silence for a few minutes before I stood up.

'I'll see you around, then?'

Jake looked up at me. 'I don't think so. Not for a while. Not until I've sorted my head out.'

I had to stop more than once as I cycled home through the trees, to gather myself together. I'd thought I was safe with Jake because he was my friend. I'd been wrong, but I had learned something. I didn't need my friends to be perfect. I didn't want them to be. I needed honesty, and to know that I didn't have to be perfect either.

* * *

It was one of those days where the sunlight never quite manages to push back the winter gloom. I found Scarlett in the reception office, surrounded by piles of scattered papers.

'Morning, Scarlett.'

She blinked at me through tortoiseshell glasses. 'Oh. Hi, Marion. Isn't this your day off?'

'Yes. I'm going into Nottingham. Do you need anything?'

Wrinkling up her brow, she thought for a moment. 'I think Valerie could do with some more thick socks. Her feet are always cold this time of year. You know she likes the stripy ones? Made of wool?'

I did know this. I had bought Valerie a three-pack of new socks when I took her shopping in the January sales only the week before.

'She needs more socks? We bought some last week, remember?'

Scarlett took her glasses off. 'Yes, of course. Forgive me, Marion, I'm a little distracted at the moment.'

I eyed the calculator next to her coffee mug. 'Can you make it work?'

'I have to, sugar. I have to.'

I bumped into Grace as I left, on her way to catch the school bus. We walked toward the campsite exit together.

'Is your mum okay? She seems tired, and – I don't know – not quite herself.'

'What, even more annoying than usual?' Grace shrugged. 'She's been staying up really late freaking out about money. She's just stressed. Either that or it's the menopause. That turned my ICT teacher into a zombie on steroids overnight.'

'Something to look forward to. Can I give you a lift to school?'

Grace sniffed. 'Well, other than that I'd rather go to school wearing cling-film than be seen in your death-trap car, I am actually meeting a friend.'

I chose to tactfully ignore the fact that Grace's nose, beneath the silver stud, had gone pink. Then I saw the boy waiting at the bus stop fifty yards along the main road. I raised my eyebrows.

'Grow up, Marion. He's a friend.' She said the word slowly, like I was a small child.

'Of course he is.' I smiled, and waved at the boy just for fun. 'He looks like a very nice *friend*. I like his hair. And his jacket. And if he smiles at all his friends like that, well—'

'If you say anything to Mum, I'll never make you a pair of shoes again!' Grace began hurrying down the grass verge, trying to go as fast as she could without it being obvious.

I grinned and backtracked to my car, resisting the urge to beep my horn as I drove past them huddling together at the bus stop.

I left the car in one of the city centre car parks and walked down to the old market square, a large pedestrianised space surrounded by shops and pubs on three sides, the grand Council House on the other. It was simple to find the road that led from there to the Central Notts Library. I ducked inside, pausing to suck in a big, comfortable breath of familiar surroundings before I climbed the stairs to the local studies section on the first floor.

Two women stood behind the help desk. One of them showed me the filing cabinets where copies of old newspapers were kept on tiny rolls of film. She pointed out where I could find the *Nottingham Evening Post*, and I pulled out the boxes containing August and

September 1981. I threaded the film through the spool and settled forwards in the chair, winding it on until the first page came into focus.

It had been a while since I used one of these machines, but it felt as familiar as tying my shoelaces. The library was far larger and busier than the one in Ballydown, but it still felt like an old friend to me: the rustle of other library users flicking through journals, the clicking of computer keyboards. I had forgotten how much I loved the warmth and the indoorsy atmosphere of libraries – how closed off and protected they are. Anything could be happening in the world outside these walls, but in here an oasis of calm prevails; the reassuring silence of strangers gathered to share a common goal of finding peace and space to browse and read, search and study. A library – the one place where talking is frowned on. What a safe haven for a recovering mute.

I got to work, scrolling through to the middle of the month, just before the date of the first festival, when I knew Henry Hatherstone was still alive. It went quicker than I thought – the newspaper was a world away from anything you could read now. I found at least a dozen different stories on every front page. In the first edition I examined carefully, on 26 August, a Wednesday, the biggest story involved a jug of water thrown over a judge during a court session investigating a riot. Page four informed readers of a local poetry evening at a village church. By page seven, the news degenerated into the utterly uninteresting wedding of a local solicitor.

I knew that the trivial nature of the stories meant that although each edition covered a lot of ground, something as serious as the accidental death of a lord's son would make front page news. The main headlines for the subsequent two days covering a twelve-year-old boy burning a house down after he sneaked in 'for a crafty fag', and a family's slightly unpleasant coaching holiday, confirmed this opinion. But I didn't rush between front pages. I dilly-dallied in the world my father had inhabited, hung around in the petty trivia, the minute details of the Nottinghamshire he had known. I got lost in the people and places of his past, wondering if he had been at that concert, or played in that cricket match. The coverage of the festival was fun, and brief. It had only been a small affair in its first year, and so many faces crammed the photograph accompanying the story that his was a tiny smudge in a Robin Hood hat.

But on September's reel, on the third day of the month, the festival came up again: 'Little John Dies in Shock Accident'. Most of the front page, and the second and third, described how local lad, Henry Hatherstone, died after falling from the roof of an abandoned tower on his family's estate. Police were still investigating, but it looked as though a verdict of accidental death would result.

Crucially, the accident had two young witnesses: one named as Daniel Miller, the other a local girl of unknown identity. A couple of comments from local residents followed, both mentioning how much everyone loved Henry. A subsidiary column reported on the tower's dangerous state of disrepair. Many villagers had believed for some time that an accident was inevitable. There had already been calls for the Hatherstones to make it safe or fence it off, particularly as everyone knew it to be a hang-out for teenagers looking for a place to meet up undisturbed.

I scrolled on, skipping through front pages now. In October, I found a follow-up story. The tower had been proved structurally sound, all except for the stone balustrade surrounding the roof, which had crumbled in certain places. Later on, I read a brief report of the inquest findings. Henry had been drinking. It was a tragic accident. The family had no comment.

I felt unsure of what this meant for my mission to find out about my father. Did witnessing the death of his best friend amount to a reason for him to leave? Maybe. But to change his name? Keep his past totally hidden? Not keep in touch with, or even mention, any of his family again?

He had left England very soon after Henry died. The two incidents must have been connected. And now I had another piece of the puzzle to pick at. The other witness, the unnamed girl: who was she? Had she too fled the scene after the accident?

Somebody must know her identity. I only hoped that if – when – I managed to find her, she would be willing to tell me what had happened.

I sat in the blue caravan with Valerie, filling vases with pink and white roses for our latest money-making venture. Except for the school half-term week, February was usually our quietest month for bookings. Valerie had suggested trying out a Valentine's special, providing flowers and chocolates, champagne, and a fridge stocked with the makings of a luxury breakfast in bed. Scarlett had arranged a great deal with a local restaurant for dinner and we had provided maps of romantic forest walks, along with a voucher for a treatment at the nearest spa. Because it was Valerie's idea, she took charge of all the finishing touches, and I worked alongside as her assistant.

'15 per cent of women buy themselves flowers on Valentine's Day.'

'Really? I wonder how many of them pretend the flowers are from a secret admirer.'

'We don't need to buy flowers. We can look through the window.'

'Absolutely. I love the snowdrops. A tiny shoot of hope poking through the snow.'

'Have you sent a card?'

'No. Have you?'

Valerie shook her head. 'I'm waiting for the right man. I haven't met him yet, but if I do, I want to be available. And if I don't, that's okay too. Enough people love me already.'

'That's a pretty good attitude!'

Valerie shrugged. She stuck another pink rose into an already overstuffed vase. 'No Man is a whole heap of trouble better than Wrong Man.'

'Sounds like something Scarlett would say.'

'She didn't have to. I've met Wrong Man. I didn't like him.'

I snipped the ends off the rest of the flowers – at a 45-degree angle as Valerie had instructed. I wondered who Wrong Man was. Maybe her father. Or Grace's.

She asked me, 'Have you?'

'What?'

'Met Wrong Man?'

I thought about that. 'I met Right Then, But Wrong Now Man. It took me years to realise that I was better off with No Man. You're way smarter than me, Valerie.'

Valerie nodded. 'Don't worry about it. You're a fast learner. You'll catch up.'

Scarlett stepped through the front door, kicking the snow off her shoes. She wore only a thin, lightweight cardigan over her red dress. Her skin was blue.

'Oooeee. They don't make winters like this back home. I got caught out a little there.'

Valerie looked down. She concentrated hard on her roses.

'How are you girls gettin' on? This all looks beautiful. Valerie, if I could afford it, I'd give you a raise. For now, I'll have to settle with a hug.'

She sat down next to her foster daughter and wrapped her arms around her. Valerie smothered a yelp as melting snow dripped off Scarlett, forming wet patches on her clothes and hair. But instead of pulling away, she pulled Scarlett toward her, fiercely holding on until Scarlett gasped out that she needed to breathe.

'I do love you, sweetheart. But I came to fetch my purse. I must get to the shops before it snows again.'

I handed Scarlett her bag from the worktop next to me. She put it down on the counter and took out a packet of paracetamol, popping two out and swallowing them dry.

'Are you sure it's safe to drive?'

'The roads past the village are gritted, and Samuel's giving me a ride in his truck. It's all kitted out for ice, snow, tornadoes, and quite possibly the end of the world, so we'll be fine.' She pulled the door open again, letting a blast of icy wind whip inside the van. 'See you girls, then. Don't forget the ribbons are in the carrier bag in the bottom cupboard.'

'Scarlett!' I called after her as she began to let the door slam behind her.

She pushed it open again. 'What, Marion? It's cold out here and Samuel's waiting.'

I handed her the bag. 'Aren't you going to wear a coat?'

'Oh.' She looked down distractedly at her shivering body and seemed to notice for the first time that she was wearing a summer outfit. Frowning, she looked about for a few minutes before spotting her coat and gloves draped over a kitchen chair. As she left the second time, I realised how disorganised the caravan looked in comparison to its usual peaceful and homely order. I hadn't noticed before. I'd been thinking about the flowers.

'Is Scarlett coping all right?'

Valerie shrugged disconsolately, her face miserable. She hadn't said one word while Scarlett was present, which answered my question.

'Is she still not sleeping?'

Valerie blew her nose. 'She has these headaches all the time.

Because of the stress. She's so busy working that she forgets to cook, or shop, or talk to us. Yesterday she didn't get up until after I'd left for college.'

'Does she often get like this?'

Valerie shook her head, bursting into tears. 'What if we lose the campsite, Marion? What will they do then? I'll have to go back and live with Mum, but what about Scarlett, and Grace, and you and Jake? And Little Johnny and Madame Plopsicle?'

I handed her another tissue. 'It won't come to that. You're smart, remember? Think about how well Christmas went, and now you've had this fab idea. The campsite will probably end up doing better than ever. And if the worst does happen, then you can all move in with Samuel and take the animals with you.'

Valerie sniffed. 'He's her Mr Right.'

'I know.'

'We'll leave Denver here, I think. And his ladies.'

'Are you sure that's safe? Have you read *Animal Farm*?' I finished the last vase, and began sweeping the rubbish into a bin bag. 'Don't worry about Scarlett. Once we start making a bit more profit, she'll be all right.'

But Scarlett was not all right. An evil, mutant tentacle had begun digging its way into her brain. Soon the tentacle would spawn more, equally evil, mutant baby tentacles, and in the days to come, her brain would be taken over by a malignant spreading mass that did not care about campsites, or profit, or daughters who needed their mother. No respecter of persons, undeterred by a kind heart, or a selfless soul, or a life unfinished. Scarlett had been betrayed by her own brain cells. She would not be all right.

20

The following day, after placing ten boxes of Sunny's homemade hazelnut chocolates in our fully booked caravans, leaving mini hampers on each table containing, among other things, expensive coffee, luxury biscuits, and locally produced cheeses, and arranging baskets of organic toiletries in each bathroom, I took Pettigrew to Hatherstone.

The trees along the path to the village had formed an arching canopy bending forward, heavy with snow, to welcome me. Cycling into the tunnel of frozen branches felt like entering fairyland, an enchanted world of silver and white. The path had been gritted, but in the deep drifts either side of me, I caught glimpses of footprints, tiny three-pronged bird prints, and larger paw marks where dogs had chased the snow-flurries. The dark-grey clouds had given way to watery sunshine, half-heartedly dissolving the snow in odd patches here and there but mostly leaving its magic to transform the forest for one more day.

I left the trees and made my way down the high street, weaving to avoid a cluster of snow people complete with not just the traditional hats and scarves, but sunglasses, bikini tops, and in the case of one muscle-bound snowman, a leopard-print thong worked in between his trunky legs. Red-cheeked children, making the most of cancelled school, pulled sledges down the centre of the deserted road toward the hill behind the chapel, while their older brothers and sisters lobbed snowballs at parked cars, each other, and unsuspecting cyclists.

I pulled up at Ada and May's picture-perfect cottage, stamping snow off my Sherwood Forest boots while I rapped the brass knocker against their yellow wooden door.

Ada called for me to come in, and I stepped inside the winter quarters of the beauty parlour set up in Ada's living room. I had an appointment. I was having a cut and blow-dry and my nails painted. Tomorrow would be Valentine's Day, which obviously I didn't care about, being footloose and fancy free for the first time in eight years; but hey, if I coincidentally felt like taking some time out to look good, that was no big deal.

I flipped through a magazine about adventure holidays in the world's most dangerous corners (which made me think about Harriet) until it was my turn in the chair.

We covered the standard chat: small talk, but a big deal for an ex-mute. I congratulated myself on not only being at a beauty parlour, which is way worse than a hairdresser's, but behaving like a normal person too. Then, as Ada stuck her face so close to mine that I could map the mini rivers of veins across her skin while she snipped my fringe, we progressed to the conversational main course.

'What have you found out about your dad?'

'I've stumbled across something, but it could hurt some people if I dig it up again. I'm trying to keep it quiet.'

'Now, girl. Didn't I tell you I've signed the official secrets act? If I was ever tempted to spill even a fraction of the secrets that are up here' – she tapped her head with the scissors – 'it would leave my clients with more than just a new cut. Hairs. Would. Curl.'

Greedy for new leads, I told her about the newspaper report, and how two teenagers had witnessed Henry's accident, one of them being my father.

'So you want to find the young lady.'

'Yes. But I don't know where to start. I know she'll be around fifty-one and was probably friends with Henry Hatherstone. She may well have done what Da did, and moved away after what happened. She could be anywhere.'

'And you can't ask Ginger or Archie? If you explained, I'm sure they'd understand.'

'I promised Reuben. I don't even feel I can ask around the village about Henry, in case it gets back to them.'

Ada wanted to try Morris again, but I couldn't stomach it. The whole subject now seemed too sensitive, and I guessed Morris Middleton didn't do sensitive very well. We settled for Ada promising to keep her eyes and ears open, and I moved across to May's station for my manicure. As always, May kept her mouth closed, her lips tightly pursed. Probably to prevent any acid from dripping off her tongue and dissolving the nail polish.

Ada had another client, Amanda of the boob tubes and bitchy remarks. I hoped the magic scissors would slip. Then told myself off for stooping to her level.

'So, Amanda.' Ada hacked off a chunk of grown-out pink, leaving a three-inch grey root behind. She tossed me a wink. Oh dear. 'How long have you lived around here?'

'Forever,' Amanda sneered. 'Never guessed I'd end up spending my life in this dump. That's what landing yerself with a baby'll do. No man wants to be saddled with a woman who's got a kid like that. What if the next one turns out just as bad?'

Ada smiled sweetly. She sneakily brushed the protective gown to one side and snipped a long thin chunk out of Amanda's fake leather waistcoat. 'So that must be, what, how long now? Nearly sixty years?'

Amanda pulled down her drawn-on eyebrows so they were now at least halfway down her forehead. 'Mind yerself! I'm only thirty-nine. Looking good for it too. You old women get so far past it, you can't remember what normal people look like.'

Ada accidentally nicked Amanda's ear, causing a ruby droplet of blood to well up on the rim of her lobe. 'Oh, my dear! I am so sorry. My doddery old hands aren't what they used to be. Here, fetch Amanda a glass of whisky, would you, May, to ward off any shock?'

Amanda calmed down once she had swigged back her second tumbler of whisky. Ada, very carefully holding her curling iron away from her client's skin, resumed the covert interrogation.

'And was the village very different when you were young?'

'No. It was just as dead.'

'And what did you get up to, you and your friends? You must have found some way of amusing yourselves. Did you have many pals? Any of them still living here?'

Amanda froze. Her eyes swivelled across the room toward me. When she spoke, it sounded as if her jaw was wired together. 'And why would you give a flying fig about that?'

I focused very hard on choosing what colour nail polish I wanted.

Ada whipped off the gown with a flourish. 'There we go; all done. That'll be ten pounds. There's a mirror in the hall. You can see yourself out? Lovely. Do come again, won't you, and we'll sort out all that grey. Goodbye.' She hustled Amanda out of the chair and through the door, simultaneously taking her money and handing back her jacket in one graceful sweep.

'Well, that was interesting! Hmm. Was she simply behaving in her usual disagreeable fashion, or is she on to us?'

May's lips twitched. 'You've just poked a rattlesnake. Let's see who gets bitten.'

* * *

Three days later, after an exhausting weekend pandering to the needs of some very frisky lovers (No, we don't stock those particular items in the campsite shop; no, we aren't going to trek through the snow at ten o'clock in the evening to find the type of sleazy shop that might sell them, and no, we definitely don't have any of our own that you can borrow), the rattlesnake bit.

I woke up to find another message, this time spray painted across the outside of my home. It said:

Shut up fat bitch

Original. I didn't want to call Brenda. I knew who had done it. We'd got Amanda angry and scared. She knew something.

Reuben came over to my caravan the following week. He brought a wooden box with him, about the same dimensions as a shoebox. Opening it up, he lifted out the papers on top and unfolded them.

'There's a lot here that isn't relevant: school certificates, Mother's Day cards and stuff like that. But I found these.'

He handed me an envelope containing a thin wad of faded photographs taken at a child's birthday party – Henry's. His cake had been made in the shape of a thirteen. The group of kids lounged along a riverbank, the boys bare-chested and wearing those tiny shorts fashionable in the mid-seventies, the girls in brightly coloured summer dresses.

'Do you see him?'

I did. In four of the photographs, my dad was there, grinning beside his best friend Henry. I drank him up until Reuben handed me one of the other pictures.

'What about here? Recognise anyone?'

I could see Ginger, her hair as vibrant as her name, curling over her shoulders in long tumbling waves. She had her head back, laughing, and I wondered if she ever laughed that freely again after Henry died.

'Look closer.'

I found her – even then wearing a skirt several inches shorter than everybody else's, her T-shirt straining against the curve of her developing body. She gazed at the camera, eyebrows arched questioningly, one side of her mouth curled up. Not beautiful, or pretty, but a girl who knew how to hook a boy's attention.

We worked backwards with the dates.

'These must have been taken in 1976.'

I shook my head. 'How does that fit? If this is Amanda, she's thirty-nine now. She would have been three in 1976. It can't be her. Does she have an older sister?'

Reuben looked at me, waiting for me to work it out for myself.

'Okay. So the chances of her telling the truth about her age are about as likely as this girl being three.' And if she was going to lie, knocking ten years off to squeeze herself into a previous decade seemed about right. 'Do you recognise anybody else?'

'No. Henry went to boarding school; most of these kids have that look about them. See how Amanda is always a little bit apart?'

There was nothing else of any use in the box. The keepsakes ended with a champagne cork, the date '15.4.81' written along the side, above the words 'Henry's eighteenth'.

I told Reuben what I had learned about the witnesses from the newspaper, and the repercussions from the conversation at Ada's cottage.

His face turned to granite. 'Marion! How many of these messages have you had?'

I showed him the first note, and told him about the second one, followed by the graffiti and the tyres.

'Please tell me the police have seen this!'

'It came the day Grace took off, wrapped around a brick through my window. Brenda assumed it was her.'

'Why would Grace chuck a brick through your window?'

I shrugged, embarrassed. 'She was going through a weird time back then. Scarlett thought she might be taking drugs.'

'And the link to you is?'

'Jake.'

'Right. That would fit. So did Grace get the blame for the rest of them?'

'I only reported the tyres. The second note was nothing, just left in my purse. And when the spray paint was done, I had already figured it was Amanda.'

'You're sure it isn't Grace?'

'We've been friends for ages now. She has a boyfriend. And she's hardly still jealous about me and Jake.' I heard my voice rising as I tried to push the image of Jake out of my head. 'And it fits. The first note came the day after I had my bag stolen at the village. Amanda was the one who picked up my photo and gave it back to me. I passed it round the traders at the festival. She doesn't want me asking about my dad. She didn't want Ada asking about her past and her friends, because they're linked. She was the other witness at Henry's accident. What is she trying to hide?'

Reuben packed away the photographs. 'We need to speak to her.' He grimaced. '*I* need to speak to her.'

'You know she'll only lie. What then?'

'I think it might be time to tell my parents.'

* * *

Three days later, on the last day of February, I came back from a run to find Grace sitting on my caravan steps, huddled against the early morning chill in an army green parka.

'Haven't you got an exam today?' I walked past her and unlocked the door. We went in and sat down.

Grace hunkered further into her coat. 'Mum left the van wearing odd shoes this morning. She woke me up at quarter past five with a cup of tea.'

'Why?'

'I don't know. When I yelled at her, she totally lost it. She chucked the mug in the sink so hard it smashed, and then left.'

'In odd shoes?'

Grace nodded. She bit hard on her bottom lip.

'Grace, I'm not sure this is just stress.' If a giant asteroid was hurtling toward the Peace and Pigs with only milliseconds to spare, Scarlett would still find a matching pair of heels. 'Go and get ready for school. I'll get changed and then we'll find her.'

I jumped in the shower, then threw on a pair of jeans and a jumper. Stuffing my wet hair under a woollen hat, I hurried over to find Grace pacing up and down outside her caravan.

'She's not inside?'

Grace shook her head.

'Where's Valerie? Did she see your mum this morning?'

'She's sorting out the pigs.'

'Come on, then.'

We found Scarlett in the office, staring at the same piles of paper that had sat there for weeks now. She was a wreck.

I gently turned Grace away. 'You need to go and take your art exam. Try to put this out of your head and we'll deal with it together when you get back.'

She stayed in the doorway. Her eyes, brimming with anguish, never left her mother.

'There's nothing you can do here that I can't do without you. You need to sit this exam, Grace.'

It took a while, but eventually I persuaded her to leave. Scarlett had been watching us, moving her head from side to side like a small child trying to follow a conversation full of words too difficult to understand.

'Hi, Scarlett.'

'Hi.'

'How are you feeling?'

She stared at me, a pen dangling from her fingers.

'Scarlett? Are you okay? Grace is worried about you.'

'What? I'm fine.' She spoke slowly, her words slurred. One side of her face looked wrong.

I sat down in a chair opposite her. 'You have odd shoes on, Scarlett.'

'What?' She looked down at her shoes, frowning, confused. 'How did that happen?'

'I think you need to see a doctor.'

'No.' She shook her head, but it was sluggish and lopsided.

I leaned forward to see if I could detect alcohol on her breath. It smelled sour, and her teeth were dark yellow. I knew she wasn't drunk.

'I need to sort out this mess. I'm tired. Please let me work.'

I put my hand on top of hers. 'You need to see a doctor.'

In the end, it wasn't hard to bundle her out of the office and into my car. She shuffled her left foot along the ground as I led her like a little girl. Or a frail old woman. Or a person who was hopelessly, desperately ill.

I called Valerie, asking her to cover for us. She would phone Samuel or the Hatherstones if anything came up. Stomach in my mouth, heart breaking, I drove Scarlett to the doctor's surgery. From there, we went to the outpatient unit at Queens Medical Centre in Nottingham. From there, it was the acute admissions ward, where we heard the news that would tear the hearts of the Peace and Pigs into tiny shreds.

21

Two days later, a grave-faced, smooth-skinned doctor with a gentle Scottish burr confirmed Scarlett's diagnosis. He spoke with us for over an hour, but only the words that mattered stuck. Inoperable. Incurable. Unstoppable. Invincible. Terminal. It would be possible to try a course of radiotherapy or chemotherapy, but this would only delay the spread of the tumour for a short time, and when it returned, it would be swift. We were talking months, not years. Probably weeks, not months.

I left Grace alone by Scarlett's bedside while Valerie and I went to the top floor of the hospital to find the restaurant. We were not the only customers with trembling hands and tear-streaked faces, Valerie's the colour of the raw dough I had kneaded that morning into bread rolls, punching and rolling my emotions into food. Valerie's eyes were still wide with shock, bloodshot and bleary. I wanted to wrap her up in a blanket and rock her. To tell her it would be all right; that I would take care of her, of them; that we would look after each other. But I knew before then would come pain and death smells, exhaustion and fear and the physical ache in your chest that hurts so much you want to prise out your heart with a spoon rather than bear the reality of what is happening. And this would be only the beginning of a long, jagged desert road.

So I told her what I knew to be true. 'I will be here. I won't leave you. And we will do our very best for Scarlett. We will love her with all the love she gave us.'

* * *

My mother told me many times that I had inherited my selective strop-ism, as she labelled my crippling psychological disorder, from my English genes. O'Gradys learned how to talk when they were babies, and kept going until their last breath. Never, she informed me with a caustic glare, had they dallied with the silent treatment. This was true; in a family that size, it would have been pointless. Nobody would even have noticed.

Instead, my Irish relatives chose continual conversation in the form of bickering, griping, yelling, bullying, and sniping. They also threw in some storytelling, joke-telling, memory-reliving and banter. But they sorely lacked any form of meaningful communication whatsoever. The most I heard said about Declan's murder was: 'It's a terrible thing, so it is. Our poor, wee Paula. And she mustn't be blamed. That one was born odd.'

True to form, no one discussed my father's illness with me, or that he was dying of some type of cancer, and that my behaviour could have no influence on that for good or bad. They told me, a seven-year-old girl, that my father was not well, and when he died, I should be happy for him because he would go to be with Jesus and not suffer any more. Nobody told me how it felt to have a chunk of your heart die with him, or how grief could cause a widow on the edge of sanity to tip right over. That and a million other things I learned the hard way, through years of reading books in the corner of the library, and hoarding titbits from the few health professionals my mother allowed near me. I grew adept at filtering the cruel taunts from my cousins and schoolmates into their three categories: truth, nasty twists on the truth, and totally made-up stuff kids will spread around to produce a reaction (like the rumour that my da was an alien who had laid a mini alien in my mother's head, so she had to have her mind probed by Martian experts from NASA).

So now, I asked the doctors to tell us everything. I read the leaflets from the cancer charities describing what could happen to the mind and body of someone with a brain tumour. I asked what 'some personality changes' might mean, and almost wished I hadn't. I went back to the library and didn't care that I sobbed as I read the blogs and questions and brain tumour websites. I would not face this blind, or in denial. I would stir up hope, cultivate optimism, and summon positivity. But this time, we would not fight an unknown enemy. Grace and Valerie asked me questions, and I did not lie or fudge my answers to them. So much remained impossible to predict, all could be softened to some extent with kindness, but I did not lie.

Scarlett only spoke to me once about her prognosis. Steroids had cleared her mind and eased her headaches, and the bewilderment had temporarily departed.

'I have a tumour. There ain't nothin' you, me or that Scottish hunk of a doctor can do about that. I could spend however long I got left worryin' about it, dwellin' on the monster chompin' its way through my brain, feelin' miserable and countin' down the days, but I don't see how that is gonna help anyone. I am goin' to die. That is old news. The only difference is that now I know how it's probably gonna happen. I choose to accept that as a gift, a chance to tidy things up and tuck in some corners. I am not goin' to spend the rest of my time here dyin'. I will, by the grace of God, grab hold of every second I got left and live it.' Her voice wavered. I reached over and took her hand. 'Although I could do with a little help.'

Yes. Despite medication, weakness, nausea, and brain tumours, Scarlett would surely live until she died.

For Grace and Valerie's sake, Scarlett didn't keep the news a secret. From that moment on, they never had to cook a meal. I borrowed a freezer and set it up in the spare employee's caravan to store all the pasta and pies and other meals deposited at reception by sympathetic Hatherstone residents. Valerie strung a hundred cards up along the edge of every wall in the blue van, and someone gave Scarlett a gift token to a spa hotel in the Peak District. The accompanying card wasn't signed, but the handwriting was almost certainly May's.

Erica brought round a card from her parents. We had been limiting visitors, as Scarlett was tired and still sometimes confused, and there are those people you want to give your time to when you don't have much left, and those it is enough to know are thinking about you. It was a good thing Erica didn't stay to see the card opened.

Inside, Fisher had written something about being sorry to hear Scarlett had received unfortunate news, and he hoped she was bearing up. He added a line expressing his concern that, for Scarlett's peace of mind, she should sew up all business regarding the campsite sooner rather than later. He had very thoughtfully offered to pay a visit to pick up all the paperwork and put it in order on her behalf. In an extraordinary step of kindness toward a terminally ill tenant, he informed her he had a suitable replacement waiting as soon as she felt ready to say goodbye to the Peace and Pigs. As if all this generosity wasn't enough, he offered to put in a good word for her with a local removals firm where he had an account.

Scarlett laughed so hard she was sick.

Her lawyer, a black-belt nutcracker who took no prisoners,

spent three consecutive afternoons with Scarlett ensuring everything was exactly as she wanted it, and would remain that way. Scarlett refused to discuss those arrangements, but it was a pretty safe bet we would not be calling Fisher's recommended removal firm any time soon.

March flew by, taken up with untangling the myriad complications that inevitably accompany serious illness. The low season was over. The Peace and Pigs had pitches booked, caravans filled, and the workload began to creep up. Grace concentrated on her last couple of months at school. Valerie needed time to be with Scarlett. Even though Samuel had taken over the livestock, we still needed help. I invited Jake back. That was not a fun phone call. For the first time in weeks, I had to work hard at my mute busters. I really, really wanted to spend the spring and summer avoiding him again, ducking behind tents and dodging round trees.

Instead, I breathed out, dropped my shoulders, breathed in, opened my mouth and said, 'Hi.'

He said hello back, and that was that. Sober, still in counselling, knocked for six by Scarlett's diagnosis, he wasted no time crawling on bended knees, and I felt grateful for that. I had no emotional energy spare to deal with trying to assuage his guilt. We were professional, with occasional forays into friendliness, and I was overwhelmed with relief that I could finally manage my own life as well as a brilliant and beautiful holiday park.

The 22 March was the Sunday before the Easter bank holiday weekend. Scarlett insisted Valerie spend the day with her mum, knowing it would be the first time since she had been in hospital. When Amanda drove Valerie home that evening, Reuben was waiting. He strode over toward the car before Valerie even had a chance to get out, and held the passenger door open, preventing the car from driving off again.

'Amanda.'

'What are you doing? Let go of my car. I've got places to be.'

'We're going to have a chat first. Come and sit down.'

Her face pinched, Amanda switched off the engine and got out. She locked the car and came to stand by the wrought-iron table and chairs outside Valerie's van.

'What?'

'Not here. Scarlett's sleeping.' Reuben led her to a picnic bench twenty or so metres away. I followed him, with Amanda huffing along behind.

When she sat down, Reuben leaned on the table and bent his head close to hers. 'What are you playing at, Amanda?'

She glanced quickly at me before narrowing her eyes straight at Reuben. 'I don't know what you're talking about.'

'We can do this now, or with the police.'

She laughed. 'Ooh! Listen to him, playing the big man! I told you: I don't know what you're on about.'

Reuben took out the first note from his jacket pocket and held it up. Amanda still smiled, but her snake eyes glittered green like toxic slime.

'Did you really think you could do all this and no one would see you? Not even once?'

The smile disappeared. 'What do you want?'

'I want to know what you're hiding. Why don't you want Marion asking questions about Daniel Miller?'

Amanda stood up to go. As she stepped away from the bench, Reuben blocked her.

'What do you know about my brother's death? You were there that night. What happened, Amanda, that you want so desperately to keep hidden?'

Something in her snapped at the mention of Henry. Clenching her fists, Amanda thrust her face in Reuben's. She bared her teeth, and when she spoke, her voice was a snarl.

'Your brother died. That's what happened. We were eighteen years old and I saw my best friend smash to pieces. His body twisted and broken on the ground. Maybe' – she jabbed her finger at me – 'I don't want her bringing that up again just to satisfy her curiosity. Maybe she would be better off going back home instead of finding out just what her dad was doing on top of that roof that meant he had to scarper and never come back.'

She turned to look at me. Saliva frothed in the corners of her mouth and her skin was mottled purple. 'Some secrets are better left that way. Some secrets you would sleep easier not knowing. The truth ain't pretty here, love. You keep your nice happy memories of your precious daddy. Do us all a favour and go home.'

She pushed past Reuben and stumbled back to her car. I lowered myself carefully onto the bench. The world seemed to be shifting under my feet and I needed to grip the table to keep upright. Reuben pushed my head down between my knees until the clanging noise had stopped.

'She meant that Da had something to do with it – with the accident.'

'She's a lying cow who'll say anything to get what she wants. Come for dinner tomorrow night. Let's see what Mum and Dad have to say.'

* * *

'Well, this is nice.' Ginger sounded as if she wasn't quite sure. She slid in beside Archie at the kitchen table while Reuben lifted a baked salmon out of the oven and placed it next to a tray of roasted vegetables. 'Where's Sunny?' She glanced anxiously at the kitchen door. 'Won't he and Katarina be joining us?'

'They're putting the kids to bed.' Reuben began dishing up the fish.

'So, what's all this about, then?' Archie furrowed his brow. 'My girl, Reuben hasn't got you pregnant, has he?'

I dropped my knife on the floor, which gave me a precious few seconds to hide under the table, scrabbling about for it. Lucy chuffed at me from her spot in front of the stove. I shook my head, warning her not to give me away.

'Not that we would mind, of course,' Ginger interrupted. 'It's just that things might be a bit awkward with Fisher and Olivia if you haven't ended things properly with Erica first. They are expecting Erica to be the next Lady Hatherstone. It all makes such good sense, with them owning the land next door. I think Fisher had some sort of grand plan for expanding the holiday park. He'll be terribly disappointed.'

'What?' Even from underneath the table, I could hear Reuben's gritted teeth. How long could I stay there before it started to look weird? 'What grand plan? Anyway, Marion is not pregnant. Or if she is, it's nothing to do with me.'

'Oh. Well, make sure you break things off gently with Erica anyway. I know you've had your ups and downs lately, but she is a lovely girl, Reuben. We brought you up better than to mess women about.'

Lucy's tongue was hanging out. She was laughing at me.

'There is nothing going on between me and Marion. That's not why I invited her here.'

'Really? Nothing going on?' I could hear the incredulity in Archie's voice, picture him grinning. 'I know that look and it always means trouble.'

I sidled back onto my chair. Reuben handed his father a plate. 'Can we eat first?'

Archie shook his head. 'What? Make awkward small talk while we shovel down our salmon as fast as possible to get to the good bit? No. You talk, we'll eat. Then you can eat while we digest both news and dinner.'

I told Archie and Ginger how my father had died leaving a mystery regarding his English past and his family, and that a photo had led me to Sherwood Forest.

'I've been asking around, but so far, I've only hit dead ends. I still don't know where Da lived, who his parents were, or why he left. But Reuben thought you might be able to help me. We think you probably knew him.'

Ginger and Archie were eagerly leaning forwards across the table, salmon forgotten.

'Well, tell us what you know. Who is it? And why do you think we would know the chap?'

I looked at Reuben. He cleared his throat. 'Because he was friends with Henry.'

The atmosphere dropped like a stone plummeting into a ravine. They sat back, Archie absent-mindedly picking up his knife and fork. Ginger closed her eyes, took a deep breath and dabbed at her lip with a napkin.

'Daniel.' Her voice was quiet but clear. The consummate lady.

'Yes.' I took the picture from my bag and offered it to her across the table. Archie was the first one to cry.

I pushed my chair back. 'I'll make some coffee.'

'No.' Reuben stood up. 'I'll do it.'

I ate some food, although every mouthful was dry and tasteless and stuck halfway down my oesophagus. Ginger stirred a heaped spoonful of sugar into her coffee, downed it in one, and seemed ready to talk.

'You're Daniel's girl. I should have seen it. You look just like him.'

I'd misread her; she wasn't ready. It took a good while longer and three of Archie's monogrammed handkerchiefs before we could resume the conversation, now sitting in the drawing room.

'I'm sorry.' Ginger wiped her nose. 'Daniel wasn't just Henry's friend. He was a son to us. His parents were our housekeeper and groundsman. They lived in the gatekeeper's cottage. Henry and Daniel grew up inseparable. When Henry had a hard time settling in at school, and then we had the robbery, we thought that could be the answer – send Daniel to school with him. We thought it would help.'

'I'm sorry. What robbery?'

'The one where... surely Daniel told you? We were away, in Switzerland. Somebody broke in and Daniel's parents interrupted them.'

'What happened?' My mind felt numb, everything seemed to be in slow motion.

'They were shot.'

How could the loss of something you never had hurt so much? I didn't want to hear any more.

'The boys found them. They were fourteen. We decided it would be best for Henry to go back to school, to get away, have some normality; but that would leave Daniel here alone. So Daniel went with him.'

No wonder he never talked about his past.

'So you paid for him to go to boarding school with Henry? And he stayed here in the holidays?'

'He was going to be a lawyer.' The tears were streaming again. Archie said nothing, his body hunched over as if he could feel the shot that had killed my grandparents.

'Daniel?'

Ginger nodded. 'They both had a place at Oxford, starting that September. We were so proud. Our boys.'

The Christmas tree flashed into my mind. *Our boys did these.*

'And then Daniel was with Henry, at the accident?' I felt bile hit the back of my throat.

Ginger nodded. 'It has taken many, many years for us to be able to forgive ourselves for what happened. Archie told you what it did to him. That we hadn't seen it coming, read the signs. That after everything, we didn't know our son at all.' She pressed one hand against her heart, as if that could prevent it from splintering apart again. 'And that, after everything, Daniel had to see it. We thought he was all right. Henry. That he had left it in the past.'

'I don't understand. What do you mean? How could it have been your fault?'

Archie lifted his head. He looked like an old, old man.

'Henry committed suicide, Marion. Your father tried to stop him. And when Daniel failed, he couldn't bear it. So we lost not one son, but two.'

* * *

Throughout the Easter weekend, the Peace and Pigs was filled to capacity. Samuel took Scarlett away from the chaos to spend her hotel spa voucher. She had become visibly weaker, especially on her left side, and her short-term memory grew increasingly worse. The day or the time, what she had planned that day or what medication she had to take – all such data were chewed up by the brain monster as quickly as she took them in. Grace, increasingly frustrated and upset by her mother's constant interruptions to ask what was going on, filled the blue van with sticky notes on every surface:

Today is Thursday. Take four blue pills with your breakfast. The district nurse is coming today. Valerie is at college. Tell Grace if you want to go out.

The only way that Valerie and Grace could cope was to carry on as normally as they could, as best they could. They had days when they cried, screamed, and threw plates, and others when they laughed, did each other's hair, and talked about boys. We worked hard to ensure they could still go out, get their work done, and do all the other stuff teenage girls do, but Scarlett was dying before their eyes and neither of them had another parent prepared to take on the job of fierce, selfless loving that Scarlett had done so well.

Scarlett's brother, Dr Drew, flew over for a few days after she came back from her break. He wanted Grace to live with him in the States after Scarlett had died. Grace considered it, but didn't want to leave Valerie. Dr Drew said that Valerie could come too, they had room. Grace still dithered, uncertain. I knew something was up, so I lured her over with the promise of coffee cake.

'Have you thought any more about going to stay with Drew?'

'Yes, I've thought about it.' She picked her hair. Bored teenager preparing to be nagged.

'I thought you loved it there. Wouldn't it be a great experience, spending some time in America?'

'What, just hopping on a plane and starting a new life as if Mum had never existed?'

'No. Taking time out to heal and grieve with people who loved her too. And when you're ready, getting on with your life. You know your mum would be furious to think you were using her as an excuse to miss out on a great opportunity.'

Grace squinted at me through her black fringe. 'What if I have a great opportunity here?'

'At the Peace and Pigs? I thought you couldn't wait to get away from this dump.'

'Not *here*. In the UK.'

I could hear something in her voice. A tiny tremble.

'And? What kind of opportunity?'

A tiny smile.

'Grace!' I thwacked her over the head with a cushion, knocking her hair out of her fingers.

It all came out in one breath. 'The London College of Fashion has offered me a place on their course in footwear design. It's a proper degree course. The London College of Fashion! People come from all over the world to train there. It's really hard to get in.'

Grace looked at me. Underneath and in between the shiny hoops and black make-up I could see hope and fear and excitement and anguish. An eighteen-year-old girl living her worst nightmare and her wildest dream.

'Get your shoes.'

We packed Grace's favourite four pairs into boxes and carried them across to the blue caravan. It was early evening, and we found Scarlett asleep on the sofa, curled up under a patchwork throw. I touched her shoulder and she opened her eyes.

'Hey, Scarlett.'

She needed help to sit up, and I fetched her a cup of tea to give her time to straighten her hair and reorientate herself.

'Here you go, Scarlett. Grace has something to show you.'

'What? Did you get a tattoo? Please let it be tasteful and time-less, not trashy.'

'No, she didn't get a tattoo!'

Grace ducked her head and blushed, one hand automatically gripping a spot on her shoulder.

'Well. Anyway. That's not what I was talking about. Grace, show your mum.'

Grace, tight with nerves, fumbled to open the first box. She took out a pair of delicate, dusky pink sandals, with six-inch heels so slender that Scarlett would have been the only woman I knew able to walk in them. Along every silky strap, she had added tiny silver-grey roses, each one only half a centimetre in diameter, and placed a crystal bead in the centre of each flower. At the tip of the strap nearest to the end, where the little toe would sit, a hummingbird perched, crafted from the same fabric as the roses. Simple, elegant, feminine, they looked a million dollars.

'Oh, Grace, honey!' Scarlett picked one up and examined it. 'These are so *beautiful*. But they must have cost a small fortune. Tell me you didn't pay for these!'

She shook her head. 'No.'

'Well, now, you didn't steal them, did ya? Somebody *gave* you shoes like this? If it was Josh, then he's an even better catch than I thought.'

Grace couldn't answer.

'She made them.'

Scarlett looked at me, her mind unable to keep up. 'What?'

'From a cheap pair of plain sandals. She unpicked the straps and resewed them in a different position, then covered them in the pink fabric and made the roses. And the bird, see, at the front.'

Scarlett leaned over to Grace, reaching out to tuck her fringe behind her ear, a gesture that would normally have Grace jerk her head away in impatience. This evening she simply lifted her hand and pressed her mother's fingers tightly to the side of her head, holding them there.

I took the lids off the other boxes, tidied away the empty cups, and left. When I glanced back from the end of the path, I could still see the outline of Scarlett's arm, reaching out across the expanse of teenage independence, stroking her daughter's hair.

Drew's flight left for the States the following day. He held on to his big sister for a long time as Samuel loaded his luggage into the truck.

'I wish I could stay.'

Scarlett shook her head, gently wiping his eyes with her thumbs. 'I bet you do. No wife wantin' the lawn mowed, the dishes done and her feet rubbed while you listen to her tell you about her day. No kids wakin' you up at the crack of dawn and hollerin' and fightin' and makin your head spin until the sun goes down. No hormonal women needin' examinin', or seventy-two-hour labours to wade through. Of course you wish you could stay.' She smiled. 'But your family needs you, honey. Life goes on. This time together was precious, and I'll think on it often, as will you. I am so grateful to have had you. My brother. And that you were willin' to offer your home to Grace, and to Valerie too? Well. Even though they won't be needin' it just now, it gives my soul peace. You couldn't have given me anythin' more.'

Drew openly wept now. 'You know I meant it, Scarlett. We would love to have them. And the offer stays open. I'll come over whenever I can, and they can visit me. I'll always be there for them, Scarlett. Anything they need.' He turned to Grace, already sitting in the back seat of Samuel's truck, ready to accompany her uncle to the airport. 'Anything, Grace. Just call. Or Skype. And not just when you need something, either. Call me anyway. And email. Facebook. Whatever it is you kids do these days.'

Scarlett took his hand and walked him the short distance to the truck. 'I love you, Drew. You take care now. Give my love to your beautiful family.'

'I love you, sis. God bless you. I'll call you when I'm home.'

Drew climbed in and shut the door. Samuel started the engine, and they slowly pulled away, Drew waving out of the window. 'You look after yourself now. See you soon!'

'See you soon.'

I walked Scarlett back to the blue van, her steps shaky, her sobs wrenching at my heart. Scarlett was weak and often confused, and time had lost all meaning, but this she did know: she would not be seeing her brother soon.

22

Spring and all its hope came to the forest while we weren't looking. The air smelled of sunshine, and the breeze, warmer each day, brought hints of long, lazy days and mild, mellow evenings.

My morning run took me through carpets of tiny flowers now. I tried to dodge trampling on them, at the same time ducking to avoid the boughs of trees, growing longer and greener every time I passed by. Everywhere the air hummed with clusters of insects: midges and butterflies and fat, furry bees. In the vegetable patch beside my caravan, I discovered feathery carrot tops and tomato shoots where I had planted seeds hardly any time ago. Onion and garlic stalks pushed straight up toward the strengthening sun, and the creeping beanstalks sent out curling, brightly verdant shoots to wrap round the canes I had pushed into the bare soil.

Enchanted by the miracle of life blooming in front of me, I wiped down my picnic chairs and table, dragging them around to the other side of the mobile home, facing the vegetables. Enraptured by the forest behind me, I moved one chair back, so when evening came, I could watch the woods. Life. Irrepressible, unconcerned with the comedy and tragedy of the humanity existing alongside it. I fell in love with it all over again.

We had decided to hold our first Fire Night of the year on the Sunday of the May Day public holiday weekend. Although the campsite was jam-packed with guests, all the preparations were running smoothly, and so far there had been no hitches or last-minute disasters, so I took the morning off and cycled to church. I had been back a few times since Christmas Eve, though I wasn't entirely sure why. Initially I hoped to find peace there, a chance to reflect and soak up some quiet; but I discovered that was not likely to happen at Hatherstone Church. The Christmas Eve service had been a one-off, by no means an accurate reflection of what usually went on inside the chapel walls on a Sunday morning.

The pointy-booted minister (whom people called Lara, with no dignifying title) seemed to believe church should resemble a large family gathering rather than a religious occasion. Everybody mucked in, whether it was serving coffee, calling out some crazy, joyous prayer of thanks, or grabbing the microphone and telling us all how God had stepped in and performed an administrative miracle at the Post Office that week. The sermons were often more like wedding speeches – energetic, conversational, passionate, frequently funny, always moving. People actually heckled – calling out jokes, or a question, or whooping. (Whooping! I think Father Francis might have appreciated a whoop.) The songs were in the style of amateur pub-band, accompanied by a gaggle of small children banging percussion instruments and dancing up and down the centre aisle.

I was welcomed but not pressured and always sent home with meals for Scarlett.

But I had a nagging guilty feeling there was another reason I got up early on a Sunday, styled my hair, and dressed up in my growing new wardrobe (growing in the number of items, still shrinking in the size of said items) to go to church. That reason usually sat two rows in front of me. He wasn't a whooper, but one week Reuben had stood at the front to remind the men to let him know if they were coming to the Hatherstone blokes' survival weekend on the Yorkshire moors. He had caught my eye across the rows of people and winked. A warm glow spread up from somewhere in the pit of my stomach that I suspected had nothing to do with the Holy Spirit or the May sunshine beaming through the stained-glass windows.

This Sunday, I hadn't hung around after the end of the service but hurried back to relieve Jake and Valerie, who had been working since eight. I found them both in reception, breaking into a carton of ice-creams.

'Hi, Marion. Ice-cream was invented around 200 BC by the Chinese.'

'I hope those aren't from the original batch. How's it going?'

'Fine. Everything's done. We sold a lot of firelighters, so I added it to the stock list.'

'Great. Do you want to go for your lunch?'

Valerie nodded, too busy licking her cone to reply. She left me with Jake.

'What time are you due to finish?'

He shrugged. 'I'm down until six, but I can stay longer if anything comes up. I was going to do some clearing up around the site, and I'll do the toilet block in a bit if you want to stay on reception.'

'I'll just grab something to eat first, if you don't mind waiting half an hour.'

'Of course. Don't rush.' Jake threw his wrapper in the bin and unfolded a newspaper.

Mr and Mrs Polite, carefully dancing around each other, trying not to step on any toes. Because I had taken on sorting out a lot of the business of the campsite while Jake still worked for Samuel, I had somehow morphed into an interim manager, and theoretically Jake's boss. Of course, Jake had worked at the Peace and Pigs three years longer than me, and while I had more administrative experience, Jake knew how to handle anything that happened beyond the office walls with his hands tied behind his back.

I hesitated at the door. 'Is this working?'

'I fixed the door last week.'

'No. Us. The campsite. Without anyone in charge.'

He grinned. 'I thought you were in charge.'

'I don't know. Scarlett hasn't said anything. I've just done the rotas and tried to get on with it. Do you think we should talk to her? What if something big goes wrong? Or something small. If *anything* goes wrong, I won't know how to deal with it. I can't tell people what to do, or make decisions. And the rent: how are we covering that?'

'You'll be fine. It's working. We're a team.'

I wished I had Jake's confidence. I wasn't authorised, qualified, or capable of running a business. I still wasn't convinced I could manage my own life. I went to see the real owner of the Peace and Pigs.

'Hi, Scarlett.' I had learned, early on, that one of the worst questions a visitor can ask a terminally ill person is 'How are you?' They are dying – that is how they are. There is not much you can say about dying that will start a friendly visit off well. Even if the well-meaning visitor is not shocked or silenced to hear the honest answer, it usually does the ill person no favours to have to spell it out. If they want to talk about it, they will, but I have learned not to ask. A grey complexion, trembling hands, and a soup-stained blouse told me how Scarlett was that Sunday. Valerie and Grace went to their rooms to give us space.

'Can we talk about the campsite? Do you feel up to it?'

A delay of several seconds followed as the words sneaked their way through Scarlett's brain tentacles to her processing neurons, then fought their way out. 'Yes. What's the problem?'

'I need to know who you want to run things while you aren't feeling up to it. What if we need to hire somebody new, or a visitor makes a complaint and asks to see the manager? Or one of us needs a telling-off? At the moment, things are fine and we're working really well together, but you ought to decide who's in charge before anything happens that causes an issue.'

Or, I didn't add, before she was too ill and confused to be able to. Scarlett sat back and closed her eyes. She had lost weight; her cheekbones stood out sharp underneath her skin. I waited while she considered.

'You're right. I thought after the summer Grace might do it, but she'll be in London. I don't think Jake can just now; he ain't strong enough.' She turned her head in my direction, eyes still closed. 'I don't wanna put pressure on you to stay, Marion. Maybe the best thing is to let Fisher have his land back, and Valerie and I'll move in with Samuel. He still seems to want me now I'm sick.'

'Samuel loves you. Next time he asks you to marry him, you should say yes.'

'Now why would I do that? I'm in no mood for sex and I can't be bothered to change my name. With this skin tone, I'd look like I was already dead if I put on a white dress. The photos would be shockin'. And what're we gonna vow? In sickness and in sickness?'

'You'd do it because it would make Samuel happy. And give Grace somewhere to call home and someone she can go to unconditionally. And we could have a party. Stop you whining about how your boobs look like deflated balloons.'

Scarlett smiled.

I said, 'I'm staying. As long as the campsite is here, I'll do my best. I'll take care of Valerie, keep an eye on Grace, and I'll figure out a way to cover the rent rise. As long as I don't have to go near the chickens.'

'You can slaughter them and eat Southern fried chicken at my funeral.'

'How about at your wedding?'

'How about at *your* wedding?' Scarlett patted my hand, slowly. 'Come back tomorrow and I'll give you your first lesson in runnin' things.'

Before I even reached the caravan door, she had fallen asleep. I descended the steps, my bones clacking together with fear. Run the campsite? Take care of Valerie? Cover the rent rise? What on earth was I thinking?

I could hear my mother's voice, braying about my incompetence as a human being, my ability to reach whole new levels of uselessness. I was a failure, a laughing stock, an embarrassment. Walking back to the reception after grabbing a sandwich, I tried to shut out the memory of her taunts, replaying the endless loop of my childhood. *Pathetic. Freak. Spineless.*

Then I stopped just behind the trees lining the rim of the car park, the sandwich in my hand forgotten. This wasn't a hideous flashback.

I could hear my mother's voice.

Either I had finally snapped from the stress, or my mother was actually here, at the Peace and Pigs. In my campsite.

I would have turned and run, but that would have been akin to leaving an escaped crocodile loose in my home. Craning my neck, I peered through a gap in the branches. Could there have been anything worse than the sight of my mother, wearing her best brown coat, standing in the Peace and Pigs car park?

How about watching her shuffle back to allow a burly taxi driver to haul not one, but two giant suitcases out of the boot of his car? Help.

My spine dissolved. I felt as though I had been karate-kicked in my solar plexus. Jake stepped out of the reception to offer some assistance. This propelled me around the treeline. I felt urgently that my mother must not meet Jake. If I could get her to leave without speaking to anyone, meeting anyone, maybe it wouldn't really have happened. She wouldn't have actually been here.

I stopped, panting, a few feet away. Jake was holding out one hand to introduce himself, no doubt explaining that we were fully booked for the bank holiday. I saw her glance across, and then look away again before she realised it was me, and turn back. I tried to lift my chin, fighting the urge to take a submissive stance, grateful I had worn my good clothes while at the same time vividly aware that I had a spot on the side of my nose.

The cogs whirred in Jake's head as we stood there, nobody making the first move.

'Do you two know each other? Shall I leave you to it?' He reversed back into the reception.

Silence like an ocean of treacle lapped between us. I heard the chaffinches calling in the woods to the right of me and the faint cry of Sunny and Katarina's children building a dam in the stream running across the bottom meadow. At the edges of my visual field, I saw the movement of green shadows as the wind rippled through the branches of the oak trees, and the flash of orange and blue where the first row of tents were pitched. Anger uncurled in my chest like an electric eel. This was my home, my haven. I knew if I had opened my mouth then, I would have let out a scream, a howl of protest. My security had been breached, my sanctuary violated.

My mother spoke. 'Hello, Marion. It's good to see you.'

Is it? Last time we talked, you were not happy with me.

'What are you doing here?' I grew even more enraged at the way my voice trembled.

She rolled her shoulders, giving the impression that her coat was too tight. 'I came to see how you were getting on.'

'I sent a card.'

'I wanted to see you, Marion. Is that so hard to believe? That a mother would want to see her daughter after nine months?'

I said nothing. Ma walked around her suitcase, carefully, and took four precise steps toward me, until we were eye to eye. She waited for a long time. She looked different, and wanted me to see it.

'What's going on, Ma? What are you doing here?'

She kept looking at me. This was a message. She had never looked at me.

'I had no other way to contact you. Harriet wouldn't give me your telephone number.'

'That's because I didn't want you to contact me.'

'So what if something had happened? What if somebody got sick, or died? You can't just disappear without any means of getting in touch.'

'Harriet would have told me.'

My mother smiled, hesitant. 'Would you mind if we found somewhere to sit down? Maybe get a cup of tea?'

'Has it?'

'Has what?'

'Has something happened?'

She shook her head. 'No. Not really.'

'Then you don't need to stay. You've seen me. I'm fine. If you need somewhere to spend tonight, then I can give you directions to a hotel. I have nothing to say to you and I don't want to hear anything you might want to say to me.'

'Ah, now, Marion. I've come all this way. Will you not even give me a cup of tea?'

With nowhere else to go, I reluctantly led her to my caravan after asking Jake to cover for me. I made tea, and tried to hide the trembling in my hands as I sliced cheese for sandwiches and buttered bread.

'How have you been?'

'Good, Ma. I've been great.' Living without your continual putdowns and cruelty has been absolute heaven.

'So, you work here?'

'Yes.' There was an awkward pause. I didn't want to fill it. This was not my doing. I spoke anyway: 'How did you find me?'

'Your postcard was sent from Nottingham. And I found the photograph was missing. I knew you would have followed him here.'

'You knew he lived here?'

'Yes. It's where we met.'

Who was this woman in Ma's brown coat who spoke about my father? I stared at her. I was waiting for the sarcasm, the bitter cackle, the jabbing finger.

'What on earth is going on? Last time I mentioned Da, you threw spaghetti at me.'

'I have been ill since you left.'

I waited.

'Worse than before. I was away for five months. The doctors there managed to sort out my medication. And I've had a lot of time to think, and talk to people. It helped me to see. I want you to come home.'

I squeezed my hands over my eyes, determined to keep a grip on myself. To remember who I was now. 'This is my home.'

23

The rest of the day stretched out into a cringe-filled eternity. We circled each other with rigid small talk and, in my case, anger simmering just below the surface. I waited for an apology. I didn't want one – I wouldn't know how to deal with it. I feared I might explode if confronted with one. But how long could this false politeness continue with so much left unsaid? Was this it now? Did I just pretend twenty years of abuse never happened? Had my mother decided to love me? Did she accept responsibility for destroying my childhood? For the damage she caused that I still lived with every day?

I went to Fire Night, introduced my mother, found a spot on a bench next to Scarlett, and ate a very large amount of chicken.

Valerie squinted at my mother. 'Marion's mum! Wow. Marion, your mum came to visit – how cool is that? There are two billion mums in the world, and look, here's yours! Come and have a drink. Did you come all the way from Ireland? Did you come on a plane or a boat? Nearly twice as many people die every year from boats as from planes, but the plane is faster. Did you have a security search?

Did a dog sniff your bag for explosives? Do you need a passport to come from Northern Ireland to England?'

My mother held up her hand. 'Stop.'

Valerie stopped.

'Yes. A plane. Yes. No. No.'

Valerie nodded her head in response to my mother's answers.

'Well? Go on.'

'Oh! Okay. Does it really rain there every day? Marion says it's like a wet towel left on the bathroom floor, but Derry is the second rainiest city in the United Kingdom, not the first; and is it fun being Marion's mum and did you really miss her?'

I ate another drumstick and tried to tune them out.

Ginger was horrified at the thought of my mother staying at a hotel. She offered her a bed for as long as she wanted it at the Hall. My mother refused, politely but firmly. She said the memories were too much. I made up a bed for her in the spare employee's caravan.

Three days later, I still hadn't grown used to my mother's presence at the campsite. Or rather, the mother who didn't criticise, demean, or ignore me. We remained cautious. I avoided spending any time alone with her and had still not ventured further than small talk, but it was just about working for now. I called Harriet, who confirmed that Ma had gone 'bonkers in a bad way' after I had left, and spent several months in hospital again. According to my second cousin's wife, Tanya, the family had been declaring their Jane to be finally her old self again. At last those doctors had managed to get it right and get her sorted. It was a miracle. Nobody made the point that the old Jane hadn't actually been that great to start with. Small mercies.

On hearing about Scarlett's illness, Mum took upon herself the role of carer: cooking, cleaning, and helping with everyday tasks. She was sympathetic toward Grace and Valerie, baking them treats, fussing over them; reminding them if they needed anything, they had only to ask.

I seethed until my volcano of resentment could be contained no longer.

'Ma, I need Valerie on reception now. She can't eat a cooked breakfast and be on time for work.'

Valerie poured herself a glass of orange juice, freshly squeezed by my mother. 'Ha, Marion. Your voice goes all Irishy when you talk to Jane.'

'Does it? That's nice.' I unclenched my teeth. 'Ma, you are making Valerie late. Stop fussing. She can get her own breakfast.'

My mother failed to hear my rising anger, or chose to ignore it. 'Well, yes, she can. But why would she want to do that when I'm here to do it for her?'

'I don't know, Ma.' Here it came, spewing forth, boiling hot lava. 'Did I want to do it when I was seven years old and you decided to lie in bed for three months? Or when I was eight, and nine, and ten, and, oh, yes – you never made me breakfast once in eighteen years. You never made me breakfast, never cleaned it up afterwards for me, and nine times out of ten, you didn't even bother to make sure there was anything in the house to even make a breakfast! I went to school hungry day after day after day when you should have *been there to do it for me*. And what about lunch, and supper, and every other meal of my life? What about my birthday? Were you there to do it then? Or Christmas? I starved because of you. I actually starved.'

I think the ducks on the far side of the lake might have heard me. 'And now, here you are, in my campsite, frying bacon in your best brown coat for a grown woman you barely know who has plenty of others to take care of her!'

She stopped cooking, but stood still facing the stove, a steel rod in her back. 'I didn't know you liked bacon.'

That was when I knew. There would be no reckoning. No apology. No great heart-to-heart where it all got laid out on the table and Ma, weeping with remorse, finally admitted that yes, she had screwed me up as well as my childhood and wrongfully taken out her bitter rage on an innocent, helpless child. That she had ensured I grew up, not without a mother, but, worse, with a cruel, unloving mother who made me believe I had killed my own da. I would never hear her say she got it wrong. I had better suck it up, get used to it, and get on with my life. Perhaps I would even learn to be grateful for the chipped, limping skeleton of a relationship she held out to me now.

I also knew this: I had lived for nine months without bitterness, unhealthy anger or twisty, warped emotions, and I was not going to allow her invasion to end that.

I went to work.

* * *

The following evening, Scarlett strolled by on my mother's arm and invited me back to her caravan for champagne. I walked back with them, trying not to let my frustration show at the slow pace, wondering what on earth we had to celebrate. Was Samuel going to be there? Had Scarlett finally said yes?

Grace was already waiting, picking at the ends of her hair in a pretence at nonchalance. Valerie had no concept of feigning indifference; she bounced up and down on the sofa while Samuel, who *was* there, uncorked a bottle.

When we had all been handed a glass, Scarlett coughed to get everybody's attention. She picked up an envelope from the table and held it out to Grace.

Grace frowned, puzzled, as she took the envelope.

Valerie called, 'Open it up, Grace – faster! What is it?'

Grace pulled out a thin sheet of A4 paper. Her puzzlement transformed into shock, her mouth dropping open. She gazed at the paper, and up at Scarlett, and back at the paper.

'Tell us what it is.' Valerie waved her glass, splashing champagne onto the carpet.

Scarlett smiled, her face glowing, and for a moment, she no longer looked like a woman ravaged by illness. She must have shone that way the first time she ever held her daughter, for she couldn't have displayed her love any clearer than in that moment.

'Grace sold her first pair of shoes.'

'What?' Valerie slopped more champagne. 'Who? Where? How? How much money did you get, Grace?'

It took a while and a lot of Samuel's promptings and reminders, but Scarlett managed to tell us. She had asked Erica to look at Grace's designs, and of course Erica had been enchanted. She had taken a dozen pairs to her office, and her manager had agreed to trial them in the Nottingham store. That was on Wednesday. The first pair had sold by Thursday lunchtime. For three figures. The manager wanted more.

It was almost a perfect evening. We drank champagne and ate cheesecake on the veranda, serenaded by the spring crickets and the bubbling of the brook. Grace got her half-finished shoes out for us to have a fashion parade, up and down the decking. We laughed, and dreamed about Grace's future world domination, when every fashion icon from pop stars to royalty would do anything to get their feet into the latest Grace Obermann.

That was the point in the evening when things got complicated.

'I'm not calling myself Grace Obermann, Mum. I'm going to be Grace Tynedale.'

Scarlett dropped her glass, which splintered on the decking, scattering across the boards. Samuel moved to pick up the pieces while my mother went inside to find a brush. Grace and Scarlett were twin statues in the deepening dusk.

'Don't freak out, okay? This is important to me. Where do you think I learned how to make shoes? And all the stuff. I couldn't have afforded tools and a bench. Do you know how much silk costs?' She took a deep breath, steadying herself.

Scarlett was shaking her head. 'How did I not see that? How could I not have known?' She snorted. 'I thought you'd run off to meet some man. And you did. But that man?'

Grace stood up, tipping her chair over. 'I knew you wouldn't understand. That's why I didn't tell you. I have a right to know him! He's part of me.'

'Oh, honey, you don't know the half of it.'

'Yes, I do. I know he went to prison and I know why. It was sixteen years ago. He's changed now. He served his time. He paid his debt.'

'Really? And what about the debt owed a young girl in a foreign country with no family, no money comin' in, and his baby growin' inside of her? He left me – not once, but twice. And the second time he left, he left you too. Underneath all that flash and charm, he is a liar, and a loser, and a weak, weak man. He will break your heart, Grace. Please don't let him.'

Grace was stark white now, tight with anger. 'He taught me this.' She jerked one of her shoes, a sky-blue court shoe covered in white clouds with a rainbow tassel. 'He gave me this. And how can I not love him? Pretty soon, he'll be the only parent I have.' She began to cry. 'Nobody else will ever love me like you do, except maybe him. I'm scared, Mum. Who will I belong to when you're gone?'

Scarlett crumpled. She opened up her frail arms, unable to lift the left one higher than her waist. Grace fell into her lap, and the rest of us stepped inside, leaving shards of broken glass still sparkling at their feet.

After a while, Scarlett got too cold to stay outside. She and Grace sat on the sofa, arms wrapped tightly around each other, twin streaks of mascara running down each face.

'Well, there you go, folks,' Scarlett drawled. 'You can always trust an Obermann-Tynedale to bring a bang to the party. Anyone else with a bomb to drop before I turn in?'

Samuel twisted his head around from where he was washing up the cheesecake plates. 'I don't suppose this would be a good time to ask you to marry me?'

'Well, heck, Samuel, it seems like as good a time as any.' She rolled her eyes. 'Come on then, I'm tired. Get it over with.'

Samuel stood for a moment, dripping soapsuds onto the kitchen floor. Scarlett sighed, and made as if to get up. He took one easy lope across the caravan and gently pushed her back down onto the sofa.

'Don't you dare.' He kneeled down in front of her, and I had to look away, his expression of tenderness was so raw, so open. 'I have loved you for twenty-one years. I loved you when you gave your heart to another man, even though I knew he would not treat it as you deserved. I loved you when you struggled alone to raise a child and build the Peace and Pigs after you dared to trust him again, and he wounded you once more. And when you swore never to love a man like that again, I loved you still. You are the most remarkable woman I have ever known. The only woman I have ever wanted. I will love you whether you like it or not until the day I die. And, God willing, for an eternity after that. And I will love your wonderful daughters as if they were my own. Now come on, girl. You know I am too old and too ugly to spin you a line or say what I don't mean. Scarlett Obermann? Stop being so darned proud and marry me.'

Scarlett blushed like a young girl. She nodded her head, and the night was perfect once more.

* * *

I had been looking through the Peace and Pigs' books and I felt worried. Christmas had helped, and Valentine's Day; I had raised prices as high as I thought seemed fair, but it wasn't enough. We needed a long-term, sustainable way to boost income, otherwise the holiday park would not be able to survive. The big question was still whether or not it needed to. Or whether, without Scarlett, anyone would want that.

I couldn't talk to Valerie about it. She loved the campsite, as she did everything she cared about, with a purity of strength and commitment most people would not be capable of feeling. Her heart was here, and I feared the pain of losing Scarlett would be the most she could bear for a long time. I spoke to Jake.

'Will you want to carry on here?'

Jake was unloading supplies into the back room. He ripped open a box of toilet rolls and began unpacking them. 'If the Pigs is still a going concern, I'll stay.'

'But?'

'I'm not up for spending the next year stressing out, watching the debt soar, desperately trying to find ways to scrabble a bit more cash together until eventually we have to give up and let the creditors move in.'

'Nice thought.'

'I'm being realistic. You've seen the figures.'

I kicked a box. 'I hate Fisher.'

Jake unpacked the box.

I relented a little. 'No, I don't really. But I hate what he's done. I want to go round to his house and yell in his face, make him understand what it will do to Valerie and Grace. That because of him Scarlett is having to spend her last months worrying about where her children are going to live after she's gone.'

'Why don't you, then?'

'What? You think I should go round and see Fisher?'

'Can't do any harm.'

'Will you come with me?'

'I suppose so,' he sighed. 'So long as you don't yell in his face.'

I spent the rest of the afternoon compiling a document outlining why the rent rise was unreasonable, and how much we could afford to pay to stay viable as a business. I made a plan, detailing the running of the campsite for the next year, and how, if he could introduce the rent increase gradually over a three-year period, we stood a chance of making it work. I even created a spreadsheet. A tiny glimmer of business-womany hope began to grow.

That evening, dressed in the closest thing I had to a suit (a pair of straight-legged navy trousers and my grey cardigan), hair pulled into a tight, professional bun, a slash of plum, I-mean-business lipstick, I picked up Jake and drove to Fisher's house. We sat in the car for a few moments, eyeing up the enemy's lair from the far side of heavy iron security gates. Situated on one of the tributaries that led off Hatherstone High Street, the red-brick house rose in a three-storey main building with a separate garage. Only a couple of years old, it sported four sets of white pillars and a circular pond with a cluster of stone fish in the centre spurting water from each of their mouths. Several stone lions had been dispersed around the edge of the gravel drive.

Jake wound down his window and pressed the intercom. After an initial crackle, someone asked who we were.

Jake leaned back in his seat, gesturing me toward the intercom with his head.

'Hello. It's Marion Miller from the Peace and Pigs Holiday Park. I wanted to talk to Fisher about the business.'

'Now?'

'Yes, please.'

'Is he expecting you?'

'Not really.'

'Wait one moment.'

We waited in the car as one moment dragged by, followed by a lot more moments. Jake kept reminding me to keep cool, present the information, and if that didn't work, to bat my eyelashes and stick my boobs out. Final resort: cry like a baby.

I breathed out, dropped my shoulders, breathed in, paused, imagined saying, 'Good evening, Mr Fisher.' Did it again. And again. Flipped through the papers I had brought. Checked my lipstick. Breathed out.

The gates eventually swung open, and we were let in through the front door by Fisher's wife, Olivia. I was expecting a butler. She led us along plush, cream carpets, past cream doors finished off with gold trim, and under a chandelier far too wide and low for the corridor, before showing us into a study.

Fisher sat behind a vast desk, in front of a wall lined with sets of thick, old-fashioned books. The type an interior decorator buys in, never expecting them to be actually opened and read. I felt angrier already. What a waste of books. He was on the phone, and carried on barking about the close of play and striking while the iron was hot, meanwhile indicating with a wave that we should sit down. A cheap trick designed to intimidate us, and make us feel the weaker party in the room. I was glad. It gave me a chance to run through my mute busters again, and straighten my spine as I reminded myself that Fisher was a pompous idiot and a bully. By the time he came off the phone, I felt ready to rumble.

'So then, Marion, is it?' He ignored Jake. 'I can spare you five.' He flicked his hand at me. 'Go. What have you got?'

'Good evening, Mr Fisher. I'm here to talk to you about the holiday park.'

'What? I can't hear you. Speak up. I don't have time to listen to everything twice.'

I couldn't even hear myself. *Come on, Marion.* Jake squeezed my elbow. I coughed, and breathed.

'I'm here to talk to you about the holiday park.'

'Well, yes, I had gathered that. Has she finally seen sense and agreed to sell?'

'No. Ms Obermann is not planning on selling the business. She wishes to pass on the running of the campsite to me, as she's not well enough.'

Fisher smiled. I now knew what a slug would look like if it had teeth.

'Really? And do you have any business experience? Relevant qualifications? I thought not. Shall we get real for a moment, dear? It is time to let go and move on. Scarlett had a nice little business going there for a while, but the number one rule in this game is knowing when to admit defeat. It's time for her to admit defeat.'

'That isn't your decision.' I blinked to clear the hot anger building behind my eyes. 'It isn't just a business. The Peace and Pigs is a home. What about Valerie and Grace? They already have to face losing their mother. Are you going to force them out as well?'

Fisher began reading a sheet of paper in front of him. 'I'm sorry – why are you here?'

'I want you to revoke the rent rise. Not altogether—' My words speeded up, I sounded garbled and frantic, but I could sense Fisher had already left the meeting. 'But, see, if you look on the spread-sheet, if we lower it by 50 per cent now, then bring in the rest of the increase gradually, over the next three years, giving us time to put up prices and find other ways to make the savings, then—'

He didn't take his eyes off the paper in front of him. 'Well, yes, that is all well and good. Just one point. You see, I neither want nor expect the Peace and Pigs' – he spat out the name – 'to still be here in three, two, or even one year's time. You'll see yourselves out?'

He picked up his phone and dialled as he spoke, swivelling his chair around to begin his conversation before I could process what he had said.

I spoke only once in the car on the way home, which was one more time than Jake.

'I'm going to find a way to meet the rent rise.'

Jake glanced at me. The determination in my voice had his attention.

'We're going to make this business so darn profitable that we can buy the land for ourselves.'

Yes, Marion, of course you are. Why don't you put a bid in for Buckingham Palace while you're at it?

24

In the make-believe world of Hollywood fantasy, once a beautiful, strong, kind woman has been given a few months to live, she writes herself a bucket list and spends those precious last days creating breathtaking memories, sharing wonderful, heart-wrenching moments and seeing her dreams come true. She lives a lifetime of experiences in a matter of weeks, assisted by the touching and achingly thoughtful gestures of her nearest and dearest.

When Scarlett was initially diagnosed, her bucket-list suggestions included a trip to Paris, skydiving (as long as she was strapped to a hunky instructor), swimming with sharks, staying in an ice-hotel to see the Northern Lights and spending the night with Clint Eastwood under the Major Oak.

As her illness took hold, the list of her hopes and dreams changed: to get up and dress herself each morning, to have a croissant for breakfast with black cherry jam, to laugh several times a day, to tell her family she loved them, to not pee on the bathroom floor, to be strong enough to walk beneath the trees again, and to spend the night with Samuel T. Waters under the Major Oak.

Scarlett was retreating. It got harder and harder for her to fight past the tumours in her head and reach us. What could we do for her before it was too late? We had a surprise picnic. I spent three days in Sunny's kitchen preparing cakes and finger foods, enjoying the added bonus of avoiding my mother, who as yet showed no signs of leaving. We put a sign up in reception and visited the midweek guests to ensure they knew there would be no staff on duty for the afternoon, leaving my mobile phone number in case of emergency. Thirty people had been invited – enough for a party but not so many as to overwhelm Scarlett or make her frailty embarrassing to her. We took blankets, picnic chairs, hampers, and ball games to the clearing around the Major Oak, in the heart of the Sherwood Forest country park. On my last trip out here, I had punched Jake and run off into the woods to have a panic attack. A lifetime ago.

The forest was reasonably empty, so we felt no guilt in sprawling out across the grass as we waited for Samuel to bring the guest of honour. We waited a long time, nervously watching the white clouds drifting back and forth across the sun, alternately plunging the clearing into shadow and lifting it with vibrant sunlight. Eventually Katarina, fussing over spoiled food, began opening hampers and laying out plates. Grace untangled herself from Josh and came to stand next to me, leaning on the fence that kept tourists at a safe distance from the ancient tree.

'She's an hour late.'

'I know. She's probably been sleeping. Or changing her mind about what to wear. You know she can't tell the time any more.'

'Samuel can. Mum thinks being late is self-important, a way of letting someone know you consider yourself of greater worth than them; that their time, and therefore their life, is less valuable than yours.'

'Maybe she decided that today she is the most important person. Perhaps she insisted on walking from the car park. You know she thinks she can do more than she actually can. She's okay, Grace. If something had happened, Samuel would have phoned.'

Grace shook her head. 'Except that you need a satellite phone to get a reception here.'

'Don't worry. Go and see if Josh wants a satay chicken stick. They are delicious, if I do say so myself.'

Two hours late, Samuel drove Archie's wagon into the forest, Scarlett waving from the seat beside him in a black and white shift dress that I hadn't seen before. He climbed down and lifted her to the ground. We all clapped and shouted, 'Surprise!'

Samuel called for everyone's attention. We quieted down, and he clasped his strong walnut arm around Scarlett.

'Actually,' she drawled, only a hint of unsteadiness in her voice, 'the surprise is on you.'

Samuel beamed, his teeth gleaming through his beard as the sun emerged from behind a cloud again.

'Ladies and gentlemen, friends and honoured guests. It is my absolute pleasure, my inexpressible delight, to present my wife: Scarlett Obermann-Waters.'

The rest of his speech was drowned out as the friends and honoured guests went wild. My eyes quickly sought out Grace and Valerie across the clearing, anxious to see how they had responded to the news of missing the wedding. With shock and relief, it appeared. They both muscled through the cluster of congratulations to embrace the newly-weds, hanging on long after others had started to hand round plastic glasses of sparkling wine.

Scarlett was ushered to a two-seater camping chair, where she curled up beside her patient husband, a soft throw around her knees, and after toasting and being toasted, she fell asleep.

Erica arrived even later than Scarlett, causing Grace to mouth 'self-important' at me with a knowing smirk. I turned away to hide my smile. Someone else didn't think Erica was perfect. That made two of us out of seven billion. She was slightly flushed, in a wholesome, outdoorsy way, but her eyes jerked about, betraying that there was more to it than that.

I have no excuse, beyond sheer nosiness, but when she swished down beside Reuben on a blanket, I wandered close enough to listen under the pretence of helping myself to another smoked salmon blini. They kissed briefly.

'I thought you had to work. Doesn't the Prebble deal need signing off today?'

Erica wriggled with suppressed excitement. 'I walked out.'

'You mean you resigned?'

'Ssshhh! Keep your voice down. I don't want my news to detract from Scarlett and Samuel's day.'

I didn't think Erica had to worry too much about that, and from the look on Reuben's face, neither did he.

'So, what are you going to do? If you resigned, you won't be entitled to a pay-out. Have you really thought this through?'

Erica leaned closer to him. 'I have another offer. It means slightly less money, and I'll have to let the flat go, so I can manage and keep the car.'

Reuben waited for her to explain. I nibbled on my third blini, willing her to hurry up before my stomach reached capacity.

'Daddy wants me to manage his new venture. It's an amazing opportunity, with tons of scope for potential. And' – she trailed one finger slowly down Reuben's bare arm – 'it means I get to work close to you. Much, much closer. Close enough to live at the Hall.'

Reuben didn't move. He took a long minute to reply. 'You can't stand the countryside. Isn't that the whole reason why for two years we've been at stalemate? Now you're inviting yourself to move in?'

Erica sat back. 'I don't have to move in if you don't want me to. I know about your old-fashioned notions of propriety. But aren't you pleased that we will actually get to see each other more than once a fortnight? We can have a proper relationship again.'

'Don't take a job simply to be near me. Your career matters too much to you, and you know it.'

'I told you, it's a great opportunity. A new challenge.'

'Round here?'

Erica looked down at her feet, demurely curled under her skirt. 'Daddy wants me to run the campsite. He's drawn up some amazing plans for expansion, to turn it from a failing, tatty trailer park into a luxury holiday village. The kind of place where people like us would want to spend our money: contemporary, hip, low carbon-footprint, but with all the latest equipment. Secluded cabins with private hot-tubs, wood-burning stoves, and a personal chef to prepare meals made with ingredients from Sherwood Organics. Like a top-class hotel but in the forest.'

I could hear the frown in Reuben's voice. 'I thought Scarlett wasn't selling.'

'Well, no, not *yet*. But in a few months.'

'Ownership of the Peace and Pigs business is passing to Samuel and Grace. Marion's going to run it. I hear she's going to look after Valerie.'

'Yes, but with the new rent increase, they can't afford to keep going as they are. Do you really think Marion can run a business, take it forward, make it into something that can grow and last? She can't even make a bowl of pasta! Oh, don't worry, I'll find something for them all to do. We'll still need cleaners and groundsmen.'

'Marion has been working at the campsite nine months longer than you. You have no idea what experience she has. Part of running a successful business is getting along with your employees. You can't just force your way in and expect it to work.'

Erica's cheeks flushed deep pink. She no longer bothered to keep her voice down. 'You don't think I can do it?'

'I don't think you *should* do it.'

'I'm doing this for us, Reuben, so that we can actually spend some time together! So I don't feel as if you have a whole separate life where you end up with other women in your kitchen half-naked. You spend enough of your time hanging around that scabby park. This way, you get to do it with me. And when you finally become Lord Hatherstone, we can use some of the wasted land on the estate to grow the business even more. Make a whole forest resort, with shops and restaurants and sports facilities. Can't you see I'm doing this for us – for our future?'

Reuben stood up. 'Of course. You can't cope without shops and restaurants on your doorstep, can you? You've got it all figured out, you and Daddy – what you're going to do with my land, my family's home, to make your fortune. Perhaps we should turn the Hall into a luxury low-carbon-footprint hotel while we're at it? Don't worry about my parents. They can clean bathrooms and make beds as well as anyone.'

Erica, chastened, scrambled to her feet and followed him as he began to walk away. 'Okay, I'm sorry. The estate land was going a bit too far. But the rest – it's going to happen anyway. At least with me in charge we can show some sympathy to the park's history.'

Reuben stopped. He removed Erica from his arm. Most of the guests were now watching from their deckchairs and blankets. 'Please can we talk about this another time?'

'All right. But where are you going?'

'Lucy needs a walk. Why don't you offer your congratulations to the happy couple before they find out you're planning on destroying their home and their business?'

* * *

I stayed awake most of that night, my head churning with figures and data and profit margins. Erica was right, of course. I had no idea how to turn a failing business around. The conclusion I reached in the end went like this: the Peace and Pigs Holiday Park was a thriving business, run well. I had checked out other rates in the area and even our previous rent had been high. Fisher trying to run us out was the only reason things had become unworkable. Still, he owned the land and had the right to fix his rent, however unfair the increase might be. And I couldn't see any way of making more money out of the business as it stood; there were no more corners to be cut. We needed some way of generating extra income. Something akin to the Christmas grotto, but lasting all year round. I kept thinking, and by morning a tiny green shoot of an idea had begun to sprout.

I decided to go into the village to speak with Jo, my friend at the café. We had chatted a few times at church now, and got on pretty well. We both enjoyed reading, and Jo had invited me along to join her book group. I had been disappointed to have to turn down my first ever potential girls' night out, but things were too hectic at the site.

I was taking my car to the village, as the bike had a puncture. As I unlocked it, my mother appeared.

'Good morning, Marion. Are you well today?'

Good morning. I was still on red alert, always watching for signs that my real mother was going to rear her vicious head.

'I'm fine. How are you?'

'Grand, thank you. Are you heading to the village?'

'Yes.'

'Would you give me a lift? I hear there's a good clothes stall at the market today, and if I don't find myself something cooler to wear, I'm never going to make it through the summer.'

This felt like a bullet barrelling through my stomach and

embedding itself in my guts. Still, I was unable to ask her what she meant. *Through the summer?* As in the whole season? Right the way out the other side? Wasn't that what 'through' meant? Was she planning on never going home?

'So? Will you give me a lift?'

'Get in.'

We drove in silence. Ma knew I was more than a little wary of her attempts at reconciliation. The truth was, I still felt angry and hurt, and annoyed that her presence reminded me constantly of my past; of who I had been, and why. I wanted nothing more than for her to leave. I mused as I sped down the country lanes that perhaps if I pretended all was forgiven and we were okay now, she might consider her mission accomplished and go. Something to think on.

I parked close to the market. It was a measure of my bitterness that I didn't want her to see where I was going. Not because it was a secret. I simply didn't want her in my life or my business, or knowing anything about me. We arranged to meet back at the car in half an hour and I slipped across to the café.

Inside felt pleasantly cool. An elderly couple sat at one table sharing a pot of tea, and four local labourers occupied another, polishing off the café's famous Outlaw's Breakfast. Jo stood behind the counter by the till, flicking through a copy of the paper.

'Hi, Marion. What can I get you?'

'Tea, please. And a piece of carrot cake.'

She deftly filled a mug and slipped a piece of cake from inside the display case onto a plain white plate, then offered me milk from a metal jug, and a sachet of sugar. I declined both.

'Do you have a few minutes to chat?'

She checked the clock. Ten-thirty, still a long while to go before the lunchtime rush.

'Sure.'

Sitting at a corner table, I described to Jo my idea of creating somewhere to eat at the campsite. Not quite a café or a restaurant, but a place that would attract visitors to stop in for food or a drink throughout the day, and provide a place for families to hang out in the evenings. I was imagining live music, a well-stocked bookcase, maybe a crate of Lego. Nothing loud or tacky, but a homely environment and high-quality food – a venue able to draw in not only campsite visitors, but local people and tourists as well.

'I don't want to compete with the café. I'm thinking more of a brasserie. Or a deli that sells food to eat in as well. What do you think?'

'It sounds like a great idea,' said Jo. 'At the moment, if anyone around here wants to go out for a meal, they have to drive for miles, or spend a fortune on a taxi. Even the local chippy is a village away. You should do take-away too.'

'You aren't worried we'd steal your customers?'

'Marion, we have a fixed market here. The people who come into my café want grease, builder's tea and sandwiches on white sliced bread. I make a comfortable living. I'm not interested in opening up evenings, and when I tried serving paninis, I sold five in a fortnight. People come here because it's tourist-free, they can hear the goss, read the paper in peace, and it's cheap. Go for it. And you can reserve me a table for opening night.'

'It's a big project. We'll need a building and tons of equipment, and then there's all the legal side of things. I was half hoping you'd tell me it's a rubbish idea and I'd better forget it.'

'Nah, not me, love. Life's too short to sit on a dream. Why don't you ask Vanessa at church to give you a hand? She used to manage a restaurant in Newark before her twins were born.'

I sat and scribbled menu options on a paper napkin until it was time to meet my mother. Could it work? What was the percentage of new businesses failing? Wasn't it 99.9 per cent or something? We would need a loan to start with. And could it even make enough to cover the rent anyway? If not, it was pointless. I had a lot of research to do, and definite figures to research and calculate. I needed to look at building costs and staffing. I felt as if I stood at the bottom of a huge snow-capped mountain, gazing up a winding track strewn with glaciers, gaping ravines and deadly beasts. If I didn't pack the correct equipment in my ruck-sack, or plot the route carefully enough, and if I didn't ensure I had the right team to come with me, it would be disastrous. But I had planted my first step on the path to the top. The summit looked inviting, and I was going to do everything I could to reach it.

My mother hadn't shown up by the car. I went to look for her at Amanda's stall, where I found her gathering together a bunch of bulging carrier bags. *Please let her not have bought leopard print or something with a fringe.*

'Sorry, Marion. It took longer than I thought to find something suitable. Strapless is not a good look on a woman my age.' She grimaced at Amanda, sporting her usual boob tube three inches below flattering. It matched her new yellow hair.

I hadn't seen Amanda since Reuben had cornered her last month. She refused to make eye contact as my mother fumbled in her purse for the right money.

'Still here, then.'

'Yes.'

'Still poking around in people's private business? Or are you too busy trying to keep Fisher's hands off the campsite?'

I ignored her, picking up two of the carrier bags and starting to move away. Amanda's partner, Jen, walked up, carrying a cardboard box. 'Can you help me sort these handbags out, Amanda? I've got three more boxes in the van.'

My mother froze, her bags dangling from each hand. She muttered to herself the name 'Amanda' and stared hard at the woman in front of her. I could see something stirring inside, a tornado gathering energy, building in intensity.

'It's you, isn't it?'

Amanda took a couple of bags out of the box and hung them on the end of one of the clothing rails.

Ma spoke louder. 'It is you. It must be.'

Amanda twisted her snaky head to look at me and then my mother. The pieces clicked into place. 'That's your mum?'

I nodded. A shadow of fear flitted across her face.

'You evil bitch!' My mother snarled the words, her withering expression everything I remembered and more. 'Look at you. Look at you! Strumping about with your market stall and your cheap clothes and trampy hair. Living your life as easy as you please. Have you no shame?' Working herself up as she spoke, she flung the bags of clothes at Amanda. 'Keep your clothes! I would freeze to death before I put on a stitch of your wares, you lying, cheating hussy. Do you know what you did to him? And what price have you paid? What price?'

Amanda recovered. She folded her arms, leaning close to my mother, her features dripping with venom. 'You don't know what you're talking about. Only one person alive knows what really happened, and that's me. You ain't got no proof of nothing. This is my town. Either keep your mouth shut or get out. If I have to make you, I will. I'll slice that pretty smile off your daughter's face to start with. You know what's at stake. You know what I'm capable of.'

Jen returned with a second box just in time to see my mother slap Amanda full in the face. Jen stepped forward smartly and grabbed Amanda's arm before she could retaliate, as I moved in front of Ma. Jen dragged Amanda away, still cursing and snapping, while I pulled Ma in the opposite direction, leaving the bags strewn across the tarmac. I shoved her into the car and sped off as fast as I dared along the main street on market day.

Ma shook uncontrollably, her teeth chattering together despite the car's baking interior, and she looked ready to pass out. It took only minutes to reach the campsite, where I hustled her out of the car and down the path to my caravan. I made us tea with two spoonfuls of sugar each and forced her to drink some before I asked her what on earth had just happened.

'That woman. It was her. I know it was.'

'This is to do with Daddy, and what happened before he left Hatherstone?'

'Yes. It was her. Her fault. She did it, she made him leave.'

'What did she do?'

'Henry told me everything.'

'What did he tell you?'

'His name wasn't even Henry. Not before that night. Before her.'

'Ma.' Running out of patience, I shook her shoulder gently. 'Tell me what happened.'

'That woman killed Henry Hatherstone.'

25

That was all Ma would say. Her lips clamped shut in their trademark scowl, and I knew nothing would prise them open. But I could think about nothing else as I prepared lunch, slicing freshly picked tomatoes and cucumbers, tossing them with balsamic vinegar before adding a hunk of feta cheese and a handful of olives. By the time I had eaten, I had made it past 'wow' to consider if what Ma said made any sense. I had a live grenade ticking in my pocket. How long was the fuse? What should I do with it?

I ran out of time to spend on the Daniel-Henry-Amanda issue that day. I'd promised to take Scarlett for her appointment at the oncology department of Nottingham City Hospital, and other things soon occupied my mind. How could she not know the time or the day, forgetting it the second after I had told her, have no awareness or interest in where we were going or why – yet she could discuss the finer details of food hygiene certificates and public liability insurance?

Dr Thakkar, sombre and sympathetic, never let us feel for a moment that she had a queue of equally desperate and dying patients waiting, who also needed her time and expertise. She answered every question, writing her responses down so they weren't forgotten. She listened to Scarlett's repetitive rambling, and sat handing over tissues as her patient uncapped the lid on all the pain and frustration she had tried to keep sealed off from Grace and Valerie.

We talked about hospice care. That was a short, sharp conversation.

The doctor offered to arrange an appointment for a Macmillan nurse to visit. That conversation took longer, but I persuaded Scarlett it was only fair to her family to accept all the professional help on offer.

She may or may not have realised that we could no longer safely leave her alone. Scarlett had filled the blue van with gas from an unlit stove, tried to eat a piece of chicken only partially cooked, and slipped twice getting in and out of the shower. Samuel had moved in, rather than the other way round, hoping familiar surroundings would support her memory and orientation in daily tasks. However, even with a manager in place, running a 150-acre farm demanded working hours similar to those of big-shot city lawyers or a mother of quadruplets. Samuel couldn't be with her all the time. Grace's final exams began in a week, and Valerie also had to divide her time between college and the campsite. I had to face the truth, much as it made me squirm: my mother was the one keeping Scarlett out of the hospice. Until we had proper carers in place, no way could I encourage her back onto a plane to Ireland.

I asked Ma to tell me what she knew about Amanda, and Henry's death.

She shook her head. 'Some things are better left forgotten. I shouldn't have said anything.'

I explained how Archie and Ginger believed Henry had committed suicide; that they blamed themselves, and the guilt had nearly destroyed Archie.

She replied, 'I'm not even sure what happened anyway. I probably got it all wrong. The coroner would have been correct.'

I ranted for another few minutes. She began to hum the theme tune to *Coronation Street*.

While imagining tightening my fingers around her throat until I had squeezed the truth out, I kept calm enough to inform her in level tones that I would be heading up to the Hall to tell Reuben what she had said that morning. She shrugged her shoulders, scrubbing the pile of freshly dug potatoes I had tipped onto Scarlett's outside table, as if I had told her I was popping to the loo. But before stalking away, I noticed the two lines etched between her brows were more pronounced than they had been since she arrived in England. Her knuckles were bright white as she scraped at the soft peel.

Reuben answered the kitchen door. A bowl of pasta in a cream sauce stood on the table.

'Have you eaten? There's plenty, if you want any.'

'No, thanks.' I hadn't eaten, but my stomach felt full of rocks.

I helped myself to a glass of water, sitting at the table while Reuben ate. He tried to make small talk, but he could see I hadn't just dropped by for a chat.

'What's happened?'

I described the scene at the market that morning and the conversation with Ma when we got back. The rest of the pasta went cold. Reuben swore softly.

'She won't tell you what she meant?'

'No. Prison and torture won't get her to open her mouth unless she wants to.'

'Amanda might crumble under the right sort of pressure.'

'Admit to murder? That'd have to be a lot of pressure. She's already threatened to maim me, without knowing what Ma has accused her of.'

I spoke casually, but inside my head my thoughts were running around in panic. *She wants to maim me!* I kept my eyes focused on the table. Reuben poured us both more water.

'I can't see much point in getting Brenda involved. She would only want to speak to your mum.'

'Ma thinks that anyone in authority is stupid, lazy, or corrupt. Except for the police. They are stupid, lazy *and* corrupt. If you want to make doubly sure she keeps schtum, call Brenda.'

Reuben thought for a moment. 'There is always a chance she was lying.'

'Why would she do that?'

'Maybe she's jealous? Amanda was an old friend of your dad's. Maybe she was more than a friend. It's hard to imagine Amanda having a platonic relationship with any man.'

I considered this. 'Even so, you didn't see her. Ma wasn't lying.'

'Okay, she believes Amanda killed Henry. That doesn't make it true.'

'My da lied? Are you saying *he* killed Henry, then fled to Ballydown, took Henry's name, and told Ma that Amanda did it?'

Reuben didn't answer.

'No. If he killed his best friend' – my voice broke on the words – 'he might have run off if he was young and scared, but he would never have blamed someone else. Not a teenage girl. His friend.'

'Even if they had something going between them, she wasn't his girlfriend by the time he spoke to your mum. Maybe something happened between Amanda and Henry? Daniel could have been the one who was jealous. Maybe he saw Amanda with Henry and lost it. Then blaming Amanda enabled him to live with it. Maybe he convinced himself it was her fault.'

'My father wasn't a murderer. And if it had been an accident, he would have confessed. He was brought up by your parents; they took him in and treated him as their son. He wouldn't have done that to them.'

'How old were you when he died, Marion?' Reuben asked it gently, but I could hear the implication behind the question.

'That doesn't matter. My father was a good man.' Whatever that meant. I thought about Father Francis, about a boat with a hole in it in the middle of a muddy lake in a storm. My father was a good man. I seethed at the injustice that he could not be here to prove it.

'If Da killed Henry, why is Amanda so keen on keeping me from finding out the truth? You can't believe she would sneak about throwing bricks through windows to protect the memory of a boyfriend from thirty years ago?'

'No, I don't. I think Amanda killed Henry.'

'Then why are you accusing my da?'

'I'm not. But next time Amanda does, I want you to be quite certain she's not telling the truth.'

'Oh.' I picked at a scratch on the table for a minute.

Reuben leaned back, comfortable with silence.

'Thanks. For listening to me about this, for helping me out.'

He shrugged. 'It's for my benefit too, if I can find out what really happened to my brother.'

'Well, anyway, it's good to know that if my bloody remains are discovered on the caravan floor, you can point Brenda in the right direction.'

'No problem.' Reuben stood up and filled the kettle, setting it to heat on the stove.

'So, will you stay for a coffee? I want to hear your grand plan to save the campsite and provide me with some extra business.'

'What? I have only told two people about that today, and one of them has no short-term memory.'

'Ah, but I happened to deliver a box of salad to the other one this afternoon.'

I told him my plans, keeping them vague and half-hearted, watching for signs that he thought I was an idiot.

'Sounds good.'

'Really?' A hot flush raced up my neck to my face. 'You think I can do it?'

'Not by yourself. But you aren't a fool, Marion. You'll get help when you need it. If I had any doubts, it would be that you're over-cautious. Don't spend so long asking for advice and making sure everything is done right that you don't get around to opening before it's too late.'

'That's why I'm going to start small, with a kiosk and an outside eating area, like we did at Christmas. I'll do drinks and homemade ice-cream, strawberries, pancakes. Maybe get Jake to build a barbeque and let his band play at weekends.'

Reuben looked at me. I couldn't read the expression in his velvet eyes. 'You owe me dinner.'

'What?'

'If you are planning on opening a professional eatery, kiosk or no kiosk, I am assuming your cooking lessons have been successful.'

'Yes, I think so.'

'So, what happened to "If you can manage to teach me how to cook, I promise I'll make you a slap-up dinner"?'

'I'm not sure Erica would like you having dinner with me.'

Reuben kept his gaze steady. 'Who I have dinner with is no longer any of Erica's business.'

I nearly choked on my coffee.

Who could I tell about cooking a three-course dinner for Reuben without them taking it the wrong way? Was there any way I could casually drop it into the conversation without it being glaringly obvious how I really felt about it?

How did I really feel about it?

Sweaty, jumpy, tongue-tied, and flappy.

Grace asked me why I was cooking crab cakes for the second time in two days.

'I'm practising.'

'For what? The annual crab cake-athon?'

'I'm cooking dinner for a friend.'

'Jo won't care how nice your crab cakes are, as long as there is a massive pudding.'

'It isn't Jo.' I turned away to hide the fact that my head had turned into a tomato.

'You haven't got any other friends.'

'Thanks for pointing that out. Aren't you my friend? Or Valerie?'

'You are practising making crab cakes for dinner with Valerie?' Grace pointed her embroidery scissors at me from the caravan sofa.

I went back to flipping my cakes.

Twenty seconds later, she gasped. 'It's a man! You have a date! It's a friend you want to be more than a friend!'

I turned off the heat and reluctantly swivelled to face her. I knew that to protest would be futile. I couldn't stop jiggling.

'Grace, I will tell you everything if you promise me two things.'

'Yes, I promise! Tell me ev-e-ry-thaaang.'

Oh dear.

'You must never, ever repeat this information or talk about it to anyone, unless I say that you can. Especially the person involved. And you mustn't take the mickey or turn this into something it's not. I am really trying to be normal and mature and nonchalant about this. I am terrified of acting like a stupid girl with a pathetic crush.'

'Hmmm. They are highly boring promises, designed to minimise any fun I could derive from this situation. That is not an easy decision. Maybe I'll have to call round every night until I catch you eating dinner with your secret lover instead.'

'Grace! If this goes wrong, the only way I can avoid dying of embarrassment is to move back to Ireland, leaving you with my mother.'

'I like Jane. She makes me breakfast. That sounds like a reasonable swap.'

I wrung my hands, trying to think of a way to keep this under control. 'I am on the brink of cancelling this as it is. I really need a friend here, Grace.'

'I thought you had a friend. One worth making crab cakes for.' She laughed. 'All right! I promise – what was it? – to never repeat anything about your new boyfriend ever to anyone, and not to tease you about it. Now spill.'

'Remember I had some cooking lessons in the autumn?'

She did.

'I made a bet with Reuben that if he managed to teach me how to cook, I would make him dinner. That's why I'm practising. Because it's like my end of course exam. It isn't a date.'

Grace's mouth had dropped open at the name Reuben.

'It isn't a date!'

'So then why all the secrecy, the red face, and the ants in your pants?' She grinned. 'You want it to be a date. You fancy Reuben.'

'All the secrecy is because I can't handle the inevitable nudges and winks and jokes because I'm cooking a posh meal for a man. Yes, I do want it to be a date. I do fancy Reuben and I am majorly freaking out about it. Happy?'

She grinned wider. 'Very.'

* * *

Friday morning, the first in June and the day of my non-date, I spent shopping in Nottingham with Grace. Not for food – I had done that already – but for what Grace described as a 'Reuben-ishous' outfit. She prepped me in the car park.

'Okay. I wrote down Mum's lesson on dressing for a first date. This is our brief.' She unfolded a scrap of paper and began to read in a perfect Southern drawl. 'One: no trashy or flashy. If he's watchin' to see if your boob pops out, he ain't listenin' to ya. Two: make an effort. Be yourself, but your best self. Three: wear shoes you can walk in. Stumblin' about or hobblin' like an old horse is not a good look. Four: wear somethin' you feel confident in. There is nothin' sexier to a man than a woman who is comfortable with herself. Not to a decent, well-adjusted man, anyhow. That's it.'

I tried on a million outfits that morning. Nothing felt right. I was looking for that perfect combination of '*Wow – I have never noticed before that you are the most gorgeous woman I have ever seen*' and at the same time appearing not to have made an effort. '*This old thing? I've had it for ages.*'

I knew that clothes couldn't transform me into a different person or add six inches to my legs. I knew Reuben had seen me sprawled in a ditch splattered with mud, covered in bruises from being hit by a car, standing in my underwear with a boiled chest, and wearing nothing but chicken poop. There was no perfect outfit. He liked me or he didn't. Or so I told myself. Then Grace handed me a deep-blue dress with a fitted waist and a full skirt. It had thin straps and a neckline that was low enough to be flattering without showing more than a hint of cleavage. It looked simple enough to be casual, but elegant enough to make me feel like an actual grown-up woman; the type of woman who has handsome male friends around for dinner without breaking into a sweat whenever she thinks about it. I swished the skirt in front of the changing-room mirror. It fitted perfectly. I even looked a teensy bit sexy.

Grace offered me the blue heels with the stars on. I accepted them tentatively, praying that Reuben wouldn't turn up in his work trousers and holey T-shirt. I would keep watch through the window and if he walked up in his muddy boots, I'd quickly swap the shoes for flip-flops.

Phew. Non-dates were exhausting. Candles? Eat inside? Or outside behind the van where no one could spot us? Music? Wine? I was out of my depth, treading water and praying for a lifeboat to come and get me out of this.

In the end, the non-date dilemmas mostly solved themselves. My tiny caravan filled up with so many dirty pots, empty food packets, and fish smells that eating outside became the only option. Candles would be pointless as it didn't get dark until after ten. Eating on the grass made music impossible unless I had it blaring so loudly through the caravan window that it would attract unwanted attention. Reuben brought a dusty bottle of wine from the Hall cellars.

'I didn't know what to bring to go with the food you've made, but most of the wines from our cellar are good enough to work with anything.'

He had dressed in a smart pair of jeans and a shirt. I had only seen him wearing a shirt once or twice before. This one was a very dark grey that made his eyes appear deep navy. Like the ocean at night. I wondered if Erica had brought him the shirt from her work.

I carefully took the bottle without touching his hand, and walked around the side of the van to put it on the table.

'Can I get you a drink?' I sounded like a puppet on the arm of a terrible ventriloquist.

'I'll open the wine, if you show me where a corkscrew is.'

'I'll fetch one. The caravan stinks of fish. It's really bad. I mean, the fish isn't bad. That'll taste great. I hope. It just smells bad. I can't stop saying bad.'

Reuben's mouth twitched. No doubt Erica never suffered from verbal diarrhoea.

By the time we settled down to eat our fishcake starters, I had begun to calm down. I pretended to have been nervous about the meal rather than the company. He seemed to buy it. Then he ruined it again.

'You look really lovely, by the way.'

I knocked over my wine glass.

After I had cleaned up the mess and picked my crab out of the wine puddle on my plate (silently praising God that it had missed my dress), Reuben took the hint and reverted back to being my cookery teacher.

'If I tell you the food is first class, will you knock the pot of sweet chilli sauce over?'

'*Is* it okay?'

He nodded. 'You must have had a mighty fine teacher.'

Oh, yes. My teacher was definitely mighty fine.

My meticulously planned, perfectly practised main course of mustard chicken and dauphinoise potatoes with Sherwood Organics' baby carrots and French beans also turned out a success. Reuben pretended to be surprised. I would carry to my grave the secret that I had eaten mustard chicken and dauphinoise potatoes every night for the past eight days.

We sat under the hazy evening sunlight, the music of crickets and songbirds far superior to anything in my music collection. Our conversation meandered through work, the Hall, and what to do about Amanda. I shared the skin on the top of the rancid custard that is my childhood. Reuben was interested to hear I had struggled with my mother, and was quietly appalled when I hinted at how deep that fissure had run. We talked until the shadows stretched out from the treeline right across the clearing to where we sat.

Then came a pause in our conversation. Reuben poured me another drink, and in that moment, an awkward tension descended over the table. Suddenly we were not two friends, a cookery teacher and his student, but a man and a woman, sitting together in the semi-darkness, alone. Every movement as Reuben leaned back in his chair and ran his fingers through his hair seemed magnified, significant. I couldn't look at him. I could sense my skin growing warmer, and suddenly my hands were too big.

'Marion. I wanted to ask you... is this a date?'

Pardon me?

'I mean, do you want it to be a date? Because, well...'

'I forgot the lemon tart.'

'What?'

I pushed back my chair and practically ran back around the caravan and stumbled up the steps. Marion Miller – just when you thought she was becoming almost normal.

When I stepped inside the living area, I noticed my phone was lit up. I had just missed a call. And five earlier calls. Valerie burst through my front door. 'Marion, why haven't you been answering your phone?'

The lemon tart remained in the fridge.

It was a pulmonary embolism. A blood clot in her lung. Samuel had found Scarlett collapsed and barely breathing on her bedroom floor. We were allowed a glimpse of her, a brief kiss and a rushed hello, I love you and goodbye, before her doctors hustled us into the relatives' room. They didn't need to tell us it was serious. When a doctor in a major A&E department looks worried, you know you should be worrying too.

So we worried, and prayed, and cried, and held each other's hands.

We called Dr Drew, who booked a seat on the next flight across the Atlantic.

We called Jake, and Katarina.

We waited.

* * *

Two hours after we had arrived, the doctor told us Scarlett's condition was far from stable. They were working hard to break up the massive clot, but the pressure on her heart was extremely dangerous. They would have to stop her heart and restart it again. Because of the severity of her condition, this would be complicated, carrying a higher-than-normal risk. It might not save her.

Grace, Valerie, and Samuel were given five minutes to say good-bye. Scarlett was nearly invisible behind the oxygen mask, wires and drips. She looked like a little girl, wrapped inside the folds of the hospital gown. The machines beeped and five doctors checked and adjusted equipment while her family tried to find a clear space on her body to stroke her skin and whisper words to convince her to stay.

Three more hours. I found a machine selling hot brown liquid it called coffee that smelled even worse than the hospital corridors. It is a strange thing, the weird flip between emotions that accompanies such an intense situation. We were in fits of laughter about Valerie's description of £500-a-cup coffee beans found in Sumatran wildcat poo and how the hospital sold shit coffee for £1.50, when the doctor returned.

She had gone.

26

Scarlett had spoken to Samuel about her funeral.

'It don't matter to me what y'all do with me. Parade me through the streets in a glass coffin pulled by six white horses, or wrap me in a blanket and bury me in the woods. I'll not be there to give an owl's hoot. But you do what's right for my girls, Samuel. They are what matters now. And I trust you to know what that is. As long as the ones who will miss me have a chance to say goodbye, and give each other a hug, you can figure out the rest however you want.'

So, ten days after he lost his wife, three and a half weeks since he had married her, twenty-one years on from giving her his heart, Samuel buried Scarlett Obermann-Waters in the depths of the forest she had loved, with the loud-laughed Lara conducting the service wearing leather trousers and a bandanna. No doubt Scarlett would have approved.

The whole of Hatherstone turned up to the back meadow where we had set up folding chairs borrowed from the church, and hung garlands in the bright colour signifying the woman we were gathering to honour. Everybody wore a red flower, and many more were laid upon her coffin and scattered across the grass. Drew and

Samuel, Archie and Reuben, Sunny and Jake bore her from the hearse to the front of the meadow as Grace and Valerie walked behind, not weeping now, but chins held high as their mother had taught them. When Katarina's children, dressed in nothing but red shorts, sang 'She'll Be Coming Round the Mountain' (for reasons known only to themselves), we all joined in through our tears.

We followed the service with a party in the Hall barn. The one rule was that everybody had to dance for at least one song. I danced for nearly every single one. And in between songs I mingled, and smiled, and hugged, and asked 'How are you?' – and really listened to the answers. That was my tribute to Scarlett.

Where on earth would I have been without her?

My conversations with Reuben had been brief and grave since our meal. The few times I had seen him, it had been hard to concentrate with that unfinished sentence yelling and thrashing about in the back of my brain. *Because, well...* what? Because I hope that it is, and that we have many more, and finish with one long date involving rings and babies and you becoming Lady Hatherstone? Or because you are a nice enough girl, but I've just come out of a serious relationship. And it isn't you, it's me and you aren't really my type, I see you as a friend, but it will never be more than that and...

I was boring myself.

I got my answer when I dashed to the loo during the 'Macarena'. Reuben stood in the shadows behind the barn, Erica in front of him. He was holding her hand, speaking with his head bent close to hers. I had seen her at the service, in a white dress covered in red roses, a pair of Grace's heels on her feet. She looked worse than she should have done, considering how well she actually knew Scarlett. She had tried to hide it with make-up, but her skin was wan, her eyes flat.

I scurried past before they saw me, and tried to smother the searing pain that ripped across my chest. I told myself that it was better to have found out before I made a fool of myself, and congratulated myself for running away the other night at precisely the right moment.

Erica was beautiful, successful, and feminine. She would make a great Lady Hatherstone one day. And at least if she stayed with Reuben, he could keep her from destroying the Peace and Pigs, if it came to it. Yes, on reflection, I thought Reuben and Erica getting back together was absolutely for the best. For the good of the campsite. Absolutely.

Another good reason to keep dancing right next to the speakers where I could hear no one's attempt at conversation. Nor think. Nor feel anything but the vibrations of the bass.

As the evening wore on, and Samuel prepared to take the exhausted Grace and Valerie back to his farm, where they had been staying since coming home from the hospital, a man stepped into the barn. I didn't recognise him, but a collective hiss, as half the partygoers sucked in their breath all at once, suggested a lot of people did. He was huge, towering over every man in the room, and carrying the kind of bulk that speaks of muscle gone to flab. Dressed in a black suit fitting smoothly over his massive frame, he wore a scarlet tie over a crisp white shirt.

He paused in the doorway, scanning the crowd, his expensive clothes at odds with his nervous demeanour. When his gaze alighted on Grace, she broke away from Samuel and moved forward.

The man smiled and held out his arms, and as Grace smiled back, I realised who he was. She grasped hold of his arm and turned to an impassive-faced Samuel. 'This is my dad.'

He tilted his head down once in acknowledgement. 'Yes. We've met.'

The man held his hand out. 'Samuel.'

Samuel hesitated before glancing at his stepdaughter, who was pumping out a mixture of fear and hope. 'Johnny. You're late. But I guess I'm glad you made it.'

Big Johnny. Otherwise known as Jonathon Edward Tynedale, the founder and owner of JET shoes. Otherwise known as the soon-to-be-saviour of the Peace and Pigs Holiday Park.

* * *

I had to admit, since Scarlett's death, I had surprised myself by feeling grateful to have Ma around. She worked harder than Jake and me put together, scrubbing the toilet block and the caravans on changeover days as if she was washing away the mistakes and the hurts of our past. She was taller now, as though the crushing grief compressing her bones and dragging her body down had begun to lift. I'd spent many hours in Ballydown library reading books about bereavement, hoping to understand my mother. I had grimaced at the repeated description of the grieving cycle, which apparently encompasses shock, denial, anger, sadness, and finally acceptance. Whatever had stuck my mother at the anger stage, whether it was me, or her illness, or her crazy family, somehow during the past year, she had become unstuck. I finally began to believe she might have changed; that she no longer hated me or blamed me. I accepted that in her own strange way she had come to Sherwood Forest, not to hunt me down and torment me, but to make amends.

The day after the funeral, Grace drove Scarlett's car – her car now – to the Peace and Pigs. It was a damp, cool afternoon, and Grace hid in the depths of her purple hoody. She found me in reception. I finished dealing with a couple of ramblers checking in for the night, and came around the counter to give Grace a hug.

'I thought you'd be at Samuel's, resting.'

She shrugged. 'I slept for twelve hours last night. Sometimes I feel like I'm wearing a lead coat, and all I can do is lie on the sofa and stare at the wall. Today – I don't know – I just wanted to come here.' Grace squinted at me. 'Do you think that's okay? Should I be crying all the time or something?'

'Do whatever you feel like doing. You'll have other days to cry.'

'Where's Jane?'

'Probably cleaning something.'

'Can I talk to you?'

I nodded.

'Did you see that man who came in at the end last night?'

'Your dad. Big Johnny.'

'Yes. I called him. It seemed wrong that he didn't know.'

'Did he know your mum was ill?'

Grace shook her head. 'I worried he would try to make peace with her if he knew she was dying. You know how she felt about him. I didn't want to cause her any more pain, or stress her out. Or waste any of her last few days dealing with all of that. She would have been angry.'

'She would. And confused. She was so weak, it would have been too much if he'd come here.'

'It's weird. Mum was so fixed on giving people millions of chances. But she wouldn't do it for him. Someone she made a baby with.'

'I think that's because protecting you came first. It wasn't about him, or her. If she had let him back in your lives, knowing there was a strong chance he would have hurt you, and he messed it up, she would have blamed herself.'

Grace considered this. 'She should have let me take that risk.'

'Yes. But if I know anything about mothers, it's that they are anything but rational.'

'He gave me a cheque.'

'Really? Well, that seems only fair. He looks like he can afford it.'

Grace pulled the cheque out of her hoody pocket and handed it to me. I nearly fell off my chair.

'Apparently, when Mum refused to take him back, or let him have anything to do with me, he opened a bank account and began putting in each month the amount he would have given us if Mum would have taken it. Even when he was just working on Hatherstone market, he still put in 30 per cent of his earnings, hoping one day he'd have the chance to give it to me. This is all that money.'

'Grace, this will pay for you to go through college! In style. It's incredible.'

She fidgeted on her seat. 'You think I should take it?'

'Of course you should take it! Why wouldn't you? It's only a shame you had to wait this long because of your mum's pride. Take it and enjoy every penny.'

Grace scrunched her face up. Two tears tumbled out of her eyes and washed twin streaks of eyeliner down her cheeks. I put my arms around her and wiped her face with a tissue.

'It feels as if I'm saying Mum wasn't good enough; that what she gave me wasn't enough. All those years she worked so hard, looking after me at the same time, all on her own, and now Big Johnny swoops in, waving his fat cheque book like a magic wand.' She swallowed hard. 'I don't want him to look after me, to make it all better. He hasn't earned that right. I want my mum. If he cared about me so much, why didn't he fight harder to see me? Why did he let Mum stop him?'

'It's never simple, or easy. And people change. Perhaps he only realises now what a mistake he made, never knowing you. And you know his money can never replace what your mum did for you – who she was.'

Grace blew her nose and pulled her hood up again. 'If I keep it, does that mean he'll think he's paid his debt? That he has the right to a relationship with me now?'

'You wanted that too, remember? You ran away to find him.'

'And he spent one hour showing me around his precious company, his real baby, before flying off to some important meeting, leaving his secretary to drive me to the station.'

'Oh, Grace. I'm sorry.'

'I didn't want some lovey daddy-daughter reunion. I just wanted to meet him. To see for myself. I didn't think Mum had the right to make the decision for me about whether or not he was worth knowing.'

'I thought he taught you how to make shoes?'

She sniffed. 'He told me a bit. Some assistant showed me a bit more and the rest I learned through the internet, and trial and error.'

'Well, you know it isn't sensible to make any big decisions at the moment. He was wrong to give you the cheque now but don't rip it up just yet; think about it for a while. And much as you love your mum, remember you need to consider your life now. She would want you to be secure.'

'I know she would. Thanks, Marion. I'm going to the blue van to blob for a bit.'

'See you later.'

Life was never simple. I hoped Grace would take the money. She would need all the help it could buy her, to make it through the next year.

* * *

A few days later, Grace and Valerie decided to move back onto the campsite. My mother spent every spare moment in the blue van looking after them. I tried not to think about a seven-year-old girl curled up on the kitchen floor, too weak to cry about the empty cupboards all around her. I got that she was doing for them what she couldn't do for me then. Even so, I still sometimes wanted to screw my thumbs into her eyeballs. I worried about how to find a way to forgive her. I knew it was the only way to let it go.

I had just kicked a chicken out of my way (not hard – she could take it) when I looked up to see Erica, the woman I currently least wanted to see, behind my mum, and possibly Amanda, skipping down the steps of the blue van. She looked horribly pleased with herself. I was instantly on my guard. Grace had no idea about Fisher's plans for the Peace and Pigs. I suspected a game play. As much as I wanted to avoid Erica right then, and as much as it was like a stake in my gut to see her perfect hair, wearing the kind of skimpy dress that would make my curves appear like a baby elephant's, and to imagine her and Reuben's make-up kisses as they laughed about the ridiculousness of him ending up on a date with me, I found myself in her path.

'Hi, Erica.'

'Hello, Marion. How are you doing? Managing to keep everything ticking over?'

'I'm fine, thanks. What are you doing here?' I didn't care that I sounded rude. I was angry, and the wounds on my heart and my pride smarted. I was glad I felt too hacked off to be polite to Erica.

Her smile vanished. 'Don't worry, Marion. I was just visiting Grace.'

'Why?'

'I had a business proposition for her. One that would help pay for her to get through college.'

'Fisher sent you. I can't believe you picked such an insensitive time.'

'No. Actually, this is all my idea. Well, mine and Reuben's.'

What? Reuben was in on it? I could feel the horror on my face.

'Oh, come on now, Marion. Don't look like that. What happened between me and Reuben is for the best. We all know it.'

Yes, if Reuben was going to be part of the master plan to take the Peace and Pigs away from Grace and chop down half the forest to turn it into a holiday village for people like Erica, it probably was. I was speechless.

'Bye, Marion. I'll probably not see you again, but for what it's worth, it was nice knowing you. The best woman won in the end.'

She smiled, striding off up the path to where she'd parked her shiny little car. I looked around for another chicken to kick. The wheelbarrow had to do instead. She wasn't going to see me again? How quickly did she plan on getting rid of us if Grace agreed to let Fisher have the campsite?

I spent half an hour taking my bad mood out on the dandelions before calming down enough to go and find out what Erica had said to Grace.

Grace and Valerie were sunbathing in the meadow. Fat bees feasted on the daisies all around their blanket. I sat down on the grass beside them.

'Hi, Marion. Did you know that 99.8 per cent of the mass of the solar system is made up of the sun?'

'No, I didn't. How are you doing, Valerie?'

'Did you know that when the person who loves you most in the whole world has been murdered by brain tentacles that made a big blood-blob get stuck in her lung and squish her heart until it stopped beating, your own heart actually aches, like the tentacles have got it too?'

'I did know that. But did you know that one of the ways to help ease the ache is to focus on the positive things you can feel, that can drown it out for a while? Like sunshine on your skin, or the sound of a beautiful piece of music, or a cup of tea that is just the right temperature?'

'Does the ache ever go away?' asked Valerie.

'Yes. It gets worse for a while, and then it begins to turn sweeter, like a strawberry becoming ripe.'

'Okay.'

'Grace, I saw Erica leaving. She said she had some business proposition to make to you, about the campsite.'

Grace tugged the headphones out of her ears and sat up. 'About the campsite? No. She was talking about college.'

'Oh. What did she say then?' She was talking about college? Then why wouldn't she be seeing me again?

'You know my shoes have been selling really well? When Erica's boss tried to get her to take her old job back, she said she only would if they agreed to sponsor me through college. Like a scholarship. And then I have to come and work for them for a couple of years when I'm finished.' Grace flushed, her voice a mixture of pride and embarrassment.

'Have to come and work for them or *get* to go and work for them? I can't believe it. No, that's not true. You are amazingly talented. I'm not surprised at all. Are you going to do it?'

She shrugged. 'Erica said the only thing I had to decide was whether or not I wanted to tie myself down to working for them for two years. She thinks by the time I graduate, I might have some better offers. She was really nice about my shoes.'

'And it's not as if you need the money. Your dad would probably offer you a job too, if you asked him. Has he seen how talented you are?'

Grace shook her head. 'I'm not working for him. At the moment, I don't really want anything from him.'

'You have some big decisions to make.'

Grace smiled, but it crumpled at one side. 'So what would Mum's lesson on all this be?'

I stretched out on my back, feeling the prickle of the grass on my bare legs and shoulders. 'I can't do the accent.'

Valerie poked me. 'You have to at least try.'

'Right. Here goes. Scarlett's lesson in choosin' whether to sell your soul to corporate bloodsuckers, take your low-life daddy's guilt money, or stand on your own two gorgeous feet and believe in yourself enough to make it. Life is hard enough, sugar. When someone offers you a helpin' hand, say, "Thank you very much," take it, and be grateful. If people recognise how darn brilliant you are, why not spend a little time workin' with them and learnin' from some experts? You might know how to make a fine pair of shoes, but let's face it, you know diddly squat about runnin' a business. You can learn the hard way, through messin' up a thousand times, or take a bit of wise advice and learn from those who actually know somethin' about what they're doin'. You might even pick up some style tips that don't involve stickin' pins in your face, or dressin' to make your complexion look as if you are digestin' rotten meat.

'And as for your daddy's money. Take it. Use it. It's too late for him to screw you up, spoil you, or buy your affection. You can forgive him and still be wise enough not to trust him.'

I stopped. Valerie and Grace were clutching each other, rolling about on the blanket. Grace managed to stop laughing for long enough to say, 'I'm sorry, Marion, I couldn't understand any of that. But I'm sure Mum would approve, whatever you said. Can you try again, without the accent? What was that meant to be? A cross between Australian and Japanese?'

'No!' Valerie squealed. 'Do the accent! Do the accent!'

'I refuse to stay here and be bullied.' I stood up, a weight falling off my shoulders at the sight of them laughing. I nudged Grace's calf with my toe before I left. 'Let me know what you decide.'

27

As we geared up for the busy season, I spent every spare moment making plans and getting things ready to open phase one of the rescue project: the outside snack bar. I met up with Vanessa, the ex-restaurant manager with twins, a couple of times. She was desperate to find something to give her a break from double nappies and feeds. Her maternity leave had nearly finished, and she was interested in working somewhere closer to home, with shorter hours and less pressure than a Michelin-starred restaurant. The only trouble was, as yet I had no way to pay her – not until we started making money, anyway.

I worked my way through organising permits and licences, calculating costs, and creating lists of equipment, until there was nothing else I could do without actually spending money. I made an appointment at the bank. They were very kind, and dreadfully sorry, but unfortunately due to the current financial climate they couldn't help me. I went to a different bank. They sneered at me for wasting their time. By the fourth 'no', I felt ready to sell the contents of my caravan just to make enough cash to get started.

I wondered what Big Johnny would think about his daughter's

home and business being run into the ground by overpriced rents. I wondered if he would consider changing the name on that enormous cheque to the Peace and Pigs Holiday Park, and if he did, if that would make Grace feel able to accept it. I wondered how I could even think about asking her to put the money into an idea that no bank in Nottinghamshire would consider backing.

Working every minute of the long summer days, too busy to think, it was only once I fell into bed each night that the challenges of learning to live with my mother floated up to the surface. For the first few weeks she had been in the forest, I couldn't think beyond the fierce desire for her to leave. Then, as Scarlett worsened, I knew we needed her here, so I just wanted her to stay out of my way until it felt reasonable to ask her to go. But things had changed with the loss of Scarlett and the brief appearance of Big Johnny. I had thought a lot about families, and forgiveness, and how refusing to let go of past transgressions hurt the person holding on more than the transgressor.

My mother had found a measure of relief; some way to live in freedom from her terrible previous life. She had a peace about her that I could only dream of. This made me angry and bitter – that she could move on and I still suffered. I knew the key was forgiveness. During her months of treatment, my mother had forgiven herself (and me, although that made me even angrier, that she might even consider I had needed to be absolved of any wrongdoing). Unless I could do the same, I would live with this resentment that fed upon my unresolved emotions. I had to figure out how to forgive her. Not for her sake, but for mine.

Growing up, it had been Father Francis who taught us about forgiveness. We said it every mass: forgive us as we forgive others. So, as my nights grew increasingly restless and I began to avoid Grace and Valerie in an attempt to stay away from Ma, I decided to turn to what I saw as my only option. I went back to church and hung around hoping for God, or an angel, or something, to tell me how to forgive her. He sent Lara instead.

She wandered over at the end of the service with two mugs of coffee in her hand and slid onto the chair beside mine. 'Here. You look like you need some caffeine. Tell me it wasn't my sermon that left you so flat.'

I sipped the hot drink. It was good coffee. 'Thanks. I've not been sleeping well.'

'Vanessa mentioned you've been working really hard.'

I had some more coffee.

'So, it's not work? In my experience, that means you're worried, you have something on your conscience, or you're in love. Tell me to mind my own business, but if you want to chat about it, listening is part of my job.'

I took a deep breath. In, then out. I paused, breathed in, and burst out crying.

I cried for what I think might have been several hours. By the time I had finished blubbing, there were only two people left in the church apart from us, and one of those was vacuuming the hall. While I cried, Lara drank her coffee, handed me tissues and very, very quietly prayed for me. Only the more she prayed, the more I cried. Big, loud, snotty sobs. I didn't care that people could hear me, or that my face looked ugly, blotchy and red. Something big inside me needed to come out, and here it was. Like evil toxins or bad bacteria, it leached out of me, until I stopped, and realised I felt not only exhausted, but clean.

'Sorry.' I was hoarse, probably dehydrated.

'No problem. Do you want to talk about it?'

Did I?

'How do you forgive someone who has done something terrible, really awful, that has messed you up for years, or broken you forever, and you know that even if they do ever feel sorry, they will never say it? How do you let that go?'

Lara puffed out a sigh. 'That's a big question. I prefer something easier like: What's the meaning of life? Or: Why do children get cancer? Seriously? That is almost impossible. But the only way I've found that works for me is to make a conscious choice. I say it out loud every day. I forgive them. I hope their life is fantastic and they have peace – and love and success and joy. Usually I start off forcing it through gritted teeth, knowing that what I really want is for them to be placed in the stocks and pelted with dirty nappies until they feel the hurt and humiliation they caused me. But when I say it enough, and I pray for them, and maybe even make myself start doing nice things for them, my heart begins to change. It's like I act and speak as if I have forgiven them, until it becomes true. But it can take a long while. It may happen only a tiny bit at a time.

'Sometimes there are no excuses. People do things that are wrong, even wicked, and they aren't sorry and are never brought to justice as far as we can see. But we can choose to love anyway. Because love wins. And it is always, without exception, better to live with love than with hate.'

I tried to say it in the car on the way home – just to see what happened. 'Ma, I forgive you for not loving me, for neglecting me, for not being there, for laughing at me, blaming me.' I couldn't do it, but I made a start with: 'Ma, I forgive you for following me to the Peace and Pigs and making me face these feelings.' I almost meant it.

Before I could change my mind, I invited her for tea that evening. With highly unforeseen consequences. See what happens when you try to do the right thing?

She arrived at six, her brown coat buttoned up tight against the oppressive July heat. The humidity had been building throughout the day as the atmosphere closed in. There would be a storm later on.

I welcomed her, and offered her a drink while the vegetables came to the boil. Broccoli, her favourite, as was the fish pie keeping warm in my little oven.

I served the food, Ma finally remembered to take her coat off and we began to eat. I tried to make conversation. It was like running up the side of a mountain with the weight of a decimated childhood dragging behind me. I told her my plans about serving food at the campsite. She nodded her head and said, 'Well, you'll be flat out with all that. I guess I'll be staying a wee while longer then.'

I stopped eating. 'There might be a problem with that.'

Ma looked at me, a crease between her eyebrows. She could sense a serious point was about to be spoken aloud – never a welcome prospect in the O'Grady family.

'Can you remember Amanda? Valerie's mum?'

She snorted.

'Before you came, I'd been asking around about Da. She did some stuff – nothing serious, it was stupid really – to try to put me off finding out about him. Which would fit, I guess, if what you said was true, that she killed Henry.'

Ma said nothing. She started scraping at her plate with her fork, even though there were only the tiniest remains of pie on there.

I told her what Amanda had done: about the brick, and the notes, and the spray paint.

Scrape.

'She slashed my tyres.'

Scraaaape.

'So, if you stay for a while longer, which would be great' (keep saying it until you mean it, Marion) 'then I'm worried it might push Amanda to do something really stupid. You did accuse her in public. She threatened to hurt me, remember?' I yanked the plate away to stop her scraping it again. 'If you stay, we need to somehow sort this out. You need to tell me what Da said about Henry's death. There are other people involved too: Reuben, and Archie and Ginger. Valerie.'

She stood up, picked her coat up off the sofa, and put it on, buttoning it deliberately from top to bottom.

'Thank you for a lovely supper, Marion. I'd better be getting back now.'

She opened the door, and I moved across to block her from leaving.

'Please, Ma. I've lost so much. I need to know this.' I reached out and took hold of her hand, realising as I did that it was unfamiliar to me; it had been so long since I had held it. 'I can't see his face properly any more. Please let me have this piece of him, of his story. Don't leave me wondering what kind of man he really was. I'll never mention it again.'

She looked down at my fingers wrapped firmly around hers, then lifting our hands up, she pressed them against her chest. 'You have his hands.' She moved them over to my torso, still gripping tightly. 'And his heart.'

We stood for a few moments, for the first time united, not divided, by our shared loss.

'There was a letter. From her. She wrote to him before he left.'

'Well? Do you still have it? What did it say?'

'It's in my caravan.'

'What? You've had it with you all this time?' I struggled to control my temper. If Ma sensed me judging or criticising her, I'd never get to see the letter.

She shrugged.

'So, can I read it? And Archie and Ginger?'

'If you must.'

28

I drove up to the Hall, the atmosphere both in and out of the car crackling with building tension. Archie welcomed us in, and we waited in the drawing room while he fetched Ginger and Reuben.

Archie spoke first. 'Jane. You have something to tell us about Daniel and Henry?'

Ma nodded, her lips pursed.

'Would you like to begin now?' What was it about Archie that made him able to sound as if he hadn't been waiting to hear this information for the past thirty years?

Ma fiddled with the zip on her cardigan. She cleared her throat.

'Why don't you start at the beginning?' Archie coaxed, so patiently.

She took a deep breath. 'You know that I was married to Daniel.'

Yes, everybody did know.

'He told me – what happened that made him leave England.'

Ginger moaned faintly. 'Henry died.'

'Yes. But it wasn't quite how you think. You'll know Daniel was going with that woman, Amanda. She'd bewitched him with her fluttering eyelashes and her tantalising outfits. He was besotted.

Thought he was in love. He would have done anything for her. But she was only using him as a stepping-stone. She wasn't interested in the lord and lady's adopted son. Or only in so far as he could lead her to the future lord. She tried more than once to ensnare your boy, but he was a grand wee lad, and wasn't having any of it. He tried to tell Daniel, but at that point, Daniel would have believed her if she'd told him she laid golden eggs.

'One day, she arranged to meet Daniel and Henry on top of that ruined tower, the one on your land, but she told Daniel the time had changed to much later. So as Daniel climbed the tower steps, he heard voices from the top. The other two were already there. When he got close enough to make out the words, he stopped and listened. She was at it again, throwing herself at your poor boy. He wouldn't have it, so she got angry. At the moment Daniel stepped up onto the roof, the two of them were struggling, the girl pushing at Henry, screaming and trying to fight him. He backed away to the edge of the tower, where the old stone had crumbled away. Henry teetered on the edge, trying to get his balance. She threw herself at him one last time and the wall gave way. He was gone before Daniel could reach him.'

Ginger and Archie looked like ghosts. They were lost thirty years in the past. If I'd stretched out my hand to touch them, surely it would have passed through the illusion of their bodies.

Reuben spoke. 'It wasn't suicide. But why... why didn't Daniel speak up? Why did he let Amanda get away with it? How could he let everyone believe Henry killed himself?'

Ma turned to face Reuben, her eyes defiant. 'He was eighteen years old. A child. And one who had lived through the murder of his parents. He was *bewitched* by her. She told him she was pregnant, and he was the father. Did he want his child to be born in prison? To be taken away? To grow up with no mother, like he had done? She swore it was an accident. What good would her going to prison do? And when he realised it was lies, that there was no baby, Amanda told him that if he said anything, she would say that Daniel had caught them together and thrown Henry off the tower in a jealous rage. He was frightened, and confused, and devastated. He hated himself for what he had done, but couldn't see how to make it right.'

'So he left.'

'Yes.'

'How do we know this is true? That Daniel *didn't* push Henry?'

'Reuben!' Ginger turned and glared at her son.

'Someone has to ask it. He ran away and changed his name.'

'Henry and Daniel were brothers in everything but blood. If you knew him, you wouldn't question it.'

'Yes, but I didn't know him, and if this is true, we need to do something about it. I'm only saying that we need to think carefully about making accusations if we have no way of proving them.'

'There is proof.'

We all looked back at my mother as she shifted on her chair.

'Go on, Ma.'

She carefully opened her bag and pulled out a small greying envelope. 'I have a letter. I'm sorry for not showing you sooner. I had my reasons and, well...'

'You're here now. And we are very grateful.' Archie leaned over and patted her knee. 'Shall you read it to us, or would you like me to?'

She handed him the letter, closing her eyes.

'Very well.' Archie began to read. 'My darling Daniel, you won't see me or talk on the phone, but this is dead important, so *please* read this and don't just chuck it in the bin. I know you think it was my fault what happened to Henry, but I didn't mean to push him off. It wasn't what it looked like – he hurt me and I was defending myself. I didn't know the tower would break. You *can't* tell anyone what you saw. Not the police or his mum and dad or anyone, Dan. Not if you love me. And even if you don't love me any more (which I hope you do because I have always loved you) you mustn't say anything. I'm pregnant. You wouldn't want our baby to be born in prison, would you? If I get done they'll take it away and you'll never get to see it. Or me. Please come and see me. I love you and need us to be together, you and me and the baby. You promised you would always take care of me. You know what Mum will do when she finds out. I love you and I never meant for this to happen. I can't stop crying. I miss you and just want to be with you. Please come so I can tell you what really happened. I need you, Dan. Your Mandy.'

Archie and Ginger went straight over to see Amanda, taking Reuben with them as back-up. We thought it best if Ma stayed at the campsite with me. By the time the Hatherstones returned, it was dark outside and the first drops of the coming storm were thudding on my caravan roof.

It took them five minutes to explain how the conversation had gone. As predicted, Amanda had refused to let them in, refused to talk about it, denied ever writing a letter, accused my mother of being a shrivelled-up, jealous old hag who was trying to frame her, and slammed the door in their faces.

What now? Did we show the letter to the police? It didn't implicate Amanda in murder, only an accident. Yes, she had lied and covered up the truth, but was it really worth raking all that up again?

And yet... her vicious threats and ugly, menacing rage simmered on the back burner of my memory. I was fearful of what Amanda might do now. I said to my mother, 'I don't think you should stay in the van by yourself tonight.'

Everybody looked at me, their faces tight with worry and exhaustion. All except for Ma, who bristled at the very thought of it. 'I'm not afraid of that woman.'

Archie frowned. 'Afraid, no. But it might be wise to feel apprehensive enough to proceed with caution. Would you consider coming to stay at the Hall for a bit, until we've agreed on a course of action?'

'Please, Ma. It'll stop the rest of us worrying about you.'

'Worrying about what? Do you think she's going to break in and murder me in my bed?'

There was a beat of silence. Ma looked at me. 'And while I'm dreaming sweet dreams all cosied up at the Hall, who will she come after then, hmm? I'm not the one whose smile she threatened to slice off.'

'What?' Reuben was incredulous. 'That's it. You're both coming.'

'We can't do that. Someone needs to be here to supervise the campsite.' I shook my head. 'This is getting ridiculous. I don't think any of us actually think Amanda's going to try to hurt anybody, do we? Maybe we'd be better off staying here and keeping an eye out, in case she decides to break another window or smash something up.'

Eventually, I persuaded Ma to let me bunk down in her van for the night. Who'd have guessed it? Me voluntarily spending the night under the same roof as my mother. I spent an anxious night, ears pricked in the anticipation of an intruder's furtive rustling.

* * *

Five more nights passed with no sign of Amanda. The torture of prolonged proximity to Ma, combined with the continual unease about what, if anything, Amanda might do, was surely more effective than any other form of retaliation she might have come up with.

The following Friday, beyond weary from my restless nights on Ma's couch, desperate for a distraction, I suggested to Grace and Valerie that we hold another Fire Night. They cautiously said yes. We agreed it would be a tribute to Scarlett, but by no means an attempt at imitation of her blissful evenings. Katarina and Sunny had taken their three gorgeous monkeys to the seaside for the week, but Ginger and Archie, Reuben, Jake, and Samuel joined us as we toasted our absent friend in the glow of the bonfire.

It was a cool evening, despite the time of year, and when the light began to go, Valerie squeezed herself in next to me on my sun lounger.

'Valerie, you're covered in goose bumps. Where's your fleece?'

'I left it on Jane's kitchen table this morning.'

Heaving her off me, I rummaged in my jeans pocket until I found my keys. 'Here, go and fetch it then. You need the big key, here.'

'The oldest lock was found in some palace ruins near Nineveh. It's 4,000 years old and made of wood. But it didn't have a key.'

'How can you remember so many amazing facts but keep forgetting your jumper? Now, hurry up and I'll make you a hot chocolate for when you get back.'

Twenty minutes later, the party was winding down, and Valerie's drink had gone cold. I waited another few minutes, wondering if she had taken a quiet moment to have a cry, then found the energy to pull myself up off the lounger again.

'Ma? Did you see Valerie come back?'

Ma, busy clearing up the remains of dessert, frowned at me. 'No. I'll go and check on her.'

'No, you're busy. I'll go. Can I take your key, just in case?'

'If you think you'll need it.'

Ma's caravan was down near the lake, tucked behind a cluster of trees and reached by a woodchip path that bypassed most of the tourist plots. Our peace-loving, quieter campers generally went to bed with the sunset, and the lack of lights glimmering through the few tents I did pass told me tonight was no exception.

Or maybe someone still remained up and about? Nearing the trees, I began to detect a scent of smoke in the air that was different to the gentle wafting of our bonfire. Harsher, more astringent. Someone was burning something they really shouldn't be. I paused, looking around for the tell-tale flicker of flame, ready to go and sort it out.

I heard it first. A muffled roar, distant pops and cracks that made my heart stutter, and all the air seemed to leave my body in one go. I ran around the edge of the copse just as Ma's caravan window exploded. Through the empty hole in the frame, wild, rampant flames danced with murderous rage.

The heat was terrifying. The smoke whirled and whooshed into the night air as I stood among the falling embers, oblivious to the hundreds of tiny shards of glass that now pierced my skin.

Valerie.

Ignoring the primal instinct that screamed at me to go, get away, jump in the lake to escape the searing heat, I pushed myself closer to the building, calling out her name before breaking off in a sudden fit of coughing.

I ran around to the furthest end, banging my fists on the bedroom and bathroom walls, shocked by how hot they were, hollering, crying, choking. A face appeared in the shadows of the bedroom window.

'Valerie!'

She put her hands on the glass, the whites of her eyes round and full of horror.

'Open the window!'

'I can't.' Her voice was a million miles away. 'It's locked and I can't find the key.'

Think, Marion. Think. I took a deep breath to try to quell my panic, sending my lungs into another spasm of violent hacking.

'You need to break the glass. Look around for something heavy to bash it with.'

She disappeared for a few seconds, returning with a shoe and a plastic hairbrush.

'Where's your phone?' I mimed making a phone call. No time to feel the helplessness of my own lack of mobile phone signal.

'In my fleece. In the other room.' The air around her was darkening with swirls of grey smoke. She tapped the hairbrush on the glass, pointlessly.

'You need to block the gap around the door frame. Use the duvet.'

'I have.'

'Okay. I'm going to find some wood to break the glass. Don't worry. We'll get you out.'

I dashed from tree to tree. July was not the month for fallen branches, but I stumbled on a rock the size of my fist on the edge of the clearing.

Valerie crouched down under a blanket while I feverishly bashed at the window with my weapon. More crashes from the other end of the van, wails and ripping sounds, and it grew hotter than I had imagined possible. We covered the bottom of the jagged frame with the blanket, and Valerie did her best to wriggle up and through the gap. I leaned in as far as I could, grabbed on to her top half and pulled, desperation overcoming the lack of breathable air in my lungs, the slick sweat that drenched our skin running into our eyes and blinding us.

As she toppled out into my arms, knocking us both to the ground, cool, dry hands took her from me, pulling and tugging at me to move away from the scorching heat and suffocating fumes. I scampered back, using my hands as well as my feet, and collapsed under the shade of an oak tree.

Archie and Ginger. They peered at us, the concern on their faces flickering in the orange glow. 'Have you called the fire brigade?'

'No phone.'

At that, Ginger clutched at her husband. 'I'll go. You get these girls away.'

'No!' Valerie sat up, her voice a painful croak. 'Mum!'

'What?' Our rescuers froze in alarm.

'Mum's in the kitchen.' Valerie fell back onto the dusty earth. She retched, bringing up thick, dark mucus. 'She fell. Bumped her head. Unconscious.'

Archie and Ginger did not hesitate. Yanking the blanket left half hanging out of the bedroom window, they plunged it in the lake before taking Ma's key off me and rushing across to the caravan door.

'Wait!' My throat felt as though I had swallowed a pincushion. I wanted to tell them not to go in; that they didn't have to do this. It was hopeless, impossible. We would end up losing three lives, not one. There was no shame in not walking into a death trap to save a woman who was surely beyond saving.

Archie and Ginger turned toward me, their silhouettes tall and straight. I didn't have to see their faces to know they understood.

'Be careful.'

Whipping the blanket around them like a superhero's cape, they unlocked the door and flung it open. A torrent of scorching black smoke surged out, engulfing the blanket.

I crawled over to Valerie, my head spinning, and curled myself around her. The thought that Valerie would be here to see Archie and Ginger bring out her mother sat like a ball of lead in the pit of my stomach. The likelihood that she wouldn't get to see it, I couldn't bear to think about.

But Archie and Ginger didn't disappear into the cackling

furnace. They stooped down, still huddled in the blanket, and began to half drag, half carry the figure of Amanda out onto the caravan veranda, before slowly lifting her down the steps and across the clearing. She must have fallen right beside the doorway.

Ginger and Archie laid her down on the grass and wrapped her gently in the blanket. Ginger began to weep. She took off her jacket and folded it up, placing it underneath Amanda's head.

'Oh!' she cried. 'Oh! You poor, poor girl. What have you done? You poor, poor girl.'

She cradled the limp body of the woman who had killed her son and lied about it for thirty years. Stroked her hair, patted her hand. Wept.

Archie pulled the letter out of his pocket. Hauling himself to his feet, he limped across to the caravan, ripping the envelope into pieces as he did so. He tossed the fragments into the air, where they floated on the hot current before disappearing into the night.

I heard the voice of Lara. *Love wins.*

The caravan still burned, rising flames dancing dangerously close to the trees. Despite my growing weakness and overwhelming nausea, the need to get help drove me to my feet, and then somehow to take enough stumbling steps through the forest to fall in a crumpled heap at Reuben's feet.

I woke up in hospital. A zillion tiny cuts covered my face and arms from the exploding window. One impressive, angry gash snaked down my chest, where a piece of glass had ripped it open as I yanked Valerie out. For three days, I was pumped full of drugs, itched beyond normal levels of human endurance and was hugged, gently, by more friends than I knew I had. They filled me in on the rest of the story.

As soon as Valerie entered the caravan, the door had opened and Amanda walked in. Taking the key off her daughter, she locked the door before proceeding to cajole, demand, and shake the whereabouts of the letter out of her. Together they turned every room upside down searching for it, Valerie terrified, her mother increasingly frenzied.

Finally accepting that Valerie knew nothing, half-crazed with the bitterness of vengeful wrath, Amanda decided to torch the van, and hopefully the letter with it. When Valerie came out of the bedroom and saw the fire starting, she tried to intervene. Amanda slipped as they wrestled, cracking her head on a metal doorstop and knocking herself out.

By this point, the curtains on the far side of the van had caught. Valerie dragged her mother to the front door, but it was locked and she couldn't find the key. As the fire grew in intensity, she could only think to build a barricade to shield Amanda from the flames, before being forced back into the bedroom. At that point, she heard me knocking on the window.

Amanda would spend a long time in hospital and rehabilitation. She pleaded guilty to breaking and entering, arson, and several smaller charges, sparing her daughter the trauma of testifying in court. Someone cleared out her house and took her things away. We didn't ask where.

The Robin Hood Festival was held during the third week of August. A thick red circle on my calendar, it marked my deadline for launching the new campsite eatery. In the days leading up to it, I spent all my time, energy and hope on getting the café kiosk fit to open. Valerie chose its name: 'Scarlett's'. Cheesy, but I could hardly argue with her about it. We towed an empty static caravan up to the grassy area behind reception, hiring builders to gut the insides and replace the fittings with all the equipment needed to run a professional kitchen, including a first-class grill for Ma to flip breakfast pancakes on. Outside, Jake built an oven for potatoes and stone-baked pizza, and a barbeque to rival the one used on Fire Nights. I scoured the local car boot sales and discount shops for tables of varying sizes, some tall enough to sit round on chairs and eat a meal, others coffee-table height. I matched them with chairs and rattan sofas, and found an antique hat stand, the perfect place to hang blankets so customers could help themselves when the evenings grew chilly sitting out under the trees.

We opted for a fire pit and chimeneas instead of gas patio heaters, stringing fairy lights through the trees to complement the table lamps. The builders deftly assembled a wooden gazebo and additional decking, fixing shutters where I had removed the glass from the main window of the van to provide a serving hatch.

I planned a menu, with Vanessa's help. She also convinced me that building a climbing frame and a sandbox would be essential if we wanted to give parents the chance to relax over their drinks. I splashed out on a giant chess set and quoits. By the second week of August, all I had left to do was purchase the stock. That, and freak out. A lot.

Oh, yes, and officially offer my mother a job.

This was not my idea, rather the terms under which Grace agreed to cash in the cheque from Big Johnny. And she insisted on using half the money to pay for Scarlett's. It was her business now, and her money. I could only graciously accept, and pray very, very hard that I didn't mess it up.

Ma said yes. I went back to my van and pictured the night of the fire. In the privacy of my caravan, I spoke out loud the now partial truth that I forgave my mother for some, if not all, of the miscellaneous iniquities she had committed. Lara was right. I barely needed to grit my teeth now as I said it.

The week before the festival, I handed out flyers to our full complement of campers, advertising our opening night on the

Friday evening. I stuck up a poster in Jo's café, and on the church noticeboard, and handed them out at the market. It took me one pre-launch haircut from Ada to realise I could have saved myself a lot of time and effort. Once I'd told her, pretty soon the whole forest would hear about the party.

Scarlett's opened at four o'clock. By 4.30 p.m., I had sold three ice-creams and a glass of homemade lemonade. By six o'clock, the queue snaked halfway around the meadow. Jake couldn't flip his steaks fast enough, and Grace and Valerie ended up taking drinks and food straight to tables, to speed things up. A couple of hours later, I left Ma to fend for herself in the kitchen and took over from Jake at the barbeque, allowing him to join his band. For a while, I could do nothing but scoop spicy lamb burgers into ciabatta rolls, hand out fish kebabs, and try to stop the chargrilled vegetables from becoming more charred than grilled. Then, as the sun began to sink beneath the trees, the line of customers temporarily all satisfied, I turned to observe the scene behind me.

A cluster of little children, three of them with bright red hair, scampered in the shadows at one end of the meadow. Older siblings languished against the bars of the climbing frame, dangling Coke cans from their hands. In front of the band, a few couples were swaying, too engrossed in one another to notice the toddlers darting around their ankles.

We had filled every table, with more people standing. The fairy lights twinkled, the breeze carried the rich scent of good food, and the sound of chatter and relaxed laughter blended with the easy rhythm of the music.

I'm not ashamed to admit I cried. We had made enough money in one evening to cover the whole month's rent.

Fortunately, Fisher had not been invited, so I didn't have to fight the temptation to laugh in his smug, toady face.

29

The final morning of the festival nearly got lost in the whirls of forest mist clinging around the tree trunks and coating every blade of grass in thick dew. I got up early, tugging a pair of jeans over my worn-out legs, wincing as the top button scraped my still-tender scar.

Armed with trays of samples from Scarlett's and a wodge of discount vouchers, I parked up at the festival site, this time using the workers' car park, and began unloading the trays into Grace and Valerie's waiting arms. It had been my decision to still have the annual employees' day out at the festival, closing the Peace and Pigs shop and kiosk for the day. The business books I had checked out at the library told me this was an idiotic decision. I didn't care. I wanted to go to the festival. I left my mobile phone number taped to the door in case of emergency. The fact that I had no mobile phone reception in the heart of Sherwood Forest was beside the point.

A man with a clipboard showed us where to find our rented stall, right at the heart of the action near the Major Oak. Valerie bobbed up and down with pent-up excitement, nearly tipping her mini muffins onto the ground.

'Do you think we'll see Robin Hood? Do you? Will the Sheriff be there? Maybe they'll have a massive fight, with real swords, and Robin will get his sword and stab the Sheriff like this, right in his guts, and all the intestines will slither out like a giant slippery sausage, and he'll die and Robin will have won once and for all!'

Grace balanced her tray onto one arm, grabbing Valerie's to stop the contents from sliding off the edge. 'You do remember that it isn't the actual Robin Hood, Val?'

Valerie ignored her.

'And that the Sheriff whose guts you want to see all over the forest is really Jake wearing a costume?'

Valerie tossed over a withering look. 'I feel sorry for you, Grace. Living in your land of no imagination must be so utterly boring.'

She leaned around Grace so that she could see me, struggling with three trays balanced on top of each other, and a carrier bag dangling from each arm producing thick red welts on my wrists. 'You're looking forward to seeing him, aren't you, Marion? I bet Robin Hood will come and stop by the stall and say, "Ooh, Lady Marion, what splendid carroty cakes I see before me. Surely they are the finest in the land!" And you'll say, "Well, I thank thee, O Prince of the Forest. You must be in sore need of a quick-release carbohydrate snack to strengthen your manly muscles for the fight that is certain to lie before you this day. Pray, do take and eat one of my humble cakes, or even two."

'And Robin will eat one – but only one because he doesn't want to be greedy – and he'll say, "Can it be true? These delightful morsels taste even more delicious than they dost appear. Dost it be magic? Or perhaps the hand of a truly skilled and able maiden? She would surely make a fine wife!" And you will say, "Sir! You do speak too kind. It was surely me that did arise this very dawn to make these cakes." And Robin will sweep you off your feet into a great big snog and everybody'll cheer, and he'll win the fight and then come back and ask you to marry him.'

Grace shook her head. 'Even in the world of Valerie, Robin Hood has to end up with Maid Marion, not *our* Marion.'

Valerie just smiled. I thought about how the actors pretending to be Robin Hood and Maid Marion had ended up together in real life, adjusting the trays pressed against my chest to squash the sudden ache back inside the secret depths of my heart where it belonged.

Our Marion. I was theirs now. I thought about that instead. For at least ten seconds.

We set up the stall in good time, and Grace and Valerie left for a quick wander about before the visitors began to arrive.

Another man with a clipboard rushed across.

'Marion?'

'Yes.'

'Can I give you this?' He held up a long, dark-red dress. Medieval style. 'Looks like it should fit. You'll need someone to fasten the stays. Do you want to use the staff cabin to change in?'

'I'm sorry. I'm not the *Maid* Marion. Marion is just my actual name. I'm here to run a stall. Don't you need Erica?'

He pulled a face. 'Erica quit. Didn't someone talk to you about this? A blonde girl told me you'd agreed to stand in.'

'A blonde girl who was bouncing on an invisible pogo stick?'

He nodded. 'That's her. So, will you do it?'

I flashed back to last year. Crowds of people. Ropes. Running. A full-blown panic attack.

'Oh, come on, duck. You'd be perfect!'

'What do I have to do?'

'Nothing really, it's a cinch. Walk about a bit, maybe have your photo taken, chat to the visitors. Stand at the edge of the field while the battle goes on, and cheer for the right side.'

Chat to the visitors? That is everything, not nothing.

'Go on, love, please. I'm desperate here. It's only one day.'

'I can't be tied up.' What am I saying? Am I going to do this? Shut up, Marion! Don't be bullied into letting him ruin the festival – for you, and all those little girls who want to meet a smiley, nice, beautiful Maid Marion. Not to mention their dads.

'No, none of that. There was an incident last year.'

I took the dress. 'I'm not doing it if this doesn't fit.'

He grinned. 'Thanks, duck, you're a life-saver.'

Maybe not that, but I am a woman whose stupid crush makes her do stupid things just to spend a bit of time indulging a stupid fantasy with a man who is in love with someone else.

I quickly changed in the temporary cabin set aside for festival staff. An older woman, dressed in what looked like a discarded flour sack, helped me with my outfit and pinned a flower garland into my hair. Images of riding off into the sunset, my arms wrapped around Reuben, kept dancing about in my brain. Thoughts like this had popped up more than I would care to admit during the weeks since our was-it-or-wasn't-it? date.

I slunk out of the cabin into the shadow of the trees. A group of lads dressed as medieval soldiers strolled past. One of them whistled at me, and another bowed with a flourish as his comrades cheered. I fought the urge to run straight back into the cabin, instead offering them a self-conscious wave. I felt like a shoddy, last-minute stand-in for the gorgeous grace of Erica. A cheap imitation and in every way a second-rate replacement. *Help.*

Sidling behind a large tree trunk, I beat myself around the head a few times for getting myself into this situation, before spending a while on my mute busters. As I slowed my breathing down, I remembered the trembly, lost girl who had tiptoed around the festival the previous year, and I felt stronger. I leaned back against the rough bark imagining my da, thirty years before, standing in the exact same place. What would he think if he could see me here now?

I could do this. I knew as much about the legend of Robin Hood and Maid Marion as anyone. This wasn't a mistake.

It was going to be brilliant.

Grace and Valerie clapped and cheered as I followed the first of the visitors back to the main clearing. As soon as they caught sight of me, people began pointing their phones at me, snapping what felt like hundreds of pictures.

I leaned across our stall and stuck my face as close to Valerie's as I could manage without squishing the goods.

'You did this!'

She giggled.

'If anything embarrassing, awkward, or unpleasant happens, I'm putting you on toilet duty for the rest of the season.'

'You look beautiful, Marion. Reuben will be dazzled. Everything will turn out excellently.'

I grimaced. 'Reuben will pretend to be dazzled. He has to. I'm quite sure he would find it much easier if it was his girlfriend wearing the ridiculous dress.'

Valerie looked confused. 'He doesn't have a girlfriend. Him and Erica broke up ages ago.'

'Yes, but they got back together. Didn't they?'

'No! Why would they do that if Reuben likes you?'

'I saw them, at the funeral.'

Before Valerie could reply, clipboard man tapped me on the shoulder.

'If you could please start making your way back down the path toward the main entrance? You can hang about there for half an hour or so, then take the longer route back here for the battle. And remember – you must stay in character at all times! For the purposes of today, you are Maid Marion!'

So, Marion's lesson on how to spend the day pretending to be your ancient namesake. One: keep smiling. And waving. Even when little boys decide it would be fun to throw mud-encrusted pinecones at you. Two: duck. Those pinecones hurt. Three: bite the bullet and stop to talk to all kids staring as you walk past. Most of them will tell you how pretty you look. They don't know you feel a complete idiot. When you see a girl in a wheelchair, so tiny she looks as if the wind could blow her away, tell her she is beautiful, and that you love her flower garland. Her incredible smile will make every second spent in an itchy, cumbersome dress, smelling of someone else's sweat, worth it.

Four: don't try to do the accent. You can't keep it up. Small talk is enough of a challenge for now. Five: clap, cheer, and forget you are meant to be a dignified noblewoman when watching a twilight-in-the-forest-eyed Robin Hood battle the super-fit, blond-haired Sheriff. Enjoy having two men fight over you for the first time ever, but not too much. Remember that when Robin Hood takes your hand, kisses it and fixes those dark, dark eyes on you as he swears to protect you, he is only acting. Slam the lid down quick on the feelings that spread from your stomach all the way to the ends of your hair.

Six: take a moment to stop and marvel at the fact that you did it. You shed your weak, worry-worn skin and actually did it.

My toes were curling with exhaustion in their silken slippers by the close of the day. I had posed for approximately 700,000 photographs, most of which would be slapped all over Facebook by the evening. I had spoken to more people in one day than all the rest of my life put together, with only a handful of weird or inappropriate things popping out of my mouth. A falcon had eaten a chunk of meat from my gloved hand. I had been serenaded by a jester, and to top it off, I had set fire to Morris Middleton's armpit hair as part of the Minstrel's Grand Finale.

After a packed afternoon, we had a two-hour gap until the evening banquet. Enough time to nip home, shower and change, drop off the empty trays, and find out why Ma had never turned up.

She was in reception. I automatically bristled at the implied criticism of my decision to give everyone the day off

'Why didn't you come to the festival?'

'I didn't want to go. I'm not interested in that sort of thing.' She started rummaging under the counter at nothing, her back to me.

'You could have helped us at the stall.'

'You didn't need me. I'd have been in the way.'

'You could have just come and enjoyed a walk, had some lunch. You didn't have to stay long.'

'I told you; I didn't want to go.'

'For goodness' sake, Ma! For the first time in my life, I invited you to spend the day with me – a chance to prove that, contrary to your actions of the past twenty-five years, you don't actually hate me; that you really are better.' I stopped. The hideous thought had struck me like a cobra. 'Are you feeling ill?'

Ma tensed like a wire brush. She straightened up, lips pursed, and looked at me for a long moment.

'I met your da at the festival. I was fourteen, on a trip with the church group. I loved him the first second I saw him. That trash had already got her claws in deep. But he promised to write to me.'

I had never known this. Of course. 'That's why he came to Ballydown.'

She nodded. 'Yes. I knew he would see she was rotten in the end.' Ma lifted her cardigan from the back of her chair, and shrugged it on. 'I'll be getting on. Grace'll be wanting her tea.'

'Thank you. For telling me this.'

'Yes, well. Maybe I'll come with you next year.'

Valerie managed to stand still long enough to lace me into my evening gown. From a short distance away, it looked lovely: rich blue velvet with pale-silver ribbons and a full skirt. Wearing it, I could feel the cheap fabric and see the coarse stitching, but I felt happy enough that it not only fit me, but actually suited me quite well too.

'You look like a princess.' Valerie fiddled with my hair, pinned up with two dozen tiny blue flower clips.

'Thanks. You look gorgeous too.' Valerie wore a long, slinky, pink dress. It was the first time I had seen her looking her age. With her thick hair curled around her shoulders, and her glowing skin, she looked a little too good. I felt glad she had Jake as her date. He would guard her with the overbearing zeal of a protective big brother.

Grace handed me my bag. She was opting to spend the evening alone in the blue caravan with Josh while Ma babysat for Sunny and Katarina. 'Robin won't be able to resist you. I'm almost sorry to miss it.'

'Did you say Robin – or Reuben?' Valerie spluttered through a fit of giggles.

'Will you shut up about me and Reuben? It's never going to happen. It embarrasses me and it makes you look childish.'

'It *is* going to happen. He couldn't stop staring at you today, like you were a massive ice cream with chocolate sprinkles and caramel sauce – like this, Marion!' She widened her eyes and let her mouth hang open.

'He was acting!'

Grace smirked. 'That was not acting. He never ogled Erica like that when she was Marion. Or any other time either.'

I pointed one of my index fingers at each girl.

'You and you. Both of you, be quiet. You, go home and wait for your boyfriend. You, put your shoes on; Jake'll be here in a minute. And if you mention this again, I'm not coming. You'll have to explain to the clipboard man why there's no Maid Marion.'

The banquet took place in a huge marquee, in an area of the forest usually closed to visitors. It had been an emergency relocation after the unseasonal rain flooded the Hall. Inside the tent, benches flanked rows of long tables laid with goblets, spoons, and wooden plates. Oak leaves had been strewn on the floor and the tent poles festooned with greenery to give the impression of dining in the forest. A group of minstrels squeaked and rattled out a tune almost drowned out by the excited hum of a hundred hungry Robin Hood fans.

I had to suffer a heralding fanfare and a steward calling out my name; evidently slipping into my seat unnoticed was not an option. Jake stayed outside, leaving me to ensure Valerie got settled with the Hatherstones. Robin Hood waited for me at the top table, wearing another billowy white shirt with a lace-up front panel instead of buttons. He had on Lincoln-green trousers and brown boots. He'd let his beard grow, to give the effect of a tough, wild man of the forest. It worked. He stood and gave a courtly bow as I took my place beside him.

'Lady Marion.'

'Robin.' My eyes stayed firmly fixed on the guests in front of us.

'I trust you had an enjoyable day?'

'It was most pleasant. Although I am a little tired. It can be quite draining, hosting such a grand event. Especially when one is new to such occasions. I only hope I performed adequately. As you know, such things are not my forte.'

'I heard you did really well.'

Reuben's voice was soft and deep. My eyes couldn't help flitting back to find his dark gaze on me.

The banquet commenced with a rousing speech from Robin Hood, and dozens of serving wenches appeared, loading up the tables with the feast. I chatted to the merry man who sat on the other side of me, a professional historical re-enactor who spent his year travelling between events, switching centuries and characters accordingly. I was happy to sit back and hear his stories while Robin mingled with the guests.

Although I felt the black hole on the bench next to me when he wasn't there, every time he returned, it sent me off-balance. I grew clumsy and red-faced, sure my stilted replies and flapping demeanour came across as unsubtle as if I had swung from the fake chandelier shouting out, 'I am not a brilliant actress! I really, really fancy him for real! And not just Robin Hood, but the real-life Reuben!'

I had to get a grip.

'Is Erica working tonight?'

'I don't know.' He furrowed his brows. 'I think she probably just couldn't face coming. It would have been pretty awkward.'

'I suppose it can't be much fun sat watching your boyfriend having to pretend to be with someone else.'

'Boyfriend?' Reuben shook his head.

At that moment, the huge double flaps at the far end of the tent were ripped open. Sheriff Jake, along with six heavily armed soldiers, burst in. Jake was riding a horse.

'Where is that foul and fiendish villain, Robin of the Hood?' He swung his sword around the top of his head in a circle.

Reuben ignored the interruption. He had his head bent down close to mine, his black hair flopping over his face. 'Marion, you know we're—'

'Stand and face me like a man!' Sheriff Jake bellowed across the marquee. The crowd fidgeted as one, waiting for their hero to respond. Their hero swore under his breath. He frowned at me again, before grabbing his bow, pulling an arrow out of the quiver on his back and leaping on top of the table in one smooth motion. Several of the maidens present fanned their hands in front of their faces and swooned. I swooned a tiny bit, but I don't think anybody saw. Surely Maid Marion was too feisty to swoon? *Get a grip!*

Robin Hood grinned across the hall. 'Come to join us, Sheriff? Supplies running a bit low in the castle? I heard you were having some money trouble.'

He sent the arrow whistling into the wall, six inches above the Sheriff's head.

'After him!' Sheriff Jake roared, as he leapt off the horse. On cue, the merry men rose to defend their leader, the soldiers rushed forwards, and some sensible soul led the poor horse back outside.

For the next few minutes, the tent overflowed with slashing blades, grunts, shouts, flailing arms and a hundred pairs of eyes riveted on the spectacle happening around them. The noise was incredible, the effect of having the battle in and out of the marquee, on top of and under the tables, both terrifying and thrilling.

I wondered if Lady Marion was supposed to join in, but then Friar Tuck tipped over the bench where I hovered, saying, 'Here, my lady, hide behind this,' before diving back into the fray.

As expected, the merry men soon had the upper hand, pinning all of the soldiers to the walls or cornering them under tables. Robin Hood, chest heaving under his ripped shirt, held an arrow in his bow, an inch from the Sheriff's throat. This was my cue. I stood up from behind the bench. A serving wench clipped a microphone to my bodice and gave me a thumbs-up. I breathed; sent an arrow of my own straight into the heart of the mute ghost still trying to hang around in my throat. Pow! Gone.

'My lords! Must we always suffer this terrible fighting? Look...' I pointed at Will Scarlet, whose tunic now glistened red to match his name, with a big splatter of fake blood. 'I invited these good people here to sup with me this night, and you have betrayed my hospitality with your brutality, dishonouring my name and that of my house. Will you not lay down your weapons for one night? For the sake of these noble, honest citizens? Can we not dine together in peace?'

Robin Hood gazed across at me, his stare unwavering, his eyes sapphires in the lamplight. I shivered.

'Would you ask me to risk my life, and the life of my men, for the sake of your supper? I have caught a rat, and rats must be dealt with. Do you ask me to forget what has passed between us? He will cut my throat even as it swallows your good wine.'

I dragged my eyes away long enough to look at Sheriff Jake. 'Well, Sheriff? Do you swear by my life to drop your charges for one evening? To grant your fine citizens a few more hours of revelry?'

He nodded. The whole thing was ridiculous, but the people had paid to see it.

'Aye, my lady. For the sake of my people, I shall grant this outlaw one night's grace. Yet be warned: at dawn, he shall be mine.'

Nobody moved. Robin Hood sighed and shook his head. 'Not for these overstuffed, overdressed peasants shall I withhold from shedding blood here this eve.' He slowly lowered his bow. 'Dear, sweet Marion, I shall do it for you.'

Over the roar of the guests, the foot-stamping and spoon-banging, came the hoarse croak of Bryan Adams's overly long number one hit, 'Everything I Do', blasting from speakers disguised as bushes. Robin and the Sheriff shook hands, and the festivities recommenced. All was well.

For about, oh, maybe four minutes.

30

There was a brief lull in the chatter as Robin Hood and the Sheriff stood side by side at the top table. Sheriff Jake waved his hands about to get everybody's attention. As he opened his mouth to speak, a ye olde profiterole whizzed over the heads of the guests and smushed right into the centre of his forehead. Jake slowly put one hand up and picked the flattened ball off his head.

A second pastry-missile zinged across, smacking into his authentic body armour. The culprit stood up, her medieval cone hat tilting at a 45-degree angle on top of her shimmering white tresses. Her nimble, magic, eighty-year-old hands clutching more food bombs, Ada pointed her chin at the dome of the tent and guffawed.

'Those wet, wimpy whippersnappers might give in to try and impress a girl, but we will never surrender!'

She launched another profiterole.

The rest of the guests, most of whom had no idea if this crazy old bat was part of the show or not, waited to see what would happen next.

What happened next was that Katarina scooped up a large blob of whipped cream on the end of her spoon and catapulted it at the nearest soldier.

The hall erupted.

It took about fifty-seven seconds for my beautiful, cheap dress to become splattered with a smorgasbord of desserts. An overenthusiastic jester tipped a tankard of lemonade down my back, and something soft and squishy got mushed into my hair.

Food fights sound like fun. They are not fun. Not unless you think having elbows and knees rammed into your organs, a table tipped onto your slippered foot, fruit juice squeezed into your eye and ending up entirely covered in sticky, squished-up food is fun.

Herded into a corner of the tent in all the mayhem, next to a bald man launching cherries over the top of an upturned table, and two of Valerie's college friends, who had painted strawberry sauce war stripes across their cheeks and noses, I hunkered down behind a chiffon net covered in flowers, covered my head with my dripping wet arms, and prepared to wait it out.

A few minutes, or possibly hours, later, I felt someone step in behind the curtain. Removing my hands from my face, I saw Reuben. One smear of powdered sugar across his cheek appeared to be his only battle scar.

'Hi.'

'Come on, get up.'

'Why?'

'I'm rescuing you.'

'Wow. Thanks.'

He had fought his way across the war zone to rescue me.

'No problem. It's my job.'

Oh. Okay.

He led me about a sixth of the way around the edge of the tent to a fire-exit flap. In the few short seconds it took us to get there, a dollop of custard hit my neck, I stepped into a puddle of chocolate sauce, and somebody stuffed a portion of cheesecake into my cleavage. The mysterious force-field that sees any good guy run through a hail of bullets and survive ensured Robin Hood remained untouched.

I fell through the flap into the startling quiet of the forest at night. Reuben pulled the flap closed behind us. He grinned at me. I flicked a chunk of pineapple off my shoulder.

'Does that happen every year?'

'Only when Ada manages to sneak a ticket. She's been banned for life. The last time was worse. She started before the Sheriff had arrived, ruining the schedule. The guests only got their first course and the managers had to give everybody a refund.'

He stopped to examine me more closely, suddenly feeling very near.

'Are you okay?'

'Urgh. I'm not hurt. Just gross.' I tugged at my bodice. The cheesecake slid down my torso and plopped out onto the ground underneath my skirt.

'Actually, you smell delicious.' Reuben sniffed, mock-seriously, and took half a step closer. I flushed hot and cold all at the same time. At least three of my vital organs flipped over. He slowly lifted a strand of hair that had sprung out of its flower clip and peered at it. 'How did you get so completely covered from behind a curtain?'

I couldn't answer. I think I swallowed my tongue when he looked straight at me. His eyes were almost black in the darkness, and I had the feeling again that they could see right into the very essence of me. Into the old fear, and the shame, and the hope and joy.

He mistook the cause of my trembling as the wet and cold. It was late August, and the temperature had dropped sharply with the sunset.

'I think you need to get out of that dress. You're sodden.' Reuben turned his head away then, shifting awkwardly. 'I mean, have you got a change of clothes?'

'It never crossed my mind that I would need one. I just came in this.'

'Here.' He removed his green jacket and handed it to me, leaving him in his ripped shirtsleeves. 'You can change in the staff cabin.'

'It's still open?'

'It should be. It's somewhere for the soldiers to hang around in, and get cleaned up after the fight.'

He walked me the short distance through the trees to the cabin. I made the foolish decision to walk straight in without warning any occupants of my arrival. Half a second later, I reversed out again. Reuben raised his eyebrow.

'It's already in use.'

'I'm sure you can ask them to leave for a minute.'

'No, I don't think so. I'm fine, really. I'm drying out already.'

'You're turning blue. Who is it? I'll ask them to leave if you're too polite. They have to obey me or I'll shoot them.'

'No! It's fine. Please don't. Don't go in there, Reuben! Stop!'

He paused at the entrance, one hand on the doorway.

'Your parents are in there,' I muttered, unable to look at him. Reuben closed his eyes and shook his head. He thumped the wall with one fist. 'You're intolerable. That's the staff cabin. *The staff cabin.*'

'I can just go behind a tree. But I need someone to undo the back.'

'Do you want me to get Val?'

'No.' I didn't want anyone else here to break the spell. I didn't want Reuben to disappear inside and leave me in the dark depths of the forest. And I definitely didn't want to go back inside, into the combat zone. 'It's not as if you haven't seen it all before.'

'That was different. It was an emergency. I was rescuing you.'

'Isn't that what you're doing now?'

I turned around, and after a lot of tugging and fiddling, some yanking and muttering, Reuben managed to loosen my bodice.

Standing there in the night, the trees all around us, the muffled whoops of the banquet in the background, it was the single most nerve-tingling, heart-stopping, sexy moment of my life. I could feel his breath on my back as he stooped to see what he was doing; sense the warmth of him through the small distance between us.

He cleared his throat. 'Listen, what you said before, about Erica.'

Well, wasn't that name a bucket of ice-cold water drenching my stupid, wrong, stupid thoughts and stupider feelings! I stepped forward quickly, the dress slipping as Reuben let go.

'That's fine, thanks. I can manage the rest.' I waved him away, my back still turned, hiding my mortification.

Five minutes later, I was covered from shoulder to mid-thigh in the jacket. My legs were freezing in thin tights, but it would do. Stepping out from the treeline, I couldn't see Reuben anywhere. I had probably driven him away with my cringy lust. How many times would I end up semi-naked – or completely naked – in front of this man? I was shameless! Brazen! He probably couldn't wait to get away before I jumped him.

In one of the deep side-pockets of the dress was my phone. I would have used it to call for a taxi, except that deep in the depths of Sherwood, there was about the same quality of phone reception as in the furthest corner of the Amazon rainforest.

Could I look for Jake, wearing nothing but Reuben's jacket? With Reuben having done a runner? I don't think so.

No problem. I would walk home. I might even jog. I just needed to follow the path to a road, and then figure out the way to the campsite. And if the sole of one of my satin slippers had already ripped open, no big deal. I could run barefoot. Grass is soft.

I half ran, half hobbled back to the marquee, hoping to find the right path on the other side. A hand grabbed me, and I screamed loud enough to silence the din from inside the tent.

'Hey! It's me. Where are you going?'

Reuben spun me around to face him, his white shirt glowing in the fake candlelight leaking through the marquee wall. He was clutching something. I followed the leather strap through the dark to find the horse. It bobbed its head, and chuffed.

'I thought it would be rude of Robin Hood not to steal the Sheriff's horse if he got the chance.'

'Not to mention an unforgiveable break from tradition.'

'My people love tradition.'

'It's what they would expect. No. It's what they deserve.'

And his people, investigating the scream, had begun to gather. They formed a huddle a short distance away, leaving plenty of room to enjoy the show.

Reuben climbed onto the horse with all the ease of the son of a lord. He stretched out his hand to me. 'Lady Marion, will you ride with me to safety?'

I hesitated, flapping about a bit. 'I've never ridden a horse before. I'm not sure I could even get on it.'

He beckoned me closer, grinning. 'Trust me. And please get a move on, before the Sheriff arrives.'

Suddenly I felt very much like a woman dressed in a man's jacket and laddered tights, with cake in her hair, who was considering riding off into the night with somebody else's boyfriend. I felt tired, and confused about what was real any more. And that horse looked at least ninety feet tall.

'It seems the fight's ended. I can wait and get a lift back with the others.'

Reuben frowned. His torn shirt fluttered in the breeze. 'That's not how it's meant to end. You getting a lift home with the Sheriff.'

'No. But I think it would be the best thing to do, under the circumstances.' I laughed, but I sounded more like a strangled piglet. 'I'd never get up there anyway.'

Reuben jumped down. He stepped right up close to me, angling his body so that the crowd wouldn't hear what he said. 'Come with me.'

'Why? For them?' I gestured at the crowd, which had shuffled a tiny bit closer. 'This isn't real, Reuben.'

'What do you mean?'

'I've had enough pretending.' I tried to walk away, but he pulled me back. 'And I don't want you to rescue me any more.'

His hand gripped my arm. 'I'm not pretending.' His face was set hard.

'Really? Does Erica know that?'

He shook his head. 'You know I finished with Erica months ago. What's she got to do with this?'

'I saw you together. At the funeral.'

'When I was asking her about Grace getting sponsorship? Erica wouldn't take me back even if I begged. She knows how I feel about you. She knew before I did.'

'How... how do you feel about me?'

And then he gently placed his hands either side of my face, leaned down, and kissed me.

Now *that* was real. The orchestra of violins and the shooting stars I wasn't so sure about.

I gave myself permission to swoon.

The crowd cheered. All except for one, who yelled out, 'What the heck is going on? Is that my horse?'

I pulled away. 'I need to get my bag from inside.'

'Don't be long. I'll meet you round the front.'

I hurried back into the tent, still glowing and giddy. There were a few guests dancing in among the aftermath of the food fight, but it felt as though the party was winding down to a close. I found my bag tucked behind a bench, and left by the front entrance. A large woman dressed in a full-length cloak swayed by herself in the clearing just in front of me.

'Oh, hellooo.' She waggled a bottle of beer in my direction. 'Want some?' Then she peered closer at me. 'Who are you?'

Who was I? I still wasn't completely sure, but then are any of us?

I was the manager of the most peaceful, piggish campsite in the forest, if not the world. I was the makings of a businesswoman. A cook. A strong, fit runner. A friend. I was the daughter of a good man, and a mother doing her best. I was loved. I was home. I was proud of myself and the life I was living.

My pride was somewhat dented when it took several hands shoving at my backside to help me onto the horse.

It was worth it.

I actually somehow ended up riding off into the night on the back of a horse. Not with Robin Hood but with Reuben Hather-stone. Where we would end up, I had no idea. But right then, I knew I was headed in the right direction.

ACKNOWLEDGMENTS

As I'm currently writing my tenth book to be published, taking time out to revisit my first, written ten years ago, has been a genuine joy as well as a time to reflect on how so many of the hopes and dreams I had when I wrote Marion's story back in 2012 have come true. And of course, that is mostly thanks to some amazing people, for whom I very grateful. So, with this in mind, I felt it right to update the acknowledgements for this new release of the book.

Firstly, huge thanks to the team at Boldwood Books for enabling the book to have a revamp, and no doubt end up in the hands of many more readers. In particular, my editor Sarah Ritherdon made suggestions which were tactful, sensitive, and always right.

I continue to be both relieved and thankful to have my brilliant agent, Kiran Kataria, who makes such a difference.

I must again thank my first editor, Jessica Tinker, who initially fell in love with the book, and went on to provide invaluable guidance and vision. For all those who have supported me over the past ten years, who are far too many to name – writing can be a lonely business and your encouragement really has made a difference. Special mention to the awesome Robbins family, including my mum, Judith. I also have to include all those who have read and shared about my books. I wouldn't be here without you, and I can't thank you enough.

Ciara, Joseph, and Dominic – the reason I started telling stories, and tried to make them good ones. And George – thank you for making me send this book to a publisher when I wanted to throw it in the bin and get a real job. Quite simply, life is better with you in it.

MORE FROM BETH MORAN

We hope you enjoyed reading *Because You Loved Me*. If you did, please leave a review.

If you'd like to gift a copy, this book is also available as an ebook, digital audio download and audiobook CD.

Sign up to Beth Moran's mailing list for news, competitions and updates on future books.

http://bit.ly/BethMoranNewsletter

Explore more uplifting novels from Beth Moran.

ABOUT THE AUTHOR

Beth Moran is the award winning author of ten contemporary fiction novels, including the top ten bestselling *Just the Way You Are*. Her books are set in and around Sherwood Forest, where she can be found most mornings walking with her spaniel Murphy. She has the privilege of also being a foster carer to teenagers, and enjoys nothing better than curling up with a pot of tea and a good story.

Visit Beth's website: https://bethmoranauthor.com/

Follow Beth on social media:

facebook.com/bethmoranauthor

twitter.com/bethcmoran

bookbub.com/authors/beth-moran

Boldw⚬⚬d

Boldwood Books is an award-winning fiction publishing company seeking out the best stories from around the world.

Find out more at www.boldwoodbooks.com

Join our reader community for brilliant books, competitions and offers!

Follow us
@BoldwoodBooks
@BookandTonic

Sign up to our weekly deals newsletter

https://bit.ly/BoldwoodBNewsletter

Lightning Source UK Ltd.
Milton Keynes UK
UKHW042147050123
414905UK00006B/84